Levi W. Yaggy

Our Home Counselor

A Practical Cyclopedia for daily use

Levi W. Yaggy

Our Home Counselor
A Practical Cyclopedia for daily use

ISBN/EAN: 9783337222987

Printed in Europe, USA, Canada, Australia, Japan

Cover: Foto ©Andreas Hilbeck / pixelio.de

More available books at **www.hansebooks.com**

OUR

Home Counselor,

A

PRACTICAL CYCLOPEDIA

FOR

DAILY USE,

Containing

Reliable Recipes, Legal Forms, Interest Tables, etc.

BY

L. W. YAGGY.

CHICAGO. ILL:

WESTERN PUBLISHING HOUSE.

1873.

Manufactured by
WESTERN PUBLISHING HOUSE,
Chicago, Ill.

EDITOR'S PREFACE.

The demand for a *practical* work upon the subjects herein treated, suggested the compilation of this volume.

In its preparation we have steadily held in view as objective points, utility, economy, and authenticity.

The recipes, which number over seven hundred, treat every variety of subjects, and are distinguished for their clearness, reliability, and usefulness.

No expense of time and money has been spared in their preparation.

A large number of them were originally sold at exhorbitant prices, and are now offered to the public, for the first time, in book form, at a price which will place them within the reach of all.

So valuable are the most of them, that the benefits arising from a *single* recipe will very often repay many times the cost of the book.

Not only are the *Recipes* truly meritorious, but we have, while considering the various Departments of the book, endeavored to throw out such hints and suggestions as cannot fail to benefit every one that will heed them.

We call especial attention to the Legal Department. In this we have not aimed to present and discuss those principles which lie at the foundation of all commercial law, but merely to give such maxims and forms as pertain to every day business life, since we feel confident that a great many of the broils, controversies, and law suits which take place in almost every community, result from an ignorance of these.

Every form in this book has been carefully prepared with the view of brevity, clearness, and precision, and worded in such language that they can be easily understood and readily applied.

The borrowing and loaning of money for interest has become an almost universal custom in this country. Hence, a book designed for a HOME COUNSELOR should be supplemented by a first-class interest table.

Accordingly, we have secured the best interest tables extant, by the use of which any person that can *add* numbers can readily compute interest, whether simple or compound, upon any amount, for any length of time, at any rate per cent.

We have called attention to only *some* of the features of this book. In a limited preface it is impossible to detail all its excellencies.

Neither do we claim that we have produced a *perfect* work, but we do think that every one that will make a fair and candid examination of the *merits* of this book, will be ready to concede that we now offer to the public a True, Economical, and Practical Home Counselor.

L. W. YAGGY.

CHICAGO, OCTOBER, 1873.

INDEX.

LEGAL DEPARTMENT.

INTEREST TABLES 321

MEDICAL DEPARTMENT.

Twelve Ways of Committing Suicide.

Before entering upon the Medical Department, we would suggest some of the fashionable modes of modern suicide:

First.—Wearing of thin shoes and cotton stockings on damp nights and in cool rainy weather. Wearing insufficient clothing, and especially upon the limbs and extremities.

Second.—Leading a life of unfeeling, stupid laziness, and keeping the mind in an unnatural state of excitement, by reading trashy novels. Going to the theatres, parties and balls, in all sorts of weather in the thinnest dress; dancing till in a complete perspiration, and then going home without sufficient over-garments through the cool, damp night air.

Third.—Sleeping on feather beds in seven by nine bed rooms, without ventilation at the top of the windows; and especially with two or more persons in the same small unventilated bed room.

Fourth.—Surfeiting on hot and very stimulating dinners; eating in a hurry, without half masticating the food, and eating heartily before going to bed, when the mind and body are exhausted by the toils of the day and the excitement of the evening.

Fifth.—Beginning in childhood on strong tea and coffee, and going from one step to another, through chewing and smoking tobacco and drinking intoxicating liquors, and personal abuse, and mental and physical excesses of other kinds.

Sixth.—Marrying in haste and getting an uncongenial companion, and living the remainder of life in mental dissatisfaction, cultivating jealousies and domestic broils, and being always in a mental ferment.

Seventh.—Keeping children quiet by giving paregoric and cordials, by teaching them to suck candy, and by supplying them with raisins, nuts and rich cakes; when they are sick by giving them mercury, tartar-emetic and arsenic, under the mistaken notion that they are medicines and not irritant poisons.

Eighth.—Allowing the love of gain to absorb our minds, so as to leave no time to attend to our health; following an unhealthy occupation, because money can be made by it.

Ninth.—Tempting the appetite with bitters and niceties when the stomach says no, and by forcing food into it when nature does not demand, and even rejects it; gormandizing between meals.

Tenth.—Contriving to keep a continual worry about something or nothing; giving way to fits of anger.

Eleventh.—Being irregular in all habits of sleeping, and eating too much, too many kinds of food, and that which is too highly seasoned.

Twelfth.—Neglecting to take proper care of ourselves, and not applying early for medical advice, when disease first appears, but by taking celebrated quack medicines to a degree of making a drug shop of the body.

The above causes produce more sickness, suffering and death, than epidemics, malaria and contagion, combined with war, pestilence and famine. Nearly all who have attained to old age have been remarkable for equanimity of temper, correct habits of diet, drink and rest—for *temperance, cheerfulness and morality.*

All commit suicide, and cut off many years of their natural life, who do not observe the means of preventing disease and of preserving health. As physical punishment is sure to visit the transgressor of nature's laws, I will add for the benefit of those who will be wise, observe and practice, the "immensely" valuable

Rules for the Preservation of Health.

Pure atmosphereic air is composed of nitrogen, oxygen, and a very small proportion of carbonic acid gas. Air once breathed has lost the chief part of its oxygen, and acquired a proportionate increase of carbonic acid gas. Therefore, health requires that we breath the same air once only. The solid part of our bodies is continually wasting, and requires to be repaired by fresh substance. Therefore, food, which is to repair the loss, should be taken with due regard to the exercise and waste of the body.

The fluid part of our bodies also wastes constantly; there is but one fluid in animals which is water. Therefore, *water only* is necessary, and no artifice can produce a better drink.

The fluid in our bodies, is to the solid in proportion, as nine to one. Therefore a like proportion should prevail in the total amount of food taken.

Light exercises an important influence upon the growth and vigor of animals and plants. Therefore our dwellings should freely admit the solar rays.

Decomposing animal and vegetable substances, yield various noxious gases, which enter the lungs, and corrupt the blood. Therefore, all impurities should be kept away from our abodes, and every precaution be observed to secure a pure atmosphere.

Warmth is essential to all the bodily functions. Therefore an equal bodily temperature should be maintained, by exercise, by clothing, or by fire.

Exercise warms, invigorates, and purifies the body; clothing preserves the warmth that the body generates; fire imparts warmth externally. Therefore, to obtain and preserve warmth, exercise and clothing are preferable to fire. Fire consumes the oxygen of the air, and produces noxious gases. Consequently the air is less pure in the presence of candles, gas, or coal fire than otherwise, and the deterioration should be repaired by increased ventilation.

The skin is a highly-organised membrane, full of minute pores, cells, blood vessels, and nerves; it imbibes moisture or throws it off, according to the state of the atmosphere and the temperature of the body. It also "breaths," as, do the lungs (though less actively). All the internal organs sympathize with the skin. Therefore, it should be repeatedly cleansed.

Late hours, and anxious pursuits exhaust the nervous system, and produce disease and premature death. Therefore, the hours of labor and study should be short.

Mental and bodily exercise are equally essential to the general health and happiness. Therefore labor and study should succeed each other.

Man will live most healthy upon simple solids and fluids, of which a sufficient but temperate quantity should be taken. Strong drinks, tobacco, snuff, opium, and all mere indulgences should be avoided.

Sudden alterations of heat and cold are dangerous, especially to the young, and the aged. Therefore, clothing, in quantity and quality, should be adopted to the alterations of night and day, and of the seasons. And also, drinking cold water, when the body is hot, and hot tea and soups, when cold, are productive of many evils.

Moderation in eating and drinking, short hours of labor and study, regularity in exercise, recreation, and rest, cleanliness and equanimity of temper, and equality of temperature, these are great essentials to that which surpasses all wealth,—health of mind and body.

Bronchitis.

This is imflammation of the lining membrane of the bronchial tubes, or air passages. Public speakers or singers are peculiarly subject to it, especially in cold weather or changeable climates. When it is of long standing it becomes chronic. It is produced in the same manner as inflammation of the lungs. Where there is a predisposition to it, very loud and continued speaking, or singing, may bring it on.

SYMPTOMS.—Acute bronchitis generally begins with a cold, slight cough, chills, oppression and tightness of the chest, accompanied with some fever. As the disease progresses the symptoms increase. The breathing becomes so difficult that there is a slight wheezing and often hoarseness. There is generally a dry cough at first, but soon there is a copious secretion of tough, white mucus thrown up, which often changes to a yellow or greenish color. There is often severe pains in the head, the tongue covered with a white, mucus coat, high pulse and dry skin. In extreme cases apply bitter herb fomentations to the breast and throat, and let the patient inhale the vapor into the lungs. Give as an expectorant and diaphoretic, a tea of pennyroyal, boneset and sanguinaria (blood root). Keep the bowels open with a mild purgative, occasionally.

For Hoarseness.

Take four ounces of grated, fresh, horseradish, saturate it in a pint of good vinegar over night, then add half a pint of honey, and bring it to a boiling point; then strain and squeeze out.

Dose.—One or two teaspoonsful several times a day. Very good for hoarseness, loss of voice, and all ordinary coughs.

Cough Mixture.

Extract of liquorice, (pound)...........................1 oz.
Nitrate of potash.......................................2 dr.
Muriate of Ammonia......................................2 "

Dissolve in half a pint of boiling water, and when cool, add:

Wine of ipecac...1 oz.
Syrup of balsam tolu.................................. 1 "
Essence of anise.......................................1 "

Dose.—From a teaspoonful to a tablespoonful, several times a day. An *excellent* remedy for bronchitis, colds and catarrhal cough.

Cough Syrup.

Take hoarhound herb, elecampane root, spikenard root, ginseng root, black cohosh and skunk cabbage roots, of each, say a good-sized handful, bruise, and cover with spirits or whisky; let stand ten days, then put all in a suitable vessel, add about four quarts of water, and simmer slowly over a fire (but don't boil) for twelve hours, or till reduced to about three pints; then strain and add one pint of strained honey, half a pint each of No. 6 tincture lobelia, and tincture of blood root, (the vinegar, or acetic tincture of blood root is the best,) and four ounces of strong essence of anise.

The above makes one of the best cough syrups known.

DOSE.—A tablespoonful three to six times a day, according to circumstances.

An Excellent Cough Syrup.

Make a pint of vinegar, a tablespoonful each of honey and molasses, and a small handful of hoarhound leaves bruised, simmer over the fire fifteen or twenty minutes, then strain, squeeze out, and add an ounce each of wine of ipecac and tincture of lobelia.

DOSE.—A teaspoonful or two as often as required.

Another.

Take syrup of squills, syrup of balsam tolu, antimonial wine, and paregoric, each one oz.

DOSE.—A teaspoonful every hour or two while the cough lasts.

Soothing Cough Mixture.

Take mucilage of gum arabic..........................1 oz.

Oil of sweet almonds.....................................1 "

Syrup of balsam tolu.....................................1 "

Wine of ipecac...1 "

Tincture of opium...½ "

Laudanum..½ "

Dose.—For a grown person, one to two teaspoonfuls as often as required.

Another.

Sweet oil...1 oz.
Acetic acid..1 "
Honey...1 "
Laudanum...½ "
Wine of ipecac...½ "

Dose.—A teaspoonful every two or three hours. Very good for coughs and colds.

Cough Tincture.

Tincture of black cohosh.............................1 oz.
Tincture of lobelia.......................................1 "
Tincture of balsam tolu...............................1 "
Acetic tincture of blood root (or vinegar)..........1 "
No. 6...½ "

Dose.—A teaspoonful three to six times a day. This is one of the best cough remedies in use. If desirable, an ounce of simple syrup may be added to the above quantity, or the syrup of tolu may be used instead of tincture. The addition of half an ounce of laudanum sometimes materially increases its beneficial properties.

Brown's Bronchial Troches.

Pulverized cubebs..2 oz.
   "   extract of conium ....½ "
   "   gum arabic...................................2 "
   "   extract of licorice..........................½ lb.
   "   sugar...¾ "

Mix well and make them of the desired shape and size. This is extensively used, especially by singers, to render the voice clear.

Boils.

Boils seldom need any treatment. In ordinary cases poultice them with linseed meal, or bread and water. Or, make a plaster of shoemaker's wax, or the white of an egg, and a little flour.

Carbuncles.

Make an incision the whole length of the carbuncle, then stuff the whole opening with cotton, saturated with with pure carbolic acid. Also paint the whole hardened surface with the acid. It will cause a slight burning sensation for a short time. Renew daily until a cure is effected.

The following is excellent:

Mix spirits of turpentine, $\frac{1}{2}$ oz, with the yolk of an egg, pulverized camphor one teaspoonful, and sufficient wheat flour to make a paste. Apply as a plaster, on a bit of muslin or oiled silk. When the dead parts slough off, heal with black or healing salve. Apply a poultice occasionally to reduce inflammation.

Canker.

Powdered goldthread..........................1 teaspoonful
Powdered sage...................................$1\frac{1}{2}$ "
Alum ....$\frac{1}{2}$ "

Water...½ teaspoonful
Honey 1   "
Loaf Sugar...................... 1   "

Mix and stir together; put into a vessel and let it simmer moderately over a steady fire. Bottle for use. Take a teaspoonful occasionally during the day.

Cancer.

Sheep sorrel..1 oz.
Red clover blossom.......................................1   "
Cinnamon bark...... ....½   "
Red oak bark...1   "
White oak bark...1   "
Poke root...1   "
Persimmon bark...1   "
Black haw bark...1   "
Blackberry root...2   "

Boil these articles in two or three gallons of water to one half gallon. Strain and add to each quart, 1 oz. of borax and 1 oz. of alum. Wash the cancer with this three or four times a day, and make a salve of beeswax, mutton suet, a small lump of turpentine, and sweet gum, and apply to the sore.

Another.

Take the narrow leaved dock root, boil it in soft water, and wash the ulcer in the strong decoction, as warm as you can bear it; pour the liquor in the cavity, and let it remain for several minutes; then scrape the hulk of the root, bruise it fine, put it on a gauze, and place it over the ulcer. Soak a linen cloth with the decoction, and place it over the gauze. Repeat this every eight hours, and let the patient take a wine glass of the tea made of the root, with a third of a glass of port wine. sweetened with honey.

Another.

Vinegar...1 oz.
Honey..1 "
Alum ....1 "

Mix with wheat flour so as to make a plaster, renew the application every twelve hours.

Another.

Take equal quantities of bread dough and old hogs lard, mix together, spread it on white leather, and apply to the sore.

Cancer (Caustic.)

Gold...1 oz.
Antimony ....1 "
Chloride of Zinc ....1 "

Mix with flour and make a paste.

Another.

Take the root of white oak, bore out the heart, and burn it to get the ashes.............................½ oz.
Salts of Nitre (Saltpetre)..............................½ "

Calomel ....½ "

Lunar Caustic...½ "

The body of a thousand-legged worm, dried, pulverized; make all fine, and mix with lard ½ lb.

Spread upon thin, soft leather, and apply to the cancer twice a day. After the cancer is killed, which will be in four or five days, apply a poultice of soaked figs until the whole tumor comes out. Then heal with a plaster of the following :—Boil red buchu leaves in water, strain and boil it thick, mix with beeswax and mutton tallow to form a salve of proper consistency. Also use something to purify the system at the same time.

Felons.

Soak the part affected in strong lye, as hot as can be borne, for half an hour at a time, several times a day; then apply a plaster of salt, soap and turpentine. If used in time this will scatter it. If it comes to a head, lance it, and poultice with lye and elm bark, and heal with some good salve; or bathe the part affected in hot ashes and water.

Apply the following:—Take the yolks of two eggs, twenty drops of spirits of turpentine, a small quantity of hard soap, and two teaspoonfuls of burnt salt and the same of Indian meal.

Another.

Stew a six-cent plug of tobacco in one pint of sweet oil until the tobacco is crisped; then press it out, and add red lead 2 ozs., and boil until black; when it is a little cool, add 2 ozs. pulverized camphor-gum.

The above has a good reputation, and is probably the best mode of using tobacco for the welfare of humanity.

Another.

Take fresh poke root (*phytolacco decambra*), roast in hot ashes until soft. This mashed and made into a poultice is an excellent application for tumors and felons and the like, to scatter them and prevent them from coming to a head, or to hasten suppuration if too late to prevent.

Liniment for Old Sores.

Gum myrrh ....1 oz.
Common salt ....1 tablespoonful.
Alcohol...1 pint.
Aqua ammonia....................... ....2 oz.
Oil of organum.................................1 "
Camphor gum...................................1 "
Opium ....1 "

Mix, and shake occasionally for a week. I have great confidence in the above. It is also very valuable for bruises, cuts, horseflesh, inflammatory rheumatism, &c.

Gum Liniment.

Alcohol...2 pints
Cayenne pepper...1 oz.
Gum myrrh ....½ "

Gum camphor...½ "
Gum opium...½ "

The above is ready for use in four or five days.

Liniment, (St. John's).

Spirits of ammonia.................................... ½ oz.
Gum camphor .... ¼ "
Seneca oil...7⅓ "
Turpentine..7⅓ "
Sweet oil ....8⅔ "
Tincture of arnica.....................................8⅔ "
Oil of organum..1⅓ "
Hemlock ....1⅓ "
Juniper ....1⅓ " .
Amber ....1⅓ "
Laudanum ....1⅓ "

The above has given general satisfaction wherever tried.

Dr. Raymond's Liniment.

Camphor gum ....1 oz.
Spirits of turpentine.....................................1 "
Tincture of cantharides..................................½ "
Oil of organum...1 "
Wormwood ....½ "
Alcohol ....1 pint

Mix, and use as required. It is said to be one of the best liniments in the world.

Enlarged Tonsils, (To Cure.)

Molasses ....1 oz.
Hot Water...2 "
No. 6 ....$\frac{1}{2}$ "

Mix.—Sip a little into the throat frequently, also swallow a little. When this leaves the tonsils hardened, as well as swollen, with tendency to inflammation of the larynx, or throat, and often with little ulcers. In that case use:

Nitrate of Silver...............................20 grains.
Water.. 2 oz.

Add six or eight drops of Creosote, and swab the throat with it, and lay a flannel wet with turpentine upon the outside. If there should be any disposition to fever, it is well to put the feet into hot water fifteen or twenty minutes, with occasionally sponging the whole surface.

Warts and Corns.

Take a small piece of potash, let it stand in the open air until it slacks, then thicken it to a paste with pulverized gum arabic. Cut off the dead skin of the corn, or seeds of the wart, apply the paste and let it remain on ten minutes, then wash it off and soak in sweet oil or sharp vinegar to neutralize the alkali. Don't squeze or jam them, but let them alone and nature will remove them.

To Remove Warts.

Cayenne ....1 oz.

Bloot root...1 "

Muriate of Ammonia........... ....1 "

Pulverize them finely, mix them and form into a plaster by melting a little beeswax and tallow and mixing together. Bind a plaster of this on the wart, protecting the surrounding surface by some adhesive plaster; apply once a day, for several days until the wart is killed or removed. Then heal with some healing salve.

For Warts and Corns.

Water ....$\frac{1}{2}$ pint.

Carbonate of Soda....................................$\frac{1}{2}$ oz.

Dissolve, and wash the warts, and surrounding surface with this solution several times a day.

This is said to be a sure cure.

Sure Cure for Corns.

Brown Sugar.........................,.....2 Teaspoonfuls.

Salt Peter....................................2 "

Tar..2 "

Warm the whole mass and spread it on a piece of leather the size of the corns. In a few days the corns will be drawn out.

Another.

Make a salve by boiling nightshade berries in hogs lard. Apply the salve to the corn once a day.

Sure Cure for Warts.

Pass a pin through the wart about half way, hold the head of the pin to the lamp until the wart is fried. This you will know when the pain ceases. A wart thus treated will leave.

Cure for a Wen.

Make a very strong brine of Turk-Island salt, by dissolving as much as possible in hot water; Double a piece of flannel two or three times and dip into the cold brine; apply to the wen and keep it constantly moist night and day until it suppurates, then apply poultices or salves to heal it.

Another.

Dissolve copperas in water sufficient to make a strong solution; prick or cut the wen in several places to make it bleed slightly, then saturate it thoroughly with the solution once daily.

Bunions.

A bunion is simply a corn on the great toe. It is produced by the same cause as the corn — tight boots, and should, consequently, be treated in a similar manner as a corn.

Spermaceti (or Lard)..¼ oz.
Iodine...6 gr.

Rub on two or three times a day and wear large boots or shoes.

Artificial Skin for Burns, Bruises, &c.

Venice turpentine...½ oz.

Gun cotton...½ "

Dissolve in sulphuric ether.............................20 "

Dissolve the cotton first, then add the turpentine. Keep it corked tightly.

"Is excellent for cracked nipples," chapped hands, surface bruises, &c.

For Burns and Scalds.

Dissolve white lead in flaxseed oil to the consistency of milk, apply over the burn or scald every five minutes. It may be applied with a soft feather. This is said to be one of the best remedies, and more permanent in its effects than any other application.

Cholera, (Dr. Paine's).

Sulphuric acid.......................................1 drachm.

Water...6 ounces.

Sulphate of morphine.............................3 grains.

Tincture gelseminum.............................. 10 drops.

Take one teaspoonful every fifteen minutes. This is an excellent remedy, and with rest, cures nearly every case.

Cholera Infantum.

Gum arabic..2 dr.

Prepared chalk...2 "

White sugar..2 "

Gum kino...1 "

Mix well and pulverize thoroughly.

DOSE.—Five to ten grains, according to age, three to six times a day.]

Used for cholera infantum and summer complaints.

Cholera.'

Golden seal...1 oz.
Bayberry ....1 "
Poplar bark..1 "
Prickly ash berries...1 "
Balmony ....1 "
Cayenne....................................... ....1 "
Cloves.................................... .. ..½ "

Boil in two quarts of water. Strain, press and add half a pint tincture of myrrh, and then an equal measure of the whole, of good loaf sugar. Scald, skim and cool; cork up for use, and set in a cool place.

DOSE.—Tablespoonful every fifteen minutes.

Another.

Tincture prickly ash berries.......................4 ounces
Gum guaiacum............................... ....4 "
Neutralizing mixture.................................½ pint
Paregoric elixir...½ ounce

Take one teaspoonful three or four times a day, as a preventative.

Egyptian Cure for Cholera.

Best Jamaica ginger root (bruised)...................2 oz.
Cayenne...4 teaspoonfuls

Boil in two quarts of water to one pint, and add suf-·
ficient loaf sugar to form a thick syrup.

Take one tablespoonful every fifteen minutes until
the patient ceases purging and vomiting; after this give
blackberry tea.

India Prescription for Cholera.

Dissolve gum camphor, $\frac{1}{4}$ oz., in $1\frac{1}{2}$ oz. of alcohol.
Second, give a teaspoonful of spirits of hartshorn in a
wine glass of water, and follow it every five minutes with
fifteen drops of camphor, in a teaspoonful of water for
three doses; then wait fifteen minutes and commence
again as before, and continue the camphor for thirty minutes, unless there is returning heat. Should this be the
case, give one more dose, and the cure is effected. Let
the patient perspire freely (which the medicine is designed
to cause), for the life depends upon this, but add no more
clothing.

Cholera Tincture.

Cloves, pulverized.................................... $\frac{1}{2}$ ounce

Guaiac,   "   ....$\frac{1}{2}$ "

Cinnamon bark...$\frac{1}{2}$ "

Best brandy...1 pint

Mix and shake occasionally for a week or two. Take
one teaspoonful to a tablespoonful at intervals of from
one to four hours.

Another.

Opium..½ dr.
Agaric...½ "
Gum camphor.......................................⅜ oz.
Sulphuric ether....................................1 "
Castor ....⅛ "
Gentian ....⅛ "

Let stand two or three days, then add one pint alcohol, and let it stand fourteen days. It is then ready for use.

DOSE.—One teaspoonful every fifteen or twenty minutes.

Isthmus Cholera Mixture.

Opium ....½ oz.
Spirits of camphor................................½ "
Essence of peppermint...........................½ "
Tinct. of rhubarb.................................½ "
Cayenne...½ "

DOSE.—From five to thirty drops every five to thirty minutes.

Colic Bilious.

Cayenne...............................24 grains
White sugar.......................... 2 scruples
Pulverized camphor.................. 8 grains

Divide into four powders. Take one in fifteen minutes and it will relieve the pain; at the same time place a mustard poultice on the belly. Croton oil, one drop in a crumb of bread, will often purge succcessfully; or, take

Spirits of turpentine.................................2 oz.

Castor oil ....2 "

DOSE.—Two large spoonfuls. This may be used before trying the other.

Wind Colic.

Take a dose of salts, or sweet tincture of rhubarb. If there is no sickness at the stomach a little essence of peppermint may be sufficient.

Cure for Cramp in Stomach.

Take warm water, sweeten with molasses or brown sugar. Drink freely. This has often given relief when opium and other remedies have failed.

Cholera Morbus.

Pulverized rhubarb root..................2 teaspoonfuls

Saleratus...2 "

Peppermint leaf..................................2 "

Put into a cup, which cover, and then pour on them one pint of boiling water; when nearly cold add two tablespoonfuls of alcohol, or twice as much brandy or other spirits. Take from two to three tablespoonfuls every twenty to thirty minutes as long as the purgations and vomiting continue.

For Colic.

A great many people are troubled occasionally with colic. A strong tea made of the roots of blue vervain is said to be an excellent remedy. If drank daily for one month will doubtless effect a permanent cure.

Flatulency, or Wind Colic in Children.

Peppermint essence.......................................1 dr.
Gelseminum ....1 "
DOSE.—One or two drops will generally give relief.

Scrofula.

Scrofula is from *Scrofa,* which means a hog, because it has been observed in swine. It chiefly affects the glands, especially those of the neck, forming hard kernels under the skin, on the neck and under the jaw, where they sometimes remain for a long time, gathering matter until they break and discharge matter.

Remedy for Scrofula.

Rectified spirits... 1 oz.
Rectified oil of amber..................................2 dr.
Iodine...10 gr.
When you add the rectified oil of amber to the iodine a combustion or flame takes place ; when this is finished the spirits should be added.

This is a valuable outward application for dispersing scrofulous tumors, or swellings of the glands or joints ;

by rubbing the parts affected gently with it, or by applying flannel moistened with it over the part.

Another.

The yellow dock has become greatly celebrated as an alterative. It is perfectly harmless. It is considered one of the best remedies.

Scrofula—Longworth's Remedy.

Take an ounce of "aquafortis" and put it on a plate, and lay in it two copper cents, when it will effervesce strongly; when it ceases, add two ounces of pure, strong vinegar; or use one tablespoonful of "aquafortis" to two of vinegar; leave the cents in. Apply to the sores twice a day, with a soft brush or rag. It will occasion pain. If it is too severe, add a little pure rain water.

Another.

Hydriodate of potash.................................30 gr.
Water.. 2 oz.

Dissolve the hydriodate in the water.

DOSE.—A tablespoonful every morning; continue for several months.

After the cure, continue giving in smaller doses, as an alterative, until the patient is perfectly cured.

Another.

Iodide of potassium............................4 scruples.
Iodine............... 2   "

Dissolve in fourteen tablespoonfuls of water. Take ten drops three times a day in a little water, gradually increasing the dose one or two times as much. Where there is much debility, the iodide of iron, in doses of twenty-five or thirty drops, in water, three times a day, should be given.

Another.

When the disease manifests itself in the form of ulcers of indolent or irritable character, the constitutional treatment should consist of the following remedies:

Scrofularin...20 gr.
Bitrate of Iron... 2 dr.
Chloride of sodium (common salt).,................. 1 "
White sugar... 3 oz.

Mix, triturate and take one teaspoonful three times a day. The diet should consist of rich animal broths, ripe fruit, &c., and a wine glass full of malt liquors should be drank with each meal. The ulcer should be stimulated by the occasional application of a mild solution of sulphate of zinc or vegetable caustic. The limb should be bandaged with moderate tightness and the ulcer covered with a soft slippery elm poultice. After pursuing the above treatment for about two weeks change it to the following:

Syrup of apocyrum....................................½ pint.
Compound syrup of stillingia.......................½ "
Syrup of iodide of potassium.......................2 oz.

Mix. Dose from one teaspoonful to a tablespoonful, three times a day. Pursue this treatment two or three weeks, when it should be omitted and the following used:

Phosphate of lime...½ oz.
Carbonate of iron.......................................3 dr.
Phytolaccin...................... ....15 gr.
White sugar...1 lb.

Mix, triturate and add one pint of water and one pint of best gin.

DOSE.—One tablespoonful three times a day. If the ulcer should still prove indolent, it may be touched with caustic of potassa, followed by a poultice of slippery elm, moistened with tincture of arnica. If it appears in the form of caries or necrosis of the bone, destroy the dead portion with sulphate of zinc or caustic potassa. The sore should be stimulated as in ulcer of the soft parts until it becomes healthy; after which collodion or a mild ointment may be applied until union takes place. In no case, however, in disease of the bones, should the ulcer be allowed to heal until the necrosed portion of bone has been entirely exfoliated and the ulcer healthy in every respect.

Asthma.

Syrup for asthmatic cough:

Hoarhound (the herb)................................2 oz.
Wild cherry tree bark................................1 "
Elecampane root ....2 "

Comfrey root ....2 "
Spikenard ....2 "

Simmer in three quarts of water down to one quart; strain, and add two pounds of brown sugar. Strain again; then add one pint of old Jamaica rum.

Dose — Half a wineglassful three times a day. Take the last on retiring to bed.

This syrup is very valuable where there is much cough and difficulty of breathing.

Powder for Asthma.

Pulverized senna...½ oz.
Cream of tartar..................... ....½ "
Sulphur...¾ "
Anise seed (pulverized) ....¼ "

Take a teaspoonful in one or two tablespoonfuls of molasses, on retiring.

If the patient requires it, take a dose occasionally during the day.

Said to be very excellent and effectual.

Another for Asthma.

Lobelia seed..1 oz.
Sulphuric ether...½ pint

Let it stand fourteen days before using.

Put one ounce on a handkerchief, and inhale freely.

Another.

Skunk cabbage.................................1 oz.
Lobelia herb..6 drachms

Lobelia seeds ....2 drachms
English valerian...2½ oz.
Skullcap ....2½ "

Make a saturated tincture. Take a teaspoonful every fifteen or thirty minutes until relieved. If the pulse be hard and firm, give veratrum viride to reduce it

Another.

Flax seed...½ oz.
Half a stick licorice.
Boneset... ....½ oz.
Slippery elm...½ "

Simmer together in one pint of water, strain carefully, add one-half pint of best molasses and one-fourth pound of loaf sugar. Simmer them all together. After it has cooled, bottle it tightly.

Another.

Make a tea of the leaves of a common chestnut which have fallen in the autumn, sweeten them well, and use as a common drink for several months. Confine yourself to a light, nutritious diet and strictly regular habits. This has effected a cure when all other remedies have failed.

Another.

Spikenard roots...¼ oz.
Hoarhound tops...½ "
Elecampane ....½ "

Angelica ....½ oz.

Comfrey ....½ "

Bruise and steep in half a pint of honey. Take a tablespoonful hot every few minutes until the patient finds relief; after which continue to take it several times a day until a cure is effected.

Another.

One or two grains myricin, repeated every two or three hours. Combined with general tonics, and alternated with small doses of ferri chlorodium, will usually effect a cure.

Another.

Veratrum viride, one drachm; oil of tar, half a drachm; syrup, one drachm; mix. Take fifteen drops three or four times a day

Pills for Asthma.

Powdered anise seed.............................2 dr.

Sulphur ....2 "

Elecampane root (powdered)....................2 "

Licorice root...2 "

Add tar sufficient to make into pills. Make the pills of the ordinary size. Take three or four at night on retiring. This is said to be an excellent remedy for Asthma and similar affections.

For Asthma.

Powdered gum ammoniac............................ ½ dr.

Asafoetida ....½ "

Add balsamac syrup sufficient to make twelve pills.

DOSE.—Three pills twice a day, or, smoke the dried leaves of the narcotic herb, stramonium. This has been found very efficacious in asthmatic affections.

Dysentery.

Vinegar..1 Tablespoonful.
Common salt..½   "

Mix it and pour upon it a gill of water. The water may be warm or cold, but leave it stand until it cools if you use warm water. Take a wineglassful every half hour.

For Bloody Flux and Dysentery.

Castor oil..½ Tablespoonful.
Loaf sugar..½   "
Exixir salutis..1   "
Add boiling water.......................................2   "

Skim it and drink hot. This is a dose for an adult, for children take less according to their ages.

Dysentery.

Tincture of camphor.....................................½ oz.
Laudanum..½ "
Tincture of rhubarb.....................................½ "
Essence of ginger.......................................½ "
Tincture of capsicum....................................½ "

Mix well and shake it.

Dose.— From ten to twenty drops every half hour until it is checked.

Diarrhea Cordial.

Capsicum..¼ oz.
Peppermint leaf..2 "
Pulverized ruhbarb root.......................................2 "

Pour on boiling water until it is covered; steep it and then strain; add essence of cinnamon...........1 oz.
Bi-carbonate of potash.......................................1 "

Take with brandy or good whiskey equal in amount to the whole, and of loaf sugar 8 oz. Take from one to two tablespoonfuls, from three to six times a day.

Another.

Take a peck of blackberries, mash thoroughly and add:
Cloves ....½ oz.
Cinnamon ....1 "
Alspice ....2 "

Pulverize well, mix and boil slowly until well done, then strain or press the juice through a homespun or flannel, and add to each pint of the juice one pound of loaf sugar, boil again for some time, take it off, and while cooling add half a gallon of the cognac brandy.

Dyspepsia.

Wild ginger...1 oz.
Golden seal ....1 "

Turkey rhubarb ....4 dr.

Cayenne pepper ....2 "

Mix and put in two pints of good wine. Take one tablespoonful before each meal.

Another.

Black alder...½ oz.

Wild cherry ....½ "

Gentian..½ "

Orange peel..½ "

Boiling Water ....½ pt.

Loaf sugar...½ lb.

Strain it; when it has cooled add sweet wine, one quart. Bottle tightly. Take a wine glass full three times a day.

Another.

Take five grains of hypophosphite of soda, triturated in three ounces of simple syrup. Makes an excellent remedy for chronic dyspepsia. It is also very highly recommended for lung affections and nervous debility.

Dysentery.

White sugar...¼ lb.

Turkey rhubarb..1 oz.

Supercarbonate of soda......................................1 "

Leptandrin ....1 "

Hot water...½ pt.

Mix them well and add essence of anise..............½ dr.

Essence of peppermint.......................................½ "

Tincture of catechu...1 "

Take one teaspoonful every half hour until the discharges cease.

Another.

Dried peppermint plant.....................½ tablespoonful.
Blackberry root..............................½   "
Scorched rhubarb root.....................½   "
 Steep in water, half a pint.

Sweeten it with loaf sugar; add prepared chalk, (well pulverized).............................. ....½ oz.
Paregoric...¼ "

Take a teaspoonful every three hours until evacuations are checked.

Another.

Take unsalted and unwashed butter just after is it churned, clarify it over the fire, and skim off all milky particles; preserve it in brandy and sweeten with loaf sugar.

DOSE.—Two tablespoonfuls twice a day.

Anti-Dyspeptic Pills.

Castile soap...1 dr.
Gamboge..1 "
Rhubarb ....1 "
Colocynth ....1 "
Socatrine aloes..2 "
Cayenne..30 "
Oil cloves...30 drops.

Make into one hundred and twenty pills, with extract of dandelion or gentian.

For dyspepsia, inactive liver, one or two pills once a day; as a cathartic, three or five pills a dose.

This is a most excellent pill. It does its work effectually without causing debility.

Another.

Rhubarb ....2 dr.
Oxide of bismuth.................................4 "
Cayenne ....1 "
Aloes...1 "
Ipecac...30 gr.

Pulverize and mix thoroughly.

Make into one hundred and twenty pills with mucilage of gum arabic. Take one pill before each meal.

Chronic Dyspepsia.

Drink freely of cold water, with a little salt in it, every morning on rising. This, and the avoidance of strong medicines, will generally give relief.

Another.

Extract nux vomica...................................... 1 gr.
Rhubarb...20 "
Quevennes powdered metallic iron....................40 "

Mix well in a mortar, and make into twenty pills, with extract of bitter root, gentian or boneset.

This pill we can highly recommend.

DOSE—One pill before each meal.

Lee's Anti-Bilious Pills.

Jalap ....60 gr.

Gamboge ....12 "

Podophyllin ....30 "

Tartar emetic.. 3 "

Take two or three pills for a dose.

Brandreth's Celebrated Pills.

Gamboge ....½ oz.

Colocynth ....2 dr.

Aloes ....1 oz.

Castile soap..2 dr.

Oil peppermint ....1 "

Make as many ordinary sized pills as the mass will allow, with mucilage of gum arabic. Take three to six pills for a purgative.

Anti-Dyspeptic Pills.

Castile soap..30 gr.

Rhubarb..30 "

Aloes ....30 "

Lobelia seed (pulverized) ....20 "

Cloves..20 "

Cayenne..20 "

Golden seal...60 "

Make into sixty pills with extract of gentian. Good for costiveness, indigestion, dyspepsia. Take one on going to bed, or more, as occasion may require.

Another.

Castile soap .... 1 dr.
Rhubarb .... 1 "
Hydrastin ....20 gr.
Ipecac ....30 gr.
Oil of cloves ....20 drops

Make into sixty pills with a little extract of boneset or gentian. If hydrastin is not to be had, use instead a drachm of powdered golden seal root. Take one pill once or twice a day.

Liver and Cathartic Pills.

Sanguinarin ....30 grs.
Ipecac..30 "
Leptandrin..30 "
Cayenne...30 "
Podophyllin ....60 "

Make into sixty pills with a little soft extract of dandelion or mandrake. This is one of the best pills in use as a liver and cathartic pill.

Cathartic Pills.

Leptandrin..20 grs.
Podophyllin ....20 "
Cayenne...10 "
Compound extract of colocynth ....60 "

May add extract of dandelion or butternut. Make into thirty pills as a laxative and to act on the liver.

Take a pill every other day; as a purgative, take two to four pills.

Cathartic and Anti-Billious Pills.

Aloes ....30 grs.
Leptandrin...30 "
Podophyllin ....30 "
Cayenne...10 "

Make into thirty pills with extract of dandelion. This is an excellent cathartic pill for ordinary purposes.

Dose.— Two to three pills.

Common Physic Pills.

Rhubarb...30 grs.
Aloes ....30 "
Jalap ....30 "

Make into thirty pills, with extract of butternut or dandelion. Take from three to five as a purgative. For habitual costiveness take one every night.

Liver Complaints.

Take powdered jalap....................................20 gr.
Extract of butternut...................................30 "
Soap ....10 "

Mix and make about fifteen pills. Three or four make a dose.

Another.

Add one grain of leptandrin to the extract of dandelion; make into pills. Take one every night. This is said to be an excellent remedy.

Another.

The extract of dandelion root is excellent for liver complaints. The following makes an excellent liver pill:

Take leptandrin..40 gr.

Podophyllin...20 "

Add sufficient of the extract of dandelion to make a pill mass. Make into about forty pills. For ordinary liver complaints or indigestion, give one pill once or twice a day. Sometimes the addition of ten or twenty grains of lobelia seed (pulverized), or sanguinarin, or ipecac, will improve them greatly.

Another.

Liverwort, (*Hipatica Triloba.*)

This is a common herb, and may be taken freely, in infusion. It is an excellent tonic and very good for affections of the liver, coughs and affections of the lungs. May be used in the form of an infusion or in a syrup.

Alterative and Hepatic Powders.

Finely powdered blue flag root........................1 oz.

"   "   blood root..........................1 "

"   "   may-apple root......................1 "

"   "   golden-seal root....................1 "

"   "   bitter-root ....1 "

Mix together and pass through a fine sieve.

DOSE.—From two to five grains, two or three times a day

Liver Powders.

White sugar...40 gr.
Leptandrin ....20 "
Podophyllin...10 "
Sanguinarin ....10 "

Triturate and rub the whole together in a small mortar, divide into twenty powders, and take one every morning and evening. If necessary, take but one per day. This is a substitute for blue pill, and entirely harmless. Is very valuable in liver complaint.

Consumption.

Almost every one knows of the dreadful ravages which this disease has produced, and all doubtless know what its symptoms are. The following receipts will be found among the best in use:

Cough Syrup.

Hoarhound ....1 oz.
Elecampane...1 "
Comfrey..1 "
Spikenard ....1 "
Wild cherry tree bark................................1 "

Boil the above in one gallon soft water, down to one quart, so as to get the strength well out of them; then pour it off and strain it, and add one pound of·honey, so as to form a syrup, and give a tablespoonful three

times a day, or as often as the cough may prove troublesome. It has been used with great success in many
cases, apparently incurable, and can be relied on as a
truly reliable remedy.

Cough Mixture.

Spikenard..1 ounce
Saltpetre ....2 teaspoonfuls
Best whisky..1 quart
 Mix.

DOSE.—Half a wine glassful, more or less, as necessary, three times a day.

This has an extensive reputation, and from the success which attends it must possess great merit.

The following has been used very successfully:

Whahoo root..1 oz.
Sarsaparilla root..1 "
Wild cherry tree bark..1 "

 Boil each of these separately, in one gallon of soft
water, down to one pint, so as to leave of each one pint.
After it is strained through a coarse towel mix the three
pints together, and add to it three pints of molasses;
boil to a thick syrup, and after the syrup has boiled sufficiently, add a teaspoonful of grated Indian turnip and
a small lump of alum, about the size of a small nutmeg.

 DOSE.—A tablespoonful three or four times a day,
or when the cough is troublesome.

Another.

Muriate of ammonia.................................... 1 dr.

Ipecacuanah ....10 gr.

Extract of liquorice................................... 3 dr.

Dissolve these three articles in half a pint of boiling water. A tablespoonful may be taken three or four times a day.

For Bronchitis.

Iodide of potash..1 dr.

Iodine ....½ "

Water...1 oz.

Gum arabic...2 dr.

White sugar...2 "

Mix and keep in a phial with a glass stopper. This wash is to be applied to the back part of the throat, the tonsils, and root of the tongue, with a camels hair brush, the tongue being depressed with a spoon handle, or suitable instrument. The above has been found a very efficient remedy for Bronchitis by many public speakers.

The following is used in the Essex and Colchester Hospitals in England:

Oil of sweet almonds (new)...........................2 oz.

Syrup of maiden-hair....................................1 "

Marsh mallows...1 "

Saffron ....1 "

And so much white sugar as will make it into a good syrup as thick as honey. A teaspoonful to be taken three or four times a day.

Another.—Bleeding at the Lungs.

1st. Eat freely of raw table salt.

2d. Or, take a tablespoonful three or four times a day, of equal parts of powdered loaf sugar and rosin.

3d. Or, boil an ounce of dried yellow-dock root in a pint of milk. Take a cupful two or three times a day.

For Consumption.

Take a teaspoonful of the expressed juice of hoarhound, the herb, and mix it with a gill of new milk; drink it warm every morning. If persevered in, it will perform wonders.

Another.

The following has performed an actual cure within one year, where all other remedies failed, and the patient pronounced incurable. Live on parched corn meal and water. Before you give up in despair give this remedy a trial.

Bleeding from the Stomach.

This disease is known as vomiting of blood. The blood is usually discharged by the mouth, in considerable quantities.

TREATMENT.—If the affection is not severe, several doses of vinegar and common table salt may be sufficient to give relief. Alum water is sometimes effectual. If these fail, give a strong tea made of the leaves of bugle-weed or of beet root. Drink cold, as occasion indicates, during the day.

Inflammation of the Stomach.

Inflammation of the stomach is usually the result of some other disease, or is connected with it.

It consequently does not often occur as a primary affection. It may be caused by taking irritating substances into the stomach, or by habitually drinking alcoholic liquors. Sometimes by drinking large quantities of water, or even by excess in eating.

TREATMENT.— Give equal parts of sweet oil and castor oil, with a little magnesia, in tablespoonful doses, repeated hourly until they operate.

Chronic Form.

In the treatment of this form of the disease the best results are obtained by strict attention to diet.

No irritating diet should be used. Use articles of food that contain much mucilage, such as arrow-root, sago, tapioca, elm-bark and decoctions of barley. If there is no fever, you may use crackers, mush and milk, boiled rice, gruels, &c. Avoid all stimulating and alcoholic drinks; also coffee, tea, &c. If there are give a pill twice a day.

Powdered sulphate of iron (copperas)................1 gr.
Extract of hyosciamus..................................3 "
Ipecac ....½ "

Continue for two or three weeks, until relief is obtained. Bathe the whole body daily, rubbing with a coarse towel.

For Dyspepsia and Weak Stomach.

Take wild cherries ....1 pint.
Pure old Jamaica spirits.............................1 "

DOSE.—Half a wine glass full twice a day. Use no sugar. This mixture has accomplished wonderful cures. Avoid all spirits after you have regained your usual health.

For Weak Stomach.

Prickly ash (*Xantoxylum Fraxincum*).

Prickly ash bark (of the root,) is a splendid article as a tonic. Used as a tincture in whisky—generally used along with other articles, such as poke-root and gum guaiac. As a stimulating bitters, and where a stimulating alterative is required, probably nothing better grows in the forest than prickly ash. The tincture of the berries is excellent for colic, pains in the bowels and stomach.

DOSE.—Take of the powder, either of the bark or of the berries, ten to thirty grains, about three times a day, and one or two teaspoonfuls of the tincture.

Pills for Dysentery.

Castile soap..30 gr.
Rhubarb ....30 "
Ipecac ....30 "
Pulverized opium..15 "

Make into thirty pills with gum arabic or some other suitable substance. In dysentery or diarrhea, take a pill every three or six hours. After you have taken three or four, don't take them oftener than once in six hours.

Another.

Rhubarb..20 gr.
Leptandrin..40 "
Morphine.. 4 "

Triturate and mix well in a mortar, so as to mix perfectly, and make twenty pills with mucilage of gum arabic.

In diarrhea and dysentery, take one pill every six to twelve hours. Two or three pills will generally cure all ordinary cases, if given in the first stages. They are very reliable in all cases and stages of dysentery and bowel diseases. Give a second pill three hours after the first; a third six hours after the second. After that give but one pill, not oftener than once in twelve hours.

For Dyspepsia.

Caraway seed...............................⅓ ounce.
Pulverized rhubarb........................⅓   "
Grated orange peel........................⅓ tablespoonful

Put into a bottle with one-third pint of best brandy. Keep it in a warm place, shaking well occasionally. Abstain from food and take a tablespoonful in the morning and upon retiring in the evening. Shake well before taking.

Itch.

SYMPTOMS.—An eruption of small pimples between the fingers, on the wrists, and over the whole body, which form matter, and are attended with an intolerable itching.

TREATMENT.—There are several varieties of this troublesome complaint, as: the rank, watery, pocky scorbutic, &c. A very bad kind of it is contracted by dogs that have the mange.

The remedy is sulphur.

It should be used internally with cream of tarter, so as to purge freely and at the same time be applied externally, in the form of an ointment. Equal portions of white vitrol, flour of sulphur and laurel berries, made into a thin liniment with olive oil, is highly recommended as a local application. The following is said to be effectual. Take of flour of sulphur two ounces, and mix it well with two drachms of nitre; throw the mixture into a warming pan containing live coals, and pass the pan between the sheets in the usual manner. The patient stripped to his skin now gets into bed, (taking care not to let the fumes escape,) when the clothes should be tucked in all around him. Repeat the process ten or twelve times. The diet in all cases should be very low. Take

Lard.. 2 oz.
Sulphur .... 1 oz.
Powdered sal ammoniac........................... 1 dr.
Oil of lemon................................ ....10 drops.

Mix well and use once a day as an ointment, first washing the parts well with strong soapsuds. Or, take

Lard..2 oz.
Red precipitate..2 dr.
Burgundy pitch...½ oz.

Melt the lard and pitch together, and while cooling stir in the precipitate and mix well. Apply of this in small quantities, once or twice a day, first cleansing well with soap and water.

Another.

Poke root (*phytolacca decandra*), commonly known as poke. The powdered root, mixed with a little lard, is a good ointment for itch, scald head and the like.

Laurel leaves stewed in lard, make an excellent ointment for scald head and that tormenting complaint, the itch.

Lotion for the Itch.

Sulphate of potash...1 oz.
Water ....1 pt.
Sulphuric acid...½ oz.

Mix. Bathe the parts affected with the disease twice a day with the lotion, first washing the parts well with soap and water. Change the clothes often, and keep the parts as clean as possible. Will soon cure.

Chilblains, or Frost-bite.

Chilblains are generally the result of slight frost-bite, and mostly occur on the feet and hands. They may be caused without even frost-bite or freezing, by exposing the parts affected alternately to extreme heat and cold. The parts affected have a purplish-red color, and are usually somewhat swollen, attended at times, especially if there is going to be a change of weather, or it is going to be moderate, with intolerable itching, and often soreness and pain. They appear usually in the spring and fall, or in the winter during mild, damp weather.

TREATMENT.—In mild cases, washing the parts in ice-cold water, or with snow, will generally be sufficient. Bathing with spirits of camphor and turpentine is also good in slight cases.

Another.

The most effectual remedy I have ever known—and it is generally effectual in all cases if persevered in—is rabbits' fat. Take the fat or tallow of a rabbit, and anoint the part well once or twice a day, especially on going to bed. Bathe it in well by holding the part to the fire. During the day, if the foot be the part affected, wear a bit of fresh rabbit's skin next the affected part, with the flesh side next the foot. If there is much swelling of the affected part, with soreness and inflammation, poultice at night with rotten apples or ginger and elm, or cover it with warm glue. In ordinary cases the use of the rabbit's fat and skin will be sufficient. Also bathe the parts at night in fresh, cold, spring or well water.

Another Method.

Take an ounce of white copperas dissolved in a quart of water, and occasionally apply it to the affected parts. This will ultimately remove the most obstinate blains.

N. B. This application must be used before they break, otherwise it will do injury.

Another.

The following ointment for this annoying disease has been attended with the most beneficial results:

Citron ointment...1 oz.
Oil of turpentine..2 dr.
Olive oil..4 "

Mix. To be well rubbed over the parts affected every night and morning.

Treatment of Corns.

When small in size, they are to be removed either by stimulants or escharotics, as the application of nitrate of silver (*lunar caustic*), merely by wetting the corn, and touching it with a pencil of the caustic every evening.

Previous to this the skin may be softened by immersion of the feet in warm water.

Another for Corns.

Rub together in a mortar:

Powder of savine leaves ....2 oz.
Verdigris ....$\frac{1}{2}$ "
Red precipitate ....$\frac{1}{2}$ "

Put some of this powder in a linen rag, and apply it to the corn at bed time.

Another.

Pare down the corn with a razor; make a poultice of cranberries and vinegar, tie this on the corn during the night, or bisect a cranberry and place it on the corn. In the morning the corn will be so thoroughly soaked that you can pick it out with a pin.

Prevention.

Corns should be secured from pressure, by means of a thick adhesive plaster, in the centre of which a hole has been made for the reception of the projecting part. This, with frequent immersion in water, will cure them.

Hiccough.

This is a spasmodic affection of the stomach and diaphragm, producing the peculiar noise which gives rise to the name. Some people and physicians claim that hiccough is the harbinger of death, immediately after an apparent recovery of a severe sickness. They however, arise frequently from acidity in the stomach, and other causes. Sometimes a sudden surprise, or fright, puts an end to them, and sometimes is also cured by swallowing in succession, a number of times without breathing. Sometimes when all other remedies fail, the following has been reverted to:

Take oil of amber in doses of five drops every ten minutes.

Heart Burn.

This common and distressing affection is only a complaint of an overloaded stomach, and we should heed it, and not only try to alleviate the pain for the moment, but be judicious in all food. Eat only moderately, and nothing which may have a tendency to sour the stomach.

Heart burn is generally supposed to be the first symptoms of dyspepsia. It should therefore be regarded as a welcome messenger, warning us against the dreadful disease, which is feasting upon the gastric juices and vitalities of our stomach. While in my collegiate course, I, (as many others do,) looked at health as of least importance, and owing to my good boarding place (Levi Manbeck, Naperville, Ill.,) and little exercise, my stomach was in great distress, and had the heart burn almost constantly.

It has been with great anxiety and care that I regained perfect health. Perhaps the cure is owing mostly to the employment which I enjoyed for nearly two years afterward (a book agent). To relieve the pain for the moment magnesia is good, or soda. Take of latter about a teaspoonful, and two of the former. To cure the complaint requires the digestive powers to be strengthened by tonics. Perhaps Vinegar Bitters is best for that purpose.

Indigestion.

Indigestion is often of different effect in its first stages. The first symptoms are generally the following:

Want of appetite, low spirits, pain and fullness in the stomach, belching, sour water raising in the mouth, the bowels are irregular and generally costive, great uneasiness after eating, troublesome dreams, &c., &c. Some Stomach Bitters, or medicine just for that purpose, is perhaps the best. I think the following is the best, Vinegar Bitters.

As this is only a book of guide, it cannot enter so deeply in treatments of such diseases, which need the best medical skill. We mean only to draw the attention of the sufferer to the danger of neglecting such symptoms, and soon fall into the incurable disease. An estimate has recently been made that there are nearly as many persons die with the disease of dyspepsia, as of any other, and it is usually the most dreadful and painful disease known.

"What I Know About"

Weak stomachs, treatment, &c. I can hardly pass over this subject without saying something more. The stomach receives, perhaps, more injustice than any other member. Many people think that man is created faulty in possessing such antagonistic organisms as the mouth and stomach, or in having a desire and relish for things that cannot be endured. But I think we are created all right. In nothing is the wisdom of Providence displayed more than in the structure of the human form. This is a murmuring and fault-finding world. People are ever ready to attribute the cause of their misfortunes, not to themselves, but their neighbors, and even to the Deity. To illustrate: A mother stuffs her child with all sorts of indigestible trash; the child, as a matter of course, is taken sick, and the doctor comes. The mother describes the difficulty, states that such were the state of things, and we must not complain, for God designed it so. In this case the Deity is blamed for making the child sick, where it was nothing but the mother's own folly and short-sightedness.

To man was given intelligence and judgment, which should be the rule and guide of his conduct, both with himself and mankind. The brute is supposed not to have judgment nor intelligence, but an instinct which controls it under all circumstances. The regularity of the brute's life is due to instinct. It is ever moderate, temperate, and seldom becomes sick from over-eating. Since man has intelligence to guide him, and no instinct, he becomes even lower than the brute when he sets aside intelligence and allows himself to be governed by a perverted taste and by unbridled passions.

People, as a general thing, eat a great deal too much and of too great a variety, and they seldom ever think of it. They do not know what a mass it makes in the stomach. Suppose we would mix up in a soup-dish as much as a person would eat. Take, for instance, a dinner meal, which is supposed to be, as it very often is, the principal meal. First, the person will eat half a pint of soup. Now, put this half a pint of soup in the soup-dish (or any empty dish), then put in a large chunk of meat; put over it two spoonfuls of dressing, then smash in a few slices of bread, and a few spoonfuls of potato, and a few spoonfuls of gravy; then dip in a dish of green sauce, throw in a few spoonfuls of green peas, and, if you please, some lettuce, and perhaps a few green onions. Now pour over this mixture a glass of water, then put in a chunk of butter and a dish of preserves, mash in a piece of fruit-cake, sponge-cake, and a piece of pie; pour over this a cup of strong tea, then throw in a dish of ice-cream and a glass of wine. Now, then, mix all this well together, stir thoroughly, and get it into a perfect mass, and let it remain for an hour or two. Then look at it, and wonder, if you can, why the stomach is so weak and so delicate. The sight of such a mass, espe-cially after it has fermented, would be enough to sicken the strongest stomach, to say nothing about eating it.

Yet it is nothing more than what a great many gormandize without the least thought, and the same in drinking, perhaps a person will go with this very mass into a saloon and drink; perhaps a glass of beer will be the first, so you can pour this right into the soup dish with the rest, and soon you can put in another, and then a glass of whisky, and just one more glass of beer at present, "well I will take another and then I go." Put all these in the former mass, then stir it up well, and then inquire, and hunt up recipes to strengthen your stomach, and if you find one, add to all the rest; now this medicine, or any other will not be of any effect, or if it will be it is only for the worse. A great many people are using medicine for dyspepsia in just similar circumstances. I think almost any case of dyspepsia can be cured if the right course be taken. I would advise the patient to eat only of simple food, not much, and not much of a variety. Milk toast for morning is very good, —some sort of soup and rare beef, &c., for dinner, mush and milk for supper, &c. If food of this kind be taken, there will be a cheap, easy and ready cure.

Poisons,—Antidotes.

As soon as it is known that a poison has been swallowed, stir salt and ground mustard, a heaping teaspoonful of each, into a glass of water, and have the patient drink it immediately. It should cause vomiting in a minute. After this give at once the white of two eggs in a cup or two of the strongest coffee. If there is no coffee, take in sweet cream, and if there is no sweet cream, take in sweet milk, if no milk down with the egg.

Snake Bites.

In the first place wash off the wound. If possible suck·out the poison forcibly with the mouth, then apply the following:

Iodine...15 grains.
Iodide of potassium.............................15   "
Water.. ½ oz.

Apply externally to the wound by saturating lint or batting, keep it moist with the same until a cure is effected, which will be in one hour and often instantly. Carbolic acid, mixed with water and taken internally, has been recommended by an Austrian physician.

Spirits of ammonia or lunar caustic, are both highly recommended, and are easily carried and applied to the wound : or, drink freely of the tea made of the bark of roots of upland ash.

Corns.

Take soft soap and thicken it with pulverized chalk until it is sufficiently thick to form a plaster. Apply to the corn for three or four times a day, and a cure will soon be effected.

Corn Extracting and Bunions. A $25 Recipe.

The following recipe I got from David Peters, Eaton, Ohio. He says it is a $25 recipe, the best ever known. This mixture is sold on street corners for 50 cents per bottle, which will cost you only a few cents at the drug store. Mr. Peters says he has known persons to do well extracting corns by this process, and I know that Mr. Peters tells the truth, because he is general agent of the Miami Valley Fire Insurance Company.

Alcohol ....$\frac{1}{2}$ oz.

Nitric acid...1 dr.

Muriatic acid...1 "

Oil of rosemary..1 "

Chloroform ....1 "

Trim the corn down well, then rub on the solution with the cork, and continue to scrape off the corn. In from three to four minutes it will be removed.

Another.

Take a piece of linen, saturate with olive oil, apply to the corn night and morning, and keep it on them during the day. This method is slow, but it will be found a sure cure.

Liquid for Curing Corns.

Pulverized blue vitriol.................................1 oz.
Nitric acid...1 "
Muriatic acid...1 "
Put these together in a glass bottle. Add
Rain water...2 oz.
Molasses ....2 "
Pearl ash..1 "

Add the pearl ash last and slowly. After it is done foaming, cork for use. Pare off the corn to the quick, apply with a feather, and bind up with a small piece of tallowed rag. Apply once a day for several days until a cure is effected. Meanwhile wear loose, easy shoes.

Another for Warts and Corns.

Take bark of the common willow, burn to ashes, mix them with strong vinegar and apply to the parts. This is a very effectual remedy.

Liniment for Rheumatism of the Joints.

Gum camphor..½ oz.
Sweet oil..½ "
Oil of linseed...1 "
Oil of cedar...1 "
Oil of amber...1 "
Spirits of turpentine..½ "
Spirits of laudanum..½ "

Stir the gum camphor and sweet oil and add a little alcohol, and grind well in a mortar. When the camphor is all dissolved, put the whole in a bottle and shake well. This will make the best liniment for joint and severe rheumatism known. It is one with which Dr. Gunn has had good success.

Liniment for Sprains, Bruises, &c.

Tincture of arnica...1 dr.
Alcohol..3 oz.

Mix, and shake well in the bottle. This is a very common and simple remedy, yet it is as useful as common. I think it is unequaled for pains in the feet and limbs from walking, and for new sprains, bruises, wounds, &c. It is perhaps, also, the best in use. The faith I have in this liniment is almost sufficient to effect relief as soon as applied.

California Liniment.

Opodeldock...2 oz.
Spirits of turpentine..2 "

Oil organum...2 oz.
Gum camphor..½ "
Red pepper..½ "
Aqua ammonia..1 "
Alcohol.............................. ....1 qt.

This is good for all acute pains, rheumatisms, sprains and swellings, either for man or beast. It is used a great deal for beasts. Some sell this receipt for $3, as the best liniment ever made.

Chilblains.

Published by order of the Government of Wurtemburg:

Lard...⅜ lb.
Mutton tallow...⅜ "

Melt in an iron vessel, and add:

Hydrated oxide of iron...............................1 oz.
Armenian bole..½ "
Oil of bergamot..½ dr.

Before putting in the bole, rub it up with a little olive oil. Apply by putting it upon lint or linen as often as convenient.

Another.

Bathe them in warm turpentine once or twice a day, wearing cotton next the feet.

Another.

Sulphate of copper (blue vitriol)....................½ oz.
Rosemary water.......................................2 gills

Dissolve them and apply as a wash.

Healing Ointment.

Olive oil..5 oz.

White wax..2 "

This ointment is used to soften the skin. It has healing qualities when the sore is not open. Mainly used to cure chaps, &c.

Balsam Salve.

A salve so commonly known, and used, can be made in the following manner. Pick the buds of the poplar trees, just before the leaves open out in the spring, put them in a frying pan with beeswax and rosin, equal quantities of each, with a little mutton tallow, or, beef tallow will also do. Then fry them until the juice or paste is about all out of the buds. Then strain while warm through coarse muslin, and stir until it is so it does not run any more. It will then be ready for use.

The tree from which these are picked are sometimes called cotton, but they are not the cotton; at least they are not so good; many use them also. The tree is sometimes also called — balsam. This tree is very common in the U. S. This salve was used by my mother to tie up our cut fingers, our sore toes, and all sorts of flesh wounds. I think it is really the best for healing qualities that has yet been discovered.

Lip Salve.

White wax..2½ oz.

Spermaceti .... 7 "

Almond oil.. 1 dr.

Balsam of peru...1½ oz.

This is supposed to be a good salve for lips—keeps them from cancer, and chapping, and heals them by a few applications.

In-growing Toe Nails,—British Oil.

Oil of amber..2 oz.

Oil of juniper...2 "

Barbadoes tar................. ....½ "

Seneca oil...½ "

Linseed oil..4 "

Turpentine.. 4 "

Mix: Is recommended for swellings, cuts, bruises, and sores of all kinds on both man and beast.

Balm of Gilead Oil.

Balm of gilead buds, any quantity, place them in a vessel for stewing, pour enough sweet oil on to cover them, stew thoroughly and press out all the oil in the buds, and bottle it for use.

Harlem Oil and Welch Mendicamentum.

Linseed oil ....½ lb.

Sublimed, or flowers of sulphur........................1 oz.

or, Vinegar ....1 gill.

Sal ammoniac ....½ oz.

For Broken Chilblains.

Oil of turpentine	2 dr.
Bole	2 "
Black oxide of iron	2 "
Sweet oil	$\frac{2}{3}$ oz.
Rosin	$\frac{2}{3}$ "
Beeswax	$\frac{2}{3}$ "

Another.

Sweet oil	$1\frac{1}{2}$ oz.
Calamine (prepared carbonate of lead)	$\frac{1}{4}$ "
Rosin	$\frac{1}{2}$ "
Beeswax	$\frac{3}{4}$ "

Melt all but the calamine together. Stir it in gradually until it is cool. The sediment at the bottom of the vessel is not used.

Rheumatic Liniment.

Alcohol	4 oz.
Spirits turpentine	3 dr.
Gum camphor	4 "
Oil cedar	3 "
Oil hemlock	4 "

This receipt is effectual in alleviating rheumatic pain. Sometimes it is used for neuralgia, sprains of joints, &c.

Liniments for Inflammatory Quinsy or Diphtheria.

Water of ammonia	$\frac{1}{2}$ oz.
Olive oil	$1\frac{1}{2}$ "

Mix them well.   In inflammatory quinsy a piece of
flannel dipped in this solution and applied to the throat,
removed every three or four hours, is one of the most
efficacious remedies.   By means of this warm, stimulating application the neck, and sometimes the whole body,
is put in a sweat.   When the skin cannot bear acrimony
of this mixture, a larger proportion of oil may be used.

Compound Soap Liniment.

Camphor ....1 oz.
Soap ....3 "
Spirits of rosemary.......................................1 pint

Digest the soap in the spirits of rosemary until it is
dissolved, and add to it the camphor.   This is useful to
excite action on the surface, and is used to disperse
scrofulous enlargements and to moisten flannel which is
applied on the throat in case of quinsy.

Cajeput Opodeldoc Liniment.

This name may seem insignificant to our readers, yet
it is of great meaning, and a liniment of excellent qualities.   Cajeput is an oil, or extract from a tree of East
India.   It has great stimulating qualities.

Almond soap...2 oz.
Alcohol ....1 pt.
Camphor..1 oz.
Cajeput oil..2 "

First dissolve the soap and camphor in the alcohol,
and when the solution is about to congeal or becomes

nearly cold, add the oil of cajeput. Shake them well together and put into the bottle to congeal.

This composition is a great improvement on the common or general liniments in cases of rheumatism, paralytic numbness, chilblains, enlargements of joints, and indolent tumors. Where the object is to arouse the action of the absorbent vessels and to stimulate the nerves, it is a very valuable external remedy. In many cases of deep-seated rheumatic pains, it has been known to succeed in giving immediate relief.

Buckeye Ointment.

Take half a dozen ripe buckeyes, remove the shells, bruise, and stew in a half pint of lard, slowly, for an hour or two. This is a splendid remedy for piles.

Ointment for Ringworm, Tetter and Itch.

Fresh butter.................................... ....4 oz.
Venice turpentine...1 "
Red precipitate..1 "

Melt the butter and turpentine together, and while warm stir in the precipitate, and mix well. Rub on a little once or twice a day for tetter, ringworm, itch, and all eruptions of the skin.

Salve for Old Sores, Ulcers, Cancers, &c.

Rosin ....1 oz.
Beeswax...1 "
Mutton tallow or hogs lard.............................4 "

Melt all together, and stir in one drachm of pulverized verdigris, and mix well.

One of the best salves known.

Common Healing Salve.

Rosin ....2 oz.
Beeswax..2 "
Sweet oil..8 "

Melt together, stirring till cold. This is a good healing salve for ordinary sores.

Bayberry Salve for Scrofulous Ulcers.

Bayberry tallow ....2 oz.
White turpentine...................................1 "
Sweet oil...1 "

Melt together, stirring well.

Catarrh.

Catarrh, or cold in the head, is a very prevalent disease, though not prevailing as an epidemic. It is caused by taking cold, which, not being promptly attended to, induces an inflammation of the lining membrane of the nostrils and windpipe, generally accompanied with a dull pain in the head and often slight chills, shivering or fever, with frequent sneezing, cough and running at the nose. It may be caused by exposing the body to a cold, damp atmosphere, by wearing insufficient clothing, or anything that disturbs the equanimity of the temperature of the body.

This disease should be attended to at once, for if it is neglected it induces inflammation of the throat and lungs, and the patient finally dies of that dread disease — consumption.

TREATMENT.—In ordinary cases but little treatment is necessary. It may be well to take a slight physic, and bathe the feet in warm water on going to bed, and drink freely of some warm herb tea, and sweat it out, taking great precaution, however, against taking additional cold. A very good plan is to "starve it out" by abstaining from food, or taking but a little for several days. When the disease has become chronic, stronger remedies and persistence in their use becomes necessary. When the disease has become seated in the mucous membrane of the nostrils, the remedies should be mainly applied to that organ. A snuff, composed of equal parts of pulverized bayberry, blood-root and Peruvian bark, a little of which should be snuffed up the nose several times a day, or used as constant snuff, will be found excellent. In addition to this, boil a handful of hops, catnip, hoarhound and chamomile flowers in a quantity of vinegar, and inhale the warm vapor arising from the decoction through the nose several times a day. If the throat and lungs are affected, inhale the same through the mouth. Keep the bowels loose by a mild purgative, or better, by dieting. Attend to the skin properly by daily bathing the whole body, and rub with a crash towel, as anything that relieves the skin also relieves the mucous membrane which lines the nostrils and throat.

Cough Mixture.

Paregoric..½ oz.
Syrup of squills...1 "
Antimonial wine ....2 dr.
Water..6 oz.

DOSE.—Two teaspoonfuls every ten minutes till the cough abates.

To those who are subject to catarrh, I recommend the following: When you rise in the morning and wash yourself, use cold water; immerse your face in the water, holding your breath so as to prevent strangling. Retain the position so long as you can easily hold your breath. This will cause the water to pass up into the nostrils, and loosen the incrustations which may have formed there during the night.· These may then be easily removed by slightly blowing the nose and washing it with water. Never blow hard. Also bathe the face and neck freely with cold water and rub with a coarse towel. This will toughen them and render them less impressible to changes of temperature in the atmosphere.

Catarrh Snuff.

Take chloride of lime, dried and pulverized, three rounding teaspoonfuls, add three ounces of Scotch snuff; mix well and put in a bottle; cork tightly. Use several times a day.

Snuff.

Lavender flowers.................................2 oz. •
Dried asarbacca leaves............................6 "
Majorum ....2 "
    Rub so as to make a fine powder.

For Catarrh.

White sugar.......................................1 oz.
Saltpetre ....½ "
    Pulverize the sugar to the fineness of flour; pulverize
the saltpetre also; mix, and use as a snuff from four to
six times a day.

Ulceration of the Tonsils.

Chlorate of potash...............................4 dr.
Pulverized sulphate of zinc.......................4 "
Strong sage tea ....1 pint
    Gargle the throat frequently. This makes an excel-
lent wash for the throat.

Gargle for Sore Throat.

Vinegar ....1 oz.
Water.. ..8 "
Tinct. of myrrh..................................4 dr.
    Mix well, and gargle the throat several times a day.

Small Pox.

Sulphate of zinc.................................1 gr.
Powdered foxglove (*digitalis*)..................1 "
Water.. .5 drops

Rub together well in a mortar; then add four or five ounces of water, and sweeten with loaf sugar.

DOSE.—For an adult, one tablespoonful, and one or two teaspoonfuls for a child. To be taken every two or three hours, until symptoms of the disease disappear.

Small Pox, (to Prevent Pitting).

The following method is practiced in China: Just at the time when the preceding fever is at its highest, and just before the eruptions appear, the chest is rubbed with croton oil and tartar emetic ointment. This will cause the whole of the eruption to appear on that part of the body to the relief of the rest. This secures a complete eruption, and thus prevents any attack of the disease on the internal organs.

Small Pox, (to Prevent Pitting).

Bisulphate of soda....................................2 dr.
Fresh glycerine.......................................1 oz.
Carbolic acid...1 scruple.

Puncture each visicle as soon as formed with a finely pointed hard wood skewer, and introduce some of the above solution. Also anoint the face freely with the same, and rub the chest with croton oil.

Scarlet Fever.

Sweetened water.........................3 tablespoonfuls
Good brewers' yeast 1   "

Give three times a day. If the throat is much swollen, apply to the throat with a poultice, mixed with

Indian meal and gargle with the yeast. Drink freely of catnip tea for several days, to keep the eruptions out.

Small Pox.

The above is very highly recommended for small pox. Use the above doses of yeast three times a day, with a milk diet. It seldom leaves a pock mark.

Dr. WILLIAM FIELDS.

Small Pox.

First give the patient an active cathartic of podophyllin and anti-bilious physic. Then give a thorough spirit sweat, after which bathe the body thoroughly in hot lye water, and place the patient in bed in a well ventilated bed room, and give the following:

Bayberry bark (pulverized)............................½ oz.
Ginger (pulverized)....................................1 "
Macrotis (pulverized).................................2 "
Capsicum..1 dr.

Mix, put in one quart of water, steep for fifteen or twenty minutes, strain, sweeten, and give two or three tablespoonfuls every hour during the development of the disease. If there is fever, give aconite to control it, and small doses of diaphoretic powder to procure rest at night if necessary.

Sun Stroke.

In every instance where you find a person fainting on the street on a hot day, remove the person to as cool and shady a place as you can find, and if possible in a draught of cool air. Keep away bystanders and idlers. If the pulse is feeble and the skin cool and moist, there is only a loss of nervous power, and relief is promptly afforded by removing the patient to a cool shady place, and applying cold water or ice to his head, and administering iced brandy and water, iced wine and water, or other stimulants. But if the skin is hot and dry, the case more fatal, and if proper treatment be not promptly resorted to, death will soon take place. His clothes should be stripped off, and his whole body rubbed with ice from head to foot, and pieces of ice should be kept under his armpits. This should be continued until a physician arrives.

Sun Stroke.

Take horseradish, bruise it, and apply to the stomach, and give him gin to drink. This is said to be a specific.

The best preventatives are temperance, regular hours, and cleanliness by frequent bathing. Wear a broadrimmed hat if you work in the sun, and see that your head is well aired.

VETERINARY MEDICINES.

Colic,—Horse.

For spasmodic colic, (gripes or frets), give once in ten minutes a pint of warm water, with one ounce of sulphuric ether, and one ounce of laudanum. If no improvement after a few doses double them. If the case is very severe an injection may be given, of one pint linseed oil, and two drachms of tincture of aloes in a quart of warm water. If these measures fail there is still another remedy supposed to be very good.

Another.

Mix some strong liquor wtih six times its quantity in warm water ; wet a cloth with it and hold it by means of a horse-blanket or something of that kind, up against the abdomen. A blister will come in from ten to fifteen minutes. This should, therefore not be held there too long, as it will remove the hide. This is often the best thing that can be done. When all these methods fail the horse has something more than colic.

Bleeding for Colic.

Some people bleed a horse in the mouth, and it is pretended that it is quite reliable. I think in some cases something more is necessary.

Splint.

The pain may be mitigated by a poultice of one drachm of opium, and one drachm of camphor. If a tendon be interfered, the skin should be opened, and the splint removed. Perhaps a veterinary surgeon should perform this operation, chloride of zinc one grain, to one ounce of water is a very good wash after the operation.

To check the growth of a splint, rub it often and thoroughly with simple ointment, mix one ounce of iodine of lead with eight ounces of ointment.

Windgalls.

When the horse is not in service, keep the galls in bandage as follows ; fold rags, wet them, put on a drachm of opium and a drachm of camphor, lay them upon the windgalls, lay over them pieces of cork, large enough to cover the windgalls, and lace on over all a bandage of vulcanized india rubber. This will sometimes give relief.

Worms,—Horses.

Teamia or tapeworm : Take a pound of quania chips, and pour on three quarts of boiling water. Take spirits of turpentine as follows : for a foal 2 drachms, for a colt three months old one-half ounce, six months one ounce, one year one and a half ounces, three years three ounces, four years or more four ounces. Make the turpentine mix with a proper quantity of the infusion, by means of the yolk of egg, and one scruple of powdered camphor,

and give early in the morning. Good food should be
supplied.

Another for Splints.

Tincture of iodine...2 oz.

Aqua ammonia..2 "

Powdered canthardies.......................................½ "

Oil of spike..1 "

Oil of hemlock..1 "

Mix this well and rub in well every other day until
a cure is effected. Shake the bottle well before using it.

Bone Spavin.

The following recipe is highly recommended for bone
spavin. It is used with a great deal of effect generally :

Take gum euphorbium................................ 1 oz.

Powdered cantharides............................... 1 "

Aqua ammonia... 2 "

Spirits of turpentine................................. 2 "

Tincture of iodine.................................... 1 "

Corrosive sublimate.................................. 3 dr.

Fresh lard...1½ lbs.

Rub on this ointment well, and let remain for a few
days, then grease the parts well with lard every day for
four days, then wash off with soap-suds, and apply the
ointment as before, and continue the same treatment
until a cure is effected. This liniment is also used some
for splints, but for that purpose the above is still better.

Bots in Horses.

Perhaps there is no disease that the horse has which is so little understood as bots; yet, owing to the great agony and distressing pain that the horse is in, the sympathetic farrier must do something. The most plausible theory that I have found yet is this: They are the grub of a fly which lays eggs on the hair of the horse's knees or sides exactly where the animal will lick them off. They pass into the stomach from the tongue, and hatch there, then hook on the inside and remain a year; at the end of that time they pass off. It is supposed that only in rare cases they are hurtful, then it is mostly serious. No medicine can be given to kill bots that will not seriously injure the horse. Perhaps the best remedy is to bleed the horse in the mouth, and after he has swallowed some blood the bots will leave the gnawing and eat the blood; then feed bran to stop the bleeding.

Distemper.

This is a contagious catarrh, and the horse having it should be kept as far from all the rest as possible, even if the rest may all get it. It is generally worse where horses are close together. The horse should be kept warm. Give him a thorough purge; feed on light food, such as clean hay, oat and wheat bran, &c. This is all that is necessary. The horse, if not subject to colds, will soon and easily recover.

Corns on Horses.

If the corn suppurates open the abscess, then poultice the foot. When the horny portion of the foot is softened about the corn by the poultice, cut away whatever of the sole is filled by the pus from the secreting surface, then tack on an old shoe and keep the foot with a solution of chloride of zinc, one grain to the ounce.

Glanders in Horses.

Glanders is what may be called the consumption of the horse. It has thus far been found incurable. It is extremely contagious, and even men have caught it and died of it. All that I mean in this recipe is to say: the horse that has the glanders should be killed at once, as it is only a danger to keep him. It seems inhuman to do so, but better relieve him from suffering and save your other horses while you can.

Scratches.

Put a teaspoonful of flour of sulphur, twice a week for two weeks, in chopped potatoes. Wash the parts clean with castile soap and water, and then rub in an ointment of sulphur and lard.

Warts on Horses.

There are three kinds. The first are enclosed in a cartilagious sack or bag. Slit this, and squeeze them out. The second are cartilagious and vasculas in their

substance.   These may be cut off, and with a red hot
iron stopped bleeding.   The third consists of a soft
granular substance in a soft skinny case.   These had
better be let alone.

Bog, Spavin and Windgall Ointment.

Take pulverized cantharides 1 oz., mecurial ointment
2 oz., tincture of iodine 1½ oz., spirits of turpentine 2
oz., corrosive sublimate 1½ dr., lard 1 lb.   This is also
supposed to be of some effect on ring-bones and bone
spavin.   The hair is first to be removed, then the liniment is applied.   It should be washed off at least twice
per week and newly applied, and this continued until a
cure is effected.

Sprain Liniment.

Oil of spike, origanum, cedar, British and spirits of
turpentine, of each 1 oz; Spanish flies, pulverized, ½ oz.
This is rather strong, and should not be used oftener than
one application in six to nine days.

Another.

Alcohol and spirits of turpentine, of each half a pint,
gum camphor, laudanum, oil of cedar, each 1 oz., oil of
hemlock and rhodium, and balsam of fir, each half an
ounce, iodine 1 drachm.   Mix.

Apply night and morning, first washing clean and
rubbing dry with a sponge, then rub the liniment into

the sprain with the hand. It may cause a gummy substance to ooze out, but without injury to the hair. This has cured the ring-bone, also removed the lumps in recent cases. It cured the lameness in a case of three years' standing. Mr. Robinson, a great farrier, says ring-bone cannot be cured. That I think is a mistake. I remember well my father had a lame horse, caused by the ring-bone, and he was cured in a few months so that he would run and stand any work, and look as well as though he never had any blemish whatever. If the disease is of old standing, it is not so easily cured, but when it is coming on, and immediate attention is paid to it, it is easily removed.

Physic for Horses.

Barbadoes aloes, pounded...............................1 oz.
Ginger..¼ "
Warm water ....1 pt.
    Mix and give as a drink.

Quick Physic for Horse.

Croton oil ....20 drops.
Crude mercury .... 5 grains.
    To be mixed in a pint of gruel or rolled in a ball of wheat dough, and forced far back in the mouth.

    This croton oil ought to be used in extreme cases only.

Healing Salve for Horses.

Rosin ....2 oz.

Beeswax ....2 "

Tallow ....2 "

Spirits of turpentine..................................1 "

Oil of spike...1 "

Gum camphor..½ "

Melt all this together over a slow fire, and stir until quite cold. You will find it best of anything ever out.

Cough Powder for Horses.

Tartar emetic ....1 oz.

Pulverized rosin.......................................2 "

Salt of tartar...2 "

Pulverized blood root..................................1 "

Ginger ....2 "

Mix these well together, and give a heaped teaspoonful twice per day. Mix it well in the feed.

Condition Powder for Horses.

Ginger..4 oz.

Black antimony...2 "

Sulphur..2 "

Saltpetre..2 "

Rosin ....2 "

This is a "tip top" recipe. It is (I was told) worth more alone than the price of the book.

MISCELLANEOUS.

Tanning Skins Soft.

The following is a good recipe. To tan and keep the skins soft and nice:

First stretch the skin over some smooth surface, and scrape it down. Then warm two quarts of milk, and mix in a teaspoonful of salt and one ounce of oil of vitriol. In this mixture soak the skin and keep it warm about forty minutes, then take out and stretch, and rub with a smooth board until dry. These ways are all excellent for tanning with fur on. The Indians tan all their deer-skins by first dressing or removing all flesh, &c., then soak it in the brain of the animal, and I think the brain is a better thing than drugs that can be put on. They generally dry the skin in smoke. It will not get so hard, and helps to tan it and keep moth out.

Tanning Furs.

This recipe has been sold again and again. Some have sold it for as much as fifty dollars. The furs should first be stretched on a table, door or board, or anything on which it can be stretched out on and nailed down; then scrape off all the adhering meat, &c., then soak it well in milk-water. It ought to be in at least one hour.

Then take saltpetre, common salt and borax, of equal
parts, and pulverize them very finely, and mix with
water to the consistency of cream, and smear the fleshy
side of the hide well; roll up and lay away, and let it
remain for three days; then take and wash it clean, and
put on the following mixture: Borax, 2 oz.; sal soda, 4
oz., and 6 oz. of good clean soap.   Smear it on the flesh
side, and double the skin, the flesh sides together, and
let it lay in a dry, warm place for two days; then wash
the skin again, and have saleratus 2 oz., dissolve in hot
rain-water, and soak the skin well in that.   Then take
alum one part, and salt 2 parts, and dissolve it in hot
rain-water, and when it is so cool that you can bear your
hands in it, put in the skin for twelve hours; then take
it out and hang up to dry for twelve hours, then put it
into the solution again for twelve hours, and hang it out
again, and before it is quite dry rub it with your hands
and work it hard, and you will have the finest tanning
that can be done.   This system not only tans the leather,
but it takes out all the properties which will cause the
hide to become hard and stiff when wet.   Sheep-fleece
may be tanned in this way and the wool washed out
clean and white, and after the tanning process the wool
may be combed out and the hide trimmed to the size
desired.   This makes one of the finest mats after it is
completed.   If you wish, you can make a solution of
purple dye (see purple dye for wool), and dip the ends of
the fur or hair in and hang it up, the fur on the lower

side, so the dye will not drip off and run into the fur.
This will dye the ends of the hair a beautiful purple, and
the roots or half inner length will be white. Such a mat
costs from $3 to $5, and is very handy about the house
as door mats and in buggies, &c.

Any fur may be used at home, and is worth a great
deal more at home than what can be had for it. For
instance, a sheep-skin, after tanned, is worth nearly as
many dollars as it is shillings to the farmer. The following mixture is very good for softening any fur or
skin: Oil of vitriol, 1 ounce; salt, 1 pint; milk, 3
quarts. Mix them well and soak the skin thoroughly,
and it will soften it very nicely.

Sheep-skin with fleece on. Take equal parts of alum
and salt, pulverize finely, then rub it thoroughly on the
flesh side of the skin, as soon as it is taken off and
scraped a little, or, if it should be dry, moisten and soak
it well. Then fold it up carefully and keep in a damp
place, three or four days; then open it and lay it on a
table and scrape it with a blunt knife to get all the adhering flesh off, then rub it with a blunt wooden instrument
until it is quite dry and soft, then give it a thorough
washing in soap-suds and hot water, in order to remove
all grease from the hair and hide, then let it dry moderately, and just before it is dry, rub it with your hands
well, and after rubbing it it will be as soft and pliable as
a kid glove, and remain so.

Another Tanning Process.

Nail the skin on some table or door, the fleshy side out, then take a broad bladed knife and scrape off all that will come without hurting the skin. Then rub in as much chalk as possible and continue until the chalk rubs off. Then take it off and fill it with finely pulverized alum; roll it up neatly and pack it in a dry place for three or four days. At the end of that time you shake out the alum and the work is done. You will have a well tanned hide.

Trapping and Hunting.

Perhaps the greatest sport, is hunting and trapping, especially in woods and new country.

I have known some who make the business very profitable, especially in trapping.

Mink Trapping.

It takes a man that is quite cunning to be successful in trapping a mink. Some sort of meat is generally used but it is not best unless it is always fresh. I think the best bate is the bladder of muskrat. Minks will scent it for two miles. A young man told me once, that he set a trap with this bate one evening and the next morning he had a large mink. He tracked the mink from his starting place, and found that he came over two miles on a straight course for the muskrat. There is no meat of which mink are so fond as muskrats. If the muskrat can not be easily obtained the extract of musk will do nearly as well. Minks are often found in muskrat piles. Where muskrats are plenty minks are few.

Muskrats Caught.

Nothing has been known to be better to bate muskrat than india rubber. You can burn or heat it in the evening, just before setting the trap. It will have a strong smell and is just what they seem to like.

Trapping Wolf.

Wolves are often hunted with a little asafoetida on the heels of boots, then walk through the woods in the vicinity of wolves. As soon as they smell this scent they will follow it up.

Hunters sometimes climb up trees and let the wolves come up to the tree and then shoot them. (I think this is the most pleasant way to kill wolves.)

Asafoetida may also be used in trapping with great effect. If a wolf is within a mile and the wind in the right direction he will be sure to find it.

For Skunks.

There is nothing more effectual than to get the trap in their way just before the hole, and cover it with ground. An egg placed on the trap will draw them most. Skunks are good bates for foxes.

Engraving on Gold or Silver.

Any one can engrave on gold or silver in the following manner: Melt wax and cast it on the article on which you wish to engrave; then take a sharp-pointed instrument and make the letters or designs you wish through the wax, on the metal you wish to engrave; then take equal parts of nitric and muriatic acid and smear it over the wax, and the acid will follow out the lines and eat close. This can be done easily, and five cents will do five dollars' worth of work. Either of these acids will do the work alone on brass, iron, copper, steel, &c., but alone they will have no effect on gold or silver, but when united they are strong enough for any metal.

Varnish for Harness.

White pine turpentine.............................¾ lb.
Gum shellac ....¾ "
Venice turpentine...............................½ gill
Ninety-eight per cent. alcohol.................. ..½ gallon
    Keep these in a jug in the sun, or by a stove, until the gums dissolve, and add
Sweet oil...½ gill
Lamp-black..1 oz.
    Rub the lamp-black first with a little of the varnish.

Varnish Amber.

Pale boiled oil ....5 oz.
Turpentine...½ pint
Amber ....½ lb.

Put the amber in an iron pot and heat until it becomes semi-liquid, then add the oil; mix and remove it from the fire. When cooled a little, stir in the turpentine. To the melted amber add shellac one ounce, and treat in the same manner as above. This makes a rather dark varnish, but is remarkably tough. The first method of making is preferable. It is excellent for covering wood.

Varnish—Cabinet Makers'.

Mastich ....3¼ oz.
Alcohol of ninety per cent.....................3 pints
Very pale shellac....................................2½ lbs.

Dissolve in the cold, stirring frequently. If prepared with weaker spirits it may be used to varnish morocco, leather book-covers, &c.

Varnish—Black Japan.

True asphaltum ....2⅓ oz.
Boiled linseed oil ....½ gal.
Burnt umber...4 oz.

Grind the umber with a little of the oil, add it to the asphaltum, which should previously be dissolved in a small quantity of the oil by heat; mix, and add the rest of the oil; boil, cool, and thin with a sufficient quantity of the oil of turpentine.

Varnish—Coach Makers.

Melt eight ounces of amber in an iron pot, add to it one gill of drying linseed oil, boiling hot, powdered rosin

1½ ounces, asphaltum 1½ ounces. Mix thoroughly by stirring over the fire, then remove. After it is cool, introduce half a pint of warm oil of turpentine.

Varnish—Colorless.

In two pints of rectified spirits of wine dissolve five ounces of shellac; boil for several minutes with ten ounces of well burned and recently heated animal charcoal. Now filter a small portion of the solution. If it is not colorless add more charcoal. After all color is removed, press the liquor through a piece of silk, and then filter through fine blotting paper.

It should be applied in a room at least 60° Fahr., perfectly free from dust. It dries in a short time, and is very good for drawings and prints that have been sized.

Varnish for Glass.

White of an egg and pulverized tragacamth, same quantity. Let it stand until dissolved. Apply carefully on glass with a brush.

Varnish—Glaze.

Alcohol, 95 per cent.....................................4 oz.
Powdered sealing wax...............................1 "
Bottle and keep in a warm place until the wax is dissolved. This gives an excellent glazed polish to straw paper, leather, &c.

Coating Sheet Iron

With varnish, to protect it from the action of the atmosphere. Dip the sheet iron plates in a solution of the chloride of iron. This will cover them with a thin tin scale. Then wash them well with warm water, and dip them into a melted composition of rosin and tallow. After which let them dry, and then dip into a hot solution composed of

Shellac...1½ lbs.
Rosin...1½ "
Dissolved in alcohol.......................................4 gals.
    Then take them out and dry them in an oven.

Oil Paste Blacking.

Ivory black..2 lbs.
Molasses...5 oz.
Oil of vitriol..⅛ lb.
Tanners' oil...5 oz.
    Mix the oil of vitriol and the tanners' oil together, let it stand one day, then add the ivory black and molasses and the whites of two eggs, and stir to a thin paste.

Liquid Blacking.

Oil of vitriol...¼ oz.
Sweet oil..½ "
Vinegar..½ gal.
Ivory black (well pulverized).............................½ lb.
Loaf sugar..¼ "

Put into a stone jug and mix the whole thoroughly by stirring. This blacking has a great reputation, and is less injurious to the leather than most blackings, and gives a very fine polish.

Black Varnish—For Straw Hats.

Rectified spirits of wine.............................1 oz.
Black sealing wax (the best) pulverized..............·¼ "

Put into a two ounce vial. Put into sand bath or near a moderate fire until the wax is dissolved; then put it on warm with a fine, soft hair brush, before a fire or in the sun. This gives a beautiful gloss to old straw hats.

Drying Paints.

Borax.. 2 oz.
Shellac.. 6 "
Water ....50 "

Apply heat carefully, and keep stirring the mixture until you obtain a colorless solution. This solution forms a varnish perfectly impermeable to water, and is not affected by atmosphere. It can be used with oil paints. To dry them quickly, add an equal part of the varnish with a little turpentine to the oil color, and rub them together until it is well mixed. It dries in from ten to fifteen minutes.

To Paint Iron.

Take sufficient lamp-black for two coats, and mix with equal quantities of boiled linseed oil and Japan varnish.

Silver Plating by Heat.

Dissolve one ounce pure silver in nitric acid, and precipitate it with common salt, to which add half a pound sal ammoniac, sandever and white vitriol, and half an ounce sublimate; or—

Dissolve one ounce pure silver in nitric acid, and precipitate it with common salt, and add, after washing, six ounces common salt, three ounces each of sandever and white vitriol, and one quarter ounce of sublimate. These are to be ground up into a paste, upon a fine stone with a muller. The substance to be silvered must be rubbed over with a sufficient quantity of the paste, and exposed to a proper degree of heat. When the silver runs it is taken from the fire and dipped into weak spirits of salts to clean it. This recipe is from J. Marquart.

Silver Plating.

The following is the most reliable of anything outside of a battery: it works fully as well, if proper attention is paid to it. Take either chloride of gold or silver, just which you choose to plate with. (If you have a piece of gold or silver you wish to use, you can prepare the chloride yourself.) You can place the piece of coin you wish to dissolve in a glass vessel, then pour on it equal parts of nitric acid and muriatic acid. Pour on just enough to dissolve all the coin. If the acid ceases to work, pour in more until it works, and so on. Then, when it is all dissolved, precipitate it by salt; that is, throw common salt in the solution, and the metal will all get on the salt. This salt wants to be rinsed with clean water, then you have chloride of gold or silver.

Then dissolve cyanuret of potassium one ounce in pure rain-water, one pint to which add the chloride of gold, or silver. One to three drachms may be used at a time. This solution is then ready. The article to be plated must then be well cleaned of all grease &c., and, for this purpose, you had better use the following solution: One ounce muriatic acid in one pint of water. Immerse the article to be cleaned in this solution, and let it remain in a few minutes, then with a brush rub it. Then take the article and put a small, clean piece of common zinc around it, letting the ends come together. Then immerse this article in the solution, and let it remain in for a few moments, say fifteen minutes; then take out and clean in clean water, and put it in again. This can be taken out and cleaned as often as you choose. This will then be as good a plate as can be put on, only the burnishing, or, the very glossy, smooth appearance will not be there; otherwise it is perfect. When I was a young boy I paid $3 for this recipe and used it very much.

Jewelry Cleaning and Polishing.

Take whiting and stir into alcohol until it is the consistency of sweet cream; this makes a very fine polish and is not very gritty. It may be used either with a fine brush, or soft rag, or buckskin; the brush is best, however.

Scouring Paste.

Aqua ammonia...1 oz.
Prepared chalk..$\frac{1}{8}$ "

Mix well and keep this, as well as the former, well corked. This recipe is similar to the former and may be used in the same way.

How to Write in Silver.

Mix finest pewter or block tin one ounce and two ounces quick-silver together till both become fluid, then grind it with gum water, and write with it. The writing will look as if done with silver.

J. MARQUART.

Whitewash Equal to Paint.

This whitewash is said to be the best of the kind ever known. It has the recommendation of being equal to the common white lead. It is attended with only a trifle expense. This is the wording in which I got the recipe.

Take half a bushel of clean white lime, put it in a barrel and pour hot water over it until it overflows three to five inches, according to the thickness of the barrel, then dissolve two pounds of sulphate of zinc, then mix them well, and add sufficient water to keep it in the consistency of lime water.

Cheap Drab Paint.

The following is also recommended to be very tena-
cious. This paint is used in great quantity for fences,
barns, &c. Mix a quantity of cement with sweet skimmed milk to the consistency of ordinary paint. This is
a very beautiful drab color, almost too cheap to be prop-
ly appreciated. It is equally good for smooth and rough
wood, for bricks or plastered walls, where no oil or paint
has been used. It becomes very hard, and is as tenac-
ious as the best of paints.

Black Ink.

Logwood.. 1 lb.
Soft water.. .... 1 gal.
Bi-chromate of potash ....24 gr.
Prussiate of potash......................................12 "

The logwood should be boiled in the soft water for
one hour before any other ingredient is added. The
bi-chromate of potash should also be dissolved in hot
water. All these should be put in the water while it
boils. This is then supposed to be the best ink in use.

Frosting or Grinding Glass.

This is a very pleasant and easy process when understood. Most of the grinding is done by throwing any
finely powdered stones on the glass, and rubbing with a
piece of copper, brass, or something of that kind. But
the easiest and best way to do is by hydrofluoric acid.

This acid will eat out the silica of the glass and thus cause it' to appear ground.

Etching on Glass.

Ornamented work is done in this way. The whole of the glass may be covered with asphaltum varnish, and in a short time, when this gets sticky so it will not run, take a sharp pointed instrument and write through the varnish on the glass. You can draw any marks or lines you may wish. Then take a feather and fill the lines with the acid, and it will eat the glass only where the varnish has been taken off. If large lettering is to be done, you can put on the varnish only between and around the letters, leaving the form of the letters clear, and then proceed as before. After the acid has worked enough, the best way is to pour on water and dilute the acid. Wash it off clean, then take off the varnish.

Another method is to melt wax and pour it on the glass (having it smoothly distributed), and scratch the designs through it. This is perhaps just as good and easier to remove when the process is completed.

Hydrofluoric Acid

Can be made in the following manner, if it is not easily found; it is in all large cities: Take flour or Derby-shire spar, pulverize and put it into sulphuric acid. The acid will dissolve. The painters or glaziers claim that the acids used in such work are very expensive, and

therefore charge very high. But this is a mistake. Dr:
Chase says an ounce will do fifty dollars' worth of work,
and it costs only seventy-five cents per pound. This
solution, or acid, can only be kept in gutta percha, or in
lead vases. Glass will, of course, not contain it.

Engraving Names on Steel with Acid.

This is a process which affords a great deal of enjoy-
ment. The hardest steel can be so easily marked as
deep as desired. The article to be marked is first covered with varnish, then a sharp-pointed instrument is
taken, and the name marked through the varnish, just
what you want the name to be. Then fill the lines with
nitric acid. Perhaps it can be best applied with a brush
or feather. The acid then eats the steel only where the
marking was made through the varnish. Wax may be
melted and poured on instead of varnish. The engraving
can be made as deep as desired. Leave the acid on from
one to ten minutes. It will make a nice, visible mark in
two minutes. When it is deep enough, first wash it off,
then take off the wax or varnish.

Varnishes.

‧Best alcohol, one quart; fine gum shellac, 10 ounces.
Put in a bottle or jug and set away where it will keep
warm, and it will soon be fit for use.

By the use of this varnish the grain in wood will
show off splendidly. Hence it is valuable for plows and

other articles where you wish to show the grain in the wood.

Linseed Oil.

Boil any quantity of linseed for an hour, and to every pint of oil add one-fourth of a pound of good clear rosin, well powdered. As soon as the rosin is well dissolved, which can be helped a good deal by stirring, add one ounce of spirits of turpentine for every pint of oil. Strain it and cool, and it will be fit for use. This is cheap and useful, and is not liable to be injured when hot water is applied.

Varnish for Tools.

Tallow two ounces, rosin one ounce; melt together, strain while hot to get the impurities out of the rosin. Apply to your tools, and it will keep off rust perfectly.

Varnish for Harness.

India-rubber ....¼ lb.
Spirits of turpentine.................................½ gal.

Put the rubber into the turpentine, heat it to milk warmth, until it forms a jelly; now add one-half gallon good linseed oil, hot, to the above, on a slow fire; stir well and it is fit for use. This forms an excellent varnish for harness and leather work.

Cheap.

Mix two pounds copal varnish, and one-half an ounce of linseed oil varnish; shake often so as to mix it well then set it away in a warm place. To use prepare the wood to be varnished by coating it with glue-water, then rub down with pumice stone, after which apply the varnish. To put on a polish, rub afterward with a solution of wax and ether. This makes a good varnish for clock-cases, picture-frames, and other articles of furniture, where a cheap varnish only is required.

Maps.

Take equal parts of genuine, pale Canada balsam, and rectified oil of turpentine; put it in a bottle and set it in warm water, at the same time shaking it well so as to mix. Set aside in a moderately warm place, and let it stand for a week, pour off what is clear and you will have a varnish that can not be beaten for maps, charts, and for transferring engravings.

Waterproof.

Pale shellac three parts by weight, spirits of sal ammoniac one part, water eight parts; put in a bottle, shake well and let stand corked for twelve hours, then place in an earthen vessel, over a fire, and boil until the shellac is fully dissolved. If you wish to use it on oil-cloths, add twelve parts of water in which some ochre or terrade scinna has been mixed; this applied, leaves when dry, a layer that is waterproof. Wood can also by this means, in a measure, be rendered waterproof.

Mahogany.

Tie or tack a rag to a stick, and dip it into aqua-fortis, and rub the furniture with this; then set into the sun to dry. This should be applied to walnut only to produce a mahogany color. Be careful not to get the aqua-fortis on the hands.

Cherry.

Rain water three quarts, annotta four ounces. Boil in a copper kettle until the annotta is dissolved, then add a piece of potash the size of a common walnut. Keep on the fire about half an hour longer and it is ready for use. Bottle for keeping. Use on poplar and other light woods, to give a cherry color. It also improves the appearance of cherry itself.

Yellow.

Water one gallon, French berries one pound, alum one-half ounce. Boil two hours, and use hot.

Ebony.

Wash the wood over two or three times with a solution of sulphate of iron, let it dry, and apply two or three coats of a strong decoction of logwood. Wipe the wood when dry, with a sponge and water, and polish with oil.

Rosewood.

Equal parts of logwood, and redwood chips, and boil in just sufficient water to make a strong stain.

Apply two or three coats to the furniture while hot, according to the depth of the color desired.

Blue.

Solution of sulphate of indigo is used hot first, and then a solution of cream of tartar, three ounces in one quart of water. This is a good stain for wooden partitions, side boards, &c., in rooms where this color is desirable.

Oak Shade for Floors.

To strong lye of wood-ashes add enough copperas for the required oak shade, which must be found out by testing. Put this on with a mop, and varnish it afterward with the waterproof varnish.

Furniture.

Take alcohol one and a half ounces, muriate acid, spirits of salts, one-half ounce, linseed oil eight ounces, best vinegar one-half pint, and butter of antimony one and a half ounces. Mix, putting in the vinegar last. Shake before using. Applied to old furniture it will make it look as well as new.

Leather.

Black, red, or blue. Pure alcohol one pint, sealing wax, whatever color you desire, three sticks. Dissolve by heat and apply it warm with a sponge.

To produce black on leather it is best to apply copperas water first, as it will serve to give it body and save
extra cost.   This can be used on any fancy work, made
of leather.

Whitewashes—Brilliant.

To sixteen pounds Paris white, add one-half pound
white transparent glue which has been previously soaked
and dissolved ; stir the Paris white in hot water until it
has the proper consistency for applying to the wall, then
add the glue and mix well.

Uncle Sam's.

Slake half a bushel of lime with boiling water, keeping it covered during the process ; strain it and add a
peck of salt, dissolved in warm water, three pounds of
ground rice put in boiling water and boiled to a thin
paste, half a pound of powdered Spanish whiting and a
pound of glue, dissolved in warm water ; mix all well
together and let stand several days.   Keep the wash thus
prepared in a portable kettle and apply hot as possible.

If the above directions are faithfully followed, you
will get a wash that will last you for years.   It is used
by the "Light House Board" at Washington who
reccommend it very highly.

Improved.

Take four ounces of glue, soak for twelve hours in
tepid water, then place it in a tin vessel in a quart of

water and bring it to a boil, in a manner usual in melting glue. Six or eight pounds of sulphate of baryta reduced to a fine powder is put in another vessel, hot water is added, and the whole stirred until it has the appearance of milk of lime, the glue is then added, and the whole stirred together and applied in the ordinary way while hot.

Stucco.

Take half a bushel of unslaked lime, slake it with boiling water, covering it during the process to keep in the steam; strain the liquor through a fine sieve, and add to it one peck of fine salt previously dissolved in warm water, three pounds of ground rice formed into a thin paste, and stirred in hot. Half a pound of Spanish whiting and one pound of clean glue, which has been soaked and dissolved in a glue kettle; add five gallons of hot water to the whole mixture, stir it well and let it stand several days, covered from dirt. It should be put on quite hot, and should for this purpose be kept in a portable furnace. This wash can also be colored to any tint desired.

Bed-bug Poison.

The following is death on bedbugs: Take a pint of spirits of wine, sal ammoniac two ounces, spirits of turpentine one pint, corrosive sublimate two ounces, and gum camphor two ounces; dissolve the gum camphor in alcohol, then pulverize the corrosive sublimate, and sal ammoniac and add to it. After which put in the spirits of turpentine and shake well. This is rather an extensive mixture, but it is good and reliable.

Another.

In eight ounces of spirits of wine dissolve two drachms of corrosive sublimate, then add one-half a pint spirits of turpentine. This is an effectual destroyer of bedbugs, but being a strong poison great care should be taken in the use of it.

Another Bed-bug Poison.

It is said by women, and therefore of good authority, that kerosene is a deadly poison on bed-bugs and their eggs. This is, perhaps, more unpleasant than handy to use.

Insect Poison.

Petroleum oil possesses the highest efficacy as a destroyer of all kinds of insects that are injurious to plants or animals. Petroleum oil is not purified, and is therefore cheaper and better.

Insects on Trees.

Trees are very much neglected, especially plum and apple. The eggs are laid on the trunk and larger branches, which, when they may easily be destroyed by the application of strong lye, soap water, or if you can go to a few cents expense, get petroleum oil and wash

them.   This will destroy the eggs, and soon the trees
are freed from them.   The most of these insects will
hatch and go to the leaves, and some to the fruit.

Moths.

I think the best way to prevent moths from getting
into furs and such things that are only worn in winter,
and consequently left undisturbed during summer, is to
put them in a tight paper bag and tie it up well.   This
prevents millers, and consequently moths.

Woolen goods may be packed in drawers with paper
around them, and saturated in turpentine.   This is an
effectual cure.   Cedar shavings, Russia leather, &c., are
also good preventives.   If the goods have been exposed,
hang them in the hot sun for a few days, and they are
destroyed.

Fleas.

I do not know but what fleas are of all torments the
most aggravating.   They bite almost as hard as a dog,
and they cannot be caught in any way, and even if you
could catch them you cannot hurt them.   You may rub
and pinch them all you please, and when you stop to
look at them they will bounce in the middle of the floor,
and just as soon as you turn your head they will seek for
revenge.   I knew a young man who tried for nearly two
hours to kill a flea which had been tormenting him.   He
finally concluded to hold it on an anvil and pound it to
pieces, but as he raised the hammer the flea saw the

serious intentions, and bit him in the finger and leaped away. His ambition was considerably embarrassed. The Hoosier schoolmaster says the only way to get rid of them is to insult them.

To Preserve Polished Iron from Rust.

Polished iron may be preserved from rust by a mixture not very expensive, consisting of copal varnish, mixed with as much olive oil as will give it a degree of greasiness, adding thereto nearly as much spirits of turpentine as varnish. This is an excellent mixture for carpenters, blacksmiths, &c., to have. Their tools will not appear greasy, yet they are sufficiently covered to keep them from rusting.

Waterproof for Leather and Cloth.

The new patent waterproof composition consists of the following materials: Boil six gallons of linseed oil, one and a half pounds of rosin, four and a half pounds of red lead, litharge, or any other substance that is used as a dryer, together, until it has the consistency to stick to your fingers when stirring. Then cool off, and thin it about the thickness of sweet oil, with spirits of turpentine, then let it stand for two days and pour off the top. Then add ivory black, or lampblack, one and a half pounds, and Prussian blue one and a half pounds, ground in linseed oil. This composition is then ready to be used on any leather or cloth, and is an excellent paint. The recipe for this has been sold for $25.

Hens Eating Eggs.

This can be prevented by feeding the chickens fresh
meats, sand and pulverized bone, oyster shells, &c.   This
will supply the calcareous matter which they crave, and
they will leave the egg shell and egg alone.

Gapes.

Gapes is caused by a small worm in the throat.   Take
a small bushy feather, strip it to within an inch of the
end, put it down the chickens wind pipe, turn it briskly
around a few times, so as to entangle the worms on the
feather, and draw them out.   If this fails, put a little
turpentine on the feather, and this will kill them.   It is
supposed by some persons that these worms come from
impure water.

Lice on Chickens.

As a preventative, use sanafear poles for roosts.
Keep them clean and warm, and give them plenty of
sharp, clean sand to rub in.   Infected premises may be
thoroughly smoked out by burning brimstone in them.
Strew some sulphur in the hen house.

Poodle Dogs.

I do not recommend the poodle dogs.   The only way
to keep them is to wash them once a week.   If this is
not done, and the dog is sick, the best remedy is to
at once cut off his tail close behind his ears.   In doing

this, there is no use in sending for the most celebrated veterinary surgeon. This method of phlebotomy will be found entirely effective.

Lice Ointment.

Mercurial ointment, says Prof. H. H. Rassweiler, is the best thing for lice out. He says, while teaching a small country school, most all the children had lice, and he got mercurial ointment and put it between the lath where the plaster was knocked off, and that cleaned them out "tip top." This, I think, is reliable, for I have never known Prof. Rassweiler to tell a lie. Any hair oil used freely, will destroy lice at once. Cream smeared on will also work with good effect.

Rat Exterminator.

Dissolve phosphorus.........................½ oz.
In butter......................................¾ " by heat.
Make a paste of water and flour...........1½ lbs.

Mix the whole, spread on bread where rats can get at it, or make it into balls, covered or rolled with sugar.

Another.

Lard...1 lb.
Phosphorus....................................½ oz.
Warm water....................................1 pint.

Mix and thicken with flour.

For the Old Sly Rat.

If the old rat gets too sharp for the former method, try the following: Get a few grains of strychnine, have a little fresh lean meat broiled, cut it in pieces, and insert a little strychnine in each, by cutting a little hole in it and closing it over again. But do not handle with your fingers else they will smell it. Then put the meat on a plate, cover with a piece of paper, and set where the rats are in the habit of going, but not too near their hole. When these are eaten up, replace and continue for several days.

Rat Poison,—From Sir Humphrey Davy.

This odorless, tasteless, and an infallible poison:
Grease..½ lb.
Carbonate of Brarytes.................................1 oz.

Mix: This produces great thirst, consequently water must be placed by it, for they die before they get back into their holes. Be careful that no other animal gets near it, as it is the most deadly poison. In this way they can be gathered up, and taken where they will not torment you with the stench of their dead carcasses.

Insects—To Exterminate.

Scatter chloride of lime on a plank in a stable, and biting fleas will be drawn away. By sprinkling beds of vegetables with a weak solution of this salt, effectually preserves them from caterpillars, slugs, &c. It has the same effect when sprinkled on fruit trees or shrubbery. If you make of it, by mixing with fatty matter, and applying in a narrow band, around the tree, it will prevent the insect from creeping up. Another good plan is, to keep all the toads in your garden, you can find. They are good insect extermin-tors. A toad will swallow the largest specimen of tomato worm, spiders, wasps; and hens destroy all insects. A duck will go up and down the rows of potatoes and tomatoes, and eat worms as fast as it can find them. Young turkeys will do the same, though they are not so easily controlled. It is also a good plan to pick the fallen fruit once or twice a day. Cook it and feed it to your cattle, and you will soon get rid of your insects.

Wine—Blackberry.

Pick berries that are fully ripe, put them into a tub or pan with a tap in it. Pour on just enough boiling water to cover them. As soon as it has cooled sufficiently to allow you to put in the hand, bruise them until all the berries are broken. Let them stand covered until the berries begin to rise toward the top, which they usually do in two or three days. Then draw off the clean liquor into another vessel, and add to every five quarts of this liquor, two pounds of sugar. Stir it thoroughly and let it stand to work a week or ten days. Filter it through

a jelly bag into a cask. Now take four ounces of isinglass, and lay it to steep for twelve hours, in a pint
of blackberry juice. The next morning, boil it over a
slow fire for half an hour, with a quart or three pints
more juice, and pour it into the cask. When cool stir it
about well and leave it to settle for a few days, then rack
it off into a clean cask and bung it down.

Wine,—Imitation of Madeira.

Prepared cider...5 galls.
Pure imported madeira wine.......................$\frac{3}{4}$ "
Sweet liquor.............. ....1$\frac{1}{2}$ qts.
Tartaric acid...$\frac{1}{2}$ oz.
Oil of bitter almonds, cut in alcohol..............$\frac{1}{8}$ dr.
Bruised raisins...1 lb.
Brandy ....1 qt.

Let stand ten days, then rack, and five days to clear.

To Remove Paint from Garments.

Saturate the spot with spirits of turpentine for a few
hours; when it gets dry repeat the process, then rub it
between the hands, and it will crumble away without the
least injury to the color of any goods, cotton, woolen or
silk.

To Remove Black Spots from Woolen Goods.

Mix sufficient tartaric acid, taste. Saturate the black
spots with it, being careful not to have it extend to the
clean parts of the garment. Rinse the spot immediately

in pure water. Weak saleratus water is good to remove spots produced by acids.

Stains from Silks.

Salts of ammonia mixed with lime will take out stains of fruits, such as cherries, grapes, &c.

Tar and Pitch Removed.

Scrape off all you can, then saturate the spots with sweet oil or lard. Rub it in well, and let it remain in the heat of the sun, or in some other warm place for an hour, then it can be cleaned as any other grease with turpentine, &c.

Stains from the Hands.

Vinegar or lemon juice are good to remove stains from the hands. The following is also found very convenient for those who are liable to stain their hands with fruits, inks, dyestuffs, &c.: Mix equal proportions of oxalic acid and cream of tartar, and keep it in a covered box, out of the way of children, as it is a poison if they eat it. When it is to be used, dip your fingers into warm water, and rub a little portion of this powder, and wash with soap.

To Remove Paint.

The above recipe is also said to remove paint-spots, no matter how long they have been standing It is even said to take paint off from a board that has been dried in. It will soften paint and absorb the oil at once. This solution should be kept in every family, as it is so useful. Some people do not like an article that will do more than one thing, but that is a poor plan. This article is as good to remove grease as it is to remove paint, and also equally good to remove dandruff, as dandruff is only a sort of a greasy secretion dried in a scab, and this is dissolved by the solution and the head perfectly cleaned. It has also an unpleasant connection with lice. The ammonia and saltpetre make them so drunk that their last move is for life. It is equally good for

Bedbugs.

Put a little of the above solution on a bedbug, and his earthly career is ended. The eggs are also destroyed by a good wash. I think no one ought to be without this solution. I am sure if I had lice or bedbugs I would get this up at once. There is only fifteen cents expense to the whole cost, and you have an article good and reliable.

To Take Grease-spots or Stains Out of Clothing.

Put a little powdered magnesia on the stain and press on the other side with a hot smoothing-iron.

CHAS. NAUMAN.

Cheap Paint.

Ground fine white lead ground in oil, one pint; water lime, one quart. Mix them thoroughly by adding best boiled linseed oil, enough to prepare it to pass through a paint-mill; after which temper with oil till it can be applied with a common paint-brush. You may vary its color as to notion, only add a little coloring of any kind. It is said it will last three times as long as any other lead paint and costs only one-fourth as much. This must make it valuable.

Grease Spots Removed.

Aqua ammonia...................................2 oz.
Soft water....................................1 qt.
Saltpetre ....1 teaspoonful
Variegated shaving soap.......................1 oz.

Scrape the soap finely, mix all, shake well, and it will be a little better to let it stand a day or so, as the ingredients will dissolve better. Soak well the grease spots with this solution and rub thoroughly, and then if necessary put it on again and sponge well, then wash off well with clean water.

Shampoo.

The solution above is also very good as a shampoo, it will remove all grease, dandruff, and if any lice it will tame them so that they wont bite any more

Floors—To Scour.

Take some clean, fine sand, scatter it on the floor, dissolve an ounce of potash in a pint of water; sprinkle this over the sand; rub the boards along their length with a scrubbing brush, and good mottled soap, change the water frequently, and use it very hot. This will clean the floor thoroughly if properly applied.

Neats-foot Oil.

In manufacturing this oil, use only the bones of the foot after rejecting the hoofs. In the hind feet of the animals the bones go up to the first joint, which bends inside; get these bones as fresh and clean as possible, and boil them for half an hour in a suitable vessel; after cooling, pour or siphon off the oil, then filter it through a piece of flannel and it is prepared for use. If the bones are not fresh, the oil may have a bad odor. It must then be purified by shaking it with a weak solution of bleaching powder, and a little hydrochloric acid, washing and filtering it with water; remove the solid fats, melt again, and pour through muslin. Is excellent for pomatums.

Oil, (Lamp,) to Purify.

Water six pounds, chloride of lime half a pound. Triturate the chloride of lime in a large mortar, adding water gradually, so as to make a smooth soap paste. Now add water so that it will have the consistency of cream. Mix this thoroughly with the oil by stirring often and carefully, in the proportion of one pint of the paste to fifty pounds of oil, or a little more. Let it remain for two or three hours, then add half a pound of sulphuric acid which has been diluted with ten or fifteen parts of water. Boil with a slow heat, stirring all the time until the oil drops clear from the end of a piece dipped in the end of it. After boiling is finished, allow it to settle for several hours, then draw off from the acidulated water. The mortar for the trituration of the chloride should be neither iron nor copper, and the boiler should be lined with lead.

Lubricating Axles, Wagon Grease.

Lard one pound, tallow three pounds, fine black lead one pound, india rubber two ounces. Cut into shreds, beat them together until they are completely mixed, when it makes a most excellent anti-friction grease for the axles of wagons. If you cannot get these materials, make a paste of wheat flour in oil, and it will answer nearly as well. Powdered soapstone and oil are excellent.

Oil Paste Blacking.

Camphene one half pint. Put in as much india rubber as it will dissolve; then add—

Lampblack..1 oz.
Tallow.......................... ....3 lbs.
Curriers' oil........ ....½ pt.

Mix well with heat. This is excellent for old harness, also for carriage tops, boots and shoes.

Waterproof Paste.

Castor or neatsfoot oil..............................1 pt.
Lampblack...1 oz.

Tallow ....2 lbs.

Beeswax...$\frac{1}{2}$ "

Mix it thoroughly by heating.

Another Blacking.

The following is very highly recommended for preserving boots and shoes:

Rosin...$\frac{1}{4}$ lb.

Tallow ....$\frac{1}{2}$ "

Put in a vessel on a hot fire, melt and mix well. Warm the boots and apply the hot mixture with a brush, until the sole and upper have taken all they will absorb. If you wish the boots to have a polish, dissolve one ounce of wax in spirits of turpentine, and add a teaspoonful of lampblack. Apply this to the boots a day after they have been treated with the rosin and tallow. Do not heat them when you apply this.

Starching.

For starching calicoes, ginghams and muslins, dissolve a piece of alum about the size of a shellbark for each pint of starch, and add to it. This will keep the colors bright for a long time, which is very desirable, when dresses must be washed often; and the cost is but a trifle.

Starch Flour.

Iix flour slowly with cold water, so as to clear it of all lumps. Stir in till it will pour easily, then stir it

into a pot of boiling water and let it boil five or six minutes; stir it frequently; add a little spermaceti to make
it smoother.   This is a good starch for cotton and linen.

Starch Glue.

Take three quarts of water, boil in it a piece of glue
four inches square; keep in a bottle well corked.   For
calicoes.

Enamel for Shirt-Bosoms.

A beautiful gloss may be made in the following way:
One ounce of white wax and two and a half ounces of
spermaceti; melt together on a gentle heat; then you
may pour it in a mould for cooling.   It is said that the
size of a pea will starch half a dozen shirts.   I think a
little more will not hurt it.   This is, perhaps, the best
article for that purpose that is in use at present.

Liquid Bluing.

Take best Prussian blue, pulverized, one ounce;
oxalic acid, also pulverized, half an ounce; soft water,
one quart; mix.   The acid dissolves the blue and holds
it equal in the water.   One to two teaspoonfuls is sufficient for a tub of water—just as you may desire it.

Starch Polish.

Take dry potato or wheat starch, enough to make a
pint of starch when boiled.   To this add:

White wax..½ dr.
Spermaceti..½ "

Then use it as a common starch.   Use the iron as hot as possible.   In this way you will produce a brilliant polish.

Starch — Lustre.

The substance known by this name is extensively used for washing purposes, which, when added to the starch, causes the linen to which it is applied to assume a high polish and a dazzling whiteness.   A portion, the size of an old-fashioned cent, added to half a pound of starch and boiled two or three minutes, will produce the best results.   This substance is nothing more than stearine.   By the addition of a small quantity of ultramarine blue the (principal ingredient being the stearine) it will be found to add very much to the beauty of linen articles, either with or without coloring.

Glycerine.

This is the name of a new preparation and is very highly recommended as an ointment for healing wounds, erysipelas, cutaneous affections and broken surfaces of all kinds.   It forms a sort of varnish over the skin and thus excludes the air.   To prepare:

Take glycerine...5 parts
The yolk of eggs 4   "

Mix.   It has the consistency of honey, feels like salve, and is not changed in the air.

Glycerine.

Glycerine is the residuum left after the making of soap and stearine candles, and which for a long time was considered worthless. The medicinal properties of glycerine are very marvelous, it being very valuable in pharmacy, and an excellent antiseptic. It is capable of preserving animal substances from decay ; keeps leather soft and pliant ; wooden vessels saturated with it, neither dry up nor shrink, and has wonderful power in healing sores and removing pains, ear-aches, &c.

To Prevent Flies from Spotting Pictures.

Boil four onions in a quart of water and wash the glass thoroughly.

To Destroy Lice on Cattle.

Dissolve camphor in spirits and apply. Is an effectual remedy.

Another.

Lard ....2 parts
Coal oil ....4 "

Melt it together and apply. This will kill the lice for sure.

Another.

Feeding the animal with onions, is said to make the lice travel "West" in ten or fifteen hours, at least it would if they dislike onions as much as I do.

To Prevent Pens from Corroding.

Put a small nail or piece of iron into the ink bottle; in a short time the free SO_3 will unite with it instead of corroding the pens.

Ink Stains—To Remove from Linen.

Take a clean sponge or rag, rub the soiled spot thoroughly with lemon juice, in which has been dissolved a small quantity of salt.

Ink—To Remove from Dress Goods.

Soft water..1 pint

Ten cents worth of oxalic acid; dissolve the acid, then dip the stained spot into it quickly, and then into clean water and rub well, repeat this until the stains are removed. If you keep the goods in the acid too long the texture will be destroyed. Be careful and dip only the spots in the liquid.

Iron Rust—To Remove.

Soak the rust with petroleum, then rub well with coarse sand paper. In this way you can remove every particle of rust.

Liniment for Paralysis.

Oil of lavender.................................$\frac{1}{2}$ oz.

Alcohol...1 "

Sulphuric ether.................................3 "

Laudanum.......................................$\frac{1}{2}$ "

Mix and cork tightly. If the case of paralysis is recent, bathe and rub the whole extent of the numbed surface, thoroughly, with this preparation for several minutes, rubbing with the hand, at least three times a day. At the same time, take, internally, 20 drops of the same, in a little sweetened water, to prevent translation upon some internal organ. It may be used to great profit in all cases. In very recent cases it may be well to keep the parts covered with flannels. Also rub the parts often with the hand. Electricity applied by some one who understands its operations. Apply the liniment freely, using about an ounce per day, on an arm or leg.

Indian Ink.

Let ivory-black or lamp-black be mixed with a small portion of Prussian blue, or indigo, for a blue black, and let the same lamp-black be mixed raw, or burnt umber, bister vandyke, or any other brown, instead of the blue, when a brown black is required. These powders should first be well mixed and powdered, then use gum water to mix them to the consistency of a thick paste. It must not be made too wet with the gum water, as the gum arabic will give it an unpleasant gloss.

Another Indian Ink.

Isinglass... 6 oz.
Soft water...12 "
Refined licorice, ground up............................1 "
Genuine ivory black.......................................1 "

These ingredients want to be prepared well, then the water must be evaporated, and the ink will be ready to be worked into sticks.

Red Ink.

Carmine..12 gr.

Spirits of ammonia................................. 2 oz.

Heat the two, and stir well, then add gum arabic eighteen grains, and stir till dissolved. This makes a fine, red ink. If any large quantities are desired the following may be the best:

Galls..40 lbs.

Gum arabic...10 "

Copperas.. 9 "

Soft water..45 gal.

This is the mixture used by almost all paper rulers that use red ink. It is good and very durable. If smaller quantities be desired, use the following:

Red Ink from Vermillion.

Gum arabic..½ oz.

Sugar ....1 teaspoonful.

Alcohol..1 oz.

Mix all these well until they are fine, then add such a proportion of vermillion as will produce a color sufficiently strong.

Green Writing Ink.

Crystals of verdigris................................1 oz.

Gum arabic..5 dr.

Dissolve both of these articles in separate vessels, then mix. This forms a good green ink.

Green ink can also be made in the following manner, if the crystals of verdigris cannot be had, or unhandy, take the powder and verdigris..........................1 oz.

White vinegar..1 qt.

White sugar ....2 dr.

Dissolve the sugar, and then let the verdigris in the quart of vinegar two or three days, and stir often, then strain through fine flannel.

Yellow Ink.

French berries...2 oz.

Alum...½ "

Gum arabic..2 dr.

White sugar...1 "

Dissolve the sugar and gum arabic, then boil until one-third evaporates, then strain. This is an English recipe and well recommended.

Blue Ink.

I remember well, when quite a little boy, I would take my mother's indigo and make good blue ink.

I would therefore recommend it.

Take one quart of rain water, and dissolve two drachms of gum arabic, then add Prussian blue until sufficiently strong.

Colorless, or Sympathetic Ink.

Nut gall is an invisible liquid. After writing has been made with this liquid, it is invisible, but as soon as it is smeared with metallic salt a black writing is seen.

Invisible Ink.

Muriatic acid is perfectly invisible, and will be so until it is brought to heat. It is the most convenient of all other invisible inks, as it needs no other solution than a few cents worth of the acid, and a heat of flat iron, or stove, lamp chimney, or any thing else will bring out the color.

To Make French Indelible Ink.

This may be prepared by dissolving Indian ink in either a mixture of dilute muriatic acid in water, or a very weak solution of caustic potash. If steel pens are to be employed in writing with it, the latter fluid is to be preferred, but if quill pens are used, the former liquid is the best.

Cements — Russian.

Russian isinglass, dissolved in pure soft water, snow water, if you can get it, is the best. Soak some 12 hours, then heat it until fully dissolved. Apply to statuary, china, glass, alabaster, &c., with a feather or soft brush, and let it remain until fully dry. Be sure and get the genuine Russian isinglass, even if it does cost more than the common, and you will have a cement that will do you good service.

Fire and Waterproof.

Take half a pint each, of vinegar and milk, mix and separate the curd, and to the whey add the whites of five eggs, beat it well together, adding quick lime until it has the consistency of thick paste. Vessels mended with this will never break where they were mended.

Another.

Apply with a small camels-hair brush carriage-oil varnish to the broken edges of the china to be mended, and let it stand till fully dry.

Japanese.

Take rice flour, mix it well with cold water, and then gently boil it until it is pretty thick. This makes a beautiful white cement, and is, when dry, almost transparent. Papers pasted with this will sooner separate in their own substance than in the joining; hence this is very desirable for pasting together articles that require successive layers to be cemented together.

Sealing for Mouths of Bottles.

Take four ounces of sealing-wax, the same quantity of rosin, and two ounces of beeswax; melt them all together, and when it froths stir it with a tallow candle.

As soon as it melts, dip in the mouths of the bottles to be sealed, and which should have been previously corked. This will exclude the air perfectly, and makes a good article for the purpose.

Aquarium.

Beat together three gills of litharge, three gills of plaster of Paris, three gills of dry white sand, one gill of finely pulverized rosin. For a greater or less quantity, take these articles in the same proportion. Sift, and keep corked tight until required for use, when it is to be made into a putty by mixing it with boiled linseed oil, adding a little patent dryer. It must be used as soon as it is mixed, for it will only keep good ten or fifteen hours. This makes a perfectly reliable cement — one that does not injure plants or fishes, and one that will hold equally good on wood, glass, stone or metal. By its use an aquarium can be readily and surely constructed, and can be used at once, although it is best to let it dry several hours.

Egg.

Thicken the white of an egg with finely powdered quick-lime. This will not resist moisture, but may be used to mend vessels that are intended to hold dry articles only.

Cutlers.

For fastening knives and forks: Melt together one pound of colophony and eight ounces of sulphur; this may afterward be reduced to a powder. To use, mix one part of the powder with half a part of fine sand, or brick dust, and fill the cavity of the handle with this mixture; then heat the stem of the knife, or fork to be mended, put it into its place, and when cold it will be found to be very tenaciously fixed.

Another good cement for this purpose may be made, as follows:

Black rosin..8 oz.
Beeswax ....2 "
Brickdust ....2 "

To be melted, well mixed, and used as before.

Stick Cement.

Dissolve one ounce common salt in one quart of water, bring to a boil and put in one and one-fourth pounds gum shellac; as soon as it is dissolved pour into cold and work like wax, moulding it in small sticks. To use, heat and apply to the articles to be mended. This is especially valuable for mending earthenware.

Leather.

Gutta-purcha..4 lbs.
India rubber..2 oz.
Pitch..2 "
Shellac...1 "
Linseed oil..2 "

Melt together these articles and always apply warm. It makes a strong and adhesive mixture to mend boots and shoes and for uniting articles of clothing. It has no equal.

Roofing and Chimney.

To one pint dry sand, ashes two pints, add dried and pulverized clay three pints; grind up fine, and work into a paste with linseed oil. Apply when soft to the leaks around your chimney and roof, and when hard you will find your roof water-proof.

Remarks.

All articles to be cemented, in order to hold well, must be well cleansed from every particle of dirt that may be in the cracks or seams. Leather, wood, and some other materials must always be scraped and then washed; then if your cement is properly made and not applied too thick—this is the secret—put it on thin, you will have success.

Glues—Spaulding's.

Soak in cold water all the glue you wish to make at one time, using only glass, earthen or porcelain dishes. Then by gentle heat dissolve the glue in the water in which it was soaked, and pour in nitric acid just enough to give the glue a sour taste. The proportions are, one ounce of nitric acid to one pound of glue.

Liquid.

Fill a bottle over half full with the best glue you can get, then fill up altogether with common whisky—cork tightly and let it stand for a week, when it will be fit for use. If kept where it will not be too cold, it will always be fit for use, and will keep for a number of years.

No. 2.

Gum arabic.. 2 oz.
Boiling water... 1 pint
Dissolve and add spirits.............................10 oz.

To keep from moulding put a few cloves into the bottle.

Bank Bill Paste.

For mending bank bills, &c., take pure glue, gallatine is best, one pound; brown sugar as coarse as you can get it, one-fourth of a pound, put into as little boiling water as will cover them; then dissolve with the aid of heat, and when perfectly liquid, remove and pour upon the surface that has been oiled a little, so that it will not adhere. It can be cut into sticks, when cold and carried in the pocket, requiring only to be wetted by the lips, before being used.

Mucilages and Pastes—Common.

Take ten cents worth of the best gum arabic, put it in a gill of vinegar, and after it is fully dissolved you will have as good an article of this kind as the best.

Glue.

To eight ounces of fine glue, add five ounces of gum arabic and one pint of water. Melt in a glue kettle in the usual manner, after which add slowly five ounces of nitric acid, and set away to cool. When bottling, if a few cloves are added, it will be kept from moulding.

Pastes—Scrap Book.

Take best laundry starch, put into a clean dish, put on enough soft water to wet it, then stir smoothly. Slowly pour on boiling water, and stir until you have a jelly-like mass. You can use this as soon as cool. For many uses this is preferable to mucilage, and is cheaply and easily made.

Rosin.

Dissolve one tablespoonful of alum in a quart of warm water. As soon as it is cool stir in a teaspoonful of rosin, and as much flour as will give it the consistency of gravy. Be careful to break up all the lumps. Now add a teacup of boiling water, stirring it all the while. It will soon be quite thick. Cover it up well and set in a tight place. When you wish to use, take out a portion and soften with warm water. This makes an excellent smooth paste and gives good satisfaction.

Label Mucilage.

Soak five ounces of good glue in twenty ounces of water, for a day or longer if necessary. Add to this mixture nine ounces of rock-candy and three ounces of gum arabic. Spread upon your paper labels while it is yet lukewarm.

When you wish to use, moisten well and it will adhere firmly to the bottles or jars.

Paints—General Remarks.

The following recipes are intended to be so complete that by their use the painter's occupation will be superceded. Painting, in order to be well done, must be done by skillful persons who have devoted time and practice to its mastery. It is just as much a trade as the carpenter's or blacksmith's, but any person of ordinary skill can, by the use of these recipes, do many a job satisfactorily.

Fire Proof.

Put a quantity of stone lime in a tub to slake, covering so as to keep in the steam. As soon as it is slaked, sift it through a fine seive. To every six quarts of it, add one quart of rock salt, and water one gallon. Now boil and skim thoroughly. To each five gallons of this add pulverized alum one pound, pulverized copperas one-half pound, and slowly add powdered potash three-quarters of a pound, and fine sand or hickory ashes four pounds.

It is to be applied with a brush, and will, when dry, make a hard, durable paint, stopping leaks in roofs, seams in walls, and make them incombustible. By adding yellow ochre or venetian red, different colors can be produced.

Whiting.

Of the best whiting take five pounds, skimmed milk two quarts, fresh slaked lime two ounces. Put the lime in a stoneware vessel, pour upon it a sufficient quantity of the milk to make a mixture resembling cream. The balance of the milk is then to be added, and lastly the whiting is then to be crumbled upon the surface of the fluid, in which it gradually sinks.

Be sure and stir it well, so that it will work up well and smooth like the above. Different tints can be produced by adding coloring matter to suit one's tastes. It must be borne in mind that, although these are cheap paints, you must in order to produce good effects, apply it well, and give it two or three coats, as you would were you using oil paints.

Waterproof.

First, take ochre ninety-six parts, lampblack sixteen parts, boiled oil enough to mix, then add yellow soap two parts, dissolved in eight parts of water. After thoroughly mixing, apply two coats at intervals of two days, by using a common paint brush. Lastly, finish it up by giving it another coat of a mixture formed of boiled oil and lampblack, of the consistency of a thick varnish. Although more expensive than the others, it is an excellent paint.

Dr. Parry's Black.

Powdered charcoal, a sufficient quantity of litharge as a dryer, to be rubbed smooth with linseed oil. Mix, and when used, thin with well boiled linseed oil.

Dr. Parry's Green.

To the above add yellow ochre, and you can produce an excellent green that will last for a number of years.

Cheap.

Slake a bushel of good, strong, white lime ; after sifting, make into a whitewash, by using forty gallons of water. Now add seventeen pounds of rock salt, and twelve pounds of brown sugar, stirring the whole together thoroughly, and it is ready for use. You must put on two or three coats in order to make it look well and lasting.

If you wish to produce fawn color, add four pounds of umber, and one pound of Indian red, and one pound of lampblack.

A stone color can be produced by adding four pounds of raw umber, and two pounds of lampblack. It is always better to mix these colors in oil before adding, so that they will work up nice and smoothly.

Petroleum.

The crude petroleum, applied to old buildings and fences, in liberal quantities, gives very satisfactory re-sults, as it fills up the pores, and thus preserves the wood.

Milk

and venetian red, mixed together, makes a cheap and lasting paint, for those that like the color, while milk

and water-lime, well mixed and evenly applied, produce a cheap paint, and one that is as good as some that
are more costly.

Ink — Black Copying.

Rain-water, half gallon; gum arabic, one ounce;
brown sugar, one ounce; clean copperas, half ounce;
powdered brown nutgalls, three ounces. Bruise all and
mix thoroughly. Let it stand for ten days, shaking
occasionally; then strain. This makes an ink that can
be depended on for years, and is therefore valuable for
records.

Black Japan.

Boil four ounces of logwood, chipped very thin and
cut across the grain, in six quarts of water; boil about
an hour, adding enough boiling water from time to time
to keep up about the same quantity you had before the
boiling commenced. Strain the liquor while hot. When
it is cool add enough cold water to make it equal five
quarts. Now add one pound of blue galls, coarsely
bruised, four ounces sulphate of iron calcined to whiteness, half ounce of acetate of copper, three ounces coarse
sugar, and six ounces gum arabic. This composition
produces the ink usually called Japan, since it exhibits
a high gloss when it is used.

Parchment.

Galls, one pound; gum, six ounces; alum two ounces;
copperas, seven ounces; kino, three ounces; logwood,

four ounces; water, eight pounds. As its name indicates, it is very useful to write on parchment.

Hainle's Black.

Two ounces of crushed gall-nuts, one ounce gum arabic, one ounce copperas, and one pound rain-water, adding a few grains of mercurial sublimate to prevent moulding. It is said that this ink will not corrode steel pens.

Cheap Black.

Prussiate of potash..1 dr.
Bichromate of potash...1 "
Extract of logwood..1 oz.
Water...1 gal.

Mix altogether and shake it well. As soon as it is dissolved it is fit for use.

Purple.

Boil one ounce of ground logwood in one-half pint of soft water, and one-half ounce pulverized alum; after boiling twenty minutes strain and it is ready for use. By bottling and keeping the air out, it will last a long time.

Violet.

One part of logwood to eight parts of water; boil down to one half, then strain and add one part chloride of tin.

Blue.

Take soft Prussian blue and oxalic acid in equal parts, powder them finely, and then add soft water to bring it to a thin paste; let it stand for a few days then add soft water to make the desired shade of color. To prevent spreading, add a little gum arabic.

Red Ruling.

Take an ounce vial and put into it a teaspoonful of aqua ammònia, gum arabic of the size of two peas, six grains of No. 40 carmine; fill up the vial with soft water, and it is ready for use. This makes a superior ruling ink, making a fine smooth line and very bright.

Dyeing Red.

To dye cotton a light red, boil in an iron kettle, one pound of camwood. This will color three pounds of cotton cloth. The cloth is to be cooked for about two hours in this solution.

Red Woolen.

Two pounds of alum to half pound of red tartar. Boil the goods in this one hour. This will dye ten pounds of woolen goods, but if you have more goods, you must boil it longer. Then boil up four and a half pounds of peachwood in clean water, cool down to a scald, then put in No. 1 tin liquor, then put in the goods and leave them in until dark enough, then the goods may be taken out once or twice, and aired a little, but not washed until they have been dyed.

Black Cotton.

Sumac, wood and bark together, three pounds. Boil half an hour, and let the goods boil eight hours. Then dip them in lime-water, and let them remain half an hour. Then take out the goods, and let them drip out an hour. Now add to the sumac liquor, copperas eight ounces, and dip an hour; then run them through the lime-water again for fifteen minutes. Now take a new dye with logwood, two and a half pounds, by boiling one hour and drip again three hours. Now add bichromate of potash two ounces to the logwood, dye and drip one hour. Then wash in clear, cold water, and dry in the shade. You say this is doing too much, but you cannot get a permanent black on cotton with less labor. At least Chase says so, and I have never known him to fail.

Bright Blue.

Three pounds of cotton cloth may be colored by this recipe:

Blue vitriol, four ounces; boil the goods a few minutes, then dip the goods in for three hours, after which, pass them through strong lime-water.

Or, Brown.

If you wish a brown color instead of a blue, you can dip the goods in a solution of prussiate of potash instead of lime-water.

Yellow on Wool.

For ten pounds of wool, bring a kettle of water to a scald or to one hundred and eighty degrees of heat, put in four pounds quer citron bark. This should not get any above one hundred and eighty degrees, as that will bring out the tanning and dull the yellow. One pound of alum, six ounces of cream of tartar, nearly one-half pint of tin liquors. Stir up the liquors well. Allow it to settle fifteen minutes. The goods keep in until dark enough.

Orange on Wool.

First, dye the pattern to a full yellow, then take a clean kettle of water, when a little warm, put in for ten pounds of goods, two pounds madder peachwood munjeet or, hypernick munjeet does very well. Put in your goods, keep them well handled, bring the goods to a boil, let boil until dark enough, wash and finish.

Coloring Thread Black.

First, take the thread and boil it in sumac and water, then let it be immersed in lime-water, cold; then in weak copperas-water, cold; then again in lime-water, cold; then in logwood liquor, warm. Take out, put some copperas liquor into your logwood liquor again, put in your goods, handle and finish.

This is from J. Marquart.

Blue for Wool.

For two pounds of goods:

Alum..5 oz.

Cream of tartar..3 "

Boil the goods in this for one hour, then throw the goods into warm water which has more or less of the extract of indigo in it, according to the depth of color desired, and boil again until it suits, adding more of the blue if needed.   It is quick and permanent.

Blue Dye — Aniline.

To one hundred pounds of fabric dissolve one and a quarter pounds of aniline blue in three quarts of hot alcohol.   Strain through a filter, add it to a bath of 130° Fahr.   Also ten pounds of glauber salts, and five pounds of acetic acid.   Put in the goods and handle them well for twenty minutes, then heat it slowly to 200° Fahr., then add five pounds of sulphuric acid diluted with water. Let the whole boil twenty minutes longer, then rinse and dry them.   If you add the aniline in two or three proportions during the process of coloring, it will facilitate the evenness of the color.   You can have any shade of blue by using different kinds of aniline.

Blue — Chromo.

Boil one hundred pounds of wool for one hour in a solution of three pounds of bichromate of potash, six pounds of alum, one pound of half refined tartar; then take it out, cool and rinse. Boil six pounds of good log-wood in a bag for half an hour in fresh water, and add three pounds of cudbear, well moistened and dissolved. Cool the dye to 180° Fahr., enter the prepared wool, handle for three-quarters of an hour, bring to a boil.

Blue Dye—Dark.

For broadcloth in the wool. This is colored in a healthy wood vat. The first dip is handled well, and boiled slow for one hour in the net. Then taken out, aired, and the vat stirred again, in two hours it can be dipped again for half an hour, and so often taken through until it has acquired the right shade. The vat ought to be strong enough in indigo to color it dark enough in three dips. About ten pounds of good in-digo is reckoned to one hundred pounds of wool. Clear indigo blue does not require anything more, but if taken through a warm bath, containing two pounds of blue vitriol, the color stands better in fulling, and is faster; after which it is rinsed, switched and dried. The dark blue, generally found in the market, is topped with fif-teen pounds of camwood, or twenty pounds of red sanders. The latter are boiled on the colored wood, as the indigo required for such dark colors would make it very expensive.

Blue Dye.

Indigo for cloth, (part logwood) one hundred pounds of cloth. First color the cloth by one or more dips in the vat of indigo blue, and rinse it well; then boil in a solution of two pounds half refined tartar, five pounds of mordanta, twenty pounds of alum, for two hours. Then take it and cool. In fresh water boil ten pounds of good logwood, for half an hour in a bag or otherwise. Cool the kettle to 170° Fahr. before entering; handle well over a reel, let it boil for half an hour; then take it out, cool and rinse. This is a fine blue, but not so permanent.

Blue Purple—Fast Color.

Dip one hundred pounds of wool into the blue vat first, to a light shade, then boil in a solution of fifteen pounds of alum and three pounds of half refined tartar for an hour and a half; take the wool out, cool and let stand twenty-four hours; now boil in eight pounds of powdered cochineal for a few minutes; cool the kettle to 170° Fahr.; handle the prepared wool in this for one hour, in which time let it boil for three-quarters of an hour; when it is ready to cool, rinse and dry. By coloring first with cochineal, as above stated, and finishing in the blue vat, the fast purple or dahlia so much admired in the German broadcloths will be produced. Use no tin acids in this color.

Blue and Purple Dye—For Stocking Yarn.

For five pounds of wool take bichromate of potash, one ounce; alum, two ounces; dissolve them, and bring the water to a boil; put in the wool and boil one hour; then throw away the dye and make another dye with logwood chips, one pound, or extract of logwood, two and a half ounces, and boil one hour. When you make a dye of logwood chips, either boil the chips half an hour and pour off the dye, or tie up the chips in a bag and boil with the wool or other goods; or take two and a half ounces of the extract in place of one pound of the chips, is less trouble and generally the better plan. In recipe, the more logwood the darker will be the shade.

Brown Dye for Wool.

1st. Make a mordant by dissolving alum and common salt in water; boil the cloth in it, then dye it in a bath of logwood to which a little green copperas has been added. Make the proportion two ounces of alum to one ounce of salt for every pound of cloth.

2d. Boil the goods in a mordant of alum and sulphate of iron, then rinse them through a bath of madder. The tint depends on the relative proportions of the alum and copperas — the more of the latter the darker will be the dye. The joint weight of the two should not exceed the one-eighth of the weight of the wool. The proportions are two parts of alum and three of copperas.

3d. Give the wool a mordant of alum and tartar, then pass it through a madder bath which will dye red. Now run it through a black bath of galls and sumac, or logwood, to which a little acetate or sulphate of iron has been added.

4th. Proceed to mordant the cloth and dye in a madder bath, then remove it and add a little acetate and sulphate of iron, and again pass it through the bath until the required tint is obtained.

5th. Give the cloth a light blue ground with indigo, then give it a mordant with alum, wash in water and run it through a bath of madder.

Brown Dye — Direct.

Make a strong decoction of oak bark. The shades will vary according to the quantity employed. You will brighten the color very much by passing it through a mordant of alum.

An infusion or decoction of walnut peels is very good for dyeing wool and silk a fine brown. First, brighten it by passing through a mordant of alum. The older the liquor the better.

Cheap Brown Dye.

The following is highly recommended, and can easily be obtained from the forests: Boil the bark of the common alder for an hour, with sufficient water to cover the goods, add a very little copperas, and put in the articles to be colored and let them remain for ten minutes; have a weak lye prepared in which you can dip them immediately after wringing them out of the former solution, then wring them immediately after dipping them and wash with soap and warm water.

To Remove Stains from Broadcloth.

Mix an ounce of fine ground pipe-clay with twelve drops of alcohol, and the same quantity of spirits of turpentine. Moisten a little of this mixture with alcohol and rub it on the spots. Let it remain until it is dry, then rub off with a woolen cloth, and the spots will disappear.

Cloth—To Raise the Nap On.

Soak the cloth in cold water for three-fourths of an hour, then put on a table board and rub the parts that are threadbare with an old hatter's card, filled with flocks, or with a prickly thistle, until you raise a nap. Let it dry in the air; and with a stiff brush lay the nap the right way.

To Extract Grease from Cloth.

Take about one-half peck of lime, add sufficient water to dissolve it, and so that it will leave about one gallon of clear water after it has been thoroughly stirred and settled, let it stand about two hours, and then pour off the clear liquid into another vessel. Add to it three ounces of pearlash for every gallon of the liquid. Stir it thoroughly, and after it has settled, bottle for use. Dilute this liquor with water to suit the strength or delicacy of the color of the cloth. Apply with a coarse sponge, rub out the grease, and wash it with clear water afterwards.

Dark Drab Dye.

For woolen yarn take one-quarter pound green tea, boil it in two quarts of water. After the strength is out add one-half teaspoonful of copperas. Put in the yarn while the solution is warm.

Crimson Dye.

Take cochineal.. 2 oz.
Wheat bran..12 "
Cream of tartar... 2 "
Pearlash (or soda)..8 dr.
Sal ammoniac..4 "

Add eight gallons of soft water in a brass kettle. After it is scalded add the cream tartar and alum. Let it boil, and put in the cloth for an hour, stirring occasionally. Take out the cloth, rinse in cool water, and air it. Empty the kettle and put in the same amount of water it contained before, add the bran, tied in a bag. The scum will raise as it boils, which remove as it rises. Then take out the bag and add the cochineal. Put in the cloth, and boil and stir for an hour, rinse the cloth in cold water, then pour out the water and pour in as much clean as before, warm it, add the sal ammoniac, put in the cloth for five minutes, stir and then drain. Now add the pearlash, and mix it. Put in the cloth again, and stir for ten minutes. Take out the cloth, air and rinse. This will give a permanent and beautiful color.

Drab Dye—Silver, (light).

For fifteen pounds of goods, take logwood three teaspoonfuls, alum three teaspoonfuls. Boil them thoroughly together, dip in the goods for an hour. The goods can be made of a darker shade by adding equal quantities of alum and logwood.

Coat Collars—(to Clean).

The following is highly recommended for cleaning coat collars and all woolen goods: Take soap tree bark (you can get it any drug store), a piece about two inches square, break it into small bits, and pour over it a half pint of boiling water. Let it stand several hours, then sponge the collar thoroughly with the liquor. After this, sponge it with clear water, and it will clean it thoroughly. Have both the washing and rinsing water as the flannel. For cleaning gray coat collars, this is one of the best articles out.

Green Dye—(for Woolen Goods.)

Steep the goods thoroughly in soap suds so as to clean them well, after which rinse several times in clean water, and lay them aside moist. Make a solution by dissolving alum in the package marked alum to mordant green on woolen, in a clean brass or copper kettle. Steep the cloth in the bath for an hour or longer, using sufficient clean water to work the goods easily. After steeping or mordanting, take the goods from the bath, drain or wring thoroughly and lay aside moist.

Green—Dye (for Silk).

Boil green ebony in water, let it settle; take the clean liquor as warm as you can bear your hands in it; handle the goods in it until it becomes of a bright yellow color; then make a solution of water, and a little sulphate of indigo. Handle the goods in it until the required shade.

Madder Red Dye—(for Wool).

For five pounds of goods:

Cream of tartar...5 oz.
Alum..25 "

Put in a kettle with water, also put in the goods; boil for half an hour; then air and boil half an hour longer. Now empty your kettle and put in five pecks of bran. Make milk warm, and let it stand until the bran rises, then skim off the bran and add madder one-half pound; put in the goods, heat slowly until it boils, and it is done. Wash them in strong soap suds.

Orange Dye—(for Cotton).

For ten pounds of goods:

Take sugar of lead eight ounces, boil a few minutes. After it gets a little cool put in the goods, dip two hours and wring out; make a new dye with bichromate of potash, sixteen ounces, madder, four ounces. Dip until it has the required shade. If it should be too red, take off a small sample, and dip it into lime-water, and you can then decide which you prefer.

Orange Dye—(for Wool).

For ten pounds of goods:

Argal eight ounces, muriate of tin twelve table-spoonfuls. Boil and dip one hour; then add to the dye two teacupfuls madder, and dip again one-half an hour. By adding cochineal instead of madder, you get a much brighter shade. This you can add in small quantities to suit your taste.

Pink Dye—(for Cotton).

For eight pounds of goods:

Solution of tin eight ounces, redwood four pounds. Boil the wood one hour, turn off into a tub, then add the tin, and put in the cloth. Let it stand five or ten minutes and a bright color will appear.

Pink Dye—(for Wool).

Alum, six ounces; boil the goods and dip one hour, then add to the dye, cream of tartar, eight ounces; also cochineal well pulverized, two ounces; boil them well, and dip the goods while boiling until you obtain the desired color. This will color six pounds of goods.

Purple Dye—(for Wool).

Alum..12 oz.

Cochineal.. 4 "

Cream of tartar...................................... 8 "

Muriate of tin ....1 teacupful

Boil the cream of tartar, alum and tin for fifteen minutes, and add the cochineal and boil five minutes; dip the goods two hours, then make a new dye, as follows:

Logwood ....28 oz.

Alum .... 8 "

Brazil wood...12 "

Muriate of tin .... 2 teacupfuls, with a little chemic. Work it until it has the desired color.

Red Dye—(for Cotton).

Take muriate of tin, one and one-third teacupfuls; add sufficient water to cover the goods well; heat it to boiling; put in the goods, and empty the kettle; put in clean water with nic-wood, two pounds; steep for half an hour at hand heat.

Rêd Dye—(for Wool).

Make a stiff paste of lac dye and sulphuric acid, and allow it to stand for a day; take two pounds of tartar, one and one-third pounds of salts of tin, and one and one-half pounds of the paste above mentioned. Boil the wool in the bath three-fourths of an hour, after which rinse and dry carefully.

Scarlet Lac Dye—(for Wool).

For one hundred pounds of flannel or wool yarn :

Tartar .... 5 lb.
Flavin .... 1 "
Tin crystals.. 1 "
Muriatic acid.. 1 "
Ground lac dye..25 "
Spirit..15 "

Boil all together for fifteen minntcs, then cool the dye to 170° Fahr.; enter the goods and handle them quickly at first; let them boil an hour; rinse them while yet hot, before the gum and impuritics harden. A small quantity of sulphuric acid may be used with this color to dissolve the gum. Regulate the quantity of lac dye by the quality.

Scarlet Dye—(for Wool).

For 100 pounds of goods.

Tin crystals.. 1 lb.
Flavine...$1\frac{1}{2}$ "
Scarlet spirit ....10 "
Ground Honduras cochineal.....................................11 "
Half-refined tartar.. 5 "
Tartaric acid .... 3 "
Oxalic acid .... 2 "

Scarlet spirit is prepared, as follows:

Take sixteen pounds muriatic acid 22° B., feathered tin one pound, water two pounds; put the acid in a stoneware pot, add the tin and allow it to dissolve. Keep the mixture a few days before using.

Slate Dye—(for Cotton or Woolen).

Boil the bark in an iron kettle; after it has boiled sufficiently, skim out the chips, then add copperas to set the dye; add more copperas if you wish it darker.

To make a slate, add about a teacupful of logwood liquor to a pan of warm water, make pretty strong, add a piece of pearlash the size of a nut; take grey colored goods and handle in this liquor a little, and it is finished.

Wine Colored Dye—(for Wool).

For ten pounds of goods, take camwood four pounds, boil fifteen minutes and dip the goods one-half an hour, then darken with blue vitriol three ounces; if it is not dark enough add one-half ounce of copperas.

Yellow Dye—(for Cotton).

1st. Steep the cloth or goods in soap-suds to cleanse them, then rinse several different messes of clean water and lay aside moist.

2d. Put the amount of clean warm water deemed necessary to work the goods easily, into a clean brass, copper or wooden vessel, then add of acetate lead (previously dissolved in a little hot water, in a basin), and stir with a wooden stick until it is well mixed; after this put in the goods, let them remain in the fluid thirty minutes, or longer, stirring frequently.

3d. Now put the amount of clean warm water required to work the goods easily into another clean earthen or metallic vessel, then add the bi chromate of potash, (previously dissolved in a little hot water, in a brass or iron kettle,) stir with a clean wooden stick till it is well mixed, then wring out the goods evenly from the acetate of lead bath, and work them in this bichromate of potash bath fifteen minutes or more, then wring out, rinse in several different messes of clean water and dry. Repeat the dipping in the different baths in the order above indicated, until the colors are even and satisfactory. One pound of cotton goods require about four gallons of water to work it easily. Larger quantities do not require so much in proportion. From Youman.

Washing Fluid.

Water...1 gal.
Unslaked lime..½ lb.
Sal soda...1 "

Put into the water and boil twenty minutes, let it stand until cool, then drain off and put into a strong jar or jug; soak your dirty clothes thoroughly, then wring them out and rub on plenty of soap, and in one boiler of clothes, well covered with water, add one teacupful of washing fluid, boil briskly for half an hour, after which wash well through one suds, rinse, and your clothes will look better than they did before you washed them.

Another.

Gum camphor..2 oz.
Alcohol ....1 pt.
Sal soda..½ lb.
Borax ....½ lb.

Dissolve the borax and sal soda in two gallons of cold rain water. Add the camphor, first dissolved in the alcohol. Stir thoroughly and bottle for use. Mix four tablespoonfuls of the preparation with a pint of soft soap and boil the clothes in this suds. If you soak the clothes over night before putting them into the suds, it is all the better.

Another.

Dissolve one-half pound of borax, two and one-half pounds of washing soda, in two gallons of water by boiling. When it is cold add about one teaspoonful of water of ammonia (hartshorn), and bottle so as to exclude the air. Use a teacupful to a pailful of water.

Hams—To Cure.

For a ham of twelve pounds, take—

Bay salt..¼ lb.
Coarse sugar ....¼ "
Common salt ....2 "
Saltpetre ....2 oz.

Reduce to a very fine powder, rub the hams thoroughly with it; then place them in a deep pan, adding a wine glassful of good vinegar. Rub them well every day with brine for three or four days, after which you can pour the brine over them with a spoon. Allow them to remain in the pickle for three weeks. After the ham is smoked, either case it with canvas to protect it against insects, or use pyroligneous acid. Apply with a brush, taking care to insinuate well into the cracks of the under surface. This will protect them thoroughly.

Hams—(Smoked) to Keep.

Put the ham into a sack made of coarse cotton c.oth for the purpose, fill it out with chopped hay all around the ham about two inches thick. The hay prevents the grease from coming in contact with the sack and keeps off all insects; hang it in the smoke-house or some other dry place and they will keep for a long time.

Hams—To Cure.

Saltpetre...1 oz.
Sugar...1¼ lbs.
Coarse salt.........   ....3½ "
Water..2 gallons

Boil together, let it cool, put on for fifty pounds of meat; keep the meat in the pickle for eight weeks. To a cask of, say from twenty-five to thirty hams, after they are closely packed, sprinkle slightly with salt; let them remain thus for several days, then cover them with brine, making it strong enough to bear an egg or potato; now add a gallon of molasses, and one-half pound saltpetre, and let them lie in the brine for six weeks, when they are all right, take them out and let them drain, and while yet damp rub the flesh side and end of the leg with pulverized red, black, or cayenne pepper; make it as fine as dust, and dust every part of the flesh side, after which hang up and smoke. Let them hang in the smoke-house, or some other cool place, for the insects will not disturb them.

Hams—(Mutton) to Pickle for Drying.

Put the hams into a weak brine for several days (say two) then pour off and apply the following:

For every five pounds,

Take water..3 gallons
Molasses.. .....½ pint
Salt..3 pounds
Saltpetre ....½ oz.
Salaratus..1 "

Let it remain from two to three weeks; this will cover them if closely packed.

Scouring.

To take stains out of silver plate: Steep the plate in soap lye for four hours, then cover it over with whiting, wet it with vinegar so that it may stick thick upon it, then dry it by a fire; then rub off the whiting and pass it over with dry bran, and the spots will disappear, and the plate will have an excellent bright appearance.

Eggs—To Preserve for Winter Use.

In one and one-half gallons of water, put one-half pint of fresh slaked lime, and three-fourths of a pint of common salt. Mix thoroughly, and let the barrel be about half full of this fluid. Let down your fresh eggs into it with a dish; tip the dish after it fills, so that they roll out without cracking the shell; for, if the shell is cracked, the egg will spoil. Be sure you put in fresh eggs. Lay a piece of board across the top of the eggs, and keep a little lime and salt upon it, so that the fluid will be as strong at the top as at the bottom. Keep them covered with brine. In this way eggs have been kept for several years.

Eggs—To Preserve.

Make a solution of gum arabic; apply it to the eggs with a brush, or immerse the egg in the solution. Let them dry, and then pack them in dry charcoal dust. This prevents their being affected by any changes of temperature.

Another.

Cream of tartar......... ....¼ lb.
Salt...1 "
Quick lime...½ bush.

Mix in a tub, or other vessel; add water to reduce it to the consistency to float an egg. Put in the eggs, keep them there, and they will be all right for two years at least.

Pickling Fruits—Apples.

Sugar...2 lbs.
Best vinegar..½ gal.

Put in as many apples as it will cover handsomely; add ground cloves and cinnamon, a tablespoonful of each. Pare and core the apples, tie up the cloves and cinnamon in a cloth, and put with the apples, into the vinegar and sugar, and only until done. Keep them in jars; they will keep a long time, and they are better and more healthy than preserves.

Pickling Peaches.

Sugar...2 lbs.
Best vinegar..1 pint
Peaches, stoned and peeled................................4 lbs.

Spice to your taste, or the same as for apples. Should they begin to ferment boil down the juice, then boil the peaches in it for a few minutes.

Pickling Plums.

Sugar...2 lbs.
Best vinegar..½ pint.
Plums...4 lbs.

Boil them in the mixture until soft. Take out the plums and boil the syrup until it is quite thick, and pour it over them again. Spice according to taste.

Pickled Cucumbers—Green.

Put one pint of rock salt into a pail of boiling water, pour it over the cucumbers, then cover it tight to keep in the steam, let them remain a night and part of a day. Make another brine same as above, and put in the cucumbers the same length of time. Scald and skim the brine and use it for the third brine, and let them remain in it as above. Now rinse and wipe them dry; add boiling hot vinegar, throw into every pail of pickles a piece of alum as large as a nut, and you will have fine green pickles. Add spices according to taste and keep the pickles under vinegar. Put a stone on the cover to keep the pickles under, and it has a tendency to collect the scum that may rise.

To Pickle Onions.

Gather the onions when quite ripe and dry, take off the thin outside skin with the fingers, and with a knife take off one more skin, and the onion will look quite clear.

Have on hand some dry bottles or jars. As fast as the onions are peeled put them in. Pour over them cold vinegar sufficient to cover them; add two teaspoonfuls of black pepper and two of allspice, taking special care that each jar has its share of the former article. Tie them down with bladder, and in two weeks they will be fit for use. They should be eaten within five or seven months after being prepared, as they are liable to get soft.

Canning Peaches.

Pare and halve the peaches. Pack them as close as possible, using no sugar. After the can is full pour in enough of pure cold water to fill up all the crevices between the peaches, up to the top. Let it stand so that the water will soak down into all the crevices, say seven hours. Pour on more water to replace that which has sunk. Now seal up the can and your peaches will retain all their freshness and flavor. Some use a cold syrup instead of water, but the peaches will not retain that natural taste as with water.

Canning Tomatoes.

Steam them sufficiently to scald or loosen the skin, then pour them on the table, and remove the skin, taking care to preserve the tomato as solid as possible. After peeling, place them in large pans, with false bottoms, perforated with holes, so as to strain off the liquid that flows from them. Pick them carefully from the pans into cans, which fill as solidly as possible; that is, put in all they will hold. Put them through the usual process, and seal hermetically.

Tomatoes when thus canned present the same appearance, and have the same fresh taste and flavor when you use them, as though they were just plucked from the vine.

Vinegar — Cider.

To realize the greatest profit on such apples as are made into cider, is to transform the juice into vinegar. In order to do this, fill the barrel completely, so that all the impurities thrown up by fermenting ("working") are thrown off by the bung hole. Complete this process before you put the barrel into the cellar. When it is done, draw off the purified juice and put it into another barrel that has a small amount of old vinegar; this will hasten the process amazingly. If you cannot obtain any vinegar to start it, it may require six months before it will be fit for table use. The longer the better.

Vinegar — German.

Boil four quarts of vinegar until reduced to two; mix the vinegar with six times its own quantity of bad vinegar in a small cask. It will mend it.

Vinegar — Raisin.

Take the pressed raisins left after making raisin wine, put them into a heap to heat; to each twenty-eight pounds, put two and one-half gallons of water and a little yeast.

Vinegar—Gooseberry.

Bruise the gooseberries when ripe, and to each quart of mashed berries add three quarts of water; let it stand for a day and night, then strain through a canvas bag. To every gallon of the juice, add one pound of brown sugar, stir them well together before you put into the cask; proceed in other respects as before. This vinegar has a very pleasant smell and taste; but raspberry vinegar, which may be made in the same manner is far superior. It is not necessary that the raspberries should be of the best sort, but they should be ripe and well flavored.

Vinegar—Cold Water.

Common molasses...................................... 2 gal.
Good hop yeast.. 1 "
Rain water...12 "

Put in a cask, set in a warm place and shake it well, once a week for several weeks, and you will have excellent vinegar; tack a piece of gauze or very thin cloth over the bunghole, to keep out dust and insects until the vinegar is made; then put in the bung, and keep it from the air, or it will lose its strength.

Vinegar—Currant.

Pick the currants from the stalks and proceed in the same manner as with gooseberries; allow it to freeze often and take the cake of ice or water from it; this purifies it and leaves it strong.

Wine—Cherry.

To make ten pints of this wine, take thirty pounds of cherries and four of currants, bruise and mix them together. Mix with them two-thirds of the kernels and put the whole of the cherries, currants and kernels into a barrel, with a quarter pound of sugar to every pint of juice. The barrel should be quite full. Cover the barrel with vine leaves, and sand above them, and let it stand until it has done working, which will be in about three weeks, then stop it with a bung, and in two months time it may be bottled.

Wine—Currant.

Put one pailful of water to every pailful of currants on the stem. Wash and strain; add three and one-fourth pounds of sugar to every gallon of the mixture of juice and water. Mix well and put into the cask, which should be placed in the cellar on the tilt, so that it can easily be racked off in October without stirring up the sediment.

Two bushels of currants will make one barrel of wine. Fill the barrel within three inches of the bung, and make it air-tight by placing wet clay over it after it is driven in.

Wine—Elderberry.

Water .... 5 gals.
Elderberry juice.................................... 5   "
White sugar.......................................22 lbs.
Red tartar.. 4 oz.

Put these into a cask, and add a little yeast and let it ferment. When undergoing fermentation, add

Ginger root..2 oz.

Allspice...2 "

Cloves...½ "

Put them into a clean cotton bag and suspend in the cask. They give a pleasant flavor to the wine, which will become clear in about two months, and may then be drawn off and bottled.

Wine — Grape.

Water...4 quarts.

Grape juice...4 "

Sugar...8 lbs.

Extract the juice in any simple way, if only a few quarts are desired. You can do it with a strainer and a pair of squeezers. If a large quantity is desired, do it to suit your own convenience, using only grapes that are perfectly ripe and free from blemish. After the first pressing put a little water with the pulp, and press a second time, using the juice of the second pressing with the water to be mixed with the clear grape juice. Put in a keg, fill even full. After fermentation has taken place and the scum removed, draw off, bottle and cork tight.

Wine — Ginger.

Ginger, best, bruised...................................2 oz.

Sugar ....6 lbs.

Water ....7 qts.

The rind of three good-sized lemons. Boil together for half an hour. When luke-warm put the whole in a cask, with the juice of the lemons and one-quarter of a pound of sun raisins. Add one teaspoonful of new yeast, and stir the wine every day for ten days.

Wine—Ginger.

Bruised ginger.. 4 oz.
Lump sugar ....10 lbs.
Water.. 5 gal.

Add two eggs. Boil well and skim. Then pour on hot three or four lemons cut in slices. Macerate for two hours, then rack and ferment. Add—

Spirits ....1 qt.
Finings ....½ pt.

Rummage well. To make color, boil—

Saleratus..½ oz.
Alum..½ "

in one pint of water, till you get a bright red color.

Wine—Lemon.

Water ....15 gals.
Raisins (bruised)....................................... 8 lbs.
Sugar ....30 "

Boil, then add—

Cider..7 gals.

Ferment and add—

Spirit...1½ gals.
White tartar... 6 oz.

Essence of lemon... 1 oz.
Finings.. ½ pt.

Shake well the essence with a pint of the spirit until it becomes milky before adding to the wine.

Wine—Apple.

To each gallon of cider, as soon as it comes from the press, add two pounds of loaf sugar; boil as long as any scum arises, then strain through a sieve and let it cool; now add some good yeast, mix well; let it work in the tub two or three weeks, then skim off the scum; draw it off close, and turn it; let it stand about a year, then rack it off and add two ounces of isinglass to the barrel; then add half a pint spirits of wine to every eight gallons.

Wine—Port.

Good imported port wine .... 3 gals.
Good prepared cider................................12 "
Juice of elderberries................................ 3 "
Good brandy..1½ "
Cochineal.. 3 oz.

Pulverize the cochineal very fine, put it with the brandy into a stone jug, let it remain at least two weeks. Have your cider ready; put six gallons of the cider into a twenty-gallon cask; add to this the elder juice, port wine, brandy and cochineal; take the remaining six gallons of cider, with part of which clean out your jug that contained the brandy, and pour the whole into the

cask, bung it tight, and in six weeks it will be all right
for use.

Wine—Raspberry.

Take six pounds of raisins, clean, wash and stone
them thoroughly; boil four gallons of spring water for
half an hour. As soon as it is taken off the fire pour
it into a deep stone jug or jar; put in the raisins with
twelve quarts of raspberries and four pounds of loaf
sugar; stir it well together, cover them closely, and set
in a cool place; stir it twice a day, then pass it through
a sieve; put the liquor in a close vessel, and one pound
more of loaf sugar; let it stand for a day and night to
settle, then bottle it, adding a little more sugar.

Wine—Unfermented.

Pick the grapes when well ripened; remove carefully
all decayed and unripe berries. You may use mixed
varieties of grapes. Express the juice and boil as long
as any scum arises; skim carefully from time to time; do
not boil over an hour; bottle it while hot, and seal either
in glass bottles, jugs or air-tight casks. It is in a condition to be used at any time, but after it is once opened
it must not be allowed to ferment. With the exception
of strawberry syrup, this will be found to be the most
delightful and exhilirating of all fermented beverages.
It needs no sugar, and may be diluted when drank.

Beer — Cottage.

Water..10 gals.
Good sweet wheat bran........................ 1 peck.
Good hops...................................... 3 handfuls.

Boil the whole together in an iron, brass or copper kettle, until the bran and hops sink to the bottom; then strain it through a hair sieve, or a thin sheet, into a cooler, and when about luke-warm, add two quarts of molasses. As soon as the molasses is melted pour the whole into a nine or ten gallon cask, with two table-spoonfuls of yeast. When the fermentation has subsided, bung up the cask, and in four days it will be fit for use.

Beer — Ginger.

Honey.. 1 lb.
Sugar..20 "
Lemon juice.................................... ....18 oz.
Yeast .... 6 pts.
Water...18 gal.
Bruised ginger root...................................22 oz.]

Boil the ginger half an hour in a gallon of water, then add the rest of the water and the other ingredients, and strain when cool. Add the whites of two eggs, beaten, and one ounce of essence of lemon. Let it stand for four days, then bottle, and it will keep a long time if you don't drink it.

Beer — Hops.

Hops..6 oz.
Water ....5 qts.

Boil three hours, then strain off the liquor, pour on four quarts of water and twelve spoonfuls of ginger, and boil the hops three hours longer. Strain it and mix with the other liquor, and stir in two quarts of molasses. Brown, very dry, half a pound of bread, and put in— rusked bread is best. Pound fine and brown in a pot, like coffee. After it has cooled so that it is luke-warm, add a pint of new yeast that is free from salt. Keep the barrel covered in a temperate atmosphere until fermentation has ceased, which you may know by the settling of the frost. Then turn into kegs or bottles, and keep in a cool place.

Beer— Philadelphia.

Water..15 gal.	
Brown sugar..................................10 lbs.	
Ginger, bruised............................. $\frac{5}{8}$ "	
Cream of tartar............................. $\frac{1}{8}$ "	
Super-carbonated soda ....1$\frac{1}{2}$ oz.	
Oil of lemon (cut in a little alcohol)...... $\frac{1}{2}$ teaspoonful.	
Hops... 1 oz.	
Yeast... 1 pint	

The whites of five eggs well beaten; boil the hops and ginger root twenty or thirty minutes in enough of water to make all milk warm, then strain into the rest; add the yeast and allow to work over night; skim and bottle.

Beer — Root.

Water at 60° Fahr...10 gal.
Molasses ....,.................. .... 3 "
    Let it stand two hours, then pour into a barrel and add—
Bruised sassafras bark.....................................½ lb.
Wintergreen bark, bruised............................½ "
Bruised sarsaparilla root...............................½ "
Yeast...1 pint
    Enough water to fill the barrel, say twenty-five gallons; let it ferment for twelve hours and bottle.

Beer — Root.

Common burdock root.................................6 lbs.
Or essence of sassafras...............................2 oz.
Good hops..1 lb.
Corn, roasted brown...................................2 pints
    Boil the whole in twelve gallons pure water until you get the strength of the material, strain while hot, into a keg, add enough cold water to make twenty gallons; when it is nearly cold add clean molasses or syrup to make it palatable; add also as much fresh yeast as would raise a batch of sixteen loaves of bread; put the keg in the cellar or some other cool place, and in two days and nights you will have a first rate sparkling root-beer.

Beer—to Cure when Ropy.

Put a handful or two of flour, and the same quantity of hops, with a little powdered alum into the beer and stir it well.

Beer—Tomato.

Gather the tomatoes once a week, take off the stems, wash and mash them well. Strain through a coarse linen bag. To every gallon of the juice, add one pound of good moist brown sugar. Allow it to stand nine days and then pour it off from the pulp, which will settle in the bottom of the jar. Bottle it closely. The older it gets the better. For use, take a pitcher that holds as much as you want to use, fill it nearly full of fresh sweetened water, add some of the preparation described, and a few drops of the essence of lemon, and you will find it equal to the best lemonade, and costs almost nothing. To every gallon of sweetened water add half tumbler of beer.

Bitters—Brandy.

Cardamons...1½ oz.

Cassia...1½ "

Cochineal ....⅛ "

Bruised gentian...4 "

Orange peel ....2½ "

Spirits .... ½ gal.

Digest for a week, then pour off the clear, and pour two and one-half pints of water on the dregs. Digest for a week longer, pour off and mix the two tinctures together.

Bitters — Stomach.

Underground Peruvian bark..........................¼ oz.

Gum kino..⅛ "

European gentian root................................¾ "

Orange peel...¾ "

Cinnamon...⅛ "

Anise seed..¼ "

Coriander seed...¼ "

Cardamon seed...⅛ "

Bruise all these articles, and put them into one-half pint of best alcohol. Let it stand for one week, and decant; then boil the dregs a few minutes in a pint of water. Strain and press out all the strength. Now dissolve loaf sugar, one-half pound, in the hot liquid, add one and one-half quarts cold water; mix with spirit tincture just poured off, or, you can add these and let it stand on the dregs if preferred.

Lemonade.

Essence of lemon....................................15 drops.

Tartaric acid.. ⅛ oz.

White sugar.............. . ...½ lb.

Water ....1½ qt.

Mix.

Lemonade — Italian.

Pare and press one dozen lemons. Pour the juice on the peels, and let it remain on them all night. In the morning add—

Loaf sugar...1 lb.
Good sherry...1 pt.
Boiling water...1½ qt.

Mix well and add one pint of boiling milk. Strain through a jelly bag until clear.

Lemonade — Milk.

Take the juice of fourteen lemons,
White sugar...1½ lb.
Sherry ....1 pt.
Boiling water...2 qt.

Mix; when cold add a quart of boiling milk; let it stand for several hours, then strain until clear, through a jelly bag and ice. It is always better if made the day before using.

Lemonade — Portable.

Take the juice of four large lemons, one pound of loaf sugar; strain the lemon juice, then mix with sugar; grate the rind of the lemon into this, and keep the mixture in a jar. If it is too sweet, add a little citric acid. Use a tablespoonful to a tumbler of water.

Lemonade — Portable.

Loaf sugar ....6 oz.
Essence of lemon...1 dr.
Tartaric acid ....1 oz.

Powder the sugar and acid; mix them, and pour the essence of lemon on them, a few drops at a time. After all is mixed, divide into twenty-four equal parts, and put them in white paper, like powders. If you wish to use them, dissolve one in a tumbler of water, and you will have a glass of lemonade. This you can carry about in your pocket.

Pop — Ginger.

Ground ginger....................................1 oz.
Hot water (boiling) ....1 gal.
Cream of tartar ....½ teaspoonful
White sugar....................... ....1 lb.
The peel of one lemon.

Let this stand until milk-warm, then put in the other part of the lemon, and
Saleratus ....½ teaspoonful
Yeast...2 tablespoonfuls
and the glair of two eggs to clear. Add cinnamon and cloves to your taste.

Pineapple-ade.

Take fresh ripe pineapples, pare and cut them into thin slices, then cut each slice into small bits; put them into a large pitcher, and sprinkle powdered white sugar among them; pour on boiling water in the proportion of half a gallon of water to each pineapple; cover the pitcher, close up the spout with a roll of paper, and let the pineapples infuse into the water till it becomes quite cool, stirring and pressing down the pineapple occasionally with a spoon to get out as much juice as possible.

When the liquid has cooled off, set the pitcher in ice for a while; then put the infusion in tumblers, and some more sugar, and put a lump of ice into each glass.

Soda Water without a Machine.

Water...1 gal.
Super-carbonate of soda...............................1 oz.
Crushed sugar..½ lb.

Fill half-pint bottles with this water. Have your corks ready. Drop into each bottle nitric acid·in crystals one-half drachm, and immediately cork and tie down. The bottles must be handled carefully, without shaking, and keep cool until needed. Use sugar according to taste.

Soda Syrup, with or without Fountains.

The common syrups are made using the following:
Pure water...½ gal.
Gum arabic...1 oz.
Crushed sugar..4 lbs.

Mix in a copper or brass kettle, boil until the gum is dissolved, then skim and strain through white flannel. After which, add tartaric acid, two and three-quarter ounces, dissolved in hot water. To flavor, use extract of orange, rose, pineapple, peach, sarsaparilla, strawberry, lemon, &c., one-half ounce to each bottle, or to suit your taste.

Cream Soda—Using Cow's Cream for Fountains.

Sweet rich cream .... 2 quarts
Water .... 3 gills
Loaf sugar ....10 lbs.

Warm gradually, so as not to burn, and add—

Extract of vanilla...1½ oz.
Extract of nutmeg.. ½ "

Bring to a boiling heat, no more; use four or five spoons of this syrup, if used without a fountain add tartaric acid one-fourth pound; keep it cool.

Ice Cream.

Rich milk.................................... ....1 gal.
White sugar..2 lbs.
Fresh cream...1 gal.

Use more or less sugar to suit yourself. Dissolve the sugar in the mixture; flavor with extract to suit your taste, or take the peal from a fresh lemon, and steep it in as little water as you can, and add this, it is the best, some prefer the juice or extract of strawberries, or raspberries for flavor; they also give a beautiful color. Have your ice well broken; take one quart of salt to a bucket of ice; about half an hour's constant stirring, and occasional scraping down and beating together, will freeze it sufficiently.

Ice Cream—Cheap.

Oswego corn-starch...................................¼ lb.
Milk ....3 quarts

Dissolve the starch in one pint of the milk, then mix all together, just simmer it a little (don't boil); flavor and sweeten according to your taste.

Another.

Pulverized sugar.......................................1 lb.

New milk, and cream (each) one quart and twelve eggs ; dissolve the sugar in milk, beat the eggs to a froth, and add to the whole; strain and bring to a scald but do not burn it; when cool flavor with oil of lemon, or extract of vanilla. Put the tin freezer in a tub with broken ice and salt, whirl the freezer, and occasionally scrape down from the side that gathers.

Pop-Corn Balls.

Pop the corn, reject all that is not nicely opened, place a peck of corn upon a table, or in a large dripping pan, put a little water in a kettle, with half a pound of sugar, boil until it becomes quite waxy in water, then remove from the fire, and dip into it three or four table-spoonfuls of thick gum solution, made by pouring boiling water upon gum arabic over night, then dip the mixture on different parts of the corn. Put a stick or hands under the corn, lift it up and mix until the corn is all saturated with candy mixture, then press the corn into balls with the hands. Do it quickly, or it will set before you get through.

Oyster Soup.

Milk ....1 gill.
Butter...½ oz.
Water ....½ pt.
Oysters..1 doz.

Crackers to thicken. Boil the oysters and water, then add the other ingredients, previously mixed together, and boil from three to five minutes. Add salt and pepper to suit individual tastes. Use the proportions for any quantity.

Oyster Stew.

Stew them in their own liquor, season to taste with salt and pepper. Butter may also improve them. Some add, also, milk or cream and condiments, such as mace, parsley or nutmeg. If thickening of the soup is desired, grated cracker is preferable to flour.

Oyster Fry.

Take them from the shell, dry them on a clean cloth or napkin. Beat up the yelks of eggs with thick sweet cream — one yelk to two tablespoonfuls of cream. Rub together some grated bread, crumbs or crackers and a little salt and pepper. Heat in a skillet three-fourths of a pound of butter until hot. Dip each oyster in the beaten yelk and cream and then roll it in the crumbs, so that they will adhere to it. Drop into the skillet and fry until of a light brown color on both sides. They ought to be crisp and light. Never pour over them the melted grease that may remain.

Oysters—Roast, Boil or Bake.

Wash the shells clean. To roast, lay the shells on a gridiron over a bed of coals. When the shells open they are done. Take off the top and serve in the under shell. To boil, put them in a pot of boiling water, serve in the shell. To bake, put in a hot oven; otherwise, treat the same as for roasting.

Honey—Artificial.

Cream of tartar.................................... 2 oz.
Water .... 3 lbs.
Coffee sugar......................................10 "

The white of an egg well beaten; Lubin's extract of honeysuckle, ten drops; bees' honey, one-half pound; strong vinegar, three tablespoonfuls. Put the water and sugar into a suitable kettle and place on the fire. When it is lukewarm, stir in the cream of tartar and vinegar, then continue to add the egg. When the sugar is almost melted put in the honey and stir until it comes to a boil, take it off, let it stand a few minutes, then strain. Add the extract of honeysuckle last, let it stand over night and it is prepared for use. This is a very delicious article.

Honey — Premium.

Water..1 qt.
Common sugar...8 lbs.
    Let them come to a boil and skim. Now add:
Pulverized alum...½ oz.
    Take from the fire and stir in
Cream of tartar..1 oz.
Water, or extract of rose ....2 tablespoonfuls,
and it is ready for use. This is a "first rate" article.
Those using it desire nothing better.

Honey — Cuba.

Water... 1 qt.
Good brown sugar...........................10 lbs.
Old bee-bread honey, in comb.............. 2 "
Cream of tartar............................. 1 teaspoonful
Oil of peppermint........................... 3 drops.
Oil of rose................................... 2 "
Gum arabic................................... 1 oz.
    Mix well, and boil two or three minutes, and pour in
one quart more of water, in which is put an egg well
beat up. As it begins to boil skim well, take it from
the fire, and when a little cool add two pounds of nice
bees' honey, and strain. This has been extensively
manufactured and shipped. If scaled up it will keep
nice and fresh for a long time.

Another Honey.

Water.. 2 qts.
Good common sugar..10 lbs.

Bring it to a boil gradually, skimming well. When cool, add two pounds bees' honey and eight drops of peppermint essence. If you wish a better article, use one-half pint less water, and one-half pound more honey and white sugar. If desired, by adding one-half ŏunce of alum to the water, you can give it the ropy appearance of bees' honey.

Tallow Candles.

Most tallow in summer is often quite yellow and soft. To avoid both, take your tallow, put in a little beeswax with it, especially if the beeswax is dark and not fit to sell; put into a suitable kettle, add weak lye and boil gently for an hour or two each day for two days, stirring and skimming well. Cut it out each morning and scrape off the bottom, which is soft; add one, two or three gallons fresh lye, according to the amount of tallow. Be sure that the lye is not too strong. The third morning use water in which there is dissolved alum and saltpetre, at the rate of half a pound each for fifteen pounds of tallow; then simmer, stir and skim again; let it cool, and you can take it off the water for use.

Candles — Imitation Wax.

Add some powdered quick-lime to melted tallow to purify it, then add two parts of wax to one of tallow, and you get a beautiful article of candle resembling wax. When making the candles, dip the wicks in lime-water and saltpetre. To a gallon of water add:

Lime ....½ lb.
Saltpetre ....2 oz.

It improves the light and prevents the tallow from running.

Candle-Wicks—Preparing.

Chloride of ammonium................................. ½ oz.
Saltpetre... ½ "
Chloride of calcium..................................... ½ "
Borax...1 "

Then dissolve in one and one-half quarts of water and filter. Soak the wicks in this solution and then dry.

Another.

Steep the wicks in the following solution:

Take saltpetre...4 oz.
Lime ·...1 lb.
Water...2 gals.

Dry the wicks well before using. It prevents the tallow from running and improves the light.

Yeast—for Bread.

Take nine medium-sized potatoes, boil in two quarts of water, and mash them fine. Steep one cup of hops in one-half pint of hot water and strain off, pressing the hops.   Now mix, hop-water, the mashed potatoes, potato-water, two tablespoonfuls of salt, two of ground ginger, one cup of sugar.   When tepid, add one cup of stock yeast.   Or, for the first, use brewers' yeast.   Put in a jar and keep in a cool place where it will not freeze. Will keep two weeks.   Let stand twenty-four hours before using.

MISCELLANEOUS TOILET.

Hair Oil.

Take alcohol...................................½ pint
Castor oil.......................................1 gill
Citrionella.....................................1 dr.

This is a fine hair dress, is also good for the hair.

Shaving Soap.

White bar-soap...........................4½ pounds
Rain water.................................1   quart ⌡
Beef's gall..................................1   gill

Cut up the soap, and boil five minutes; stir while boiling, and color with one-half ounce vermillion; scent with oil of roses, or almonds.

Windsor Soap.

This soap may be made by cutting nice white bar soap, and dissolving it over a slow fire, and scent it with oil of caraway; when it is well mixed, pour it into your mold, and let remain for a few weeks.

Freckles.

Freckles are yellowish brown spots on the skin, usually upon the exposed parts of the body, as the face, neck, hands, and arms; they usually occur upon persons

of fair complexions and sandy or red hair; they are
probably owing to the derangement of the liver more
than any other cause; sometimes also to other causes;
exposure to the sun also increases them. They are
generally very difficult to remove and often impossible.
Various washes have been recommended, and used for
their removal, among which, the following are probably
the best:

Rose water....................................4 oz.
Pulverized borax.............................2 drachms

Mix: Dissolve and wash the parts twice a day, with
a little of this solution, rain water may be used instead
of rose-water. The following wash is probably still
better:

Take beef's gall..............................1 oz.
Pulverized saleratus.........................½ "
Pulverized borax.............................½ "
Gum guaiac...................................⅓ "
Alcohol.......................................½ pint
Rose or rain water...........................½ "

Mix, and let stand ten days, shaking occasionally;
use as a wash twice a day. A solution of citric acid,
made by dissolving half an ounce of the acid in a pint
of rose, or rain water, is also good; to be used same as
the others. It will be well to attend to the liver, by
taking daily, at the same time, the liver pills or powders;
avoid exposure to the sun. A cold infusion of cleavers,
(*Galium aparine*) drank three times a day, and the parts

washed with the same, will remove freckles from the skin, if continued for two or three months.

Golden seal..4 dr.

Orris root..4 "

Add honey until it is a stiff paste.

Toothache and Neuralgia.

When this affection befalls any one we can practically sympathize, knowing what the suffering is. We would for their comfort recommend the following:

Sal volatile..3 dr.

Laudanum ....1 "

Mix, and rub the part affected frequently, or if the tooth which is affected be hollow, drop some of this on a piece of cotton and put it into the tooth. For a general faceache or sore throat, moisten a bit of flannel with it, and put it at night to the part affected.

Coral Tooth Powder.

Take four ounces of coral, reduced to an impalpable powder, eight ounces of very light Armenian bole, one ounce of Portugal snuff, one ounce Havana snuff, one ounce of good burnt tobacco ashes, and one ounce of gum myrrh well pulverized. Mix them together and sift them twice.

A Good Powder.

To make a good tooth powder, leave out the coral, and in its place put in pieces of brown stoneware, reduced to a very fine powder.

This is the common way of making it.

Tooth Powders.

Many persons, while laudably attentive to preserve
their teeth, do them hurt by too much officiousness.
They daily apply to them some dentrifice powder, which
they rub so hard as not only to injure the enamel by excess-
ive friction, but to hurt the gums even more, than by
abuse of the tooth-pick.   The quality of some of the dentrifice powders advertised in the newspapers is extremely
suspicious, and there is reason to think that they are not
altogether free from corrosive ingredients.   One of the
safest and best compositions for the purpose is a mixture
of two parts of cuttle-fish bone and one of Peruvian
bark, both finely powdered, which is calculated not only
to clean the teeth without hurting them, but to preserve
the firmness of the gums.

Besides the advantage of sound teeth, for their use
in mastication, a proper attention to their treatment
conduces not a little to the sweetness of the breath.
This is, indeed, often affected by other causes, existing
in the lungs, the stomach, and sometimes even in the
bowels; but a rotten state of the teeth, both from the
putrid smell emitted by carious bones and the impurities
lodged in their cavities, never fails of aggravating an
unpleasant breath, wherever there is a tendency of that
kind.

Tooth Paste.

The following is an excellent tooth paste. This has the finest cleansing qualities, a healthy influence on the gums, and prevents the teeth from decaying:

Charcoal ....3 drachms,
Chinchona 3   "

Hair Vigorators — Baldness.

In this, as well as all diseases, it is always better to work at the cause than the effect. Baldness is sometimes caused by one thing and sometimes by another. The dress of the head is often the cause. It is mostly too warm and heavy, not allowing enough fresh air, keeping the head in a damp and sweaty condition. That is most always the cause of dandruff, and that of baldness. Dandruff is much more injurious than generally supposed. It heats the head and burns up the oils and moisture of the head, and soon destroys the root of the hair, which causes the hair to turn gray and fall out. Hair should be kept short as practicable, and cleaned often, washed with soapsuds, and rinsed with cold water, and then the head rubbed with a brush or coarse towel until it is real warm. If a stiff brush is used often while the hair is dry, it will help it wonderfully. The most reliable recipe to restore hair, perhaps, is the following:

Take glycerine .... 2 oz.
Tinct. of myrrh... 1 "

Cologne .... 1 oz.

Tinct. of cantharides.................................... ½ "

Distilled water...24 "

Mix well, and use once or twice per day. Apply with a sponge.

Some also use the following mixture, and recommend it:

Take red wine ....1 lb.

Salt ....1 dr.

Sulphate of iron ....2 "

Nut-gall ....2 "

This is all to be boiled for a few minutes on a gentle fire. Wash the head gently, and in an hour wash off with cold water. If this practice is kept up a month the hair will be sure to come out in full force. A fine growth can be sure in six weeks. My father and mother have both used this recipe with much satisfaction.

Another.

Lac sulphur....................... .... 3 dr.

Sugar of lead .... 2 "

Tannin...40 gr.

Pulverized copperas ....40 "

Rose water.. 6 oz.

Apply once a day until the hair is quite well colored, then three times per week, and finally once per week. This recipe is intended to color the hair, also to invigorate it. The use of it will soon strengthen and aid the hair so it will not want any coloring. I have heard of instances where the hair got its original color.

French Restoratives and Vigorators.

Sugar of lead...1 oz.
Lac sulphur...2 "
Borax...1½ dr.
Aqua ammonia...1 "
Alcohol...½ gill.
Bergamot...1 oz.

Shake these articles until well mixed, and let them stand a few days. Then put in three pints of soft water. If the quantity is too large, you can take only half of each quantity. This is surely one of the best Hair Restoratives ever out. The lac sulphur and sugar of lead also have the properties of coloring the gray hair to a dark brown, and even if greater quantities are used of each, it will turn it jet black.

MODE OF APPLYING.—Wash your head clean each morning and dry with a rough towel; then moisten the bald part of the head well. Be sure the roots are reached as the work is there.

The following recipe we can highly recommend:

To Remove Freckles.

Alum ....1 oz.
Lemon juice...1 "

Mix with one pint of rose water. Apply to the face with a sponge three times a day. This solution is very effectual and perfectly harmless, and removes from the face all impurities, such as freckles, blotches and pimples.

Face Powder.

Starch..6 oz.
Oxide of bismuth............... ....2 "

This is not so deleterious as most powders and paints, yet it is a nuisance.

The following is my choice recipe : To set off the complexion with all the advantage it can attain, nothing is more useful than to wash the face with pure water. A little soap may be found excellent occasionally.

Pearl Powder.

These are of several sorts. The finest is the least hurtful to the skin. It gives the most beautiful appearance, but is too dear for common use. Still perfumers keep it for those that are curious and rich. The next best to this, perhaps, is the following :
Magistery of bismuth ....4 oz.
Fine starch powder ....2 "

Mix well and pour over proof spirits until it overflows the powder. Stir frequently, so that the impurities will rise and may be removed. Continue stirring until all impurities have risen and are removed: After this pour off the spirits and set the paste in the sun to dry.

Another Hair Tonic.

Take good brandy.........................¼ pint,

Bay rum...............................¼ "

Fine salt.............................1 tablespoonful,

Alum 1   "

Mix well and stir often for a few days. Then add one-fourth pint of soft rain-water.

Apply with a soft sponge if the head is bald, if not, rub in well. If this amount is used and well applied it will surely be effective.

Oil to Make Hair Curl.

Olive oil................................1 lb.

Oil organum...........................1 dr.

Oil of rosemary.......................1¼ "

Use it freely, twice per day will not be too often, but only a little at a time. Using this only for a few weeks will be of great benefit.

Razor Strap Paste.

Emery reduced to an impalpable powder, two parts; spermaceti ointment, one part; mix together and rub over the strap. This usually costs twenty-five cents per box; according to the above recipe, will cost you about three cents.

Hair Dye.

The following recipe is from one of our best barbers. He says:

Take gallic acid...2 dr.

Alcohol ....4 oz.

Soft water ....8 "

Mix this all and put in one bottle. Then mix the following:

Nitrate of silver.. ½ oz.

Good ammonia...12 dr.

Gum arabic .... 2 "

Soft water... 4 oz.

First dissolve the nitrate of silver in the ammonia, then add the gum arabic which must first be dissolved in the water; this is put in another bottle; the bottle No. 1, or first mixture is kept separate from the second bottle No. 2. The hair is then first cleansed with a good shampoo, or soap-suds, removing all grease from it, then rub quite dry, and No. 1 rubbed on with a sponge, then take a towel again, and rub until it is only nice and moist. Then take a small tooth-brush (that is what barbers use) and a comb, and put on the silver, or No. 2. Be careful not to get it on the skin, as it is hard to remove. Cyanuret of potassium, one-half drachm, to one ounce of water will remove it. However it is a poison, and should not be used much. This dye is a sure permanent dye. As soon as the process is over the whiskers are dyed. The shade can be as desired. If only brown, the No. 2 is to be diluted by water. I think I can speak practically about its fast color. When I was a boy I of course wanted to "show off" with moustache, but owing to my age, my moustache could not be seen unless colored, so I resorted to this recipe, and I found that it was rather tedious to touch only the moustache, and still more tedious in cleaning my face. I found it rather a "botch." My dignity was considerably embarrassed. The moustache was somewhat colored, and so was my face. This recipe I would by no means recommend for the hair. It is perhaps more injurious than any other. Instead of it being somewhat like the others —a tonic, it is rather a poison, but it is a good fast color and used by all barbers.

Perfumery — Ambergris Perfume.

Melt two pennyweights of fine ambergris in a brass mortar, very gently, stir in quickly eight drops of green lemon juice, and the same of behn-nut oil. Add, ready powdered, with fine loaf sugar:

Musk...12 grains
Civet..12   "

And twenty-four grains of the residuum from the making of ambergris; add one ounce of spirits of ambergris. Mix and incorporate them well, and add sixteen pounds of fine dry hair powder. Pass the whole twice through a fine hair seive; then lay it open for three days in a dry room, stir it often, that the spirits may entirely evaporate; otherwise it may turn sour, which, however, will go off by keeping. Bottle and cork well.

Musk and Civet Perfumes.

Pure musk..2 pwts.
Civet...2 grains
Residuum of ambergris............................1 pwt.

Make this into a paste, with two ounces of musk, made by infusion. Powder it with loaf sugar and mix in sixteen pounds of fine hair powder.

Orris Perfume.

Take best dried and scraped orris roots, free from mould. Bruise or grind them. The latter is best, as being very tough, they require great labor to pound. Sift the powder through a fine hair seive, and put the remainder in a baker's oven to dry the moisture. A violent heat will turn the roots yellow. When dry, grind again and sift, and repeat the same until the whole has passed through the seive. Mix nothing with it.

Violet Perfume.

Drop twelve drops of genuine oil of rhodium on a lump of loaf sugar; grind this well in a glass mortar and mix it thoroughly with three pounds of orris powder. This will in its perfume have a resemblance to a well flavored violet. If you add more rhodium oil, a rose perfume instead of a violet one, will be produced. The orris powder is a most agreeable perfume, and only requiring to be raised by addition to the above named quantity of the oil. Keep this perfume in the same manner as the others. What is at the druggists' shop is generally adulterated.

Rose Perfume.

Take two pecks of fresh, dry damask rose leaves, strip them from their leaves and stalks; have ready six pounds of fine hair powder; strew a layer of rose leaves on sheets of paper at the bottom of a box, cover them over with a layer of hair powder, then strew alternately a layer of roses and powder, until the whole of each has been used. When they have lain twenty-four hours, sift the powder out and expose it to the air twenty-four hours more. Stir it often, add fresh rose leaves twice as before, and proceed in the same way. After this dry the powder well by a gentle heat, and pass it through a fine sieve. Lastly, pour ten drops of oil of rhodium, or three drops of otto of roses, on loaf sugar, which triturate in a glass mortar, and stir well into the powder, which put into a box or glass for use. This hair powder perfume will be excellent, and will keep well.

Bergamot Perfume.

Take sixteen pounds of hair powder, and forty drops of Roman oil of bergamot, and proceed in all respects as before, but do not leave the compound exposed to the air, for in this case the bergamot is so volatile that it will quickly fly off.

To Perfume Clothes.

Take of oven-dried best cloves, cedar and rhubarb root, each one ounce, beat them to a powder, and sprinkle them in a box or chest, where they will create a most beautiful scent, and preserve the apparel against moths.

Sun Burn.

A cosmetic made from elder flowers, steeped in boiling water, and then suffered to cool, is excellent for the hands and face.

Pastils for Perfuming Sick Rooms.

Powder separately the following ingredients and then mix on a marble slab:

Gum benzoin...1 lb.

Gum storax...8 oz.

Frankincense...1 lb.

Fine charcoal...2 "

Add to this composition the following liquids:

Tincture of benzoin.......................................6 oz.

Essence of ambergris ....2 "

Essence of musk...1 "

Almond oil...2 "

Clear syrup..4 "

Mix the whole into a stiff paste, and form into pastils of a conical shape which, dry in the heat of the sun. If more liquid should be required for the paste add warm water.

Lip Salve.

Dissolve a small lump of white sugar in a large spoonful of rose-water (common water may be substituted); mix it with a couple of large spoonfuls of oil, a piece of spermaceti of half the size of a butternut; simmer the whole eight or ten minutes.

Sore Eyes.

Sugar of lead...½ drachm
Sulphate of zinc.....................................½   "
Salt 1   "
Loaf sugar 1   "
Clean rain water.....................................½ pint

Let stand and shake occasionally for two days, then filter through white flannel; it is then ready for use. This is an excellent eye wash. It may be used two or three times a day. An excellent wash is also used, which is made in the following way: A strong decoction of green tea and yellow root, of each, one-half an ounce, and the addition of one drachm of sulphate of zinc all well mixed and filtered as before.

Eye Water.

Extract of lead.....................................10 drops
Rose water ....6 oz.

Mix, and wash them night and morning.

Another.

Extract of lead..................................10 drops
Spirits of camphor............................20   "
Rose water.. ½ pint

This eye-water is very useful in ophthalmia attended with much inflammation. Use as the other.

Another.

Opium ....10 gr.
Camphor .... 6 "
Boiling water...12 oz.

Rub the opium and camphor in the boiling water, and stir the water a long time, then strain. This collyrium abates the pain and irritation attendant on severe cases of inflammation of eyes.

Another.

White vitriol ....½ dr.
Spirits of camphor ....1 "
Rose-water...4 oz.

Dissolve the vitriol in warm water, and then mix all well. This is a good tonic for the eye, especially in weak eyes after inflammation.

Another.

Opium ....10 gr.
Distilled water..................................... 6 oz.
Liquor acetate of ammonia .... 2 "

The water is to be warmed, and the opium dissolved and strained through a white flannel, then mixed with the ammonia. This water is very good in case of great pain.

Warts.

These troublesome excrescences can easily be removed if only a little attention is paid. I have known some people to be annoyed exceedingly with warts on hands, neck, &c. It is something I never could bear on me. The first appearance of one would make me very uneasy until it was removed. The way I would do was, to cut the wart down until it would bleed a little, then lay the head of a match on it and ignite it, allowing it to burn on the wart. The phosphorous burning so slowly would seldom ever fail to destroy all the roots. But this operation was attended with a great deal of pain, not only at the moment, but it would inflame the part very much. Some people use nitric acid, by touching the wart until it is all eaten off. This is a simple and easy remedy, only it is sometimes dangerous, as the acid is not always taken off in due time. The following is a recipe from a doctor, (who states in the *Journal of Health*,) after the practice of nearly twenty years, he has never known this to fail:

Take nitrate of silver (lunar caustic), dip the end of the caustic into water, then rub the wart with it. By doing this a few times, the wart will be gone. If the caustic is too severe, you can destroy its effects by smearing on a little cream.

Bark of a common willow burnt to ashes, says Dr. Gunn, will, if mixed with strong vinegar and applied on warts or corns, remove them at once.

Hair Restorative—(Mrs. Allen's.)

Soft water ....8 oz.
Rose water...8 "
Sugar of lead..$\frac{1}{8}$ "
Sulphur ....$\frac{1}{8}$ "

Prepare the compound and let it stand seven days before using.

Wood's Restorative.

Sugar of lead..1 dr.
Lac sulphur...2 "
Rose water..$\frac{1}{2}$ pt.

Mix well, and apply as occasion may require.

Phalon's.

To four ounces of ninety per cent. alcohol, colored by a few drops of tincture of alkanet root, add half an ounce of castor oil, and perfume with a compound of neroli, orange, bergamot and verbena.

Hair Wash—Saponaceous.

Rose water..$\frac{1}{2}$ gal.
Extract of rondeletia..$\frac{1}{4}$ pt.
Rectified spirits...$\frac{1}{2}$ "
Hay saffron ....$\frac{3}{8}$ dr.
Transparent soap...$\frac{3}{8}$ oz.

Cut up the soap very fine; boil it and the saffron in a pint of rose-water; after it is dissolved add the rest of the water, then the spirits, and last the rondeletia. To perfume it, leave it stand four or five days, then bottle it for use.

Toilet—Hair Wash for Dandruff.

Castor oil..$\frac{1}{2}$ teaspoonful
Alcohol...$\frac{1}{2}$ pt.

Scent it with a few drops of lavender. This is an excellent hair wash. The alcohol seems to dissolve castor oil better than any other.

Chapped Hands.

Take the white of an egg and four ounces of blanched almonds; beat the almonds to a smooth paste in a mortar, then add the white of egg and sufficient rose-water, mixed with one-half its weight of spirits of wine, to give the proper consistency.

Cure for Sore Mouth.

Sulphur ....2 teaspoonfuls
Armenian bole.............................2   "
Burnt copperas 2   "
Burnt alum 2   "
Honey ....2 teacupfuls

Mix them thoroughly; take a small quantity in the mouth, let it dissolve in the mouth, and then swallow it. Repeat this often until the mouth is healed.

Hair Dye.

Sugar of lead...................... ....—........6 drachms
Lac sulphur...4   "
Glycerine oil ....2 oz.
Rain water...1 qt.
Sage...1 handful
    Fifteen cents worth of perfume—citronella.

Hair Invigorator.

Carbonate of ammonia...................................½ oz.
Tincture of cantharides..............................½ "
Bay rum...2 pts.
Alcohol......................................1 "
Castor oil...2 oz.
    Mix well and shake it before using.

Another.

Cologne water..½ oz.
Rose water...½ "
Vinegar of cantharides...........................½ "
    Mix well and rub the roots of the hair thoroughly.
Use daily.   Is good for bald heads, and to prevent hair
from falling off.

Another Invigorator.

    Strong sage tea has also been recommended to pre-
vent the hair from falling off, and if persevered in will
make the hair grow very luxuriantly.

Hair Dye—(Dr. Hanman's.)

Quicklime...6 oz.

Starch ....4 "

Litharge ....1 "

Mix in a powder; mix it in warm water and rub the hair well. Cover the hair with wadding or oil skin on retiring.

Hair Dye—(Batchelor's.)

Dissolve one-half ounce of gallic acid in four ounces of alcohol, add one ouart of soft water.

Another.

Concentrated ammonia..............................$\frac{1}{2}$ oz.

Soft water...$\frac{1}{2}$ "

Add nitrate of silver................................$\frac{1}{2}$ "

Let it dissolve. To this add:

Gum arabic ....$\frac{1}{2}$ oz.

Soft water..2 "

Hair Dye—(Warren's.)

White lime..$\frac{1}{4}$ oz.

Lime..2 "

Litharge ....$\frac{1}{2}$ dr.

Mix in a powder. Apply with a sponge and water to dye black. To dye brown, apply with milk.

COOKING AND BAKING.

Cooking may be defined thus: The best and most efficient ways of preparing raw food so as to preserve its natural qualities unimpaired, and render it most palatable and nutritious.

A choice meal does not necessarily imply great expense and great skill in its preparation. The first requisite for a good meal is *good sense*. The best authorities should be consulted, and instruction given by them should be carried out with care and patience; the materials being chosen with taste should be cooked with a judicious regard to their appearance at the table. Promptness, too, in preparing a meal adds much to its being well prepared. Also having one part ready long before the other impairs that part of its nutrition. A meal served on time is more palatable to guests than one for which they have been waiting. Waiting for meals is a trying time. We have experienced—

> "How sad it is to sit and pine,
> The long half hour before we dine;
> Upon our watches oft to look,
> Then wonder at the clock and cook!"

The art of cookery might be based on philosophical principles, but the means and circumstances of the masses are so different that a work of this kind would not be practical. The recipes in this work are not of such a character as to imply great expense, so that none but the wealthy could use them. A judicious economy was kept in view, and recipes were valued according as they were practical. Mrs. P. Y. Dundore, of Plainfield, Ill., has prepared and selected the various recipes with much care. She being a good cook herself, to which the writer can testify, they can be relied upon, and some even bear the impress of actual experience; and of those into whose hands this book may fall, she would ask a fair trial of the recipes before passing judgment.

General Rules and Directions for Preserving.

1st. Let everything that is used for this purpose be delicately clean and dry.

2d. Never place a preserving pan flat upon the fire, as this will render the preserves liable to burn; it should rest on the lower bar of the kitchen range.

3d. After the sugar is added to them, stir the preserves gently at first, and more quickly towards the end, without quitting them until they are done. This precaution will always prevent the chance of their being spoiled.

4th. All preserves should be perfectly cleansed from the scum as it rises.

5th. Fruit which is to be preserved in syrup, must first be blanched or boiled gently, until it is sufficiently softened to absorb the sugar, and a thin syrup must be poured on it at first, or it will shrivel instead of remaining plump, and becoming clear. Thus, if its weight of sugar is to be allowed, and boiled to a syrup with a pint of water to the pound, only half the weight must be taken at first, and this must not be boiled with the water more than fifteen or twenty minutes at the commencement of the process; a part of the remaining sugar must be added every time the syrup is re-boiled, unless it should be otherwise directed in recipe.

6th. To preserve both the true flavor and the color in jams and jellies, boil them rapidly.

Patent Yeast.

Take three tablespoonfuls of flour, three of sugar, one of ginger, half a tablespoonful of salt, put all together into a pan, boil four good sized potatoes in a quart of water; when tender, pour the water from the potatoes into the jar, mash the potatoes very fine and add to the rest. Boil a handful of hops in a quart of water, strain the water into the mixture, stir it briskly five minutes; when lukewarm, add one cup of good yeast, let it rise, and then stir it down several times through the day; next day put it into a fruit can or jug, cork up pretty tight and put it into a cool cellar ready for use.

One teacupful of this is sufficient for four loaves of bread. Yeast made in this way will keep five or six

weeks in cool weather, and three in hot. In summer
omit the flour. Is the very best. Try it.

Pickling Cherries.

Take nice ripe cherries with the stems on, add one
pint of cider vinegar, two pounds of sugar. Put all
together; let it come to the boiling point, pour into a jar,
let it stand two days; then boil the juice briskly one hour,
add the fruit and scald it well. Be careful that it does
not cook to pieces.

Pickle Chow-Chow.

Take two quarts of green tomatoes, two quarts of
white onions, two quarts of pickling beans, one dozen
green cucumbers, one dozen peppers, one head of cabbage.
Season with mustard, celery seed, and salt to suit the
taste. Boil two hours slowly, continually stirring, and
add two tablespoonfuls of salad oil while hot.

Pickling Tomatoes.

Slice green tomatoes a quarter of an inch thick, put
into a jar, and sprinkle salt over each layer. Let them
remain twenty-four hours, lift them into a colander, and
let them drain well; then, to one quart of vinegar add
two pounds of sugar, two teaspoonfuls of cinnamon, one of
cloves. Boil all together until the tomatoes are tender.

Pickling Siberian Crab Apples.

For one gallon of fruit take one quart of best vinegar,
one pound of sugar, a small handful of cinnamon; boil

until the apples are tender, but not boiled to pieces; let them stand four or five days, pour off the juice, boil it half an hour, add the fruit and let it come to a boil. The flavor is retained best if sealed up tight.

Ripe Pickled Cucumbers.

Peel ripe cucumbers, cut them in two, and scrape out the seeds; cut them into slices, put them into a preserving kettle with sufficient vinegar to cover them, and a little molasses; heat them gradually to the boiling point, but do not boil; put them into a jar and let them remain two or three days; then take one quart of vinegar to every two quarts of cucumbers, one cup of sugar, a dozen cloves and a few pieces of cinnamon; boil all together a few minutes, drain the vinegar off from the cucumbers, and pour the fresh vinegar, boiling hot, over them. They will always be ready for use.

Pickling Apples.

Fill a two-gallon jar with pared and cored sweet apples, one gallon of best vinegar, four pounds of sugar, one tablespoonful of ground cinnamon and one of cloves. Put all together in a preserving-kettle and boil till barely tender.

Pickling Plums.

One quart of best vinegar, four pounds of sugar, eight pounds of plums; boil them in the mixture until tender, then take out the plums and boil the syrup until quite thick, and pour it over them again.

Pickling Cabbage.

Slice the cabbage into a jar, and sprinkle salt over each layer; let it remain two days, then put it into a colander to drain one day; put it into the jar again, and cover with boiling vinegar, adding a few slices of red-beet root.

Pickling Mushrooms.

Clean the mushrooms and put them into cold vinegar, and allow it to come slowly to a boil; drain and lay them in a cloth till cold, then put them into fresh vinegar, and simmer slowly a few minutes; dry them again, and put into the vinegar, after it has been cooled, with a little mace added.

Another Mode of Pickling Cucumbers.

Take fresh cucumbers and put into a weak brine a week, add mustard-pode and horseradish leaves to keep them green; take out and drain, covering with vinegar for a week, at which time take out and drain again, and put into new vinegar. For a barrel of pickles, add two ounces of each mustard seed, ginger root, cloves, pepper, and red pepper pods.

Sour-Krout.

Take solid cabbages, strip off the outer leaves and shave fine into a jar or keg. To each layer of cabbage sprinkle over it a piece of salt, and pack it down tight with a potato-masher. Proceed in this way until the jar is full; lay a dozen of clean cabbage leaves on top, have a tight-fitting cover to cover with, and put a weight of about five pounds on top to press it down. It will be ready for use in five or six weeks. Boil about two hours, add a little butter or some pork.

Pickling Capers.

As soon as gathered, put them into a jar with strong vinegar and salt. Tie a skin over the jar and keep in a cool place.

Pickled Cucumbers.

Pick the cucumbers when only two or three inches long; wash them and lay them into a jar or keg; make a strong salt brine, strong enough to bear up an egg, pour over the cucumbers, cover them up and put weights on top to keep them in the brine. When wanted for use, soak them in fresh water three or four days, changing the water twice a day. When sufficiently freshened put them in good cider vinegar.

Sweet Pickled Peaches.

Three pounds of sugar, seven pounds of fruit, one pint of vinegar. When on the boil, put in the fruit; whole cloves and ground cinnamon put in a bag; cook twenty minutes. Put into a jar and cover it up tight.

If they should ferment at any time, simply boil down the juice, then boil the peaches in it for a few minutes only.

Fried Bread.

Beat four eggs, add half a teacupful of rich sweet milk, half a teaspoonful of salt, cut bread into slices, (dry bread will do,) dip it into the mixture and fry in butter or lard; when brown on one side, turn it over.

Waffles.

To a quart of milk add five eggs, one and one-fourth pounds of flour, half pound of butter, beat them well together; when baked sift cinnamon and sugar on them. If you make the waffles before it is time to bake them, add a spoonful of yeast.

Graham Biscuit.

Take one quart of graham flour, one tablespoon half full of salt, sufficient water stirred in to stir easily with the spoon; drop it into hot cast-iron moulds and bake in a hot oven. If the oven is not hot the biscuit will not be good; the heat makes them light. These are the healthiest biscuit made.

French Rolls.

One spoonful of lard or butter, three pints of flour, one cup of yeast, and as much milk as will work it up to the stiffness of bread; just before baking them take a clean cloth or brush and rub them over with a little sweetened milk.

Pan Cakes.

Two cups of sweet milk, four eggs, one teaspoonful of salt, half a teaspoonful of soda, two cups of flour. Do not stir more than is necessary to mix.

Johnny Cake.

Take one pint of sweet milk, one pint of sour, one teacupful of cream, or, if cream can not be had, take half a teacupful of lard, four eggs, one teaspoonful of saleratus, add corn meal to the consistency of pancake batter; bake quick in a hot oven; it is nice, try it.

Graham Bread.

Take some of your light bread sponge, mix graham flour into it sufficient to prevent its sticking to the hands while kneading it, make into loaves, let it rise, and bake one hour; if there is no sponge on hand, make the yeast as for light bread.

Jumbles.

Take one and a half pounds of flour, one pound of sugar, one cup of butter, three eggs, with a wine-glass of rose water; roll them thick with fine powdered sugar; bake on tins.

One pint of lukewarm milk, half a cup of butter, one of yeast, flour enough to make a stiff batter, and set it to rise; when light, add two beaten eggs, one cup of sugar, flour to make a stiff dough, when light make into small cakes.

Indian Bread.

To two quarts of Indian meal, add boiling water enough to wet the same; when sufficiently cooled, add one teaspoonful of salt, half a pint of yeast, one tea-cupful of molasses, and flour enough to form it into a loaf; (it should not be kneaded hard); when light, bake two hours in a well heated oven. Half a cup of butter or lard is an addition.

Breakfast Corn Cake.

Four teacups of corn meal, two of sour milk, two tablespoonfuls of cream or butter, one teaspoon even full of saleratus, two eggs, a teaspoonful of salt; bake in "'em nans" and serve hot, like rolls.

Light Bread.

Take five or six ordinary sized potatoes, boil till tender in a quart of water; take one pint of flour, pour boiling water over it, stirring it briskly, meanwhile, to prevent it being lumpy; pour the water from the pota-toes into it, mash the potatoes fine and add those; mix it well; have the mixture the consistency of pancake batter; when warm add one teacupful of patent yeast, and let it rise over night; in the morning take one

quart of sweet or buttermilk, previously warmed; mix
with one quart of flour, add the yeast and stir well ten
minutes; set it in a warm place to rise; when quite light
add flour, and knead up stiff. It should be worked at
least half an hour. Let it rise a little, and knead it
again; when light the second time mould out and put
into the bread-pans. Let it rise, and bake one hour in
a moderate oven.

Dry Yeast.

Take one pint of good yeast, stir sufficient corn meal
into it to roll out; roll thin, cut it into cakes, put them
in the sun to dry. If dried by the stove, care should be
taken not to scald them. When thoroughly dry, put
away in a dry place. It will keep three or four months.

Marble Cake.

One cup of butter, one of milk, two of sugar, whites
of eight eggs, five cups of flour, half a teaspoonful of
saleratus, spice.

One cup of butter, two of brown sugar, one of sour
milk, yelks of eight eggs, one egg, one cup of molasses,
spice, four cups of flour, one teaspoonful of saleratus.
Put in pans together.

Sweet Fried Cakes.

Two and a half cups of buttermilk or sour milk, one
cup of butter or lard, one cup of sugar, one teaspoonful

of soda, one teaspoonful of brandy, two eggs, a little salt; mix flour to the consistency of biscuit dough, cut them in strips, twist them and double them over, press the ends together. Fry them in hot lard.

Lemon Cake.

Three cups of loaf sugar, one of butter, one of milk, one teaspoonful of soda, two of cream of tartar, the yelks of five eggs, five cups of flour, the juice and grated peel of one lemon.

A Good Seed Cake.

Beat to a cream one pound of sugar and one of butter; next add the whites of eight eggs beaten to a stiff froth, and the well-beaten yelks of twelve, add these by degrees, beating continually till are well mixed; then gradually add a pond and a half of flour, into which two ounces of nicely cleaned caraway seed have been strewn, and a good-sized nutmeg grated. Beat another quarter of an hour, then pour into a buttered mould and bake for an hour and a half.

Philadelphia Cake.

One and a half pounds of flour, three-quarters of a pound of sugar, half a pound of butter, three eggs, two teaspoonfuls of baking powder, mixed with the flour, or, half a teaspoonful of soda and one teaspoonful of cream of tartar, one cup of sweet milk, a wineglass of wine, the same quantity of brandy, a pound and a half of seeded raisins, a quarter of an ounce of pounded mace, or, a couple of nutmegs and a little cloves or cinnamon. Stir to cream the butter and sugar, then add the eggs, previously beaten to a froth. If soda is used, dissolve it in the milk; stir the whole together a few minutes; bake in pans lined with buttered paper.

Spanish Puffs.

Put into a saucepan a teacupful of water, one tablespoonful of powdered sugar, half a tablespoonful of salt and two ounces of butter. While it is boiling add sufficient flour for it to leave the saucepan, stir in one by one the yelks of four eggs, drop a tablespoonful at a time into boiling lard and fry a light brown.

Cream Muffins.

One quart of rich milk, or, half cream and half milk is better; a quart of flour, six eggs, a tablespoonful of butter, one of lard softened together. Beat whites and yelks separately, very light, then add flour and shortening and a teaspoonful of salt; stir the flour in the last thing, lightly as possible, and have the batter free from lumps. Fill dishes half full well buttered muffin-rings and bake immediately in a hot oven.

Muffins.

One quart of flour, three cups warm milk, one of yeast and a little salt; stir well together and let rise;

mix flour enough in to knead it with the hands. Knead it well and let it rise one hour; roll it into balls, set them to rise, then bake.

Rich Mince Meat.

Cut the root of a neat's tongue, rub the tongue well with salt, let it lie four days, wash it perfectly clean, and boil it till it becomes tender; skin, and when cold chop it finely; mince as small as possible, two pounds of fresh beef suet from the sirloin, stone and cut small two pounds of bloom raisins, clean nicely two pounds of currants, pound and sift half an ounce of mace, and a quarter of an ounce of cloves, grate a large nutmeg; mix all these ingredients thoroughly together with a pound and a half of good brown sugar; pack it in jars. When it is to be used, allow for the quantity, sufficient to make twelve small mince pies, five finely minced apples, the grated rind and juice of a large lemon, add a wine glass and a half of wine; put into each a few bits of citron, and preserved lemon peel. Three or four whole, green lemons, preserved in brown sugar, and cut into thin slices, may be added.

To Broil.

This culinary branch is very confined, but excellent as respects chops or steaks, to cook which in perfection the fire should be clear and brisk, and the gridiron set on it slanting, to prevent the fat dropping in it. In addition, quick and frequent turning will insure good flavor in the taste of the article cooked.

To Fry Meats, &c.

Be always careful to keep the frying-pan clean, and see that it is properly tinned. When frying any sort of fish, first dry them in a cloth and then flour them. Put into the pan plenty of dripping or hog's lard, and let it be boiling hot before putting in the fish. Butter is not so good for the purpose, as it is apt to burn and blacken and make them soft. When they are fried, put them in a dish or hair sieve to drain, before they are sent to table. Olive oil is the best article for frying, but it is very expensive, and bad oil spoils everything that is dressed with it. Steaks and chops should be put in when the liquor is hot, and done quickly, of a light-brown, and turned often. Sausages should be done gradually, which will prevent their bursting.

To make a savory dish of veal, cut some large scollops from a leg of veal, spread them on a dresser, dip them in rich egg batter; season them with cloves, mace, nutmeg and pepper, beaten fine; make force-meat with some of the veal, some beef suet, oysters chopped, sweet herbs shred fine; strew all these over the scollops, roll and tie them up, put them on skewers and roast them. To the rest of the force-meat add two raw eggs, roll them in balls and fry them; put them into the dish with the meat when roasted, and make the sauce with strong

broth—an anchovy of a shalot, a little white wine and
some spice; let it stew, and thicken it with a piece of
butter rolled in flour; pour the sauce into the dish, lay
the meat in with the force-meat balls, and garnish with
lemon.

To Roast a Duck.

Ducks may be roasted as soon as killed. Keep a
clear bright fire; let them be done of a light brown,
but if wild, they should not be much roasted or the flavor will be spoiled. They take about an hour to roast,
and should be well basted. The livers and gizzard are
parboiled, chop fine and thrown into the gravy. Can-
vass-back ducks are roasted in half an hour; they
should always be served with currant jelly. For tame
ducks, apple sauce is more appropriate. A duckling
will require proportionally more roasting.

To Broil a Fowl.

Split the fowl down the back; season it very well
with pepper, and put it on the gridiron with the inner
part next the fire, and allow the fowl to remain until it
is nearly half done, then turn it, taking great care that
it does not burn; broil it of a fine brown, and serve it
up with stewed mushrooms, or a sauce with pickled
mushrooms. A duck may be broiled in the same way.
If the fowl is very large, half roast it, then cut it into
four quarters and finish it on the gridiron; it will take
from half an hour to three-quarters of an hour to cook.

To Fry Chickens.

Cut up the chickens, and season them with salt and cayenne pepper; roll them in flour, and fry them in hot lard; when fried, pour off the lard, and put in a quarter of a pound of butter, one teacupful of cream, a little flour and some scalded parsely chopped fine for the sauce.

To Regulate Time in Cookery — Mutton.

A leg of eight pounds will require two hours and a half; a chine or saddle of ten or eleven pounds, two hours and a half; a shoulder of seven pounds, one hour and a half; a loin of seven pounds, one hour and three-quarters; a neck and breast, about the same time as a loin.

Beef.

The sirloin of fifteen pounds, from three hours and three-quarters to four hours; ribs of beef from fifteen to twenty pounds, will take from three hours to three hours and a half.

Veal.

A fillet from twelve to sixteen pounds will take from four to five hours, at a good fire; a loin upon the average, will take three hours; a shoulder from three hours to three and a half; a neck, two hours; a breast, from one and a half to two hours.

Lamb.

Hind quarter of eight pounds will take from an hour and three-quarters to two hours; fore quarter of ten pounds, about two hours; leg of five pounds, from an hour and a quarter to an hour and a half; shoulder, or breast, with a quick fire, an hour.

Pork.

A leg of eight pounds will require about three hours; griskin, an hour and a half; a spare-rib of eight or nine pounds will take from two hours and a half to three hours, to roast it thoroughly; a bald spare-rib of eight pounds, an hour and a quarter; a loin of five pounds, if very fat, from two hours to two hours and a half; a sucking pig, of three weeks old, an hour and a half.

Poultry.

A very large turkey will require about three hours; one of ten pounds, two hours; a small one, an hour and a half; a full-grown fowl, an hour and a quarter; a moderate sized one, an hour; a pullet, from half an hour to forty minutes; a goose, full-grown, from an hour and a half to two hours; a green goose, forty minutes; a duck. full-size, from thirty to fifty minutes.

Venison.

A buck haunch, which weighs from twenty to twenty-five pounds, will take about four hours and a half roasting; one from twelve to eighteen pounds, will take three hours and a quarter.

Green Peas—a la Francaise.

Take two quarts of fresh shelled peas, put them into cold water with three ounces of butter, and stir them about until they are well covered with the butter, drain them in a colander and put them in a stew-pan with parsley; dredge over them a little flour, stir the peas well and moisten them with boiling water; boil them quickly over a large fire for twenty minutes, or until there is no liquor remaining.   Dip a small lump of sugar into some water that it may soon melt; put it with the peas and add a half a teaspoonful of salt.   Take a piece of butter the size of a walnut, work it together with a teaspoonful of flour and add this to the peas, which should be boiling when it is put in.   Serve hot.

Fruit Cake.

One cup of butter, one of thick cream, three of sugar, four of raisins, five cups of flour, four eggs; one teaspoonful of saleratus, one of nutmeg and two of cinnamon; stir the sugar and butter to a cream, beat the eggs to a stiff froth and mix with the sugar and butter. Dissolve the saleratus in a tablespoonful of water, pour it into the cream, stir but very little; mix all and stir a few minutes, and bake one hour.

Tea Cake.

One cup of sweet cream, one of sugar; two eggs, three cups of flour, one heaping teaspoonful of baking powder mixed with the flour; bake twenty or thirty minutes.

Paste for Tarts.

One ounce of fine loaf sugar to one pound of flour, a pinch of salt; make it into a stiff paste with a gill of boiling cream and three ounces of butter. Work it well and roll out thin.

Paste for Chicken Pie.

Take one quart of flour, one pound of butter; mix it well together; add two cups of milk, with half a teaspoonful of saleratus and one teaspoonful of salt; roll out and line a deep dish with it; have a young chicken dressed and cut in pieces, put into the lined dish, with a teacup of wáter, one teaspoonful of salt, one tablespoonful of butter, a little pepper and some parsley; put on the top crust and bake one hour. If an old chicken is used, boil it tender first and then bake into a pie.

Pie Crust

Take one quart of flour and eight ounces of butter or lard, one teaspoonful of salt; work them well together, then mix it up with as little water as possible, so as to have it a stiff paste; roll out thin for use.

Puff Paste.

Take two quarts of flour and one pound of butter, one teaspoonful of salt; rub the flour and butter well together, add sufficient water to make a paste stiff enough to roll out; when rolled out, put a layer of butter all over it, then sprinkle a little flour on, double it up and roll out again; double and roll it with layers of butter three times, and it will be ready for use.

Beefsteak Pie.

Take tender steak that has been broiled, cut in small pieces; season to taste; make a paste same as for chicken pie and bake one hour.

Raised Lamb Pie.

Bone a loin of lamb, cut them nicely, and lay them in the bottom of a stew-pan, with an ounce of butter, a teaspoonful of lemon-juice and some pepper and salt; put them over a fire and turn them, and put them to cool. Then raise four or five small pies with paste about the size of a teacup, put some veal force-meat at the bottom and the cutlets upon it; roll out the top an eighth of an inch thick, close and pinch the edges, bake them half an hour, and when done take off the top and pour in some good brown sauce.

Omelet.

Whisk up three eggs, a sprinkling of parsley, a pinch of salt and a taste of black pepper, with two ounces of bacon cut into half dice, and turn the frothing mixture into the omelet pan, in which a spoonful of butter has been heated, without browning. When it is brown on one side take a flat spoon and turn it over; brown nicely on the other side, then tip the whole mass upon a plate.

Another.

Beat four eggs, add half a teacup of sweet milk, half a teaspoonful of salt, melt two tablespoonfuls of butter in a frying-pan, add one pint of bread-crumbs, stir until the bread is hot through, then pour on the egg mixture and stir a few minutes longer. Serve hot.

Air-Castle Pie.

Take one pint of cream, half a teaspoonful of soda, one teaspoonful of salt; mix in flour enough to make a stiff paste; take two-thirds of the paste, roll out and line deep round or oval dishes with it; take a deep plate that will exactly cover the dish, roll out the rest of the paste, lay the plate bottom side up, butter the plate, lay the paste on and ornament it with leaves made of the paste; rub it over with the yolk of an egg; bake it a nice brown; when done take it off the deep dish and put it on a plate; have ready some previously stewed chicken, rabbits or pigeons well seasoned with some gravy; put it into the crust, take the cover from the plate and cover it up, and serve hot. This makes an excellent pie, and is quite showy.

Raised Pork Pie.

Make a raised crust as for chicken pie; take the rind and chine bone from a loin of pork, chop it fine, season with pepper, salt and powdered sage, and fill your pie; put on the top, fasten the edges well, rub the top over with the yelk of an egg, and bake it two hours, with a paper over it to prevent the crust from burning.

Rabbit Pie.

Make a crust as for chicken pie, or mince fine a pound of boiled bacon with the livers of the rabbit, one tablespoonful of butter, one pint of bread-crumbs, some pepper and salt, some pounded mace, some chopped parsley, and a challot thoroughly beaten together; cover the bottom of the dish with it, put in neatly dressed rabbits, and cover with thinly sliced ham or bacon.

To Cook White Beans.

Take one quart of white beans, wash clean, put into a kettle with three quarts of water and one teaspoonful of saleratus; boil fifteen or twenty minutes, pour the water off, add three quarts of fresh water, and boil till done.   Saleratus is quite an improvement in cooking beans.

Boiled Turnips.

Peel, and if large, cut in two or three pieces; boil them till very tender, then drain the water off thoroughly and mash them very fine; then stir them constantly over the fire a few minutes so as to get them dry, then add a little salt, a little good butter, and a little cream, and a little pepper; continue to simmer and stir a few minutes longer, and serve quite hot.

Pickled Beets.

Wash the beets very clean, but neither scrape nor cut them, as not a fiber even should be cut away, until after they are boiled, then boil from one and a half to two and a half hours, according to their size. When quite tender, peel and slice thick, and put them into an earthen or glass jar; sprinkle a little black pepper over them, and let stand until next day, pour the vinegar off and boil it, pour it on boiling hot. Boiling the vinegar keeps them longer.

Green Peas.

Take one quart of fresh shelled peas, boil them in a quart of water twenty or thirty minutes, when done add a little salt, three tablespoonfuls of cream, and one of butter. Serve hot.

Tomatoes.

Take fresh ripe tomatoes, pour boiling water over them; let them remain in the water a minute or two, take them out and peel and slice them, and serve with loaf sugar, or a little vinegar, sugar and salt.

Stewed Tomatoes.

Take good ripe tomatoes, peel and slice them, put them into a stew-pan with a little water and some butter; boil them fifteen or twenty minutes; take three or four butter-crackers, crumb them up fine and stir in; if crackers can not be had, light bread crumbs will do; add sugar to taste.

Camphor Ice.

One-half ounce spermaceti, one ounce oil of sweet almonds, one drachm powdered camphor; melt the oil and spermaceti together, then add the camphor, previously dissolved in a little of the oil.

Superior Sponge Cake.

Take twelve eggs, beat the yelks with one pint of pulverized white sugar twenty minutes; beat the whites to a stiff froth and mix them with the yelks and sugar; stir the whole together for a few minutes, then add gradually one pint of flour and the grated rind of a lemon. Butter white paper to line the cake pans, turn into the pans and bake in a middling hot oven thirty or forty minutes. If it browns too fast, cover with thick paper; do not move it while in the oven or it will be heavy.

Frosting.

Beat to a stiff froth the whites of two eggs, stir into it eight tablespoonfuls of pulverized white sugar, flavor with lemon or vanilla.

Raised Luncheon Cake.

Mix one and a half pounds of light bread dough, knead well into a half pound of currants, three-quarters of a pound of sugar, quarter of a pound of candied peel, put it into a tin mould, let it rise an hour; bake till done.

Washington Cake.

One and three quarter pounds of flour, one and a half pounds of sugar, three-quarters of a pound of butter, one pint of milk, one nutmeg, one and a half pounds of raisins, six eggs, one teaspoonful of soda, two of cream of tartar, and one glass of wine.

Sponge Cake.

Take five eggs, one cup of sugar ; beat the eggs and sugar briskly fifteen minutes, stir in one cup of flour. Bake half an hour.

White Mountain Jelly Cake.

One-half a cup of butter, one cup of milk, two cups of sugar, three cups of flour, two eggs, two teaspoonfuls of cream of tartar, one teaspoonful of soda; beat the sugar and eggs together, put the soda in the milk and the cream of tartar in the flour, stir all together and bake quick. Instead of jelly, put frosting between each layer.

Cream Jell Cake.

Take one cup of cream, one cup of sugar, two eggs, half a teaspoonful of soda, and flour to make it the thickness of cream; butter white paper and put in a long dripping-pan, put the cake in and bake quick. When done, spread on the jelly and roll it up.

Italian Sponge Cake.

Put into a large basin a pound of powdered loaf sugar and nine eggs, beat briskly for ten minutes with an egg-whisk, then place the basin in a large vessel containing hot water, add nine more eggs, and continue beating the mixture ten minutes longer, sprinkle in one pound of potato flour and go on beating, taking care that it is mixed very smoothly with the eggs and sugar. Pour the mixture into a buttered mould and bake the cake in a slow oven.

Bun Cake.

One pound of flour, half a pound of currants, half a pound of sugar, half a pound of butter, three eggs, one gill of milk, one teaspoonful of baking powder and twenty-five drops of essence of lemon.

Fruit Cake.

One pound of sugar, one pound of butter, nine eggs, one teacup of milk, one teacup of molasses, one wineglass of wine, one teaspoonful of soda, one and a half pounds of flour, three pounds of raisins, two pounds of currants, and citrons, flour a little to prevent their sinking, one teaspoonful of cloves, two teaspoonfuls of allspice, one nutmeg. This will keep good a long time.

Another of Same.

One and three-fourths pounds of flour, one and three-fourths pounds of butter, one pound of raisins, one pound of currants, half a pound of citron, half a pint of sweet milk, one teaspoonful of soda, six eggs, one teaspoonful of cloves, two of cinnamon, three of allspice. Bake one hour.

Fruit Canning, &c.

Pare and core the fruit, then put among it enough sugar to make it palatable — say several pounds for each bushel; let it stand until the sugar is dissolved, using no water, then heat to a boil; continue the boiling carefully for twenty or thirty minutes, or long enough to heat through to expel the air; now dip the can into a kettle of hot water long enough to heat it, fill in the fruit while hot, cork it immediately, and dip the end of the cork into a cement used for canning fruit; after it has cooled dip it a second time, so as to insure the closing of all air-holes, which would spoil the fruit. Keep all canned fruit in a very cool cellar.

For Berries, Plums, Cherries, &c.

You need not boil over ten or fifteen minutes, using sugar to make palatable.

Strawberries require about one-half a pound for every pound of berries. Use the same precaution in heating cans, &c., as in canning other fruits.

To Can Pine Apples.

Take those that are ripe, and free from decay; pare them, cut into small pieces, leaving out the hard centre. To one pound of the apple add six ounces of fine white sugar, let it stand for several hours, that the juice will run freely to form a syrup; boil over a slow fire, and add a small quantity of water if there is not enough syrup. As soon as tender fill in glass jars and seal immediately.

To Can Vegetables.

Green corn, peas, beans, tomatoes, &c., get fresh, and ripe vegetables, boil them as you do for eating, with a little salt. Put tomatoes in scalding water until the skins can be easily taken off; after they are skinned stir them slowly with a little salt; stew them for nearly an hour, then put in cans.

Fruit Drying.

If you have much fruit to dry, you ought to have a house; if you have hot-bed sashes, you can easily arrange them into a drying apparatus, and at the same time they will keep off insects. A hot-bed frame that has a bottom to it raised above the ground makes a capital drying box.

Dried Fruits—To Protect from Worms.

If you put a little sassafras bark with the dried fruit, when you store it away, it will not be molested by insects. This is a cheap and simple remedy, and very effectual.

Grapes—To Keep.

The grapes must be taken as soon as ripe. All the imperfect ones should be picked from the bunch. Put a layer of thoroughly dried bran upon the bottom of a keg, put a layer of grapes on the bran; between the layers have sufficient bran so that the bunches will not come in contact. Thus fill the keg and close air-tight.

Another.

Select the best bunches, picking off the imperfect grapes; put a layer of paper in a box, then a layer of grapes, continue thus alternating with a layer of paper and grapes until the box is full, then put on several layers or folds of paper or cloth; nail down the lid and set in a cool place where they will not freeze; do not crowd the bunches, but give them plenty of room, don't use papers on which there is print; it may be well to put a little sealing wax on the ends of the stems. It is advisable to look after them several times during the winter, and if any are mouldy remove them and box up the good ones

Arrowroot Pudding.

Mix four tablespoonfuls of arrowroot to a smooth batter with half a pint of milk. Put a pint of milk on the fire with two tablespoonfuls of sugar. When it boils add the batter and keep stirring it till sufficiently thick to leave the sauce-pan. Pour it into moulds previously soaked in cold water. When cold it will turn out easily. A tablespoonful of brandy, poured in just before it is moulded, much improves the flavor.

Amber Pudding.

One pound of butter, three-quarters of a pound of sugar, the yelks of fifteen eggs, one orange peel; mix the butter and sugar well together, then line a dish with paste, fill with the mixture, lay a crust over the top and bake in a slow oven.

Another Dressing for Turkey.

Take one pint of pork sausage meat, one pint of bread crumbs, one beaten egg, one onion, a little salt, pepper and sage.

Boiled Turkey.

A turkey for boiling should be prepared in the same manner as for roasting. Tie it up in a cloth, in order to have it look white, unless rice is boiled with it. It will require about two-thirds of a cup of rice if a soup is to be made of the water in which it is boiled; if no rice is boiled with it, mix a little flour in and serve for gravy.

A Christmas Dinner.

Roast turkey, boiled ham, or fresh sausages, turnips, potatoes, cabbage, squash, beets, mince pies, and cranberry sauce.

To Roast a Turkey.

After the turkey is singed and well cleaned, prepare stuffing in the following manner: Take a quart of light bread crumbs, half a teacupful of butter, a little salt and pepper, some grated nutmeg, a small handful of parsley; put all together into a dish and pour nearly a quart of boiling water over it, let it stand a few minutes, then stir the bread crumbs fine; beat two eggs and mix with it. Stuff the turkey full and sew up; tie the wings to its body, and put it into a dripping pan with a pint of water and half a teacupful of butter; rub some salt and pepper on the outside of the turkey, put it in a hot oven to bake, baste it with the gravy in the pan every fifteen minutes. Roast a large turkey three hours; smaller ones less. If not sufficient water in the dripping pan, add some more and stir in one tablespoonful of flour and serve with the turkey.

Family Mince Pie.

Boil three pounds of lean beef till tender and when cold chop it fine. Chop two pounds of clean beef suet and mix the meat; sprinkle in a tablespoonful of salt. Pare, core and chop fine six pounds of good apples, stone four pounds of raisins and chop them, wash two pounds of currants and mix them all well with the meat, season with powdered cinnamon, one spoonful of powdered nutmeg, a little mace, and a few cloves pounded, and one pound of sugar, one quart of Madeira wine and eight ounces of citron chopped fine. This mixture, put down in a stone jar and closely covered, will keep several weeks.

To Tell Good Eggs.

Put them into water. If the butt-end turns up they are not fresh. This is said to be a certain test.

Queen of Puddings.

Soak one pint of bread crumbs in one quart of rich milk, beat the yelks of eight eggs and the whites of four with one cup of sugar, add one teaspoonful of butter, flavor to taste and bake it. Beat the whites of four eggs that were left and mix with sugar as for icing. As soon as the pudding is baked, spread lightly over it a layer of cranberry, grape, or any jelly slightly acid, then put the icing on thick, place it back in the oven until the meringue is slightly browned, which will depend on the temperature of the oven. Send to the table in the pudding dish in which it was baked.

Cherry Cordial.

Twenty pounds of cherries and six of sugar; stone and lay the fruit in the sugar over night; boil down to a thick jam, adding two large tablespoonfuls of bruised fruit kernels, (apricot or peach kernels,) add three gallons of brandy, put it into a demijohn and at the end of six months strain and bottle it. This is a delicious cordial.

Raspberry Tart with Cream.

Roll out some thin puff paste and lay it in a patty-pan; put in raspberries, strew over them fine sugar, cover with a thin lid, and then bake; cut it open, and have ready the following mixture, warm: Half a pint of cream, the yelks of two eggs well beaten, and a little sugar. When this is added to the tart, return it to the oven five or six minutes.

Cranberry Jelly.

Put the cranberries (which should be ripe) in a jar, cover it close and set in a kettle of boiling water; boil it until the fruit is soft, and to each pint of juice put three-fourths of a pound of sugar — brown will do; boil briskly ten or fifteen minutes.

Calf's-Feet Jelly.

Take four feet that have been previously cleaned, boil them in four quarts of water till very soft and the water is reduced to one quart; take it from the fire and let it remain till perfectly cool, then scrape off the dregs which adhere to the bottom of the jelly; put it in a pre-serving kettle and set it where it will melt slowly; when melted take it from the fire, mix with it half a pint of white wine, the juice and grated rind of a fresh lemon, and a stick of cinnamon; beat the whites of six eggs to a stiff froth, stir them into the jelly; when cool set it on a moderate fire; when hot sweeten to your taste. It should boil slowly fifteen minutes.   If the weather is hot it will not keep over two days.

Apple Jelly.

Peel and stew some tart, juicy apples, strain them as for other jellies; to one pint of juice add one pint of white sugar; boil very rapidly ten or fifteen minutes. Boil only a pint at a time.   Flavor with peach or lemon.

Lemon Jelly of Cooper's Isinglass.

Pour a quart of boiling water on an ounce of Cooper's isinglass, a pound and a half of white sugar, and the juice and grated rind of two fresh lemons; when the isinglass and sugar are dissolved stir the whole up well, let it simmer over a moderate fire for three or four minutes, then strain it and mix with it a glass of white wine; fill your jelly glasses and set where it will cool.   If you wish a yellow color, use tincture of saffron.   For red, use raspberry, elderberry, or currant juice.

Grape Jelly.

Grapes should be picked as soon as fully ripe.   Bruise them and strain through thin muslin.   The muslin should be thin enough to allow all of the pulp of the grape to be pressed through; to one pint of the juice add one pint of sugar.   Boil ten to fifteen minutes.

Rhubarb Jelly.

Peel, slice and stew the rhubarb, bruise some of the

stalks and take the juice, so as not to be obliged to put any water in to stew it. When tender, strain through muslin. To one pint of juice take one pint of white sugar and a little grated lemon.

Currant Jelly.

Pick fine ripe currants, but not too ripe. (The first or second week in July is the best time to make it in the vicinity of Chicago.) Bruise and strain them through thin strong muslin. To a pint of juice add a pint of white sugar, or, a pound of sugar to a pound of juice; boil very briskly for eight or ten minutes. Pour into your jelly dishes. Never boil more than a pint of juice at a time. It will not jell as quick if too much is boiled at once. Have your currants dry when used for jelly.

Siberian Crab Apple Jelly.

Pick out the good ones, wash and stew them till quite tender; strain them through thin muslin; to a pint of juice add a pint of sugar and a little grated lemon peel. Boil ten minutes, pour into the jell dishes; let it stand twelve hours before putting it away.

Sweet Corn.

Corn is in the best condition when the kernels are full-grown, and of a milky substance. It is much the sweetest when boiled on the cob; boil it half an hour. For succotash, cut it from the cob, and boil it with

beans, add a little butter and salt. If the beans are
not very young and tender, boil the beans half an hour
before putting in the corn.

Asparagus.

Take that which is very young and tender, boil in
water with a little salt, as soon as it is tender add a little butter, and souse cream, or have ready a large slice
of toast, put the asparagus on the toast, and pour some
melted butter over it; or, take a teacupful of the liquor
in which the asparagus was boiled, and half a teacupful
of milk, and one tablespoonful of butter, let them scald
up and turn over the asparagus.

String Beans.

Cut off the ends and take off the strings, wash them
clean, put them in a kettle with sufficient water to cover
them; boil them briskly one hour. Ten minutes before
taking them out, add a little salt and some butter; some
cream or milk may be added if preferred.

Boiled Cabbage.

Take off all the green leaves, cut it in quarters and
boil one hour; add a little salt and butter. It is very
excellent boiled with corn beef, and will then not require
any butter or salt.

Cold Slaw.

Take off the green leaves, cut it into small strips

with a cabbage-cutter or knife; to about a quart of the fine-cut cabbage, take a half a teacupful of sugar, half a teacupful of sweet cream, and half a cupful of vinegar.

Hot Slaw.

Melt in a frying pan a piece of butter the size of a hen's egg, or beef drippings. Put in the cabbage, and half a teacupful of water and a little salt; boil twenty or thirty minutes; when tender add half a teacupful of vinegar.

Delicate Cake.

Take half a pound of white sugar, and four ounces of butter; mix butter and sugar to a cream; then add the whites of eight eggs, well beaten; stir in half a pound of sifted flour; flavor to suit the taste; bake immediately in a quick oven; remove from the oven as soon as it is done, and frost it at once. The yolks of the eggs may be used for custard or gold cake.

Boston Cup Cake.

Three cups of sugar, one of butter, one of milk, five eggs, two teaspoonfuls of cinnamon, one nutmeg, half a cup of wine, one teaspoonful of soda; mix to the consistency of pound cake.

Sponge Cake.

One teacup of sugar, one of flour, three eggs. Bake quickly.

Ginger Cake.

Two eggs, one cup of sugar, half a cup of butter, half a cup of milk, three tablespoonfuls of molasses, one tablespoonful of ginger, one teaspoonful of soda, two and a half cups of flour.

This is an excellent recipe.

Cocoa-Nut Cake.

Rasp a fresh cocoa-nut on a grater, add to it double its weight of fine white sugar, and the whites of eight eggs beaten to a stiff froth and a teacupful of flour for every pound; put the mixture into small drop tins and bake them in a very gentle oven about twenty minutes; move them out of the tins while warm.

Gold Cake.

Take the yelks of eight eggs, beat them to a froth. Take one cup of white sugar and three-quarters of a cup of butter; stir the sugar and butter to a cream before adding to the eggs. Dissolve half a teaspoonful of soda in half a cup of milk; one teaspoonful of cream of tartar mixed with two cups of flour. Mix all together; flavor with extract of lemon, or mace. Care must be taken to have the oven quite hot.

Cup Cake.

One cup of cream, two cups of sugar, three cups of

flour, half a teaspoonful of saleratus, four eggs, one teaspoonful of brandy ; beat the sugar and eggs together,
then dissolve the saleratus in the cream ; stir the cream
as little as possible, mix all together, but no more ; the
less you stir it the better the cake will be. Bake half
an hour in a quick oven.

Silver Cake.

Two cups of fine white sugar, three-quarters of a cup
of butter; mix the sugar and butter to a cream, then add
the whites of eight eggs beaten to a stiff froth; dissolve
half a teaspoonful of soda in three-quarters of a cup of
sweet milk, one teaspoonful of cream of tartar mixed
with three cups of sifted flour; stir all together a few
moments. Flavor with lemon, peach or vanilla. Line
your cake pan with buttered white paper; bake immediately. If it browns too fast, cover with thick paper.

Plain Cookies.

One cup of sugar mixed with half a cup of butter
and half a nutmeg; dissolve a teaspoonful of soda in a
spoonful of water stirred into a cup of sour milk; mix
all together, and add flour enough to roll out. Do not
work it much. Bake quick.

Rich Loaf Cake.

Mix a pound of sifted flour with a pint of lukewarm
milk, a cup of good light yeast, and set it where it will

keep warm till risen. When light, take one pound of sugar and one pound of butter stirred to a cream, and work it into the dough, together with four eggs, the whites and yelks beaten separately to a froth; a wineglass of wine, one of brandy, a quarter of an ounce of mace, and a teaspoonful of cinnamon; add another pound of flour and two pounds of seeded raisins, quarter of a pound of citron; let it rise, and bake.

Rich Cookies.

One pound of sugar, half a pound of butter, one teacup of water, one teaspoonful of soda; boil the sugar in the water; while hot add the butter; when cold stir in flour enough to roll out; bake in a quick oven. These will keep a long time.

Cookies.

One cup butter, two cups sugar, one cup of milk, two teaspoonfuls cream tartar, one teaspoonful soda, flour to roll out; roll thin and cut in small cakes; bake quickly. These are very good if not too stiff and not worked much.

Another.

Same as above, adding two eggs, two tablespoonfuls of caraway seed, and some nutmeg; mix, and bake same as above.

Raised Doughnuts.

Heat a pint of milk lukewarm, and stir into it a cup

of melted lard, and sifted flour, till it is thick batter, add a small cup of good yeast, and keep it warm-till the batter is light, then work into it four beaten eggs, two cups of sugar, a teaspoonful of salt, and two of cinnamon. When the whole is well mixed, knead in flour till about as stiff as biscuit-dough; set it where it will keep warm, till of a spongy lightness, then roll the dough out, half an inch thick, and cut it into cakes two inches wide, and two or three inches long; let them remain a few minutes after rolling out, then fry them in a pot of three or four pounds of lard; the lard should be so hot that it will boil up around them as they are dropped in ; they will cook in four or five minutes; the lard can be used again for the same purpose.

Apple Fried Cakes.

Two cups sweet milk, one cup sweet cream, half a teaspoonful of soda, heat together near boiling, yet not quite; pour over one quart of flour; the flour should be as near the scalding point as possible, yet not scalded. When cool enough so as not to scald the eggs, beat four eggs and stir in, with a little salt; pare and slice crosswise, one dozen mellow tart apples, dip them in the batter, and fry in hot lard ; the batter should be as thick as pancake batter.

Fried Cakes.

Two cups of cream, one teaspoonful of soda, three

eggs, and a little salt, flour enough to roll out; roll thin and fry in lard.

Plain Crullers.

Beat four eggs and mix with six tablespoonfuls of sugar and four spoonfuls of butter or lard. Dissolve half a teaspoonful of soda in half a cup of milk; grate some nutmeg, mix all together, roll out and fry in lard.

Rich Crullers.

One cup of sugar, one cup of butter, six eggs, mix flour enough to roll out, cut them into shapes and fry them in hot lard; the lard should be hot enough to boil up as the crollers are put in; as soon as brown on the under side, turn over. When nicely browned on both sides they are done.

Cocoa-Nut Cake.

Beat to a cream two cups of fine white sugar and one of butter; add five eggs beaten to a froth, half a teaspoonful of soda, dissolved in a cup of sweet milk, one teaspoonful of cream of tartar stirred in five cups of flour; grate the white part of one cocoa-nut. Bake in square pans; have the batter one inch thick.

Crullers.

One cup of sugar, half a cup of cream, half a cup of butter, three eggs, half a teaspoonful of soda; stir flour in to make it stiff enough to roll out; cut in strips, or any fanciful shape, and fry in fresh lard.

Black Fruit Cake.

One pound of dark brown sugar, one of flour, one
of butter, twelve eggs, two large spoonfuls of molasses,
a wineglass of wine, one of French brandy, a teaspoonful of cloves, one of mace, two of allspice, and two of
cinnamon, two pounds of raisins, two pounds of zante
currants, and half a pound of citron; stir the sugar and
butter together, then add the eggs, the yelks and whites
beaten separately. Flour the fruit to prevent its sinking to the bottom of the cake; stir all together ten
minutes, bake in pans lined with white paper, buttered.
If the leaves are thick, let them bake from two to three
hours; the oven must not be too hot; a brick oven is
best.

Greens.

Beets, spinach, cowslip, young dandelions, water
cresses, and the tops of small beets, are good for greens;
boil them with a little salt, in the water until they sink
to the bottom.

Lettuce.

Take young, tender lettuce, wash clean, leave in the
water about an hour; drain off the water and press
it dry, add a little salt, pour over it some melted butter
or lard and a little vinegar or take half a teacupful of
sweet cream, one tablespoonful of sugar and four tablespoonfuls of vinegar; mix well together and pour over
the lettuce.

General Rules for Meat.

To keep meat fresh in winter it should be packed in snow. It will keep for months if the snow does not melt; set it in a cold place and keep it covered with plenty of snow.

Meat that is frozen should be soaked in cold water before it is boiled or roasted, to take out the frost. Meat is improved by being kept a few days. Fresh meat will not keep long in hot weather, and should be packed in weak brine.

Meat — Boiled.

All kinds of meat are best if not boiled too fast. Put in hot water and boil gradually till done. Fresh meat requires less cooking than salt meats. As soon as it begins to boil take off the scum. In boiling fresh meat add one tablespoonful of salt to five pounds of meat, half a teaspoonful of pepper, a few leaves of parsley, one quart of water. Add more water as it boils down. Boil three hours over a moderate fire.

Roast Meat.

For five pounds of meat take one tablespoonful of salt, rub it on the meat; put it into a dripping pan with a pint of water, add more water as it cooks away, baste the meat often and turn it several times. Be careful not to burn it; have it a nice brown all around; stir two tablespoonfuls of flour into the drippings for gravy. If too thick, add more water. Season with pepper and parsley.

Turnips.

Peel them and cut in pieces if large, and boil one hour if young and tender; if old boil longer. Pour off the water, add butter and salt and mash them fine. Serve hot.

Squash.

Cut in large pieces, and bake in a hot oven till quite tender; scrape off the stringy part, then scrape that which is mealy and tender into a dish, mash it fine, add some salt, a little piece of butter, and cream. If it is not convenient to bake it, steam it. If squash is boiled in water, it should be placed in the oven a few minutes to dry before using it.

Beets.

Beets should not be cut or scraped before boiling. Wash clean and boil till quite tender, peel and cut in slices quarter of an inch thick, and put them in good vinegar with a little pepper sprinkled over the top.

Parsnips.

Scrape them and cut in two lengthwise; boil till tender; melt some butter in a frying-pan, skim the butter and put them into the frying-pan; fry them a nice brown and sprinkle a little salt over them.

Onions.

Peel and boil in milk and water, with a little salt; when tender take them up and butter them.

Cauliflower.

Boil nearly tender, then put it in good vinegar, or if to be eaten warm, boil in milk and water mixed, and a little salt.

Tomatoes Stewed.

Take six large, nice ripe tomatoes, pour boiling water over them, let them remain two or three minutes, then pour off the water, and peel the skins off, cut them in small pieces, boil them thirty minutes in a little water; when tender add two tablespoonfuls of sugar, one of butter and a few crackers.

Tomatoes Baked.

Peel as above, cut in thick slices, sprinkle a little salt and pepper over them; bake in a quick oven twenty or thirty minutes. Serve to your taste.

Tomato Sauce.

Peel and cut in slices and serve with plenty of white sugar, or, add vinegar, a pinch of salt, the same of black pepper, and a little sugar.

Tomato Catchup.

Take one peck of ripe tomatoes, wash them clean,

and boil till tender; strain them through a coarse cloth, or a wire seive, add two teacups of sugar, one teacup of ground allspice, and one of cinnamon, one tablespoonful of cloves, and one quart of good vinegar; boil all together one hour; stir it constantly to prevent it burning, bottle, and seal up tight for use.

Tomato Preserves.

Take ripe peeled tomatoes, (the small or cherry varieties are the best,) weigh your fruit, take as many pounds of white sugar as you have of fruit. To every five pounds add one lemon, or some lemon essence. Boil thirty or forty minutes.

Potatoes.

New potatoes are best when put into boiling water without peeling them. As soon as done, pour off the water and serve hot. They do not soak as much water without peeling as when they are peeled. If old, they are improved by turning off the water as soon as they are tender.

Pork Sausage.

Take one-third fat and two-thirds lean of pork, chop it very fine. To forty pounds of meat add one pound of fine salt, four heaping tablespoonfuls of black pepper and four tablespoonfuls of sage rubbed fine. Or, a heaping tablespoonful of salt, half a teaspoonful of pepper and half a teaspoonful of sage to one pound of pork.

Fill casings that have been cleaned thoroughly. Sausages should be cooked slowly.

Beef Sausage.

Take two-thirds of beef and one-third of pork, chop it fine and season as pork sausage, make them into cakes and fry a nice brown.

Bologna Sausage.

Take equal parts of ham, beef and veal, chop it very fine and season with salt and pepper, cloves and allspice, fill some clean casings.

To Cure Hams.

In six or eight hours after the pork has been killed and the hams are cooled off, make a salt brine, strong enough to bear up an egg, make it boiling hot and pour over the hams that have been previously packed in a clean barrel or tub. The hot brine closes the pores of the meat and preserves the nutrition.

Bread Pudding.

One pint of bread crumbs, soaked in a quart of rich new milk, add two eggs well beaten, one tablespoonful of butter, two tablespoonfuls of sugar, one teacupful of raisins; bake one hour in a hot oven; to be served with sweet sauce.

Sweet Sauce for Puddings.

One tablespoonful of butter, two of sugar, and two

of flour; mix well together; grate some nutmeg over it, pour boiling water over it until it is about as thick as gravy.

Common Plum Pudding.

Beat together three-quarters of a pound of flour, the same quantity of raisins, six ounces of beef suet, finely chopped, a small pinch of salt, some grated nutmeg and three eggs, well beaten, with about a quarter of a pint of milk. Pour the whole into a buttered dish and bake an hour and a quarter.

Another Plum Pudding.

Mix a quarter of a pound of raisins and the same of currants, one pint of flour and three-quarters of a pint of milk, six ounces of chopped suet and three table-spoonfuls of molasses. Boil three hours.

Unrivaled Plum Pudding.

One and three-fourths pounds of currants, two and a half pounds of raisins, two pounds of sugar, two pounds of bread crumbs, sixteen eggs, two pounds of finely chopped suet, six ounces of candied peel, the rinds of two lemons, one ounce of grated nutmeg, one ounce of ground cinnamon, half an ounce of powdered bitter almonds, a half pint of brandy. Mix all the dry ingredients well together and moisten with the eggs, which should be well beaten. Stir in the brandy, and when all is thoroughly mixed, butter and flour a stout pudding

cloth, put in the pudding, tie it down tightly, boil from
six to eight hours and serve with brandy sauce.   Half
this quantity will do for a small family.

Lemon Pudding.

The juice and peel of two lemons, the peel to be
rubbed off with lumps of sugar, six ounces of pounded
loaf sugar, except what has been used for the lemon peel,
a good sized teacupful of bread crumbs; whilst these are
soaking, beat up four eggs, leaving out two of the whites,
melt two ounces of fresh butter, and mix all the above
ingredients together; edge and trim a dish with puff
paste, and pour in the above mixture and bake it in a
quick oven for three quarters of an hour.

SICK-ROOM COOKERY.

Gruels.

For a sick person various preparations of oatmeal, flour, &c., can at any time be made. When these are cooked nicely and prepared neatly they are very palatable to an invalid.

Rice Gruel.

Soak two tablespoonfuls of rice in cold water for half an hour. Turn off the water and to the rice add a pint or more of new milk, simmer slowly till the rice is soft and tender, then pulp it through a sieve and put milk in it. Warm it over the fire and add a little more milk gradually, pour off to cool, then it may be flavored with salt and sugar; in some cases white wine or sherry may be put in.

Scraps.

Be very neat and clean in all preparations for the sick. Every article of food must be served on snow-white cloths. A dirty saucer, tray or cloth is very irritating to the sick. Remember that a sheet soiled, or a pillow-case daubed by glasses, basins filled too full, is a perfect worry to the sick.

Gruel Water.

Mingle two tablespoonfuls of fresh oatmeal in two
pints of water and place it over a good fire. When it is
about to boil, take it from the fire and pour backward
and forward from one pan into another. Then place it
over the fire again, and when about to come to a boil it
should be poured into a basin and left until it has settled.
If thoroughly cooked it will not be necessary to steam
it; should it have lumps in it, steam through a hair sieve.
Add a little salt to taste.

Another.

In a small quantity of cold water mix a little oatmeal,
add enough water so as to make the whole put in one
quart; boil it very gently until it is sufficiently thick to
be agreeable; season either with sugar or salt.

Bread Pap.

Over white bread pour boiling water; then mash,
strain and add new milk seasoned with sugar.

Another Method.

In a pint of water mix three tablespoonfuls of oat
meal; when cleared, pour off. To the oat meal put a
pint of fresh water, mix well and leave till next day;
strain the liquor through a sieve and place it over a good
fire. While it is warming add about half as much milk,
and when about to boil take it off and put it in a basin
till it is cool. Flavor with salt or sugar.

Oat-Meal Pap.

Add one-third of unboiled new milk to two-thirds of water gruel when cool; warm it well, and flavor with salt or sugar.

Let every article of food intended for the sick be well and carefully prepared with due regard to its appearance. Fat is always disagreeable to the sick.

Millet Milk.

In cold water wash three tablespoonfuls of millet seed, and put in one quart of new milk; simmer gently until it is moderately thick; to cool, pour in a basin, and use salt or sugar for flavoring.

Ground-Rice Milk.

With new milk mix a large spoonful of ground rice to form a batter. Set a pint of new milk over the fire; when boiling hot mix it in the batter, and continue stirring it one way until thick, yet let it not boil; let it cool in a basin, and flavor with salt or sugar.

Rice Milk.

Put clean rice in a little water, and put over a good fire; add some milk to form the whole into a proper consistency; use salt or sugar for flavoring.

Sago.

In cold water put a tablespoonful of sago for half an hour, then turn off the water and add some fresh; boil

gently until the quantity is about half as large, then put
it into a basin and leave it to cool.   Use sugar, salt or
wine, according to taste.

Barley Water.

Add three pints of water to about a handful of barley;
when cooked gently to a proper thickness, strain it, and
flavor with sugar and salt.

Apple Water.

Four or five ripe apples sliced into a jug with some
boiling water on it, and when cool and seasoned with
sugar makes a good drink.

Toast and Water.

Toast a slice of new bread quite brown, yet do not
burn it, then put it in a jug of hot water; when cold
remove the bread and use the water.   Burnt bread spoils
the drink.

Lemon Water.

Put two or three slices of lemon, with a lump of
sugar and a spoonful of capillaire into a covered jug,
and pour to this a pint of boiling water.   For two or
three hours keep closed.   This forms a very fine drink
for a patient afflicted with fever.

Jelly — Sago.

Boil a teacupful of sago in four pints of water, till it
is quite thick; after it is cool, pour in it a pint of

raspberry juice, pressed from new fruit, or perhaps half as much of syrup of raspberry, put in enough sugar to sweeten it, boil fast for five minutes and put into a shape which has been steeped in cool water, add a little cream over the jelly.

The smaller the quantity and the greater the variety, the more acceptable will it be to the sick. Do not leave food near the patient's bedside, if it is not wanted; carry it away, as leaving it will only make it distasteful.

Jelly—Chicken.

Take quite a large fowl, and place it into a pan with about two quarts of water, one blade of mace, one onion, and some salt, reduce it to three pints by boiling, strain it and leave it until next day; take off the fat very clean, take the whites of six eggs, one-half ounce of isinglass, the juice of two lemons, beat them well together, bring the scum to the top by boiling, let it settle for a few minutes, then strain it through a jelly bag. This is claimed to be one of the most invigorating preparations that is known. It may be taken cold or warm, just as it suits the patient best.

Tapioca Jelly.

The tapioca must first be well washed in three or four waters, then again soaked in fresh water for five hours, and placed over a gentle fire till quite clear; lemon juice, wine, and sugar may be added.

Mulled Egg.

Beat the yelk of a fresh egg in a teacup, add some milk and sugar or cream, then fill the cup with tea or coffee, at the same time stirring it well to prevent the egg from coagulating. This forms a very good breakfast for an invalid. It is quite nutritious and light, without creating heat.

Chicken Panada.

Skin a fowl, cut it to pieces, but leave the breast whole, boil it gently in some water, not too much, till it is perfectly tender, pick the meat from bones, pound it very fine in a mortar, and mix it with the water in which it was boiled; put it through a sieve and season it with salt.

Beef Tea.

Take two pounds of the best beefsteak, cut it in very small pieces and put in a bottle, pour enough cold water over it to cover the meat, then cork the bottle and put it into a pan of water for several hours, by which time the best of the meat will be extracted. This then is the best essence of beef. It is very nutritious and wholesome, to which the writer's experience will testify.

Rabbits Stewed in Milk.

Take two teaspoonfuls of flour and a little milk and make into a smooth paste; then add, perhaps, nearly a quart of new fresh milk; cut up into small pieces two quite young rabbits; put into a stew-pan with the milk a blade of mace, some salt and pepper; stir from time to time and boil gently for about half an hour. It may be eaten either hot or cold just as it suits the taste of the patient.

LEGAL DEPARTMENT.

A competent knowledge of the laws of the society in which we live, is the proper accomplishment of every gentleman and scholar. As every person is interested in the preservation of the laws of his country, it is incumbent upon every man to be acquainted, at least with those with which he is immediately concerned. This should apply in a measure to *every man* in the country; and I think we can safely say that the form of American government and universal suffrage demands that the citizen of the States shall be educated, to a reasonable degree, in the Constitution and laws of the country.

In the limited space of this department we cannot enter into a discussion of those legal principles upon which the laws of the country are based, or into the principles of self-government. The common rules and legal forms in general and constant use in the ordinary transactions of business life, are only given. Every legal form in this book has been carefully prepared, and it is hoped they will commend themselves, so far as they go, to the busy and earnest men, in whose interest they have been prepared.

There is a work sold by the Western Publishing House, at Chicago, called "American Commercial Law," by Chamberlin, which contains full and accurate information upon thousands of business matters. It is not merely a work for entertaining and instructive reading, but it is a book for constant reference and *every-day use*. On a single point it will often save from ten to fifteen times its cost, and should be in every office, every store, in the hands of every mechanic and every family in the country. It is simply a matter of economy to possess it. There is scarcely a week in the business of any man in which some question or other does not come up, in regard to which a correct understanding of those principles of law which this book explains would save much anxiety, embarrassment and very frequently financial ruin.

Legal Principles in Merchantile Law.

The following general rules are worthy of preservation:

1st. That which is originally void, does not by lapse of time become valid.

2d. A personal right of action dies with the person.

3d. The law compels no one to do impossibilities.

4th. No one shall be twice vexed for one and the same cause.

5th. The greater contains the less.

6th. The law favors things which are in the custody of the law.

7th.   The husband and wife are one person.

8th.   Every act shall be taken most strongly against the maker.

9th.   When two titles occur the elder should be preferred.

10th.   Agreement overrules the law.

11th.   He who derives the advantage ought to sustain the burden.

12th.   No man shall take advantage of his own wrong.

13th.   When the right is equal, the claim of the party in actual possession shall prevail.

14th.   He has the better title who was first in the point of time.

15th.   A right of action cannot arise out of fraud.

16th.   It is fraud to conceal fraud.

17th.   The law assists those who are vigilant, and not those who sleep over their rights.

18th.   Ignorance of the law excuses no one.

19th.   Who does not oppose what he might oppose, seems to consent.

20th.   When contrary laws come in question the inferior law must yield to the superior; the law general to the law special; an old law to a new law; man's law to God's law.

21st.   If there is any other legal principle which I have not mentioned it is embraced in this: "Do unto others as you would wish them to do unto you."

Forms of Contracts or Agreements.

Every agreement should be written and signed by both parties, and witnessed, where this can be done; although the law absolutely requires witnesses in very few cases, and in none of mere contract.

It is prudent, however, to have them, for it is a rule of law, that things which cannot be proved and things which do not exist, are the same in law. Everything agreed upon should be written out distinctly, and care should be taken to say all that is meant, and just what is meant, and nothing else, for it is a rule of law that no oral testimony shall control a written agreement, unless fraud can be proved. Against fraud nothing stands.

A General Agreement — Mutual Agreement of Two.

A. B. (give place of residence, and business or profession), and C. D. of (as before), have agreed together, at (place), on (the day should always be named), and do hereby promise and agree to and with each other, as follows: A. B., in consideration of the promises hereinafter made by C. D. (if there are any such promises), and of (here state any other consideration which A. B. has), promises and agrees to and with C. D., that (here set forth, as above directed, the whole of what A. B. undertakes to do.)

And C. D., in consideration (set forth consideration and promise as before.)

Witness our hands to two copies of this agreement interchangeably.   A. B.

C. D.

Signed and interc-anged in ⎰ R. W.
    presence of   ⎱ E. G.

Tenant's Agreement.

This is to certify that I have hired of John Long, of the Village of Plainfield, in the County of Will, and State of Illinois, a house and lot known as number twenty-three, in the Village of Plainfield aforesaid, for the term of one year, from the first day of July, one thousand eight hundred and seventy-three, at the yearly rent of two hundred dollars, payable quarter-yearly. And I hereby promise to make punctual payment of the rent in manner aforesaid, and quit and surrender the premises at the expiration of said term, in as good state and condition as reasonable use and wear thereof will permit, damages by the elements excepted, and engage not to let or underlet the whole or any part of said premises, without the written consent of the landlord, under the penalty of forfeiture and damages; and also not to occupy the said premises for any business deemed extra hazardous without the like consent under the like penalty

Given under my hand and seal, the ninth of August, one thousand eight hundred and seventy-three.

JOHN RICE. [SEAL.]

Witness, ⎰ PETER BOND,
    ⎱ JACOB JONES.

Landlord's Agreement.

This is to certify that I have let and rented unto John Rice, of the Village of Plainfield, in the County of Will, and State of Illinois, my house and lot, known as number twenty-three, in the Village of Plainfield aforesaid, for the term of one year from the first day of July, one thousand eight hundred and seventy-three, at the yearly rent of two hundred dollars, payable quarter-yearly. The premises are not to be used or occupied for any business deemed extra hazardous on account of fire; nor shall the same, or any part thereof, be let or underlet without the written consent of the landlord, under the penalty of forfeiture and damages.

Given under my hand and seal the ninth day of August, one thousand eight hundred and seventy-three.

JOHN LONG.

Witness, { PETER BOND,
          { JAMES JONES.

Letter of Credit.

This is a letter frequently given by a person of known responsibility to a friend, to enable that friend to procure goods on time. It is usually somewhat in this form: (See form Letter Credit.)

An Agreement

for making a quantity of manufactured articles.

Articles of agreement between.........(the buyer) of the one part and.........of the other part.

The said.........(the manufacturer) for the consideration herein after mentioned doth covenant that he will, at his own charge, make for the said.........(describe the articles to be made) of the same quality of materials and goodness, as, and in all other respects according to a pattern agreed between the said parties [.........], and deliver the same to the said at.........within....,...months from the date hereof. And the said.........in consideration thereof doth covenant to pay to the said.........at the rate of.........after.........months from the delivery of the said.........as aforesaid. And it is agreed, that if any of the said.........shall not be made agreeable to the said pattern, and for that reason shall be rejected by the said.........he the said.........shall take back such as shall be so refused, and deliver the said........ the like quantity of the goodness and make, according to the pattern aforesaid.

In witness whereof, &c.,

(Signature.) [SEAL.]

Agreement for Hiring a Clerk or a Workman.

This agreement, made this first day of September, one thousand eight hundred and seventy three, between P. Y. Dundore, of the Village of Plainfield, in the County of Will, in the State of Illinois, of the first part, and George Taber of the same place aforesaid, of the second part.

Witnesseth, that the said George Taber, has agreed to enter the service of said P. Y. Dundore, as clerk (or workman), and covenants and agrees, to and with the said P. Y. Dundore, that he will faithfully, honestly, and diligently, apply himself, and perform the duties of a clerk, (or workman), in the store, (or shop), of said P. Y. Dundore, and faithfully obey all the reasonable wishes and commands, of said P. Y. Dundore, for and during the space of one year from the first day of September, for the compensation of five hundred dollars per annum, payable quarterly.

And the said P. Y. Dundore, covenants with the said George Taber, that he will receive him as his clerk, (or workman), for the term of one year aforesaid, and will pay him for his service as such clerk, (or workman), the sum of five hundred dollars per annum, in quarter yearly payments.

We witness our hand and seal.

[SEAL.]

[SEAL.]

Agreement for Copartnership.

Articles of copartnership, made this twenty-second day of September, in the year one thousand eight hundred and seventy-three, between John Jones, of the first, and Charles Dickens, of the second part, both of Chicago, in the County of Cook, State of Illinois.

It is the intention of said parties to form a copartnership for the purpose of carrying on the business of......, for which purpose they have agreed on the following terms, to the faithful performance of which they mutually bind and engage themselves to each other, his executors and administrators:

First. The style of copartnership shall be......(and Company), and it shall continue for the term of ten years from the above date, except in case of death of either of said parties within the said term, or earlier mutual agreement to dissolve.

Second. The said John Jones and Charles Dickens are proprietors of the stock, a schedule of which is contained in their stock book, in the proportion of five hundred to the said John Jones, and seven hundred to the said Charles Dickens; and the said owners shall continue to be owners of their joint stock in the same proportions; and in case of any additions being made to to the same, the said John Jones shall advance......, and the said Charles Dickens......of the cost thereof.

Third. All profits which may accrue to said partnership shall be divided, and all loss happening to said firm, whether from bad debts, or depreciation of goods, or any other cause, and all expenses of the business, shall be borne by the said parties in the aforesaid proportions of their interest in the said stock.

Fourth. The said Charles Dickens shall devote and give all his time and attention to the business of the said firm, as a junior member, and generally to the care and superintendence of the house; and the said John Jones shall devote so much of his time as may be requisite in advising, overseeing and directing the said business.

Fifth. All the purchases, sales, transactions, and accounts, of the said firm, should be kept in regular books, which shall be always open to the inspection of both parties, and their legal representatives. An account of stock shall be taken, and an account between said parties shall be settled as often as once in two years ...., and as much oftener as either party may desire and, in writing, request.

Sixth. Neither of said parties shall subscribe any bond, sign, or endorse, any note of hand, accept, sign, or endorse, any draft or bill of exchange, or assume any other liability, verbal or written, either in his own name, or the name of the firm, for the accommodation of any other person or persons whatsoever, without the consent in writing of the other party; nor, shall either party lend any of the funds of the copartnership without such consent of the other partner.

Seventh. No importation, or large purchase of stock property, shall be made, nor any transaction out of the usual course of the business be undertaken, by either of the partners, without previous consultation and the approbation of the other partner.

Eighth. Neither party shall withdraw from the joint stock, at any time more than his share of the profits of the business there earned, nor shall either party be entitled to his share of the capital, but if, at the expiration of the year, a balance of profits be found due to either partner, he shall be at liberty to withdraw the said balance, or to leave it in the business, provided the other partner consent thereto, and in that case he shall be allowed interest on the said balance.

Ninth. At the expiration of the aforesaid or earlier dissolution of this copartnership, if the said parties, or their legal representatives, cannot agree in the division of the stock then on hand, the whole copartnership effects, except the debts due to the firm, shall be sold at public auction, at which both parties shall be at liberty to bid and purchase like other individuals, and the proceeds shall be divided after payment of the debts of the firm, in the proportions aforesaid.

Tenth. For securing the performance of the foregoing agreements, it is agreed that either party, in the case of any violation of them, or either of them, by the other, shall have the right to dissolve this partnership forthwith, on his becoming informed thereof, and also to recover his damages for such violation.

In witness whereof, we the said John Jones and Charles Dickens, have hereunto set our hands, the day and year above written.

Executed in the ⎱ L. M.
   presence of   ⎰ C. Y.

A Brief Building Contract.

Contract for building made this.........day of.........
one thousand eight hundred and.........by and between
.........of.........in the county of.........and.........of
.........in the county of.........builder. And the said
.........covenant and agrees to and with the said.........
to make, erect, build, and finish in a good substantial
manner,.........upon.........situate.........said.........to
be built agreeable to the draught, plans, explanations
or specifications furnished or to be furnished to said
.........by.........of good and substantial materials,
and to be finished and complete on or before the.........
day of .... And said.........covenant and agrees to
pay to said.........for the same.........dollars, as follows:

Security against mechanics', or other lien, is to be
furnished by said.........prior to.........payment by said
........., and for the performance of all and every one
of the articles and agreements above mentioned, the said
.........and.........do hereby bind themselves, their
heirs, executors and administrators, each to the other, in
the penal sum of.........dollars, firmly by these presents.

In witness whereof, we, the said.........and.........
have hereunto set our hands the day and year first
above written.

(Signatures.) [SEALS.] .

Executed and delivered in ⎱
  the presence of,   ⎰

General Contract for Mechanics' Work.

Contract made this.....day of......A. D. 18..., by and between......of......of the first part, and......of......of the second part: .

Witnesseth,. That the party.of the first part,.for the consideration hereinafter mentioned, covenants and agrees with the party of the second part [to perform in a faithful and workmanlike manner, the following .specified.work, viz: And in addition to the above to become responsible for all materials delivered and receipted for. The work to be commenced...:....and to be completed and delivered, free from mechanic or other liens, on or before the...... day of......]. And the party of the second.part covenants and agrees, with the party.of .the first part, in consideration of the faithful performance of the above specified work, to pay.the party of the first part the sum of.........dollars, as follows:

And it is further mutually agreed by and between both parties, that in case of disagreement in reference to the performance of said work, all questions of disagreement shall be referred to........., and the award of said referees, or a majority of them, shall be binding and final on all parties.

In witness whereof, we hereunto set our hands and seals on the day and year first above written.

JOHN B. [SEAL.]

Executed in pres- { W. E. W.   JAMES L. [SEAL.]
ence of   { R. B. D.

Power to Collect Debts.

Know all men, that I, Ira Jones, of the City of Aurora, in the County of Kane and State of Illinois, have made, constituted and appointed, and by these presents do make, constitute and appoint William King, of the same place, my true and lawful attorney, for me, and in my name, place and stead, to demand, ask, sue for, collect and receive all sums of money, debts, rents, dues, accounts and demands of every kind, nature and description whatever, which are due, owing or payable to me from any person or persons whomsoever, and to give good and sufficient receipts, acquittances and discharges therefor; giving and granting unto my said attorney full power and authority to do and perform all and every act and thing whatsoever requisite and necessary to be done in and about the premises, as fully, to all intents and purposes, as I might or could do if personally present, with full power of substitution and revocation, hereby ratifying and confirming all that my said attorney or his substitute shall lawfully do or cause to be done by virtue hereof.

In witness whereof, I have hereunto set my hand and seal this fifth day of September, one thousand eight hundred and seventy-three.

IRA JONES. [SEAL.]

Sealed and delivered   } ROBERT WRIGHT,
in the presence of   } GEORGE TABOR.

Form of Letter of Credit.

JOLIET, Ill., November 20, 1873.

MESSRS. G. N. CHITTENDEN & Co., *Joliet, Ill.:*

GENTLEMEN — Please deliver to John Long, of this place, goods, silks and merchandise, to any amount not exceeding five hundred dollars, and I will hold myself accountable to you for the payment of the same, in case Mr. Long should fail to make payment therefor. You will please notify me of the amount for which you may give him credit; and if default should be made in the payment, let me know it immediately.

I am, gentlemen, your most obedient servant,

GEORGE KING.

Power to Sell and Convey Real Estate.

Know all men by these presents, that I, Ira Jones, of the City of Aurora, in the County of Kane, and State of Illinois, have made, constituted and appointed, and by these presents do make, constitute and appoint William King, of the same place, my true and lawful attorney, for me, and in my name, place and stead, to enter into, and take possession of all the real estate belonging to me, situate in the City of Aurora, in the County of Kane, and State of Illinois, and to bargain, sell, grant, convey and confirm, the whole or any part thereof, for such price or sum of money, or on such terms as he may think best, and for me and in my name to make, execute, acknowledge and deliver unto the purchaser or purchasers thereof, good and sufficient conveyances, with warranty of the same; and to demand, receive and collect all sums of money which shall become due and payable to me by reason of such sale or sales; giving and granting unto my said attorney full power and authority to do and perform all and every act and thing whatsoever requisite and necessary to be done in and about the premises, as fully, to all intents and purposes, as I might or could do if personally present, with full power of substitution or revocation, hereby ratifying and confirming all that my said attorney or his substitute shall lawfully do or cause to be done by virtue hereof.

In witness whereof, I have hereunto set my hand and seal this fifth day of September, one thousand eight hundred and seventy-three.

IRA JONES, [SEAL.]

Sealed and delivered in } ROBERT WRIGHT.
presence of } GEORGE TABOR.

Brief General Form of a Will.

I, John Richards, of Joliet, in the State of Illinois, hereby make this, my last will and testament:

First. I direct that my just debts be paid by executors hereinafter named, as soon after my death as may by them be found convenient.

Second. I give to my wife the dwelling house and land connected therewith and now occupied by us as a homestead, and all the furniture, pictures, ornaments, &c., contained therein, and used by us in connection therewith; fifteen shares of stock of the Chicago, Alton and St. Louis Railroad Company.

Third. I give to my son James all my real estate in Plainfield, and $10,000 in cash.

Fourth. I give to my daughter Jane all my stock in the First National Bank of Joliet, and four thousand dollars in cash, to be held by her sole and separate use, and to the use of her heirs and assigns, free from the interference and control of her husband.

Fifth. I give to my daughter Lucy a life estate in my farm in Plainfield, and three cows, four yoke of oxen and two horses now on said farm, and all the tools, implements and utensils used in working the same, and three thousand dollars in cash.

Sixth. I hereby appoint my son James to be executor of this will.

In testimony whereof I hereto set my hand, this 5th day of September, A. D. 1873.

JOHN RICHARDS.

Signed and published as his last will by the said John Richards, in the presence of us, who, in his presence, and in the presence of each other, have hereto subscribed our names as witnesses.

AMOS ROSE, Joliet street, Joliet.
GEORGE WOODWARD, Joliet.
AMOS KING, Joliet.

Assignment.

Brief form of an assignment to be indorsed on a note, or any similar promise or agreement :

I hereby, for value received, assign, and transfer the within written (or the above written)........., together with all my interest in and all my rights under the same, to (name of the assignee).

(Signature.)

General Form of Assignment.

Know all men by these presents, that I, T. L. Hains, within named, in consideration of fifty dollars, to me in hand paid, by E. D. Einsel, of the City of Lafayette, in the County of Tipeconoe, and State of Indiana, the receipt whereof is hereby acknowledged, have sold and assigned and by these presents, do sell and assign, to the said E. D. Einsel, the within instrument in writing, and all my right, title and interest, in and to the same, authorizing him, in my name or otherwise, but at his own expense, to enforce the same according to the tenor thereof.

In witness whereof, I have hereunto set my hand and seal, this first day of September, one thousand eight hundred and seventy-three.

In the presence of.....................................
....

[SEAL.]

Form of Affidavit.

An affidavit is a written statement, subscribed by the party making it, and sworn to and affirmed before the the proper officer.

STATE OF ILLINOIS, ⎱ to wit:
   County of Will. ⎰

Charley Freizer, of the town of Plainfield, in the county and state aforesaid, being duly sworn, says (here state the facts,) and further says not.

CHARLES FREIZER.

Sworn to, this tenth day of September, A. D., 1873, ⎱
   before me E. Corbin, Commissioner of Deeds. ⎰

Bill or Draft at a certain time after date.

$1,150.00   Chicago, September 10th, 1873.

Thirty days after date pay to the order of C. D. Hill, one thousand one hundred and fifty dollars.

Value received and charge the same to account of,

Yours, &c.,

SOL. SCHWAB, Chicago, Ill.

To J. L. Rocky, Chicago, Ill.

Check or Draft on a Bank.

No. 84.   Chicago, September 11th, 1873.

Cashier of the Bank of Chicago:

Pay to G. C. Knoble, or bearer, three hundred and fifty dollars.

$350.   C. DALE ARMSTRONG.

Short Form of Mortgage with Power of Sale.

This indenture, made the eighth day of November, in the year one thousand eight hundred and seventy-three, between John Lowe, of the Town of Plainfield, in the County of Will and State of Illinois, of the first part, and Richard Janes, of the Village of Crete, in the County of Kane and State of Illinois, of the second part;

Witnesseth, That the said party of the first part, in consideration of the sum of one thousand dollars, lawful money of the United States, to him duly paid, has sold, and by these presents does grant and convey, to the said party of the second part, all that certain piece or parcel of land situate in the town of, &c., [here describe the land], with the appurtenances, and all the estate, title and interest of the said party of the first part therein.

This grant is intended as a security for the payment of one thousand dollars, on the first day of January, one thousand eight hundred and seventy-four, with interest thereon, payable semi-annually, at the rate of seven per cent. per annum, which payment, if duly made, will render this conveyance void. And if default shall be made in the payment of the principal or interest above mentioned, then the said party of the second part, and his assigns, are hereby authorized to sell the premises above granted, or so much thereof as will be necessary to satisfy the amount then due, with the costs and expenses allowed by law.

In witness whereof, &c.

Mortgage to Secure a Note.

This indenture, made the tenth day of October, in the year of our Lord one thousand eight hundred and seventy-three, between John Lowe, of Aurora, in the County of Kane, in the State of Illinois, of the first part, and Alfred Wagner, of the Town of Wheatland, in the County of Will, and the State of Illinois, of the second part: Witnesseth, that the said party of the first part, in consideration of the sum of five hundred dollars, lawful money of the United States, to him in hand paid, the receipt whereof is hereby acknowledged, 'hath granted, bargained, sold, aliened, remised, released, conveyed and confirmed, and by these presents doth grant, bargain, still, alien, remise, release, convey, and confirm, unto the said party of the second part and to his heirs and assigns forever, all that piece, or parcel of land, &c., [here describe the property mortgaged], together with all and singular, the tenements, heredita-ments, and appurtenances, thereunto belonging or in any wise appertaining, and the reversion, and reversions, remainder and remainders, rents, issues, and profits, thereof; and also all the estate, right, title interest, claim and demand whatsoever, as well in law as in equity, of the said party of the first part, of, in, and to the same. To have and to hold, the above granted and described premises, with the appurtenances, unto the said party of the second part, his heirs and assigns, to his and their own proper use, benefit, and behoof, for over: *Provided always*, and these presents are upon this condition, that if the said party of the first part, shall well and truly pay his certain promissory note, *bearing even date herewith* given to the said party of the second part for the sum of five hundred dollars, lawful money as aforesaid, according to the tenor of said note, then these presents shall become void, and the estate hereby granted shall cease and utterly determine.

In witness whereof, the said party of the first part to these presents has hereunto set his hand and seal, the day and year first above written.

JOHN LOWE. [SEAL.]

Sealed and delivered in ⎫ JOHN SMITH,
the presence of   ⎭ JAMES JONES.

Bond for the Payment of Mone

Know all men by these presents, that I, Will Canton, of the Town of Oswego, in the County of Kendle, and the State of Illinois, am held and firmly bound unto Tonny Tomphson, of the Town of Plainfield, in the County of Will, and the State of Illinois, in the sum of two thousand five hundred dollars, lawful money of the United States, to be paid to the said Tonny Tomphson, his executors, administrators or assigns, for which payment well and truly to be made, I bind myself, my heirs, executors and administrators, and each of them, firmly by these presents.

Sealed with my seal, dated the first of October, one thousand eight hundred and seventy-three.

The condition of the above obligation is such, that if the above bounden Will Canton, or his heirs, executors or administrators, shall well and truly pay, or cause to be paid, unto the above named Tonny Tomphson, his executors, administrators or assigns, the just and full sum of *fifteen hundred dollars on the first day of July next, with interest thereon at the rate of seven per cent. per annum,* then the above obligation to be void, otherwise to remain in full force and virtue.

WILL CANTON. [SEAL.]

Sealed in the pres-⎱ WINT. RIGHT.
ence of   ⎰ F. R. TOBIAS.

Bonds for a Deed.

Know all men, &c. [as in the preceding].

Now the condition of this obligation is such that if the bounden obligor shall, on the tenth day of July next, make, execute and deliver unto the said Tonny Tomphson, (provided the said Tonny Tomphson shall, on or before that day, have paid to the said obligor the sum of fifteen hundred dollars, the price by said Tonny Tomphson agreed to be paid therefor), a good and sufficient conveyance in fee simple, with the usual covenants, of all that certain piece or parcel of land [here describe the land], then the obligation to be void; otherwise to remain in full force, virtue and effect.

WILL. CANTON. [SEAL.]

Sealed and delivered in ⎱ WINT. RIGHT,
the presence of ⎰ F. R. TOBIAS.

Simple Deed, without Warranty.

This indenture, made the fifth day of November, ·in the year one thousand eight hundred and sixty, between John Gage, of the City of Chicago, in the County of Cook, and State of Illinois, of the first part, and James Richards, of the same place, of the second part:

Witnesseth, that the said John Gage, for and in consideration of one thousand dollars, lawful money of the United States, to him in hand paid by the said James Richards, the receipt whereof is hereby acknowledged, hath granted, bargained and sold, and by these presents doth grant, bargain, sell, convey and confirm, unto the said James Richards, his heirs, executors, administrators and assigns forever, all and singular that certain piece or parcel of land situate in the Town of Lockport, in the County of Will, and State of Illinois, [here describe the land,] together with all and singular the tenements, hereditaments and appurtenances thereunto belonging; and the reversions, remainders, rents, issues and profits thereof, and all the estate, title and interest of the said John Gage, to the said premises, or any part thereof.

In witness whereof, I have hereunto set my hand and seal, this fifth day of November, one thousand eight hundred and sixty.

JOHN GAGE. [SEAL.]

Sealed and delivered in ⎱ JOHN SMITH.
   presence of   ⎰ JAMES JONES.

Simple Deed, with Warranty.

· This indenture, made the tenth day of September, in the year of our Lord one thousand eight hundred and seventy-three, between Jacob Musselman, in the Town of Wheatland, in the County of Will, and State of Illinois, of the first part, and Elmer Emory, of the same place, of the second part:

Witnesseth, that the said party of the first part, for and in the consideration of the sum of eight thousand dollars, lawful money of the United States, to him duly paid before the delivery hereof, hath bargained and sold, and by these presents doth grant and convey to the said party of the second part, his heirs and assigns forever, all that certain piece or parcel of land lying and being, &c., [here describe the land, its location, &c.,] together with all and singular the tenements, hereditaments and appurtenances, and all the estate, title and interests of the said party of first part therein; and the said party of the first part doth hereby covenant and agree with the said party of second part, that at the time of the delivery thereof, the said party of the first part is the lawful owner of the said premises above granted, and seized thereof in fee simple absolute, and that he will warrant and defend the above granted premises in the quiet and peaceable possession of the said party of the second part, his heirs and assigns forever.

In witness whereof, I have hereunto set my hand and seal the day and year above written.

JACOB MUSSELMAN. [SEAL.]

Sealed and delivered in) AL. CORBIN.
   presence of   } WILL. CHIT.

Quit-Claim Deed by Husband and Wife.

This indenture, made the tenth day of April, in the year one thousand eight hundred and sixty, between John Lowe, of the City of Joliet, in the County of Will, and State of Illinois, and Susan, his wife, parties of the first part, and Richard Rowe, of the Town of Jackson, in the County of Cook, and State of Illinois, party of the second part.

Witnesseth, that the said parties of the first part, for and in consideration of the sum of two thousand dollars, lawful money of the United States, to them in hand paid by the said party of the second part, at or before the ensealing of these presents, the receipt whereof is hereby acknowledged, have remised, released, and quit-claimed, and by these presents, do remise, release, and quit-claim unto the said party of the second part and to his heirs and assigns, forever, all that certain piece or parcel of land lying and being situated in the town, &c., [here describe the land], together with all and singular the tenements, hereditaments, and appurtenances thereunto belonging, or in anywise appertaining, and the reversion, and reversions, remainder and remainders, rents, issues, and profits thereof; and also all the estate, right, title, interest, dower, and right of dower, property possession, claim, and demand whatsoever, as well in law as in equity, of the said parties of the first part of, in, or to the above described premises, and every part and parcel thereof with the appurtenances. To have and to hold all and singular the above mentioned and described premises, together with the appurtenances, unto the said party of the second part, his heirs, and assigns, forever.

In witness whereof, the said parties of the first part have hereunto set their hands and seals the day and year first above written.

JOHN LOWE.   [SEAL.]
SUSAN LOWE.   [SEAL.]

Sealed and delivered in } JOHN SMITH,
  the preseence of   } JAMES JONES.

Of the Interest which a Husband acquires in the Personality of his Wife.

At common law, the husband by marriage acquires an absolute title to all personal property *then in her possession.* He does not acquire a mere life estate in it, as by courtesy he sometimes does in her real estate, but it goes to his executors and heirs in case of his death, she surviving him, unless he has given it to her by will. As a necessary accompaniment of his acquisition of her estate, he is, at common law, bound to pay her debts; this rule, however, is universal, and not at all dependent upon his receiving estate of any left with her. All wages earned by the wife while she is married, belong to the husband; so that she can acquire nothing by her services.

As to personality not in possession of the wife, as things in action, for which she holds notes, bonds, or other securities, the husband has at common law, the right to reduce them to his possession, by voluntary payment to him by the debtor, or by adverse action at law, if they are so reduced to possession by the husband, the property then becomes his, as absolutely as that which was in her possession and control at the time of the marriage. He may also assign them, and such assignment, even before their avails are reduced to possession, will, if made upon good consideration, be valid against the wife; but, if not reduced to possession, during his life-time, he cannot devise them by will; for unless they are collected (*i. e.* reduced to possession) or assigned before his death, they belong to the wife. The husband also has right to all the rents and profits of the real estate of his wife during the marriage, and they may be taken adversely, for his debts. All her leases of land and other chattels real, are his, and may be transferred by him.

In fact, at common law, the wife has, during coverture, no separate rights in, or control of, her own property, but may, with her husband's consent, and jointly with him make sale and conveyance thereof.

Deed to a Married Woman to her Separate Use.

I, A. B., of........., in consideration of.........dollars, to me paid by C. D., wife of E. D., of........., the receipt of which is hereby acknowledged, do grant and convey unto the said C. D., her heirs and assigns, a lot of land situated in........., with the dwelling-house thereon standing, bounded and described as follows, to-wit: [here insert the description,] with the appurtenances thereto belonging:

To have and to hold, the above granted premises, to the said C. D., wife of the said E. D., to her separate use, free from the interference or control of her present or any future husband, and to her heirs and assigns, to her and their sole use forever. [Here insert covenants of warranty as in a common deed.]

In witness whereof, I, the said A. B., &c.

A. B. [SEAL.]

Signed, sealed and delivered }
in presence of   }

Complaint to a Magistrate by a Master.

To A. B., a Justice of the Peace, &c.:

I, C. D., of..........in said..........machinist, hereby make complaint that E. F., an apprentice lawfully indentured to me, whose term of service is still unexpired, with whom I have not received, nor am I entitled to receive, any sum of money as compensation for his instruction, (or if he has received money, set forth the sum and his own discharge of duty), refuses to serve me and conducts himself in a disorderly and improper manner, in this, to wit: (set forth the wrong doing), and utterly refuses to perform the conditions of said indenture, as required by law. Dated the.......day of..........A. D. 18... C. D.

To Continue a Partnership.

Whereas, the partnership agreed upon in the within written articles has this day expired by the limitations herein contained (or will expire on the..........day of ....next), it is hereby agreed that the same shall be continued on the same terms, and with all the provisions and restrictions herein contained, for the further term of ....years from this date (or from any other date.)

Agreement for Dissolution.

We mutually agree that the copartnership formed between us by the within articles, be, and the same is hereby, dissolved, except for the purpose of final liquidation and settlement of the business thereof; and upon such settlement then wholly to determine.

Witness our hands [as before.]

For Purchase of House and Lot.

This agreement, made this......day of........., in the year 18..., between A. B., of........and C. D., of........:

Witnesseth, that the said A. B. agrees to sell, and the said C. D. agrees to purchase, for the price of......... dollars, the house and lot known and distinguished as number twenty-four in Bill Street, in the city of De Pue. The possession of the property is to be delivered on the ......day of.........next, when.....per cent. of the purchase money is to be paid in cash, and a bond or note and mortgage on the premises, bearing......per cent. interest, payable in......years, is to be executed for the balance of the purchase money; at which time, also, a deed of conveyance, in fee simple, containing the usual full covenants and warranty, is to be delivered, executed by the said A. B. and wife, and the title made satisfactory to said C. D. It is to be understood that this agreement shall be binding upon the heirs and assigns of the respective parties, and, also, that the aforesaid premises are now insured for.........dollars, and in case the said house should be burnt before the said......day of......... next, that the said A. B. shall hold the said insurance in trust for, and will then transfer the same to the said C. D., with the said deed.

In witness whereof, the parties have hereunto set their hands the day and year aforesaid.

A. B.
C. D.

Lease — A Short Form.

This indenture, made the.........day of.........in the year of our Lord one thousand eight hundred and seventy......

Witnesseth, That I (name and residence of the lessor) do hereby lease, demise and let unto (name and residence of lessee) a certain parcel of land, in the city (or town) of.........county of.........and State of......... with all the.........buildings thereon standing, and the appurtenances to the same belonging, bounded and described as follows (or, a certain house in said city, giving the street and number, with the land and adjoining the same):

(The premises need not be described so minutely or fully as is proper in a deed or mortgage of land, but must be so described as to identify them perfectly, and make it certain just what premises are leased.)

To hold for the term of.........from the.........day of.........yielding and paying therefor the rent of......... And said lessee does promise to pay the said rent in four quarterly payments, on the.........day of.........(or state otherwise just when the payments are to be made) and to deliver up the premises to the lessor, or his attorney, peaceably, and quietly, at the end of the term, in as good order and condition, reasonable use and wearing thereof, fire, and other unavoidable casualties excepted, as the same now are or may be put into by the said lessor, and to pay the rent as above stated, and all taxes and duties levied or to be levied, thereon, during the term, and also the rent and taxes, as above stated, for such further time as the lessee may hold the same, and not make or suffer any waste thereof, nor lease, nor underlet, nor permit any other person or persons to occupy or improve the same, or make or suffer to be made any alteration therein but with the approbation of the lessor thereto, in writing having first been obtained; and that the lessor to view or make improvements, and to expel the lessee, if he shall fail to pay the rent and taxes as aforesaid, or make or suffer any strip or waste thereof.

In witness whereof, the said parties have hereunto interchangeably set their hands and seals, the day and year first above written.

(Signature.)   [SEAL.]

(Signature.)   [SEAL.]

Signed, sealed and delivered }
    in presence of   }

Short and General Form of Lease.

I, A. B., of.........hereby lease to C. D., of.........for the term of one year, to commence on the...........day ....next, the dwelling house (or store) numbered...... ....street, in the city of Chicago, with appurtenances, for the yearly rent of.........dollars, to be paid in quarterly payments of.........dollars each, on. the first days of April, July, October and January.

Said C. D. agrees to pay A. B. said rent at the times above specified, and to surrender the premises at the expiration of the term in as good a condition as reasonable use will allow, fire and unavoidable casualties excepted.

In witness whereof, the said parties have hereto set their hands, this 22d day of.........A. D. 18.....

A. B.
C. D.

In presence of.........

Lease of Rooms, with Special Privileges, with Guaranty

A. B., of.........hereby leases to C. D., of.........one room in the...........story, and one room in the........... story, with privilege in kitchen, yard and cellar, being part of the house now occupied by tenants, situate in...... street, No......, in the City of.........; said room to be pointed out and possession given:

To hold the same for the term of two years from the ......day of.........next, said lessee paying therefor a rent of.........dollars a year, payable weekly (or monthly), in equal proportions; the first payment to be made on the ......day of.........next.

Said C. D. agrees to pay the said A. B. the above rent as aforesaid, and at the end of the term quit said premises in as good condition as they are now in, reasonable wear, accidental fire, unavoidable casualties excepted.

Witness our hands this......day of.........A. D. 18...

A. B.
C. D.

Executed in presence of

Landlord's Notice to Quit for Non-payment of Rent.

JOLIET, September 3d, A. D. 18...

STATE OF ILLINOIS, }
Will County.   } ss.

To (name of tenant):

You being in possession of the following described premises, which you occupy as my tenant (here describe the premises sufficiently to identify them), in the City (or Township) of........., and County of........., aforesaid, are hereby notified to quit and deliver up to me the premises aforesaid, in fourteen days from this date, according to law, your rent being due and unpaid. Hereof fail not, or I shall take a due course of law to eject you from the same.

(Signature.)

Witness:

Agreement to Cultivate Land on Shares.

This agreement, made this 16th day of September, one thousand eight hundred and seventy-three, between Dan. Higgins, of the County of Du Page, and the State of Illinois, of the first part, and Chas. Naumann, of the Village of Naperville, in said County and State, of the second part:

Witnesseth, that the said Dan. Higgins agrees with the said Chas. Naumann, that he will properly plough, harrow, till, fit and prepare for sowing, all that certain field of ground belonging to said Chas. Naumann, which field lies, &c., (here insert description of the field,) containing about fifty acres, and to sow the same with good winter wheat, finding one-half the seed wheat necessary therefor, on or before the fifth day of September next; and that he will at the proper time cut, harvest and thresh the said wheat, and properly winnow and clean the same, and deliver the one-half part of the said wheat to the said Chas. Naumann, at his barn in the Town of Naperville aforesaid, within ten days after the same shall have been cleaned; and will carefully stack the one-half part of the straw on the premises of the said Chas. Naumann, near to his barn aforesaid.

And the said Chas. Naumann, in consideration of the foregoing agreement, promises and agrees, to and with the said Dan. Higgins, that he may enter in and upon the said field for the purpose of tilling and sowing the same and of harvesting the crops, and free ingress and egress have and enjoy for the purpose aforesaid; and that he will furnish to said Dan. Higgins one-half of the seed wheat necessary to sow the same on or before the fifth day of September next, and permit the said Dan. Higgins to thresh and clean the wheat upon the premises of the aforesaid Chas. Naumann.

We set our hands and seals on this the aforesaid date.

[SEAL.]

[SEAL.]

Marriage Certificate.

This is to certify, that James Earnest, and Emma Daniels, were, with their mutual consent, lawfully joined together in holy matrimony, which was solemnized by me, in the presence of credible witnesses.

Given at................., this......day of........., in the year of our Lord one thousand eight hundred and........

DUNCAN McGREGOR.

Bill of Exchange.

Exchange for $5,000.

Ten days after sight, pay to the order of John Quinn Five Thousand Dollars, value received, and charge the same to account of

JAMES JONES.

To ALFRED COOK,

Chicago, Ill.

Notes Negotiable—On Time.

$150.00.   KINGSTON, November 1st, 187...

Four months from date, for value received, I promise to pay Wm. Whipple, or order, One Hundred and Fifty Dollars.   WM. HOLBROOK.

Notes *on time* are liable to interest after they become due, whether demand is made for their payment or not.

Payable at Bank.

$500.00.   KINGSTON, November 1st, 187...

Ninety days from date, for value received, I promise to pay E. E. Spangler, or order, Five Hundred Dollars, at the Will County Bank.

ROGER KING.

Payable by Instalments.

$200.00.   RALSTON, GA., November 1st, 187...

For value received, I promise to pay Philip Hoffer, or order, Two Hundred Dollars, in the following manner: fifty dollars in two months, fifty dollars in six months, and one hundred dollars in one year from date, with interest.   A. H. MCGREGOR

On Time, with Interest.

$100.00.   PLAINFIELD, November 1st, 187...

One month from date, for value received, I promise to pay G. W. Koach, One Hundred Dollars, with interest.

W. H. SMITH.

With Security.

$75.00.   PLAINFIELD, November 1st, 187...

Six months from date, for value received, I, James Koch, as principal, and I, John Snow, as surety, promise to pay Geo. Bond Seventy-Five Dollars.

JAMES KOCH.

JOHN SNOW.

Order for Merchandise.

$10.00.   PLAINFIELD, November 1st, 187...

Messrs. Jones & King:

GENTS: Please let the bearer have Ten Dollars in merchandise, and place the same to the account of

Yours, &c.,

WM. WHIPPLE.

JULIAN'S

INTEREST TABLES,

CONTAINING AN

ACCURATE CALCULATION OF INTEREST,

AT 5, 6, 7, 8, 9 AND 10 PER CENT.,

BOTH SIMPLE AND COMPOUND,

ON ALL SUMS FROM 1 CENT TO $10,000,

AND FROM ONE DAY TO SIX YEARS.

ALSO,

SOME VERY VALUABLE TABLES.

BY ERAN JULIAN,
LANCASTER, OHIO.

LANCASTER, OHIO:
ERAN JULIAN.
1873.

A TABLE, GIVING THE DATE A NOTE OR BILL MATURES WHEN GIVEN FOR A STATED TIME.

THE intention of this table is to show correctly what month and day of the month that promissory notes, bills, etc., mature, when drawn for any certain length of time, with or without the three days of grace.

Should you give a note for 100 days on the 25th day of August, and wish to know when it becomes due, turn to Time Table, run across top of table from left corner until you get to August, run down August column first line of figures until you get to 25th day; opposite 25th day, in same column, you will find 237, which amount put down, and add to it the 100 days, which will make 337; then look for the 337th number of the table, opposite which you will find the 3d day of December, the day your note or bill becomes due.

You can add three days grace to the 100 days if you wish; it will then come due on the 6th December.

This table is designed for ordinary years; therefore when you pass over February in leap year, your note falls due one day sooner.

Should your note fall due on Sunday, it must be presented and paid the day previous.

EXPLANATIONS OF TIME TABLE.

SHOULD you want to find the number of days from October 20th to June 12th, turn to Time Table, and run your finger across the top until you come to October; run down the days of the month, which is the left hand row of figures, in October column until you get to 20; opposite 20, in same column, you will find 293, which number put down; then run across top to the right as before until you get to June; run down June column until you get to 12, opposite which you will find 528. Said number place above the figures 293, and subtract 293 from 528, which leaves 235 days.

Should you want to reduce that to months, divide 30 into 235, which will make 7 months 25 days.

EXAMPLE.

528
293
———
30)235
———
7 mos. 25 days.

In counting interest on a note that is given a certain number of days from date, the actual number of days must be taken without regard to the month; but in counting interest by months, the number of months must be used.

In passing over February in leap year, add 1 day.

TIME TABLE.

Day	JAN.	FEB.	MAR.	APRIL	MAY	JUNE	JULY	AUG.	SEPT.	OCT.	NOV.	DEC.
1	1	32	60	91	121	152	182	213	244	274	305	335
2	2	33	61	92	122	153	183	214	245	275	306	336
3	3	34	62	93	123	154	184	215	246	276	307	337
4	4	35	63	94	124	155	185	216	247	277	308	338
5	5	36	64	95	125	156	186	217	248	278	309	339
6	6	37	65	96	126	157	187	218	249	279	310	340
7	7	38	66	97	127	158	188	219	250	280	311	341
8	8	39	67	98	128	159	189	220	251	281	312	342
9	9	40	68	99	129	160	190	221	252	282	313	343
10	10	41	69	100	130	161	191	222	253	283	314	344
11	11	42	70	101	131	162	192	223	254	284	315	345
12	12	43	71	102	132	163	193	224	255	285	316	346
13	13	44	72	103	133	164	194	225	256	286	317	347
14	14	45	73	104	134	165	195	226	257	287	318	348
15	15	46	74	105	135	166	196	227	258	288	319	349
16	16	47	75	106	136	167	197	228	259	289	320	350
17	17	48	76	107	137	168	198	229	260	290	321	351
18	18	49	77	108	138	169	199	230	261	291	322	352
19	19	50	78	109	139	170	200	231	262	292	323	353
20	20	51	79	110	140	171	201	232	263	293	324	354
21	21	52	80	111	141	172	202	233	264	294	325	355
22	22	53	81	112	142	173	203	234	265	295	326	356
23	23	54	82	113	143	174	204	235	266	296	327	357
24	24	55	83	114	144	175	205	236	267	297	328	358
25	25	56	84	115	145	176	206	237	268	298	329	359
26	26	57	85	116	146	177	207	238	269	299	330	360
27	27	58	86	117	147	178	208	239	270	300	331	361
28	28	59	87	118	148	179	209	240	271	301	332	362
29	29		88	119	149	180	210	241	272	302	333	363
30	30		89	120	150	181	211	242	273	303	334	364
31	31		90		151		212	243		304		365

Day	JAN.	FEB.	MAR.	APRIL	MAY	JUNE	JULY	AUG.	SEPT.	OCT.	NOV.	DEC.
1	366	397	425	456	486	517	547	578	609	639	670	700
2	367	398	426	457	487	518	548	579	610	640	671	701
3	368	399	427	458	488	519	549	580	611	641	672	702
4	369	400	428	459	489	520	550	581	612	642	673	703
5	370	401	429	460	490	521	551	582	613	643	674	704
6	371	402	430	461	491	522	552	583	614	644	675	705
7	372	403	431	462	492	523	553	584	615	645	676	706
8	373	404	432	463	493	524	554	585	616	646	677	707
9	374	405	433	464	494	525	555	586	617	647	678	708
10	375	406	434	465	495	526	556	587	618	648	679	709
11	376	407	435	466	496	527	557	588	619	649	680	710
12	377	408	436	467	497	528	558	589	620	650	681	711
13	378	409	437	468	498	529	559	590	621	651	682	712
14	379	410	438	469	499	530	560	591	622	652	683	713
15	380	411	439	470	500	531	561	592	623	653	684	714
16	381	412	440	471	501	532	562	593	624	654	685	715
17	382	413	441	472	502	533	563	594	625	655	686	716
18	383	414	442	473	503	534	564	595	626	656	687	717
19	384	415	443	474	504	535	565	596	627	657	688	718
20	385	416	444	475	505	536	566	597	628	658	689	719
21	386	417	445	476	506	537	567	598	629	659	690	720
22	387	418	446	477	507	538	568	599	630	660	691	721
23	388	419	447	478	508	539	569	600	631	661	692	722
24	389	420	448	479	509	540	570	601	632	662	693	723
25	390	421	449	480	510	541	571	602	633	663	694	724
26	391	422	450	481	511	542	572	603	634	664	695	725
27	392	423	451	482	512	543	573	604	635	665	696	726
28	393	424	452	483	513	544	574	605	636	666	697	727
29	394		453	484	514	545	575	606	637	667	698	728
30	395		454	485	515	546	576	607	638	668	699	729
31	396		455		516		577	608		669		730

EXPLANATIONS OF INTEREST TABLES.

THE principal or amount on which you want to count interest, will be found on the top of each page, with the word Dollars attached to it.

The figures 5, 6, 7, 8, 9 and 10 at the head of columns, are the different rates per cent.

The time for which you want to count interest will be found in the first column of each page, headed time.

Above the double line, near the bottom of each page, is Simple Interest; below the double line is Compound Interest.

To find the interest on 100 dollars, at 10 per cent., for 2 years, 6 months and 18 days, turn to 100 dollars page, run down to 18 days, and across to 10 per cent. column, where you will find 50 cents, which is the interest for 18 days; go on down to 6 months, and across to 10 per cent. column, as before, and you will find the interest on 6 months is five dollars; go on down to 2 years, and across to 10 per cent. column, and you will find that the interest for two years is 20 dollars, making in all 25 dollars and 50 cents.

EXAMPLE FIRST.

Interest on 100 dollars for 2 years 6 months and 18 days:

Interest for 18 days   50
"   "   6 mos.   5.00
"   "   2 yrs.   20.00
———
　　　　　　　　　　[mos. and 18 days.
$25.50, Interest on $100 for 2 yrs. 6

To find the interest on 150 dollars for 2 years 6 mos. 18 days, get the interest on 100 dollars as in first example, then turn to page 50 dollars, and calculate same as in first example, and add together.

EXAMPLE SECOND.

Interest on 150 dollars for 2 years 6 months and 18 days:

Int. on
$100. { For 18 days   50
         "   6 mos.   5.00
         "   2 yrs. 20.00
Int. on
$50. { "   18 days   25
         "   6 mos.   2.50
         "   2 yrs. 10.00
       ——————
                        [6 mos. 18 days.
       $38.25 Interest on $150 for 2 yrs

To find the interest on $150.50 for 2 years 6 months 18 days, get the interest on $150, same as example second, then turn to page 50 dollars, and run down to 18 days, and across to 10 per cent. column, and you find 25 cents, which is $\frac{25}{100}$ part of a cent interest, and of which you will keep no account; then run down to 6 months as before, and across to 10 per cent. column, you will find $2.50, which in cents will be $2\frac{50}{100}$ cents, which you will put down 3 cents, having a fraction to carry from 18 days; go on down to 2 years, opposite which you find $10, which in cents will be 10 cents; put said amount under three cents, which will make 13 cents, the interest on 50 cents for that time.

It is but $12\frac{75}{100}$ cents, but as we do n't count fractions, we will call it 13 cents.

EXAMPLE THIRD.

Interest on $150 for 2 yrs. 6 mos. 18 days, . 38.25
"   50 cents for 6 mos., ...   03
"   50 cents for 2 years, ...   10

Interest on 150\frac{50}{100}$ for 2 yrs. 6 mos. 18 days, $38.38

The interest on dollars is shown in dollars and cents, and on cents in cents and hundredths of a cent.

All other per cents. are calculated same as 10 per cent.

Compound Interest is computed same as Simple Interest.

1 Dollar.

TIME.	5 %	6 %	7 %	8 %	9 %	10 %
Days 1	0	0	0	0	0	0
" 2	0	0	0	0	0	0
" 3	0	0	0	0	0	0
" 4	0	0	0	0	0	0
" 5	0	0	0	0	0	0
" 6	0	0	0	0	0	0
" 7	0	0	0	0	0	0
" 8	0	0	0	0	0	0
" 9	0	0	0	0	0	0
" 10	0	0	0	0	0	0
" 11	0	0	0	0	0	0
" 12	0	0	0	0	0	0
" 13	0	0	0	0	0	0
" 14	0	0	0	0	0	0
" 15	0	0	0	0	0	0
" 16	0	0	0	0	0	0
" 17	0	0	0	0	0	0
" 18	0	0	0	0	0	1
" 19	0	0	0	0	0	1
" 20	0	0	0	0	1	1
" 21	0	0	0	0	1	1
" 22	0	0	0	0	1	1
" 23	0	0	0	1	1	1
" 24	0	0	0	1	1	1
" 25	0	0	0	1	1	1
" 26	0	0	1	1	1	1
" 27	0	0	1	1	1	1
" 28	0	0	1	1	1	1
" 29	0	0	1	1	1	1
Mos. 1	0	1	1	1	1	1
" 2	1	1	1	1	2	2
" 3	1	2	2	2	2	3
" 4	2	2	2	3	3	3
" 5	2	3	3	3	4	4
" 6	3	3	4	4	5	5
" 7	3	4	4	5	5	6
" 8	3	4	5	5	6	7
" 9	4	5	5	6	7	8
" 10	4	5	6	7	8	8
" 11	5	6	6	7	8	9
Yrs. 1	5	6	7	8	9	10
" 2	10	12	14	16	18	20
" 3	15	18	21	24	27	30
" 4	20	24	28	32	36	40
Com. 2	10	12	14	17	19	21
" 3	16	19	23	26	30	33
" 4	22	26	31	36	41	46
" 5	28	34	40	47	54	61
" 6	34	42	50	59	68	77

2 DOLLARS.

TIME.	5 %	6 %	7 %	8 %	9 %	10 %
Days 1	0	0	0	0	0	0
" 2	0	0	0	0	0	0
" 3	0	0	0	0	0	0
" 4	0	0	0	0	0	0
" 5	0	0	0	0	0	0
" 6	0	0	0	0	0	0
" 7	0	0	0	0	0	0
" 8	0	0	0	0	0	0
" 9	0	0	0	0	0	1
" 10	0	0	0	0	1	1
" 11	0	0	0	0	1	1
" 12	0	0	0	1	1	1
" 13	0	0	1	1	1	1
" 14	0	0	1	1	1	1
" 15	0	1	1	1	1	1
" 16	0	1	1	1	1	1
" 17	0	1	1	1	1	1
" 18	1	1	1	1	1	1
" 19	1	1	1	1	1	1
" 20	1	1	1	1	1	1
" 21	1	1	1	1	1	1
" 22	1	1	1	1	1	1
" 23	1	1	1	1	1	1
" 24	1	1	1	1	1	1
" 25	1	1	1	1	1	1
" 26	1	1	1	1	1	1
" 27	1	1	1	1	1	2
" 28	1	1	1	1	1	2
" 29	1	1	1	1	1	2
Mos. 1	1	1	1	1	2	2
" 2	2	2	2	3	3	3
" 3	3	3	4	4	5	5
" 4	3	4	5	5	6	7
" 5	4	5	6	7	8	8
" 6	5	6	7	8	9	10
" 7	6	7	8	9	11	12
" 8	7	8	9	11	12	13
" 9	8	9	11	12	14	15
" 10	8	10	12	13	15	17
" 11	9	11	13	15	17	18
Yrs. 1	10	12	14	16	18	20
" 2	20	24	28	32	36	40
" 3	30	36	42	48	54	60
" 4	40	48	56	64	72	80
Com. 2	21	25	29	33	38	42
" 3	32	38	45	52	59	66
" 4	43	52	62	72	82	93
" 5	55	68	81	94	1.08	1.22
" 6	68	84	1.00	1.17	1.35	1.54

TIME.	5 %	6 %	7 %	8 %	9 %	10 %
Days 1	0	0	0	0	0	0
" 2	0	0	0	0	0	0
" 3	0	0	0	0	0	0
" 4	0	0	0	0	0	0
" 5	0	0	0	0	0	0
" 6	0	0	0	0	0	1
" 7	0	0	0	0	1	1
" 8	0	0	0	1	1	1
" 9	0	0	1	1	1	1
" 10	0	1	1	1	1	1
" 11	0	1	1	1	1	1
" 12	1	1	1	1	1	1
" 13	1	1	1	1	1	1
" 14	1	1	1	1	1	1
" 15	1	1	1	1	1	1
" 16	1	1	1	1	1	1
" 17	1	1	1	1	1	1
" 18	1	1	1	1	1	2
" 19	1	1	1	1	1	2
" 20	1	1	1	1	2	2
" 21	1	1	1	1	2	2
" 22	1	1	1	1	2	2
" 23	1	1	1	2	2	2
" 24	1	1	1	2	2	2
" 25	1	1	1	2	2	2
" 26	1	1	2	2	2	2
" 27	1	1	2	2	2	2
" 28	1	1	2	2	2	2
" 29	1	1	2	2	2	2
Mos. 1	1	2	2	2	2	3
" 2	3	3	4	4	5	5
" 3	4	5	5	6	7	8
" 4	5	6	7	8	9	10
" 5	6	8	9	10	11	13
" 6	8	9	11	12	14	15
" 7	9	11	12	14	16	18
" 8	10	12	14	16	18	20
" 9	11	14	16	18	20	23
" 10	13	15	18	20	23	25
" 11	14	17	19	22	25	28
Yrs. 1	15	18	21	24	27	30
" 2	30	36	42	48	54	60
" 3	45	54	63	72	81	90
" 4	60	72	84	96	1.08	1.20
Com. 2	31	37	43	50	56	63
" 3	47	57	68	78	89	99
" 4	65	79	93	1.08	1.23	1.39
" 5	83	1.01	1.21	1.41	1.62	1.83
" 6	1.02	1.26	1.50	1.76	2.03	2.31

TIME.	5 %	6 %	7 %	8 %	9 %	10 %
Days 1	0	0	0	0	0	0
" 2	0	0	0	0	0	0
" 3	0	0	0	0	0	0
" 4	0	0	0	0	0	0
" 5	0	0	0	0	1	1
" 6	0	0	0	1	1	1
" 7	0	0	1	1	1	1
" 8	0	1	1	1	1	1
" 9	1	1	1	1	1	1
" 10	1	1	1	1	1	1
" 11	1	1	1	1	1	1
" 12	1	1	1	1	1	1
" 13	1	1	1	1	1	1
" 14	1	1	1	1	1	2
" 15	1	1	1	1	2	2
" 16	1	1	1	1	2	2
" 17	1	1	1	2	2	2
" 18	1	1	1	2	2	2
" 19	1	1	1	2	2	2
" 20	1	1	2	2	2	2
" 21	1	1	2	2	2	2
" 22	1	1	2	2	2	2
" 23	1	2	2	2	2	3
" 24	1	2	2	2	2	3
" 25	1	2	2	2	3	3
" 26	1	2	2	2	3	3
" 27	2	2	2	2	3	3
" 28	2	2	2	2	3	3
" 29	2	2	2	3	3	3
Mos. 1	2	2	2	3	3	3
" 2	3	4	5	5	6	7
" 3	5	6	7	8	9	10
" 4	7	8	9	11	12	13
" 5	8	1C	12	13	15	17
" 6	10	12	14	16	18	20
" 7	12	14	16	19	21	23
" 8	13	16	19	21	24	27
" 9	15	18	21	24	27	30
" 10	17	20	23	27	30	33
" 11	18	22	26	29	33	37
Yrs. 1	20	24	28	32	36	40
" 2	40	48	56	64	72	80
" 3	60	72	84	96	1.08	1.20
" 4	80	96	1.12	1.28	1.44	1.60
Com. 2	41	49	58	67	75	84
" 3	63	76	90	1.04	1.18	1.32
" 4	86	1.05	1.24	1.44	1.65	1.86
" 5	1.11	1.35	1.61	1.88	2.15	2.45
" 6	1.36	1.67	2.00	2.35	2.71	3.10

TIME.	5 %	6 %	7 %	8 %	9 %	10 %
Days 1	0	0	0	0	0	0
" 2	0	0	0	0	0	0
" 3	0	0	0	0	0	0
" 4	0	0	0	0	1	1
" 5	0	0	0	1	1	1
" 6	0	1	1	1	1	1
" 7	0	1	1	1	1	1
" 8	1	1	1	1	1	1
" 9	1	1	1	1	1	1
" 10	1	1	1	1	1	1
" 11	1	1	1	1	1	2
" 12	1	1	1	1	2	2
" 13	1	1	1	1	2	2
" 14	1	1	1	2	2	2
" 15	1	1	1	2	2	2
" 16	1	1	2	2	2	2
" 17	1	1	2	2	2	2
" 18	1	2	2	2	2	3
" 19	1	2	2	2	2	3
" 20	1	2	2	2	3	3
" 21	1	2	2	2	3	3
" 22	2	2	2	2	3	3
" 23	2	2	2	3	3	3
" 24	2	2	2	3	3	3
" 25	2	2	2	3	3	3
" 26	2	2	3	3	3	4
" 27	2	2	3	3	3	4
" 28	2	2	3	3	4	4
" 29	2	2	3	3	4	4
Mos. 1	2	3	3	3	4	4
" 2	4	5	6	7	8	8
" 3	6	8	9	10	11	13
" 4	8	10	12	13	15	17
" 5	10	13	15	17	19	21
" 6	13	15	18	20	23	25
" 7	15	18	20	23	26	29
" 8	17	20	23	27	30	33
" 9	19	23	26	30	34	38
" 10	21	25	29	33	38	42
" 11	23	28	32	37	41	46
Yrs. 1	25	30	35	40	45	50
" 2	50	60	70	80	90	1.00
" 3	75	90	1.05	1.20	1.35	1.50
" 4	1.00	1.20	1.40	1.60	1.80	2.00
Com. 2	51	62	72	83	94	1.05
" 3	79	96	1.13	1.30	1.48	1.66
" 4	1.08	1.31	1.55	1.80	2.06	2.33
" 5	1.38	1.69	2.01	2.35	2.69	3.06
" 6	1.70	2.09	2.50	2.93	3.39	3.86

TIME.	5 %	6 %	7 %	8 %	9 %	10 %
Days 1	0	0	0	0	0	0
" 2	0	0	0	0	0	0
" 3	0	0	0	0	0	1
" 4	0	0	0	1	1	1
" 5	0	1	1	1	1	1
" 6	1	1	1	1	1	1
" 7	1	1	1	1	1	1
" 8	1	1	1	1	1	1
" 9	1	1	1	1	1	2
" 10	1	1	1	1	2	2
" 11	1	1	1	1	2	2
" 12	1	1	1	2	2	2
" 13	1	1	2	2	2	2
" 14	1	1	2	2	2	2
" 15	1	2	2	2	2	3
" 16	1	2	2	2	2	3
" 17	1	2	2	2	3	3
" 18	2	2	2	2	3	3
" 19	2	2	2	3	3	3
" 20	2	2	2	3	3	3
" 21	2	2	2	3	3	4
" 22	2	2	3	3	3	4
" 23	2	2	3	3	3	4
" 24	2	2	3	3	4	4
" 25	2	3	3	3	4	4
" 26	2	3	3	3	4	4
" 27	2	3	3	4	4	5
" 28	2	3	3	4	4	5
" 29	2	3	3	4	4	5
Mos. 1	3	3	4	4	5	5
" 2	5	6	7	8	9	10
" 3	8	9	11	12	14	15
" 4	10	12	14	16	18	20
" 5	13	15	18	20	23	25
" 6	15	18	21	24	27	30
" 7	18	21	25	28	32	35
" 8	20	24	28	32	36	40
" 9	23	27	32	36	41	45
" 10	25	30	35	40	45	50
" 11	28	33	39	44	50	55
Yrs. 1	30	36	42	48	54	60
" 2	60	72	84	96	1.08	1.20
" 3	90	1.08	1.26	1.44	1.62	1.80
" 4	1.20	1.44	1.68	1.92	2.16	2.40
Com. 2	62	74	87	1.00	1.13	1.26
" 3	95	1.15	1.35	1.56	1.77	1.97
" 4	1.29	1.57	1.86	2.16	2.47	2.78
" 5	1.67	2.03	2.42	2.82	3.23	3.66
" 6	2.04	2.51	3.00	3.52	4.06	4.63

7 DOLLARS.

TIME.	5 %	6 %	7 %	8 %	9 %	10 %
Days 1	0	0	0	0	0	0
" 2	0	0	0	0	0	0
" 3	0	0	0	0	1	1
" 4	0	0	1	1	1	1
" 5	0	1	1	1	1	1
" 6	1	1	1	1	1	1
" 7	1	1	1	1	1	1
" 8	1	1	1	1	1	2
" 9	1	1	1	1	2	2
" 10	1	1	1	2	2	2
" 11	1	1	1	2	2	2
" 12	1	1	2	2	2	2
" 13	1	2	2	2	2	3
" 14	1	2	2	2	2	3
" 15	1	2	2	2	3	3
" 16	2	2	2	2	3	3
" 17	2	2	2	3	3	3
" 18	2	2	2	3	3	4
" 19	2	2	3	3	3	4
" 20	2	2	3	3	4	4
" 21	2	2	3	3	4	4
" 22	2	3	3	3	4	4
" 23	2	3	3	4	4	4
" 24	2	3	3	4	4	5
" 25	2	3	3	4	4	5
" 26	3	3	4	4	5	5
" 27	3	3	4	4	5	5
" 28	3	3	4	4	5	5
" 29	3	3	4	5	5	6
Mos. 1	3	4	4	5	5	6
" 2	6	7	8	9	11	12
" 3	9	11	12	14	16	18
" 4	12	14	16	19	21	23
" 5	15	18	20	23	26	29
" 6	18	21	25	28	32	35
" 7	20	25	29	33	37	41
" 8	23	28	33	37	42	47
" 9	26	32	37	42	47	53
" 10	29	35	41	47	53	58
" 11	32	39	45	51	58	64
Yrs. 1	35	42	49	56	63	70
" 2	70	84	98	1.12	1.26	1.40
" 3	1.05	1.26	1.47	1.68	1.89	2.10
" 4	1.40	1.68	1.96	2.24	2.52	2.80
Com. 2	72	87	1.01	1.16	1.32	1.47
" 3	1.10	1.34	1.58	1.82	2.07	2.32
" 4	1.51	1.84	2.18	2.52	2.88	3.25
" 5	1.93	2.37	2.82	3.29	3.77	4.27
" 6	2.38	2.93	3.51	4.11	4.74	5.40

TIME.	5 %	6 %	7 %	8 %	9 %	10 %
Days 1	0	0	0	0	0	0
" 2	0	0	0	0	0	0
" 3	0	0	0	1	1	1
" 4	0	1	1	1	1	1
" 5	1	1	1	1	1	1
" 6	1	1	1	1	1	1
" 7	1	1	1	1	1	2
" 8	1	1	1	1	2	2
" 9	1	1	1	2	2	2
" 10	1	1	2	2	2	2
" 11	1	1	2	2	2	2
" 12	1	2	2	2	2	3
" 13	1	2	2	2	3	3
" 14	2	2	2	2	3	3
" 15	2	2	2	3	3	3
" 16	2	2	2	3	3	4
" 17	2	2	3	3	3	4
" 18	2	2	3	3	4	4
" 19	2	3	3	3	4	4
" 20	2	3	3	4	4	4
" 21	2	3	3	4	4	5
" 22	2	3	3	4	4	5
" 23	3	3	4	4	5	5
" 24	3	3	4	4	5	5
" 25	3	3	4	4	5	6
" 26	3	3	4	5	5	6
" 27	3	4	4	5	5	6
" 28	3	4	4	5	6	6
" 29	3	4	5	5	6	6
Mos. 1	3	4	5	5	6	7
" 2	7	8	9	11	12	13
" 3	10	12	14	16	18	20
" 4	13	16	19	21	24	27
" 5	17	20	23	27	30	33
" 6	20	24	28	32	36	40
" 7	23	28	33	37	42	47
" 8	27	32	37	43	48	53
" 9	30	36	42	48	54	60
" 10	33	40	47	53	60	67
" 11	37	44	51	59	66	73
Yrs. 1	40	48	56	64	72	80
" 2	80	96	1.12	1.28	1.44	1.60
" 3	1.20	1.44	1.68	1.92	2.16	2.40
" 4	1.60	1.92	2.24	2.56	2.88	3.20
Com. 2	82	99	1.16	1.33	1.50	1.68
" 3	1.26	1.53	1.80	2.08	2.36	2.65
" 4	1.72	2.10	2.49	2.88	3.29	3.71
" 5	2.21	2.71	3.22	3.75	4.31	4.88
" 6	2.72	3.35	4.01	4.70	5.42	6.17

TIME.	5 %	6 %	7 %	8 %	9 %	10 %
Days 1	0	0	0	0	0	0
" 2	0	0	0	0	0	1
" 3	0	0	1	1	1	1
" 4	1	1	1	1	1	1
" 5	1	1	1	1	1	1
" 6	1	1	1	1	1	2
" 7	1	1	1	1	2	2
" 8	1	1	1	2	2	2
" 9	1	1	2	2	2	2
" 10	1	2	2	2	2	3
" 11	1	2	2	2	2	3
" 12	2	2	2	2	3	3
" 13	2	2	2	3	3	3
" 14	2	2	2	3	3	4
" 15	2	2	3	3	3	4
" 16	2	2	3	3	4	4
" 17	2	3	3	3	4	4
" 18	2	3	3	4	4	5
" 19	2	3	3	4	4	5
" 20	3	3	4	4	5	5
" 21	3	3	4	4	5	5
" 22	3	3	4	4	5	6
" 23	3	3	4	5	5	6
" 24	3	4	4	5	5	6
" 25	3	4	4	5	6	6
" 26	3	4	5	5	6	7
" 27	3	4	5	5	6	7
" 28	4	4	5	6	6	7
" 29	4	4	5	6	7	7
Mos. 1	4	5	5	6	7	8
" 2	8	9	11	12	14	15
" 3	11	14	16	18	20	23
" 4	15	18	21	24	27	30
" 5	19	23	26	30	34	38
" 6	23	27	32	36	41	45
" 7	26	32	37	42	47	53
" 8	30	36	42	48	54	60
" 9	34	41	47	54	61	68
" 10	38	45	53	60	68	75
" 11	41	50	58	66	74	83
Yrs. 1	45	54	63	72	81	90
" 2	90	1.08	1.26	1.44	1.62	1.80
" 3	1.35	1.62	1.89	2.16	2.43	2.70
" 4	1.80	2.16	2.52	2.88	3.24	3.60
Com. 2	92	1.11	1.30	1.50	1.69	1.89
" 3	1.42	1.72	2.03	2.34	2.66	2.98
" 4	1.94	2.36	2.80	3.24	3.70	4.18
" 5	2.49	3.04	3.62	4.22	4.85	5.49
" 6	3.06	3.77	4.51	5.28	6.09	6.94

10 DOLLARS.

TIME.	5 %	6 %	7 %	8 %	9 %	10 %
Days 1	0	0	0	0	0	0
" 2	0	0	0	0	1	1
" 3	0	1	1	1	1	1
" 4	1	1	1	1	1	1
" 5	1	1	1	1	1	1
" 6	1	1	1	1	2	2
" 7	1	1	1	2	2	2
" 8	1	1	2	2	2	2
" 9	1	2	2	2	2	3
" 10	1	2	2	2	3	3
" 11	2	2	2	2	3	3
" 12	2	2	2	3	3	3
" 13	2	2	3	3	3	4
" 14	2	2	3	3	4	4
" 15	2	3	3	3	4	4
" 16	2	3	3	4	4	4
" 17	2	3	3	4	4	5
" 18	3	3	4	4	5	5
" 19	3	3	4	4	5	5
" 20	3	3	4	4	5	6
" 21	3	4	4	5	5	6
" 22	3	4	4	5	6	6
" 23	3	4	4	5	6	6
" 24	3	4	5	5	6	7
" 25	3	4	5	6	6	7
" 26	4	4	5	6	7	7
" 27	4	5	5	6	7	8
" 28	4	5	5	6	7	8
" 29	4	5	6	6	7	8
Mos. 1	4	5	6	7	8	8
" 2	8	10	12	13	15	17
" 3	13	15	18	20	23	25
" 4	17	20	23	27	30	33
" 5	21	25	29	33	38	42
" 6	25	30	35	40	45	50
" 7	29	35	41	47	53	58
" 8	33	40	47	53	60	67
" 9	38	45	53	60	68	75
" 10	42	50	58	67	75	83
" 11	46	55	64	73	83	92
Yrs. 1	50	60	70	80	90	1.00
" 2	1.00	1.20	1.40	1.60	1.80	2.00
" 3	1.50	1.80	2.10	2.40	2.70	3.00
" 4	2.00	2.40	2.80	3.20	3.60	4.00
Com. 2	1.03	1.24	1.45	1.66	1.88	2.10
" 3	1.58	1.91	2.25	2.60	2.95	3.31
" 4	2.16	2.62	3.11	3.60	4.12	4.64
" 5	2.76	3.38	4.03	4.69	5.39	6.11
" 6	3.40	4.19	5.01	5.87	6.77	7.72

11 DOLLARS.

TIME.	5 %	6 %	7 %	8 %	9 %	10 %
Days 1	0	0	0	0	0	0
" 2	0	0	0	0	1	1
" 3	0	1	1	1	1	1
" 4	1	1	1	1	1	1
" 5	1	1	1	1	1	2
" 6	1	1	1	1	2	2
" 7	1	1	1	2	2	2
" 8	1	1	2	2	2	2
" 9	1	2	2	2	2	3
" 10	2	2	2	2	3	3
" 11	2	2	2	3	3	3
" 12	2	2	3	3	3	4
" 13	2	2	3	3	4	4
" 14	2	3	3	3	4	4
" 15	2	3	3	4	4	5
" 16	2	3	3	4	4	5
" 17	3	3	4	4	5	5
" 18	3	3	4	4	5	6
" 19	3	3	4	5	5	6
" 20	3	4	4	5	6	6
" 21	3	4	4	5	6	6
" 22	3	4	5	5	6	7
" 23	4	4	5	6	6	7
" 24	4	4	5	6	7	7
" 25	4	5	5	6	7	8
" 26	4	5	6	6	7	8
" 27	4	5	6	7	7	8
" 28	4	5	6	7	8	9
' 29	4	5	6	7	8	9
Mos. 1	5	6	6	7	8	9
" 2	9	11	13	15	17	18
" 3	14	17	19	22	25	28
" 4	18	22	26	29	33	37
" 5	23	28	32	37	41	46
" 6	28	33	39	44	50	55
" 7	32	39	45	51	58	64
" 8	37	44	51	59	66	73
" 9	41	50	58	66	74	82
" 10	46	55	64	73	83	92
" 11	50	61	71	81	91	1.01
Yrs. 1	55	66	77	88	99	1.10
" 2	1.10	1.32	1.54	1.76	1.98	2.20
" 3	1.65	1.98	2.31	2.64	2.97	3.30
" 4	2.20	2.64	3.08	3.52	3.96	4.40
Com. 2	1.13	1.36	1.59	1.83	2.07	2.31
" 3	1.73	2.10	2.48	2.86	3.25	3.64
" 4	2.37	2.89	3.42	3.97	4.53	5.11
" 5	3.04	3.72	4.43	5.16	5.92	6.72
" 6	3.74	4.60	5.51	6.46	7.45	8.49

TIME.	5 %	6 %	7 %	8 %	9 %	10 %
Days 1	0	0	0	0	0	0
" 2	0	0	0	1	1	1
" 3	1	1	1	1	1	1
" 4	1	1	1	1	1	1
" 5	1	1	1	1	2	2
" 6	1	1	1	2	2	2
" 7	1	1	2	2	2	2
" 8	1	2	2	2	2	3
" 9	2	2	2	2	3	3
" 10	2	2	2	3	3	3
" 11	2	2	3	3	3	4
" 12	2	2	3	3	4	4
" 13	2	3	3	3	4	4
" 14	2	3	3	4	4	5
" 15	3	3	4	4	5	5
" 16	3	3	4	4	5	5
" 17	3	3	4	5	5	6
" 18	3	4	4	5	5	6
" 19	3	4	4	5	6	6
" 20	3	4	5	5	6	7
" 21	4	4	5	6	6	7
" 22	4	4	5	6	7	7
" 23	4	5	5	6	7	8
" 24	4	5	6	6	7	8
" 25	4	5	6	7	8	8
" 26	4	5	6	7	8	9
" 27	5	5	6	7	8	9
" 28	5	6	7	7	8	9
" 29	5	6	7	8	9	10
Mos. 1	5	6	7	8	9	10
" 2	10	12	14	16	18	20
" 3	15	18	21	24	27	3.
" 4	20	24	28	32	36	40
" 5	25	30	35	40	45	50
" 6	30	36	42	48	54	60
" 7	35	42	49	56	63	70
" 8	40	48	56	64	72	80
" 9	45	54	63	72	81	90
" 10	50	60	70	80	90	1.00
" 11	55	66	77	88	99	1.10
Yrs. 1	60	72	84	96	1.08	1.20
" 2	1.20	1.44	1.68	1.92	2.16	2.40
" 3	1.80	2.16	2.52	2.88	3.24	3.60
" 4	2.40	2.88	3.36	3.84	4.32	4.80
Com. 2	1.23	1.48	1.74	2.00	2.26	2.52
" 3	1.89	2.29	2.70	3.12	3.54	3.97
" 4	2.59	3.15	3.73	4.33	4.94	5.57
" 5	3.32	4.06	4.83	5.63	6.46	7.33
" 6	4.08	5.02	6.01	7.04	8.13	9.26

13 Dollars.

TIME.	5 %	6 %	7 %	8 %	9 %	10 %
Days 1	0	0	0	0	0	0
" 2	0	0	0	1	1	1
" 3	1	1	1	1	1	1
" 4	1	1	1	1	1	1
" 5	1	1	1	1	2	2
" 6	1	1	2	2	2	2
" 7	1	2	2	2	2	3
" 8	1	2	2	2	3	3
" 9	2	2	2	3	3	3
" 10	2	2	3	3	3	4
" 11	2	2	3	3	4	4
" 12	2	3	3	3	4	4
" 13	2	3	3	4	4	5
" 14	3	3	4	4	5	5
" 15	3	3	4	4	5	5
" 16	3	3	4	5	5	6
" 17	3	4	4	5	6	6
" 18	3	4	5	5	6	7
" 19	3	4	5	5	6	7
" 20	4	4	5	6	7	7
" 21	4	5	5	6	7	8
" 22	4	5	6	6	7	8
" 23	4	5	6	7	7	8
" 24	4	5	6	7	8	9
" 25	5	5	6	7	8	9
" 26	5	6	7	8	8	9
" 27	5	6	7	8	9	10
" 28	5	6	7	8	9	10
" 29	5	6	7	8	9	10
Mos. 1	5	7	8	9	10	11
" 2	11	13	15	17	20	22
" 3	16	20	23	26	29	33
" 4	22	26	30	35	39	43
" 5	27	33	38	43	49	54
" 6	33	39	46	52	59	65
" 7	38	46	53	61	68	76
" 8	43	52	61	69	78	87
" 9	49	59	68	78	88	98
" 10	54	65	76	87	98	1.08
" 11	60	72	83	95	1.07	1.19
Yrs. 1	65	78	91	1.04	1.17	1.30
" 2	1.30	1.56	1.82	2.08	2.34	2.60
" 3	1.95	2.34	2.73	3.12	3.51	3.90
" 4	2.60	3.12	3.64	4.16	4.68	5.20
Com. 2	1.33	1.61	1.88	2.16	2.45	2.73
" 3	2.05	2.48	2.93	3.38	3.84	4.30
" 4	2.80	3.41	4.04	4.69	5.35	6.03
" 5	3.59	4.40	5.23	6.10	7.00	7.94
" 6	4.42	5.44	6.51	7.63	8.80	10.03

14 Dollars.

TIME.	5 %	6 %	7 %	8 %	9 %	10 %
Days 1	0	0	0	0	0	0
" 2	0	0	1	1	1	1
" 3	1	1	1	1	1	1
" 4	1	1	1	1	1	2
" 5	1	1	1	2	2	2
" 6	1	1	2	2	2	2
" 7	1	2	2	2	2	3
" 8	2	2	2	2	3	3
" 9	2	2	2	3	3	4
" 10	2	2	3	3	4	4
" 11	2	3	3	3	4	4
' 12	2	3	3	4	4	5
" 13	3	3	4	4	5	5
" 14	3	3	4	4	5	5
" 15	3	4	4	5	5	6
" 16	3	4	4	5	6	6
" 17	3	4	5	5	6	7
" 18	4	4	5	6	6	7
" 19	4	4	5	6	7	7
" 20	4	5	5	6	7	8
" 21	4	5	6	7	7	8
" 22	4	5	6	7	8	9
" 23	4	5	6	7	8	9
" 24	5	6	7	7	8	9
" 25	5	6	7	8	9	10
" 26	5	6	7	8	9	10
" 27	5	6	7	8	9	11
" 28	5	7	8	9	10	11
" 29	6	7	8	9	10	11
Mos. 1	6	7	8	9	11	12
" 2	12	14	16	19	21	23
" 3	18	21	25	28	32	35
" 4	23	28	33	37	42	47
" 5	29	35	41	47	53	58
" 6	35	42	49	56	63	70
" 7	41	49	57	65	74	82
" 8	47	56	65	75	84	93
" 9	53	63	74	84	95	1.05
" 10	58	70	82	93	1.05	1.17
" 11	64	77	90	1.03	1.16	1.28
Yrs. 1	70	84	98	1.12	1.26	1.40
" 2	1.40	1.68	1.96	2.24	2.52	2.80
" 3	2.10	2.52	2.94	3.36	3.78	4.20
" 4	2.80	3.36	3.92	4.48	5.04	5.60
Com. 2	1.44	1.73	2.03	2.33	2.63	2.94
" 3	2.21	2.67	3.15	3.64	4.13	4.63
" 4	3.02	3.67	4.35	5.05	5.76	6.50
" 5	3.87	4.74	5.64	6.57	7.54	8.55
" 6	4.76	5.86	7.01	8.22	9.48	10.80

TIME.	5 %	6 %	7 %	8 %	9 %	10 %
Days 1	0	0	0	0	0	0
" 2	0	1	1	1	1	1
" 3	1	1	1	1	1	1
" 4	1	1	1	1	2	2
" 5	1	1	1	2	2	2
" 6	1	2	2	2	2	3
" 7	1	2	2	2	3	3
" 8	2	2	2	3	3	3
" 9	2	2	3	3	3	4
" 10	2	3	3	3	4	4
" 11	2	3	3	4	4	5
" 12	3	3	4	4	5	5
" 13	3	3	4	4	5	5
" 14	3	4	4	5	5	6
" 15	3	4	4	5	6	6
" 16	3	4	5	5	6	7
" 17	4	4	5	6	6	7
" 18	4	5	5	6	7	8
" 19	4	5	6	6	7	8
" 20	4	5	6	7	8	8
" 21	4	5	6	7	8	9
" 22	5	6	6	7	8	9
" 23	5	6	7	8	9	10
" 24	5	6	7	8	9	10
" 25	5	6	7	8	9	10
" 26	5	7	8	9	10	11
" 27	6	7	8	9	10	11
" 28	6	7	8	9	11	12
" 29	6	7	8	10	11	12
Mos. 1	6	8	9	10	11	13
" 2	13	15	18	20	23	25
" 3	19	23	26	30	34	38
" 4	25	30	35	40	45	50
" 5	31	38	44	50	56	63
" 6	38	45	53	60	68	75
" 7	44	53	61	70	79	88
" 8	50	60	70	80	90	1.00
" 9	56	68	79	90	1 01	1.13
" 10	63	75	88	1.00	1.13	1.25
" 11	6C	83	96	1.10	1.24	1.38
Yrs. 1	75	90	1.05	1.20	1.35	1.50
" 2	1.50	1.80	2.10	2.40	2.70	3.00
" 3	2.25	2.70	3.15	3.60	4.05	4.50
" 4	3.00	3.60	4.20	4.80	5.40	6.00
Com. 2	1.54	1.85	2.17	2.50	2.82	3.15
" 3	2.36	2.87	3.38	3.90	4.43	4.97
" 4	3.23	3.94	4.66	5.41	6.17	6.96
" 5	4.14	5.07	6.04	7.04	8.08	9.16
" 6	5.10	6.28	7.51	8.80	10.16	11.57

16 Dollars.

TIME.	5 %	6 %	7 %	8 %	9 %	10 %
Days 1	0	0	0	0	0	0
" 2	0	1	1	1	1	1
" 3	1	1	1	1	1	1
" 4	1	1	1	1	2	2
" 5	1	1	2	2	2	2
" 6	1	2	2	2	2	3
" 7	2	2	2	3	3	3
" 8	2	2	2	3	3	4
" 9	2	2	3	3	4	4
" 10	2	3	3	4	4	4
" 11	2	3	3	4	4	5
" 12	3	3	4	4	5	5
" 13	3	3	4	5	5	6
" 14	3	4	4	5	6	6
" 15	3	4	5	5	6	7
" 16	4	4	5	6	6	7
" 17	4	5	5	6	7	8
" 18	4	5	6	6	7	8
" 19	4	5	6	7	8	8
" 20	4	5	6	7	8	9
" 21	5	6	7	7	8	9
" 22	5	6	7	8	9	10
" 23	5	6	7	8	9	10
" 24	5	6	7	9	10	11
" 25	6	7	8	9	10	11
" 26	6	7	8	9	10	12
" 27	6	7	8	10	11	12
" 28	6	7	9	10	11	12
" 29	6	8	9	10	12	13
Mos. 1	7	8	9	11	12	13
" 2	13	16	19	21	24	27
" 3	20	24	28	32	36	40
" 4	27	32	37	43	48	53
" 5	33	40	47	53	60	67
" 6	40	48	56	64	72	80
" 7	47	56	65	75	84	93
" 8	53	64	75	85	96	1.07
" 9	60	72	84	96	1.08	1.20
" 10	67	80	93	1.07	1.20	1.33
" 11	73	88	1.03	1.17	1.32	1.47
Yrs. 1	80	96	1.12	1.28	1.44	1.60
" 2	1.60	1.92	2.24	2.56	2.88	3.20
" 3	2.40	2.88	3.36	3.84	4.32	4.80
" 4	3.20	3.84	4.48	5.12	5.76	6.40
Com. 2	1.64	1.98	2.32	2.66	3.01	3.36
" 3	2.52	3.06	3.60	4.16	4.72	5.30
" 4	3.45	4.20	4.97	5.77	6.59	7.43
" 5	4.42	5.41	6.44	7.51	8.62	9.77
" 6	5.44	6.70	8.01	9.39	10.83	12.34

TIME.		5 %	6 %	7 %	8 %	9 %	10 %
Days	1	0	0	0	0	0	0
"	2	0	1	1	1	1	1
"	3	1	1	1	1	1	1
"	4	1	1	1	2	2	2
"	5	1	1	2	2	2	2
"	6	1	2	2	2	3	3
"	7	2	2	2	3	3	3
"	8	2	2	3	3	3	4
"	9	2	3	3	3	4	4
"	10	2	3	3	4	4	5
"	11	3	3	4	4	5	5
"	12	3	3	4	5	5	6
"	13	3	4	4	5	6	6
"	14	3	4	5	5	6	7
"	15	4	4	5	6	6	7
"	16	4	5	5	6	7	8
"	17	4	5	6	6	7	8
"	18	4	5	6	7	8	9
"	19	4	5	6	7	8	9
"	20	5	6	7	8	9	9
"	21	5	6	7	8	9	10
"	22	5	6	7	8	9	10
"	23	5	7	8	9	10	11
"	24	6	7	8	9	10	11
"	25	6	7	8	9	11	12
"	26	6	7	9	10	11	12
"	27	6	8	9	10	11	13
"	28	7	8	9	11	12	13
"	29	7	8	10	11	12	14
Mos.	1	.7	9	10	11	13	14
"	2	14	17	20	23	26	28
"	3	21	26	30	34	38	43
"	4	28	34	40	45	51	57
"	5	35	43	50	57	64	71
"	6	43	51	60	68	77	85
"	7	50	60	69	79	89	99
"	8	57	68	79	91	1.02	1.13
"	9	64	77	89	1.02	1.15	1.28
"	10	71	85	99	1.13	1.28	1.42
"	11	78	94	1.09	1.25	1.40	1.56
Yrs.	1	85	1.02	1.19	1.36	1.53	1.70
"	2	1.70	2.04	2.38	2.72	3.06	3.40
"	3	2.55	3.06	3.57	4.08	4.59	5.10
"	4	3.40	4.08	4.76	5.44	6.12	6.80
Com.	2	1.74	2.10	2.46	2.83	3.20	3.57
"	3	2.68	3.25	3.83	4.42	5.02	5.63
"	4	3.66	4.46	5.28	6.13	7.00	7.89
"	5	4.70	5.75	6.84	7.98	9.16	10.38
"	6	5 78	7.11	8.51	9.98	11.51	13.12

TIME	5 %	6 %	7 %	8 %	9 %	10 %
Days 1	0	0	0	0	0	1
" 2	1	1	1	1	1	1
" 3	1	1	1	1	1	2
" 4	1	1	1	2	2	2
" 5	1	2	2	2	2	3
" 6	2	2	2	2	3	3
" 7	2	2	2	3	3	4
" 8	2	2	3	3	4	4
" 9	2	3	3	4	4	5
" 10	3	3	4	4	5	5
" 11	3	3	4	4	5	6
" 12	3	4	4	5	5	6
" 13	3	4	5	5	6	7
" 14	4	4	5	6	6	7
" 15	4	5	5	6	7	8
" 16	4	5	6	6	7	8
" 17	4	5	6	7	8	9
" 18	5	5	6	7	8	9
" 19	5	6	7	8	9	10
" 20	5	6	7	8	9	10
" 21	5	6	7	8	9	11
" 22	6	7	8	9	10	11
" 23	6	7	8	9	10	12
" 24	6	7	8	10	11	12
" 25	6	8	9	10	11	13
" 26	7	8	9	10	12	13
" 27	7	8	9	11	12	14
" 28	7	8	10	11	13	14
" 29	7	9	10	12	13	15
Mos. 1	8	9	11	12	14	15
" 2	15	18	21	24	27	30
" 3	23	27	32	36	41	45
" 4	30	36	42	48	54	60
" 5	38	45	53	60	68	75
" 6	45	54	63	72	81	90
" 7	53	63	74	84	95	1.05
" 8	60	72	84	96	1.08	1.20
" 9	68	81	95	1.08	1.22	1.35
" 10	75	90	1.05	1.20	1.35	1.50
" 11	83	99	1.16	1.32	1.49	1.65
Yrs. 1	90	1.08	1.26	1.44	1.62	1.80
" 2	1.80	2.16	2.52	2.88	3.24	3.60
" 3	2.70	3.24	3.78	4.32	4.86	5.40
" 4	3.60	4.32	5.04	5.76	6.48	7.20
Com. 2	1.85	2.22	2.61	3.00	3.39	3.78
" 3	2.84	3.44	4.05	4.67	5.31	5.96
" 4	3.88	4.72	5.59	6.49	7.41	8.35
" 5	4.97	6.09	7.25	8.45	9.70	10.99
" 6	6.12	7.53	9.01	10.57	12.19	13.89

TIME.	5 %	6 %	7 %	8 %	9 %	10 %
Days 1	0	0	0	0	0	1
" 2	1	1	1	1	1	1
" 3	1	1	1	1	1	2
" 4	1	1	1	2	2	2
" 5	1	2	2	2	2	3
" 6	2	2	2	3	3	3
" 7	2	2	3	3	3	4
" 8	2	3	3	3	4	4
" 9	2	3	3	4	4	5
" 10	3	3	4	4	5	5
" 11	3	3	4	5	5	6
" 12	3	4	4	5	6	6
" 13	3	4	5	5	6	7
" 14	4	4	5	6	7	7
" 15	4	5	6	6	7	8
" 16	4	5	6	7	8	8
" 17	4	5	6	7	8	9
" 18	5	6	7	8	9	10
" 19	5	6	7	8	9	10
" 20	5	6	7	8	10	11
" 21	6	7	8	9	10	11
" 22	6	7	8	9	10	12
" 23	6	7	8	10	11	12
" 24	6	8	9	10	11	13
" 25	7	8	9	11	12	13
" 26	7	8	10	11	12	14
" 27	7	9	10	11	13	14
" 28	7	9	10	12	13	15
" 29	8	9	11	12	14	15
Mos. 1	8	10	11	13	14	16
" 2	16	19	22	25	29	32
" 3	24	29	33	38	43	48
" 4	32	38	44	51	57	63
" 5	40	48	55	63	71	79
" 6	48	57	67	76	86	95
" 7	55	67	78	89	1.00	1.11
" 8	63	76	89	1.01	1.14	1.27
" 9	71	86	1.00	1.14	1.28	1.42
" 10	79	95	1.11	1.27	1.43	1.58
" 11	87	1.05	1.22	1.39	1.57	1.74
Yrs. 1	95	1.14	1.33	1.52	1.71	1.90
" 2	1.90	2.28	2.66	3.04	3.42	3.80
" 3	2.85	3.42	3.99	4.56	5.13	5.70
" 4	3.80	4.56	5.32	6.08	6.84	7.60
Com. 2	1.95	2.35	2.75	3.16	3.57	3.99
" 3	2.99	3.63	4.28	4.93	5.61	6.29
" 4	4.09	4.99	5.91	6.85	7.72	8.82
" 5	5.25	6.43	7.65	8.92	10.23	11.60
" 6	6.46	7.95	9.51	11.15	12.87	14.66

TIME.	5 %	6 %	7 %	8 %	9 %	10 %
Days 1	0	0	0	0	1	1
" 2	1	1	1	1	1	1
" 3	1	1	1	1	2	2
" 4	1	1	2	2	2	2
" 5	1	2	2	2	3	3
" 6	2	2	2	3	3	3
" 7	2	2	3	3	4	4
" 8	2	3	3	4	4	4
" 9	3	3	4	4	5	5
" 10	3	3	4	4	5	6
" 11	3	4	4	5	6	6
" 12	3	4	5	5	6	7
" 13	4	4	5	6	7	7
" 14	4	5	5	6	7	8
" 15	4	5	6	7	8	8
" 16	4	5	6	7	8	9
" 17	5	6	7	8	9	9
" 18	5	6	7	8	9	10
" 19	5	6	7	8	10	11
" 20	6	7	8	9	10	11
" 21	6	7	8	9	11	12
" 22	6	7	9	10	11	12
" 23	6	8	9	10	12	13
" 24	7	8	9	11	12	13
" 25	7	8	10	11	13	14
" 26	7	9	10	12	13	14
" 27	8	9	11	12	14	15
" 28	8	9	11	12	14	16
" 29	8	10	11	13	15	16
Mos. 1	8	10	12	13	15	17
" 2	17	20	23	27	30	33
" 3	25	30	35	40	45	50
" 4	33	40	47	53	60	67
" 5	42	50	58	67	75	83
" 6	50	60	70	80	90	1.00
" 7	58	70	82	93	1.05	1.17
" 8	67	80	93	1.07	1.20	1.33
" 9	75	90	1.05	1.20	1.35	1.50
" 10	83	1.00	1.17	1.33	1.50	1.67
" 11	92	1.10	1.28	1.47	1.65	1.83
Yrs. 1	1.00	1.20	1.40	1.60	1.80	2.00
" 2	2.00	2.40	2.80	3.20	3.60	4.00
" 3	3.00	3.60	4.20	4.80	5.40	6.00
" 4	4.00	4 80	5.60	6.40	7.20	8.00
Com. 2	2.05	2.47	2.90	3.33	3.76	4.20
" 3	3.15	3.82	4.50	5.19	5.90	6.62
" 4	4.31	5.25	6.22	7.21	8.23	9.28
" 5	5.53	6.76	8.05	9.39	10.77	12.21
" 6	6.80	8.37	10.01	11.74	13.54	15.43

TIME.	5 %	6 %	7 %	8 %	9 %	10 %
Days 1	0	0	0	0	1	1
" 2	1	1	1	1	1	1
" 3	1	1	1	1	2	2
" 4	1	1	2	2	2	2
" 5	1	2	2	2	3	3
" 6	2	2	2	3	3	4
" 7	2	2	3	3	4	4
" 8	2	3	3	4	4	5
" 9	3	3	4	4	5	5
" 10	3	4	4	5	5	6
" 11	3	4	4	5	6	6
" 12	4	4	5	6	6	7
" 13	4	5	5	6	7	8
" 14	4	5	6	7	7	8
" 15	4	5	6	7	8	9
" 16	5	6	7	7	8	9
" 17	5	6	7	8	9	10
" 18	5	6	7	8	9	11
" 19	6	7	8	9	10	11
" 20	6	7	8	9	11	12
" 21	6	7	9	10	11	12
" 22	6	8	9	10	12	13
" 23	7	8	9	11	12	13
" 24	7	8	10	11	13	14
" 25	7	9	10	12	13	15
" 26	8	9	11	12	14	15
" 27	8	9	11	13	14	16
" 28	8	10	11	13	15	16
" 29	8	10	12	14	15	17
Mos. 1	9	11	12	14	16	18
" 2	18	21	25	28	32	35
" 3	26	32	37	42	47	53
" 4	35	42	49	56	63	70
" 5	44	53	61	70	79	88
" 6	53	63	74	84	95	1.05
" 7	61	74	86	98	1.10	1.23
" 8	70	84	98	1.12	1.26	1.40
" 9	79	95	1.10	1.26	1.42	1.58
" 10	88	1.05	1.23	1.40	1.58	1.75
" 11	96	1.16	1.35	1.54	1.73	1.93
Yrs. 1	1.05	1.26	1.47	1.68	1.89	2.10
" 2	2.10	2.52	2.94	3.36	3.78	4.20
" 3	3.15	3.78	4.41	5.04	5.67	6.30
" 4	4.20	5.04	5.88	6.72	7.56	8.40
Com. 2	2.15	2.60	3.04	3.49	3.95	4.41
" 3	3.31	4.01	4.73	5.45	6.20	6.95
" 4	4.53	5.51	6.53	7.57	8.64	9.75
" 5	5.80	7.10	8.45	9.86	11.31	12.82
" 6	7.14	8.79	10.51	12.32	14.22	16.21

TIME.	5 %	6 %	7 %	8 %	9 %	10 %
Days 1	0	0	0	0	1	1
" 2	1	1	1	1	1	1
" 3	1	1	1	1	2	2
" 4	1	1	2	2	2	2
" 5	2	2	2	2	3	3
" 6	2	2	3	3	3	4
" 7	2	3	3	3	4	4
" 8	2	3	3	4	4	5
" 9	3	3	4	4	5	6
" 10	3	4	4	5	6	6
" 11	3	4	5	5	6	7
" 12	4	4	5	6	7	7
" 13	4	5	6	6	7	8
" 14	4	5	6	7	8	9
" 15	5	6	6	7	8	9
" 16	5	6	7	8	9	10
" 17	5	6	7	8	9	10
" 18	6	7	8	9	10	11
" 19	6	7	8	9	10	12
" 20	6	7	9	10	11	12
" 21	6	8	9	10	12	13
" 22	7	8	9	11	12	13
" 23	7	8	10	11	13	14
" 24	7	9	10	12	13	15
" 25	8	9	11	12	14	15
" 26	8	10	11	13	14	16
" 27	8	10	12	13	15	17
" 28	9	10	12	14	15	17
" 29	9	11	12	14	16	18
Mos. 1	9	11	13	15	17	18
" 2	18	22	26	29	33	37
" 3	28	33	39	44	50	55
" 4	37	44	51	59	66	73
" 5	46	55	64	73	83	92
" 6	55	66	77	88	99	1.10
" 7	64	77	90	1.03	1.16	1.28
" 8	73	88	1.03	1.17	1.32	1.47
" 9	83	99	1.16	1.32	1.49	1.65
" 10	92	1.10	1.28	1.47	1.65	1.83
" 11	1.01	1.21	1.41	1.61	1.82	2.02
Yrs. 1	1.10	1.32	1.54	1.76	1.98	2.20
" 2	2.20	2.64	3.08	3.52	3.96	4.40
" 3	3.30	3.96	4.62	5.28	5.94	6.60
" 4	4.40	5.28	6.16	7.04	7.92	8.80
Com. 2	2.26	2.72	3.19	3.66	4.14	4.62
" 3	3.47	4.20	4.95	5.71	6.49	7.28
" 4	4.74	5.77	6.84	7.93	9.05	10.21
" 5	6.08	7.44	8.86	10.33	11.85	13.43
" 6	7.48	9.21	11.01	12.91	14.90	16.97

TIME.	5 %	6 %	7 %	8 %	9 %	10 %
Days 1	0	0	0	1	1	1
" 2	1	1	1	1	1	1
" 3	1	1	1	2	2	2
" 4	1	2	2	2	2	3
" 5	2	2	2	3	3	3
" 6	2	2	3	3	3	4
" 7	2	3	3	4	4	4
" 8	3	3	4	4	5	5
" 9	3	3	4	5	5	6
" 10	3	4	4	5	6	6
" 11	4	4	5	6	6	7
" 12	4	5	5	6	7	8
" 13	4	5	6	7	7	8
" 14	4	5	6	7	8	9
" 15	5	6	7	8	9	10
" 16	5	6	7	8	9	10
" 17	5	7	8	9	10	11
" 18	6	7	8	9	10	12
" 19	6	7	8	10	11	12
" 20	6	8	9	10	12	13
" 21	7	8	9	11	12	13
" 22	7	8	10	11	13	14
" 23	7	9	10	12	13	15
" 24	8	9	11	12	14	15
" 25	8	10	11	13	14	16
" 26	8	10	12	13	15	17
" 27	9	10	12	14	16	17
" 28	9	11	13	14	16	18
" 29	9	11	13	15	17	19
Mos. 1	10	12	13	15	17	19
" 2	19	23	27	31	35	38
" 3	29	35	40	46	52	58
" 4	38	46	54	61	69	77
" 5	48	58	67	77	86	96
" 6	58	69	81	92	1.04	1.15
" 7	67	81	94	1.07	1.21	1.34
" 8	77	92	1.07	1.23	1.38	1.53
" 9	86	1.04	1.21	1.38	1.55	1.73
" 10	96	1.15	1.34	1.53	1.73	1.92
" 11	1.05	1.27	1.48	1.69	1.90	2.11
Yrs. 1	1.15	1.38	1.61	1.84	2.07	2.30
" 2	2.30	2.76	3.22	3.68	4.14	4.60
" 3	3.45	4.14	4.83	5.52	6.21	6.90
" 4	4.60	5.52	6.44	7.36	8.28	9.20
Com. 2	2.36	2.84	3.33	3.83	4.33	4.83
" 3	3.63	4.39	5.18	5.97	6.79	7.61
" 4	4.96	6.04	7.15	8.29	9.47	10.67
" 5	6.35	7.78	9.26	10.79	12.39	14.04
" 6	7.82	9.63	11.52	13.50	15.57	17.75

TIME.	5 %	6 %	7 %	8 %	9 %	10 %
Days 1	0	0	0	1	1	1
" 2	1	1	1	1	1	1
" 3	1	1	1	2	2	2
" 4	1	2	2	2	2	3
" 5	2	2	2	3	3	3
" 6	2	2	3	3	4	4
" 7	2	3	3	4	4	5
" 8	3	3	4	4	5	5
" 9	3	4	4	5	5	6
" 10	3	4	5	5	6	7
" 11	4	4	5	6	7	7
" 12	4	5	6	6	7	8
" 13	4	5	6	7	8	9
" 14	5	6	7	7	8	9
" 15	5	6	7	8	9	10
" 16	5	6	7	9	10	11
" 17	6	7	8	9	10	11
" 18	6	7	8	10	11	12
" 19	6	8	9	10	11	13
" 20	7	8	9	11	12	13
" 21	7	8	10	11	13	14
" 22	7	9	10	12	13	15
" 23	8	9	11	12	14	15
" 24	8	10	11	13	14	16
" 25	8	10	12	13	15	17
" 26	9	10	12	14	16	17
" 27	9	11	13	14	16	18
" 28	9	11	13	15	17	19
" 29	10	12	14	15	17	19
Mos 1	10	12	14	16	18	20
" 2	20	24	28	32	36	40
" 3	30	36	42	48	54	60
" 4	40	48	56	64	72	80
" 5	50	60	70	80	90	1.00
" 6	60	72	84	96	1.08	1.20
" 7	70	84	98	1.12	1.26	1.40
" 8	80	96	1.12	1.28	1.44	1.60
" 9	90	1.08	1.26	1.44	1.62	1.80
" 10	1.00	1.20	1.40	1.60	1.80	2.00
" 11	1.10	1.32	1.54	1.76	1.98	2.20
Yrs. 1	1.20	1.44	1.68	1.92	2.16	2.40
" 2	2.40	2.88	3.36	3.84	4.32	4.80
" 3	3.60	4.32	5.04	5.76	6.48	7.20
" 4	4.80	5.76	6.72	7.68	8.64	9.60
Com. 2	2.46	2.97	3.48	3.99	4.51	5.04
" 3	3.78	4.58	5.40	6.23	7.08	7.94
" 4	5.17	6.30	7.46	8.65	9.88	11.14
" 5	6.63	8.12	9.66	11.26	12.93	14.65
" 6	8.16	10.04	12.02	14.08	16.25	18.52

25 Dollars.

TIME.	5 %	6 %	7 %	8 %	9 %	10 %
Days 1	0	0	0	1	1	1
" 2	1	1	1	1	1	1
" 3	1	1	1	2	2	2
" 4	1	2	2	2	3	3
" 5	2	2	2	3	3	3
" 6	2	3	3	3	4	4
" 7	2	3	3	4	4	5
" 8	3	3	4	4	5	6
" 9	3	4	4	5	6	6
" 10	3	4	5	6	6	7
" 11	4	5	5	6	7	8
" 12	4	5	6	7	8	8
" 13	5	5	6	7	8	9
" 14	5	6	7	8	9	10
" 15	5	6	7	8	9	10
" 16	6	7	8	9	10	11
" 17	6	7	8	9	11	12
" 18	6	8	9	10	11	13
" 19	7	8	9	11	12	13
" 20	7	8	10	11	13	14
" 21	7	9	10	12	13	15
" 22	8	9	11	12	14	15
" 23	8	10	11	13	14	16
" 24	8	10	12	13	15	17
" 25	9	10	12	14	16	17
" 26	9	11	13	14	16	18
" 27	9	11	13	15	17	19
" 28	10	12	14	16	18	19
" 29	10	12	14	16	18	20
Mos. 1	10	13	15	17	19	21
" 2	21	25	29	33	38	42
" 3	31	38	44	50	56	63
" 4	42	50	58	67	75	83
" 5	52	63	73	83	94	1.04
" 6	63	75	88	1.00	1.13	1.25
" 7	73	88	1.02	1.17	1.31	1.46
" 8	83	1.00	1.17	1.33	1.50	1.67
" 9	94	1.13	1.31	1.50	1.69	1.88
" 10	1.04	1.25	1.46	1.67	1.88	2.08
" 11	1.15	1.38	1.60	1.83	2.06	2.29
Yrs. 1	1.25	1.50	1.75	2.00	2.25	2.50
" 2	2.50	3.00	3.50	4.00	4.50	5.00
" 3	3.75	4.50	5.25	6.00	6.75	7.50
" 4	5.00	6.00	7.00	8.00	9.00	10.00
Com. 2	2.56	3.09	3.62	4.16	4.70	5.25
" 3	3.94	4.78	5.63	6.49	7.38	8.28
" 4	5.39	6.56	7.77	9.01	10.29	11.60
" 5	6.91	8.46	10.06	11.73	13.47	15.26
" 6	8.50	10.46	12.52	14.67	16.93	19.29

34

TIME.	5 %	6 %	7 %	8 %	9 %	10 %
Days 1	0	0	0	1	1	1
" 2	1	1	1	1	1	1
" 3	1	1	2	2	2	2
" 4	1	2	2	2	3	3
" 5	2	2	3	3	3	4
" 6	2	3	3	3	4	4
" 7	3	3	4	4	5	5
" 8	3	3	4	5	5	6
" 9	3	4	5	5	6	7
" 10	4	4	5	6	7	7
" 11	4	5	6	6	7	8
" 12	4	5	6	7	8	9
" 13	5	6	7	8	8	9
" 14	5	6	7	8	9	10
" 15	5	7	8	9	10	11
" 16	6	7	8	9	10	12
" 17	6	7	9	10	11	12
" 18	7	8	9	10	12	13
" 19	7	8	10	11	12	14
" 20	7	9	10	12	13	14
" 21	8	9	11	12	14	15
" 22	8	10	11	13	14	16
" 23	8	10	12	13	15	17
" 24	9	10	12	14	16	17
" 25	9	11	13	14	16	18
" 26	9	11	13	15	17	19
" 27	10	12	14	16	18	20
" 28	10	12	14	16	18	20
" 29	10	13	15	17	19	21
Mos 1	11	13	15	17	20	22
" 2	22	26	30	35	39	43
" 3	33	39	46	52	59	65
" 4	43	52	61	69	78	87
" 5	54	65	76	87	98	1.08
" 6	65	78	91	1.04	1.17	1.30
" 7	76	91	1.06	1.21	1.37	1.52
" 8	87	1.04	1.21	1.39	1.56	1.73
" 9	98	1.17	1.37	1.56	1.76	1.95
" 10	1.08	1.30	1.52	1.73	1.95	2.17
" 11	1.19	1.43	1.67	1.91	2.15	2.38
Yrs. 1	1.30	1.56	1.82	2.08	2.34	2.60
" 2	2.60	3.12	3.64	4.16	4.68	5.20
" 3	3.90	4.68	5.46	6.24	7.02	7.80
" 4	5.20	6.24	7.28	8.32	9.36	10.40
Com. 2	2.67	3.21	3.77	4.33	4.89	5.46
" 3	4.10	4.97	5.85	6.75	7.67	8.61
" 4	5.60	6.82	8.08	9.37	10.70	12.07
" 5	7.18	8.79	10.47	12.20	14.00	15.87
" 6	8.84	10.88	13.02	15.26	17.60	20.06

TIME.	5 %	6 %	7 %	8 %	9 %	10 %
Days 1	0	0	1	1	1	1
" 2	1	1	1	1	1	1
" 3	1	1	2	2	2	2
" 4	2	2	2	2	3	3
" 5	2	2	3	3	3	4
" 6	2	3	3	4	4	5
" 7	3	3	4	4	5	5
" 8	3	4	4	5	5	6
" 9	3	4	5	5	6	7
" 10	4	5	5	6	7	8
" 11	4	5	6	7	7	8
" 12	5	5	6	7	8	9
" 13	5	6	7	8	9	10
" 14	5	6	7	8	9	11
" 15	6	7	8	9	10	11
" 16	6	7	8	10	11	12
" 17	6	8	9	10	11	13
" 18	7	8	9	11	12	14
" 19	7	9	10	11	13	14
" 20	8	9	11	12	14	15
" 21	8	9	11	13	14	16
" 22	8	10	12	13	15	17
" 23	9	10	12	14	16	17
" 24	9	11	13	14	16	18
" 25	9	11	13	15	17	19
" 26	10	12	14	16	18	20
" 27	10	12	14	16	18	20
" 28	11	13	15	17	19	21
" 29	11	13	15	17	20	22
Mos. 1	11	14	16	18	20	23
" 2	23	27	32	36	41	45
" 3	34	41	47	54	61	68
" 4	45	54	63	72	81	90
" 5	56	68	79	90	1.01	1.13
" 6	68	81	95	1.08	1.22	1.35
" 7	79	95	1.10	1.26	1.42	1.58
" 8	90	1.08	1.26	1.44	1.62	1.80
" 9	1.01	1.22	1.42	1.62	1.82	2.03
" 10	1.13	1.35	1.58	1.80	2.03	2.25
" 11	1.24	1.49	1.73	1.98	2.23	2.48
Yrs. 1	1.35	1.62	1.89	2.16	2.43	2.70
" 2	2.70	3.24	3.78	4.32	4.86	5.40
" 3	4.05	4.86	5.67	6.48	7.29	8.10
" 4	5.40	6.48	7.56	8.64	9.72	10.80
Com. 2	2.77	3.34	3.91	4.49	5.08	5.67
" 3	4.26	5.16	6.08	7.01	7.97	8.94
" 4	5.82	7.09	8.39	9.73	11.11	12.53
" 5	7.46	9.13	10.87	12.67	14.54	16.48
" 6	9.18	11.30	13.52	15.85	18.28	20.83

TIME.	5 %	6 %	7 %	8 %	9 %	10 %
Days 1	0	0	1	1	1	1
" 2	1	1	1	1	1	2
" 3	1	1	2	2	2	2
" 4	2	2	2	2	3	3
" 5	2	2	3	3	4	4
" 6	2	3	3	4	4	5
" 7	3	3	4	4	5	5
" 8	3	4	4	5	6	6
" 9	4	4	5	6	6	7
" 10	4	5	5	6	7	8
" 11	4	5	6	7	8	9
" 12	5	6	7	7	8	9
" 13	5	6	7	8	9	10
" 14	5	7	8	9	10	11
" 15	6	7	8	9	11	12
" 16	6	7	9	10	11	12
" 17	7	8	9	11	12	13
" 18	7	8	10	11	13	14
" 19	7	9	10	12	13	15
" 20	8	9	11	12	14	16
" 21	8	10	11	13	15	16
" 22	9	10	12	14	15	17
" 23	9	11	13	14	16	18
" 24	9	11	13	15	17	19
" 25	10	12	14	16	18	19
" 26	10	12	14	16	18	20
" 27	11	13	15	17	19	21
" 28	11	13	15	17	20	22
" 29	11	14	16	18	20	23
Mos. 1	12	14	16	19	21	2³
" 2	23	28	33	37	42	4?
" 3	35	42	49	56	63	70
" 4	47	56	65	75	84	93
" 5	58	70	82	93	1.05	1.17
" 6	70	84.	98	1.12	1.26	1.40
" 7	82	98	1.14	1.31	1.47	1.63
" 8	93	1.12	1.31	1.49	1.68	1.87
" 9	1.05	1.26	1.47	1.68	1.89	2.10
" 10	1.17	1.40	1.63	1.87	2.10	2.33
" 11	1.28	1.54	1.80	2.05	2.31	2.57
Yrs. 1	1.40	1.68	1.96	2.24	2.52	2.80
" 2	2.80	3.36	3.92	4.48	5.04	5.60
" 3	4.20	5.04	5.88	6.72	7.56	8.40
" 4	5.60	6.72	7.84	8.96	10.08	11.20
Com. 2	2.87	3.46	4.06	4.66	5.27	5.88
" 3	4.41	5.35	6.30	7.27	8.26	9.27
" 4	6.03	7.35	8.70	10.09	11.52	12.99
" 5	7.74	9.47	11.27	13.14	15.08	17.09
" 6	9.52	11.72	14.02	16.44	18.96	21.60

TIME.	5 %	6 %	7 %	8 %	9 %	10 %
Days 1	0	0	1	1	1	1
" 2	1	1	1	1	1	2
" 3	1	1	2	2	2	2
" 4	2	2	2	3	3	3
" 5	2	2	3	3	4	4
" 6	2	3	3	4	4	5
" 7	3	3	4	5	5	6
" 8	3	4	5	5	6	6
" 9	4	4	5	6	7	7
" 10	4	5	6	6	7	8
" 11	4	5	6	7	8	9
" 12	5	6	7	8	9	10
" 13	5	6	7	8	9	10
" 14	6	7	8	9	10	11
" 15	6	7	8	10	11	12
" 16	6	8	9	10	12	13
" 17	7	8	10	11	12	14
" 18	7	9	10	12	13	15
" 19	8	9	11	12	14	15
" 20	8	10	11	13	15	16
" 21	8	10	12	14	15	17
" 22	9	11	12	14	16	18
" 23	9	11	13	15	17	19
" 24	10	12	14	15	17	19
" 25	10	12	14	16	18	20
" 26	10	13	15	17	19	21
" 27	11	13	15	17	20	22
" 28	11	14	16	18	20	23
" 29	12	14	16	19	21	23
Mos. 1	12	15	17	19	22	24
" 2	24	29	34	39	44	48
" 3	36	44	51	58	65	73
" 4	48	58	6S	77	87	97
" 5	60	73	85	97	1.09	1.21
" 6	73	87	1.02	1.16	1.31	1.45
" 7	85	1.02	1.18	1.35	1.52	1.69
" 8	97	1.16	1.35	1.55	1.74	1.93
" 9	1.09	1.31	1.52	1.74	1.96	2.18
" 10	1.21	1.45	1.69	1.93	2.18	2.42
" 11	1.33	1.60	1.86	2.13	2.39	2.66
Yrs. 1	1.45	1.74	2.03	2.32	2.61	2.90
" 2	2.90	3.48	4.06	4.64	5.22	5.80
" 3	4.35	5.22	6.09	6.96	7.83	8.70
" 4	5.80	6.96	8.12	9.28	10.44	11.60
Com. 2	2.97	3.58	4.20	4.83	5.45	6.09
" 3	4.57	5.54	6.53	7.53	8.56	9.60
" 4	6.25	7.61	9.01	10.45	11.94	13.46
" 5	8.01	9.81	11.67	13.61	15.62	17.70
" 6	9.86	12.14	14.52	17.02	19.64	22.38

TIME.	5 %	6 %	7 %	8 %	9 %	10 %
Days 1	0	1	1	1	1	1
" 2	1	1	1	1	2	2
" 3	1	2	2	2	2	3
" 4	2	2	2	3	3	3
" 5	2	3	3	3	4	4
" 6	3	3	4	4	5	5
" 7	3	4	4	5	5	6
" 8	3	4	5	5	6	7
" 9	4	5	5	6	7	8
" 10	4	5	6	7	8	8
" 11	5	6	6	7	8	9
" 12	5	6	7	8	9	10
" 13	5	7	8	9	10	11
" 14	6	7	8	9	11	12
" 15	6	8	9	10	11	13
" 16	7	8	9	11	12	13
" 17	7	9	10	11	13	14
" 18	8	9	11	12	14	15
" 19	8	10	11	13	14	16
" 20	8	10	12	13	15	17
" 21	9	11	12	14	16	18
" 22	9	11	13	15	17	18
" 23	10	12	13	15	17	19
" 24	10	12	14	16	18	20
" 25	10	13	15	17	19	21
" 26	11	13	15	17	20	22
" 27	11	14	16	18	20	23
" 28	12	14	16	19	21	23
" 29	12	15	17	19	22	24
Mos. 1	13	15	18	20	23	25
" 2	25	30	35	40	45	50
" 3	38	45	53	60	68	75
" 4	50	60	70	80	90	1.00
" 5	63	75	88	1.00	1.13	1.25
" 6	75	90	1.05	1.20	1.35	1.50
" 7	88	1.05	1.23	1.40	1.58	1.75
" 8	1.00	1.20	1.40	1.60	1.80	2.00
" 9	1.13	1.35	1.58	1.80	2.03	2.25
" 10	1.25	1.50	1.75	2.00	2.25	2.50
" 11	1.38	1.65	1.93	2.20	2.48	2.75
Yrs. 1	1.50	1.80	2.10	2.40	2.70	3.00
" 2	3.00	3.60	4.20	4.80	5.40	6.00
" 3	4.50	5.40	6.30	7.20	8.10	9.00
" 4	6.00	7.20	8.40	9.60	10.80	12.00
Com. 2	3.08	3.71	4.35	4.99	5.64	6.30
" 3	4.73	5.73	6.75	7.79	8.85	9.93
" 4	6.47	7.87	9.32	10.81	12.35	13.92
" 5	8.29	10.15	12.08	14.08	16.16	18.32
" 6	10.20	12.56	15.02	17.60	20.31	23.15

TIME.	5 %	6 %	7 %	8 %	9 %	10 %
Days 1	0	1	1	1	1	1
" 2	1	1	1	1	2	2
" 3	1	2	2	2	2	3
" 4	2	2	2	3	3	3
" 5	2	3	3	3	4	4
" 6	3	3	4	4	5	5
" 7	3	4	4	5	5	6
" 8	3	4	5	6	6	7
" 9	4	5	5	6	7	8
" 10	4	5	6	7	8	9
" 11	5	6	7	8	9	9
" 12	5	6	7	8	9	10
" 13	6	7	8	9	10	11
" 14	6	7	8	10	11	12
" 15	6	8	9	10	12	13
" 16	7	8	10	11	12	14
" 17	7	9	10	12	13	15
" 18	8	9	11	12	14	16
" 19	8	10	11	13	15	16
" 20	9	10	12	14	16	17
" 21	9	11	13	14	16	18
" 22	9	11	13	15	17	19
" 23	10	12	14	16	18	20
" 24	10	12	14	17	19	21
" 25	11	13	15	17	19	22
" 26	11	13	16	18	20	22
" 27	12	14	16	19	21	23
" 28	12	14	17	19	22	24
" 29	12	15	17	20	22	25
Mos. 1	13	16	18	21	23	26
" 2	26	31	36	41	47	52
" 3	39	47	54	62	70	78
" 4	52	62	72	83	93	1.03
" 5	65	78	90	1.03	1.16	1.29
" 6	78	93	1.09	1.24	1.40	1.55
" 7	90	1.09	1.27	1.45	1.63	1.81
" 8	1.03	1.24	1.45	1.65	1.86	2.07
" 9	1.16	1.40	1.63	1.86	2.09	2.33
" 10	1.29	1.55	1.81	2.07	2.33	2.58
" 11	1.42	1.71	1.99	2.27	2.56	2.84
Yrs. 1	1.55	1.86	2.17	2.48	2.79	3.10
" 2	3.10	3.72	4.34	4.96	5.58	6.20
" 3	4.65	5.58	6.51	7.44	8.37	9.30
" ·4	6.20	7.44	8.68	9.92	11.16	12.40
Com. 2	3.18	3.83	4.49	5.16	5.83	6.51
" 3	4.89	5.92	6.98	8.05	9.15	10.26
" 4	6.68	8.14	9.63	11.17	12.76	14.39
" 5	8.56	10.48	12.48	14.55	16.70	18.92
" 6	10.54	12.97	15.52	18.19	20.99	23.92

TIME.	5 %	6 %	7 %	8 %	9 %	10 %
Days 1	0	1	1	1	1	1
" 2	1	1	1	1	2	2
" 3	1	2	2	2	2	3
" 4	2	2	2	3	3	4
" 5	2	3	3	4	4	4
" 6	3	3	4	4	5	5
" 7	3	4	4	5	6	6
" 8	4	4	5	6	6	7
" 9	4	5	6	6	7	8
" 10	4	5	6	7	8	9
" 11	5	6	7	8	9	10
" 12	5	6	7	9	10	11
" 13	6	7	8	9	10	12
" 14	6	7	9	10	11	12
" 15	7	8	9	11	12	13
" 16	7	9	10	11	13	14
" 17	8	9	11	12	14	15
" 18	8	10	11	13	14	16
" 19	8	10	12	14	15	17
" 20	9	11	12	14	16	18
" 21	9	11	13	15	17	19
" 22	10	12	14	16	18	20
" 23	10	12	14	16	18	20
" 24	11	13	15	17	19	21
" 25	11	13	16	18	20	22
" 26	12	14	16	18	21	23
" 27	12	14	17	19	22	24
" 28	12	15	17	20	22	25
" 29	13	15	18	21	23	26
Mos 1	13	16	19	21	24	27
" 2	27	32	37	43	48	53
" 3	40	48	56	64	72	80
" 4	53	64	75	85	96	1.07
" 5	67	80	93	1.07	1.20	1.33
" 6	80	96	1.12	1.28	1.44	1.60
" 7	93	1.12	1.31	1.49	1.68	1.87
" 8	1.07	1.28	1.49	1.71	1.92	2.13
" 9	1.20	1.44	1.68	1.92	2.16	2.40
" 10	1.33	1.60	1.87	2.13	2.40	2.67
" 11	1.47	1.76	2.05	2.35	2.64	2.93
Yrs. 1	1.60	1.92	2.24	2.56	2.88	3.20
" 2	3.20	3.84	4.48	5.12	5.76	6.40
" 3	4.80	5.76	6.72	7.68	8.64	9.60
" 4	6.40	7.68	8.96	10.24	11.52	12.80
Com. 2	3.28	3.96	4.64	5.32	6.02	6.72
" 3	5.04	6.11	7.20	8.31	9.44	10.59
" 4	6.90	8.40	9.95	11.54	13.17	14.85
" 5	8.84	10.82	12.88	15.02	17.24	19.54
" 6	10.88	13.39	16.02	18.78	21.67	24.69

TIME.	5 %	6 %	7 %	8 %	9 %	10 %
Days 1	0	1	1	1	1	1
" 2	1	1	1	1	2	2
" 3	1	2	2	2	2	3
" 4	2	2	3	3	3	4
" 5	2	3	3	4	4	5
" 6	3	3	4	4	5	6
" 7	3	4	4	5	6	6
" 8	4	4	5	6	7	7
" 9	4	5	6	7	7	8
" 10	5	6	6	7	8	9
" 11	5	6	7	8	9	10
" 12	6	7	8	9	10	11
" 13	6	7	8	10	11	12
" 14	6	8	9	10	12	13
" 15	7	8	10	11	12	14
" 16	7	9	10	12	13	15
" 17	8	9	11	12	14	16
" 18	8	10	12	13	15	17
" 19	9	10	12	14	16	17
" 20	9	11	13	15	17	18
" 21	10	12	13	15	17	19
" 22	10	12	14	16	18	20
" 23	11	13	15	17	19	21
" 24	11	13	15	18	20	22
" 25	11	14	16	18	21	23
" 26	12	14	17	19	21	24
" 27	12	15	17	20	22	25
" 28	13	15	18	21	23	26
" 29	13	16	19	21	24	27
Mos. 1	14	17	19	22	25	28
" 2	28	33	39	44	50	55
" 3	41	50	58	66	74	83
" 4	55	66	77	88	99	1.10
" 5	69	83	96	1.10	1.24	1.38
" 6	83	99	1.16	1.32	1.49	1.65
" 7	96	1.16	1.35	1.54	1.73	1.93
" 8	1.10	1.32	1.54	1.76	1.98	2.20
" 9	1.24	1.49	1.73	1.98	2.23	2.48
" 10	1.38	˙1.65	1.93	2.20	2.48	2.75
" 11	1.51	1.82	2.12	2.42	2.72	3.03
Yrs. 1	1.65	1.98	2.31	2.64	2.97	3.30
" 2	3.30	3.96	4.62	5.28	5.94	6.60
" 3	4.95	5.94	6.93	7.92	8.91	9.90
" 4	6.60	7.92	9.24	10.56	11.88	13.20
Com. 2	3.38	4.08	4.78	5.49	6.21	6.93
" 3	5.20	6.30	7.43	8.57	9.74	10.92
" 4	7.11	8.66	10.26	11.90	13.58	15.32
" 5	9.12	11.16	13.28	15.49	17.77	20.15
" 6	11.22	13.81	16.52	19.37	22.34	25.46

TIME.	5 %	6 %	7 %	8 %	9 %	10 %
Days 1	0	1	1	1	1	1
" 2	1	1	1	2	2	2
" 3	1	2	2	2	3	3
" 4	2	2	3	3	3	4
" 5	2	3	3	4	4	5
" 6	3	3	4	5	5	6
" 7	3	4	5	5	6	7
" 8	4	5	5	6	7	8
" 9	4	5	6	7	8	9
" 10	5	6	7	8	9	9
" 11	5	6	7	8	9	10
" 12	6	7	8	9	10	11
" 13	6	7	9	10	11	12
" 14	7	8	9	11	12	13
" 15	7	9	10	11	13	14
" 16	8	9	11	12	14	15
" 17	8	10	11	13	14	16
" 18	9	10	12	14	15	17
" 19	9	11	13	14	16	18
" 20	9	11	13	15	17	19
" 21	10	12	14	16	18	20
" 22	10	12	15	17	19	21
" 23	11	13	15	17	20	22
" 24	11	14	16	18	20	23
" 25	12	14	17	19	21	24
" 26	12	15	17	20	22	25
" 27	13	15	18	20	23	26
" 28	13	16	19	21	24	26
" 29	14	16	19	22	25	27
Mos. 1	14	17	20	23	26	28
" 2	28	34	40	45	51	57
" 3	43	51	60	68	77	85
" 4	57	68	79	91	1.02	1.13
" 5	71	85	99	1.13	1.28	1.42
" 6	85	1.02	1.19	1.36	1.53	1.70
" 7	99	1.19	1.39	1.59	1.79	1.98
" 8	1.13	1.36	1.59	1.81	2.04	2.27
" 9	1.28	1.53	1.79	2.04	2.30	2.55
" 10	1.42	1.70	1.98	2.27	2.55	2.83
" 11	1.56	1.87	2.18	2.49	2.81	3.12
Yrs. 1	1.70	2.04	2.38	2.72	3.06	3.40
" 2	3.40	4.08	4.76	5.44	6.12	6.80
" 3	5.10	6.12	7.14	8.16	9.18	10.20
" 4	6.80	8.16	9.52	10.88	12.24	13.60
Com. 2	3.49	4.20	4.93	5.66	6.40	7.14
" 3	5.36	6.49	7.65	8.83	10.03	11.25
" 4	7.33	8.92	10.57	12.26	13.99	15.78
" 5	9.39	11.50	13.69	15.96	18.31	20.76
" 6	11.56	14.23	17.02	19.95	23.02	26.23

TIME.	5 %	6 %	7 %	8 %	9 %	10 %
Days 1	0	1	1	1	1	1
" 2	1	1	1	2	2	2
" 3	1	2	2	2	3	3
" 4	2	2	3	3	4	4
" 5	2	3	3	4	4	5
" 6	3	4	4	5	5	6
" 7	3	4	5	5	6	7
" 8	4	5	5	6	7	8
" 9	4	5	6	7	8	9
" 10	5	6	7	8	9	10
" 11	5	6	7	9	10	11
" 12	6	7	8	9	11	12
" 13	6	8	9	10	11	13
" 14	7	8	10	11	12	14
" 15	7	9	10	12	13	15
" 16	8	9	11	12	14	16
" 17	8	10	12	13	15	17
" 18	9	11	12	14	16	18
" 19	9	11	13	15	17	18
" 20	10	12	14	16	18	19
" 21	10	12	14	16	18	20
" 22	11	13	15	17	19	21
" 23	11	13	16	18	20	22
" 24	12	14	16	19	21	23
" 25	12	15	17	19	22	24
" 26	13	15	18	20	23	25
" 27	13	16	18	21	24	26
" 28	14	16	19	22	25	27
" 29	14	17	20	23	25	28
Mos. 1	15	18	20	23	26	29
" 2	29	35	41	47	53	58
" 3	44	53	61	70	79	88
" 4	58	70	82	93	1.05	1.17
" 5	73	88	1.02	1.17	1.31	1.46
" 6	88	1.05	1.23	1.40	1.58	1.75
" 7	1.02	1.23	1.43	1.63	1.84	2.04
" 8	1.17	1.40	1.63	1.87	2.10	2.33
" 9	1.31	1.58	1.84	2.10	2.36	2.63
" 10	1.46	1.75	2.04	2.33	2.63	2.92
" 11	1.60	1.93	2.25	2.57	2.89	3.21
Yrs. 1	1.75	2.10	2.45	2.80	3.15	3.50
" 2	3.50	4.20	4.90	5.60	6.30	7.00
" 3	5.25	6.30	7.35	8.40	9.45	10.50
" 4	7.00	8.40	9.80	11.20	12.60	14.00
Com. 2	3.59	4.33	5.07	5.82	6.58	7.35
" 3	5.52	6.69	7.88	9.09	10.33	11.59
" 4	7.54	9.19	10.88	12.62	14.41	16.24
" 5	9.67	11.84	14.09	16.43	18.85	21.37
" 6	11.90	14.65	17.53	20.54	23.70	27.00

36 Dollars.

TIME.	5 %	6 %	7 %	8 %	9 %	10 %
Days 1	1	1	1	1	1	1
" 2	1	1	1	2	2	2
" 3	2	2	2	2	3	3
" 4	2	2	3	3	4	4
" 5	3	3	4	4	5	5
" 6	3	4	4	5	5	6
" 7	4	4	5	6	6	7
" 8	4	5	6	6	7	8
" 9	5	5	6	7	8	9
" 10	5	6	7	8	9	10
" 11	6	7	8	9	10	11
" 12	6	7	8	10	11	12
" 13	7	8	9	10	12	13
" 14	7	8	10	11	13	14
" 15	8	9	11	12	14	15
" 16	8	10	11	13	14	16
" 17	9	10	12	14	15	17
" 18	9	11	13	14	16	18
" 19	10	11	13	15	17	19
" 20	10	12	14	16	18	20
" 21	11	13	15	17	19	21
" 22	11	13	15	18	20	22
" 23	12	14	16	18	21	23
" 24	12	14	17	19	22	24
" 25	13	15	18	20	23	25
" 26	13	16	18	21	23	26
" 27	14	16	19	22	24	27
" 28	14	17	20	22	25	28
" 29	15	17	20	23	26	29
Mos. 1	15	18	21	24	27	30
" 2	30	36	42	48	54	60
" 3	45	54	63	72	81	90
" 4	60	72	84	96	1.08	1.20
" 5	75	90	1.05	1.20	1.35	1.50
" 6	90	1.08	1.26	1.44	1.62	1.80
" 7	1.05	1.26	1.47	1.68	1.89	2.10
" 8	1.20	1.44	1.68	1.92	2.16	2.40
" 9	1.35	1.62	1.89	2.16	2.43	2.70
" 10	1.50	1.80	2.10	2.40	2.70	3.00
" 11	1.65	1.98	2.31	2.64	2.97	3.30
Yrs. 1	1.80	2.16	2.52	2.88	3.24	3.60
" 2	3.60	4.32	5.04	5.76	6.48	7.20
" 3	5.40	6.48	7.56	8.64	9.72	10.80
" 4	7.20	8.64	10.08	11.52	12.96	14.40
Com. 2	3.69	4.45	5.22	5.99	6.77	7.56
" 3	5.67	6.88	8.10	9.35	10.62	11.92
" 4	7.76	9.45	11.19	12.98	14.82	16.71
" 5	9.95	12.18	14.49	16.90	19.39	21.98
" 6	12.24	15.07	18.03	21.13	24.38	27.78

TIME.	5 %	6 %	7 %	8 %	9 %	10 %
Days 1	1	1	1	1	1	1
" 2	1	1	1	2	2	2
" 3	2	2	2	2	3	3
" 4	2	2	3	3	4	4
" 5	3	3	4	4	5	5
" 6	3	4	4	5	6	6
" 7	4	4	5	6	6	7
" 8	4	5	6	7	7	8
" 9	5	6	6	7	8	9
" 10	5	6	7	8	9	10
" 11	6	7	8	9	10	11
" 12	6	7	9	10	11	12
" 13	7	8	9	11	12	13
" 14	7	9	10	12	13	14
" 15	8	9	11	12	14	15
" 16	8	10	12	13	15	16
" 17	9	10	12	14	16	17
" 18	9	11	13	15	17	19
" 19	10	12	14	16	18	20
" 20	10	12	14	16	19	21
" 21	11	13	15	17	19	22
" 22	11	14	16	18	20	23
" 23	12	14	17	19	21	24
" 24	12	15	17	20	22	25
" 25	13	15	18	21	23	26
" 26	13	16	19	21	24	27
" 27	14	17	19	22	25	28
" 28	14	17	20	23	26	29
" 29	15	18	21	•24	27	30
Mos. 1	15	19	22	25	28	31
" 2	31	37	43	49	56	62
" 3	46	56	65	74	83	93
" 4	62	74	86	99	1.11	1.23
" 5	77	93	1.08	1.23	1.39	1.54
" 6	93	1.11	1.30	1.48	1.67	1.85
" 7	1.08	1.30	1.51	1.73	1.94	2.16
" 8	1.23	1.48	1.73	1.97	2.22	2.47
" 9	1.39	1.67	1.94	2.22	2.50	2.78
" 10	1.54	1.85	2.16	2.47	2.78	3.08
" 11	1.70	2.04	2.37	2.71	3.05	3.39
Yrs. 1	1.85	2.22	2.59	2.96	3.33	3.70
" 2	3.70	4.44	5.18	5.92	6.66	7.40
" 3	5.55	6.66	7.77	8.88	9.99	11.10
" 4	7.40	8.88	10.36	11.84	13.32	14.80
Com. 2	3.79	4.57	5.36	6.16	6.96	7.77
" 3	5.83	7.07	8.33	9.61	10.92	12.25
" 4	7.97	9.71	11.50	13.34	15.23	17.17
" 5	10.22	12.51	14.89	17.37	19.93	22.59
" 6	12.58	15.49	18.53	21.71	25.05	28.55

TIME.	5 %	6 %	7 %	8 %	9 %	10 %
Days 1	1	1	1	1	1	1
" 2	1	1	1	2	2	2
" 3	2	2	2	3	3	3
" 4	2	3	3	3	4	4
" 5	3	3	4	4	5	5
" 6	3	4	4	5	6	6
" 7	4	4	5	6	7	7
" 8	4	5	6	7	8	8
" 9	5	6	7	8	9	10
" 10	5	6	7	8	10	11
" 11	6	7	8	9	10	12
" 12	6	8	9	10	11	13
" 13	7	8	10	11	12	14
" 14	7	9	10	12	13	15
" 15	8	10	11	13	14	16
" 16	8	10	12	14	15	17
" 17	9	11	13	14	16	18
" 18	10	11	13	15	17	19
" 19	10	12	14	16	18	20
" 20	11	13	15	17	19	21
" 21	11	13	16	18	20	22
" 22	12	14	16	19	21	23
" 23	12	15	17	19	22	24
" 24	13	15	18	20	23	25
" 25	13	16	18	21	24	26
" 26	14	16	19	22	25	27
" 27	14	17	20	23	26	29
" 28	15	18	21	24	27	30
" 29	15	18	21	24	28	31
Mos. 1	16	19	22	25	29	32
" 2	32	38	44	51	57	63
" 3	48	57	67	76	86	95
" 4	63	76	89	1.01	1.14	1.27
" 5	79	95	1.11	1.27	1.43	1.58
" 6	95	1.14	1.33	1.52	1.71	1.90
" 7	1.11	1.33	1.55	1.77	2.00	2.22
" 8	1.27	1.52	1.77	2.03	2.28	2.53
" 9	1.43	1.71	2.00	2.28	2.57	2.85
" 10	1.58	1.90	2.22	2.53	2.85	3.17
" 11	1.74	2.09	2.44	2.79	3.14	. 3.48
Yrs. 1	1.90	2.28	2.66	3.04	3.42	3.80
" 2	3.80	4.56	5.32	6.08	6.84	7.60
" 3	5.70	6.84	7.98	9.12	10.26	11.40
" 4	7.60	9.12	10.64	12.16	13.68	15.20
Com. 2	3.90	4.70	5.51	6.32	7.15	7.98
" 3	5.99	7.26	8.55	9.87	11.21	12.58
" 4	8.19	9.97	11.81	13.70	15.64	17.64
" 5	10.50	12.85	15·30	17.83	20.47	23.20
" 6	12.92	15.90	19.03	22.31	25.73	29.32

TIME.	5 %	6 %	7 %	8 %	9 %	10 %
Days 1	1	1	1	1	1	1
" 2	1	1	2	2	2	2
" 3	2	2	2	3	3	3
" 4	2	3	3	3	4	4
" 5	3	3	4	4	5	5
" 6	3	4	5	5	6	7
" 7	4	5	5	6	7	8
" 8	4	5	6	7	8	9
" 9	5	6	7	8	9	10
" 10	5	7	8	9	10	11
" 11	6	7	8	10	11	12
" 12	7	8	9	10	12	13
" 13	7	8	10	11	13	14
" 14	8	9	11	12	14	15
" 15	8	10	11	13	15	16
" 16	9	10	12	14	16	17
" 17	9	11	13	15	17	18
" 18	10	12	14	16	18	20
" 19	10	12	14	16	19	21
" 20	11	13	15	17	20	22
" 21	11	14	16	18	20	23
" 22	12	14	17	19	21	24
" 23	12	15	17	20	22	25
" 24	13	16	18	21	23	26
" 25	14	16	19	22	24	27
" 26	14	17	20	23	25	28
" 27	15	18	20	23	26	29
" 28	15	18	21	24	27	30
" 29	16	19	22	25	28	31
Mos. 1	16	20	23	26	29	33
" 2	33	39	46	52	59	65
" 3	49	59	68	78	88	98
" 4	65	78	91	1.04	1.17	1.30
" 5	81	98	1.14	1.30	1.46	1.63
" 6	98	1.17	1.37	1.56	1.76	1.95
" 7	1.14	1.37	1.59	1.82	2.05	2.28
" 8	1.30	1.56	1.82	2.08	2.34	2.60
" 9	1.46	1.76	2.05	2.34	2.63	2.93
" 10	1.63	1.95	2.28	2.60	2.93	3.25
" 11	1.79	2.15	2.50	2.86	3.22	3.58
Yrs. 1	1.95	2.34	2.73	3.12	3.51	3.90
" 2	3.90	4.68	5.46	6.24	7.02	7.80
" 3	5.85	7.02	8.19	9.36	10.53	11.70
" 4	7.80	9.36	10.92	12.48	14.04	15.60
Com. 2	4.00	4.82	5.65	6.49	7.34	8.19
" 3	6.15	7.45	8.78	10.13	11.51	12.91
" 4	8.40	10.24	12.12	14.06	16.05	18.10
" 5	10.77	13.19	15.70	18.30	21.01	23.81
" 6	13.26	16.32	19.53	22.89	26.41	30.09

TIME.	5 %	6 %	7 %	8 %	9 %	10 %
Days 1	1	1	1	1	1	1
" 2	1	1	2	2	2	2
" 3	2	2	2	3	3	3
" 4	2	3	3	4	4	4
" 5	3	3	4	4	5	6
" 6	3	4	5	5	6	7
" 7	4	5	5	6	7	8
" 8	4	5	6	7	8	9
" 9	5	6	7	8	9	10
" 10	6	7	8	9	10	11
" 11	6	7	9	10	11	12
" 12	7	8	9	11	12	13
" 13	7	9	10	12	13	14
" 14	8	9	11	12	14	16
" 15	8	10	12	13	15	17
" 16	9	11	12	14	16	18
" 17	9	11	13	15	17	19
" 18	10	12	14	16	18	20
" 19	11	13	15	17	19	21
" 20	11	13	16	18	20	22
" 21	12	14	16	19	21	23
" 22	12	15	17	20	22	24
" 23	13	15	18	20	23	26
" 24	13	16	19	21	24	27
" 25	14	17	19	22	25	28
" 26	14	17	20	23	26	29
" 27	15	18	21	24	27	30
" 28	16	19	22	25	28	31
" 29	16	19	23	26	29	32
Mos. 1	17	20	23	27	30	33
" 2	33	40	47	53	60	67
" 3	50	60	70	80	90	1.00
" 4	67	80	93	1.07	1.20	1.33
" 5	83	1.00	1.17	1.33	1.50	1.67
" 6	1.00	1.20	1.40	1.60	1.80	2.00
" 7	1.17	1.40	1.63	1.87	2.10	2.33
" 8	1.33	1.60	1.87	2.13	2.40	2.67
" 9	1.50	1.80	2.10	2.40	2.70	3.00
" 10	1.67	2.00	2.33	2.67	3.00	3.33
" 11	1.83	2.20	2.57	2.93	3.30	3.67
Yrs. 1	2.00	2.40	2.80	3.20	3.60	4.00
" 2	4.00	4.80	5.60	6.40	7.20	8.00
" 3	6.00	7.20	8.40	9.60	10.80	12.00
" 4	8.00	9.60	11.20	12.80	14.40	16.00
Com. 2	4.10	4.94	5.80	6.66	7.52	8.40
" 3	6.31	7.64	9.00	10.39	11.80	13.24
" 4	8.62	10.50	12.43	14.42	16.46	18.56
" 5	11.05	13.53	16.10	18.77	21.54	24.42
" 6	13.60	16.74	20.03	23.47	27.08	30.86

41 Dollars.

TIME.	5 %	6 %	7 %	8 %	9 %	10 %
Days 1	1	1	1	1	1	1
" 2	1	1	2	2	2	2
" 3	2	2	2	3	3	3
" 4	2	3	3	4	4	5
" 5	3	3	4	5	5	6
" 6	3	4	5	5	6	7
" 7	4	5	6	6	7	8
" 8	5	5	6	7	8	9
" 9	5	6	7	8	9	10
" 10	6	7	8	9	10	11
" 11	6	8	9	10	11	13
" 12	7	8	10	11	12	14
" 13	7	9	10	12	13	15
" 14	8	10	11	13	14	16
" 15	9	10	12	14	15	17
" 16	9	11	13	15	16	18
" 17	10	12	14	15	17	19
" 18	10	12	14	16	18	21
" 19	11	13	15	17	19	22
" 20	11	14	16	18	21	23
" 21	12	14	17	19	22	24
" 22	13	15	18	20	23	25
" 23	13	16	18	21	24	26
" 24	14	16	19	22	25	27
" 25	14	17	20	23	26	28
" 26	15	18	21	24	27	30
" 27	15	18	22	25	28	31
" 28	16	19	22	26	29	32
" 29	17	20	23	26	30	33
Mos. 1	17	21	24	27	31	34
" 2	34	41	48	55	62	68
" 3	51	62	72	82	92	1.03
" 4	68	82	96	1.09	1.23	1.37
" 5	85	1.03	1.20	1.37	1.54	1.71
" 6	1.03	1.23	1.44	1.64	1.85	2.05
" 7	1.20	1.44	1.67	1.91	2.15	2.39
" 8	1.37	1.64	1.91	2.19	2.46	2.73
" 9	1.54	1.85	2.15	2.46	2.77	3.08
" 10	1.71	2.05	2.39	2.73	3.08	3.42
" 11	1.88	2.26	2.63	3.01	3.38	3.76
Yrs. 1	2.05	2.46	2.87	3.28	3.69	4.10
" 2	4.10	4.92	5.74	6.56	7.38	8.20
" 3	6.15	7.38	8.61	9.84	11.07	12.30
" 4	8.20	9.84	11.48	13.12	14.76	16.40
Com. 2	4.20	5.07	5.94	6.82	7.71	8.61
" 3	6.46	7.83	9.23	10.65	12.10	13.57
" 4	8.84	10.76	12.74	14.78	16.87	19.03
" 5	11.33	13.87	16.50	19.24	22.08	25.03
" 6	13.94	17.16	20.53	24.06	27.76	31.63

TIME.	5 %	6 %	7 %	8 %	9 %	10 %
Days 1	1	1	1	1	1	1
" 2	1	1	2	2	2	2
" 3	2	2	2	3	3	4
" 4	2	3	3	4	4	5
" 5	3	4	4	5	5	6
" 6	4	4	5	6	6	7
" 7	4	5	6	7	7	8
" 8	5	6	7	7	8	9
" 9	5	6	7	8	9	11
" 10	6	7	8	9	11	12
" 11	6	8	9	10	12	13
" 12	7	8	10	11	13	14
" 13	8	9	11	12	14	15
" 14	8	10	11	13	15	16
" 15	9	11	12	14	16	18
" 16	9	11	13	15	17	19
" 17	10	12	14	16	18	20
" 18	11	13	15	17	19	21
" 19	11	13	16	18	20	22
" 20	12	14	16	19	21	23
" 21	12	15	17	20	22	24
" 22	13	15	18	21	23	26
" 23	13	16	19	21	24	27
" 24	14	17	20	22	25	28
" 25	15	18	20	23	26	29
" 26	15	18	21	24	27	30
" 27	16	19	22	25	28	32
" 28	16	20	23	26	29	33
" 29	17	20	24	27	30	34
Mos. 1	18	21	25	28	32	35
" 2	35	42	49	56	63	70
" 3	53	63	74	84	95	1.05
" 4	70	84	98	1.12	1.26	1.40
" 5	88	1.05	1.23	1.40	1.58	1.75
" 6	1.05	1.26	1.47	1.68	1.89	2.10
" 7	1.23	1.47	1.72	1.96	2.21	2.45
" 8	1.40	1.68	1.96	2.24	2.52	2.80
" 9	1.58	1.89	2.21	2.52	2.84	3.15
" 10	1.75	2.10	2.45	2.80	3.15	3.50
" 11	1.93	2.31	2.70	3.08	3.47	3.85
Yrs. 1	2.10	2.52	2.94	3.36	3.78	4.20
" 2	4.20	5.04	5.88	6.72	7.56	8.40
" 3	6.30	7.56	8.82	10.08	11.34	12.60
" 4	8.40	10.08	11.76	13.44	15.12	16.80
Com. 2	4.31	5.19	6.09	6.99	7.90	8.82
" 3	6.62	8.02	9.45	10.91	12.39	13.90
" 4	9.05	11.02	13 05	15.14	17.29	19.49
" 5	11.60	14.21	16.91	19.71	22.62	25.64
" 6	14.28	17.58	21.03	24.65	28.44	32.41

TIME.	5 %	6 %	7 %	8 %	9 %	10 %
Days 1	1	1	1	1	1	1
" 2	1	1	2	2	2	2
" 3	2	2	3	3	3	4
" 4	2	3	3	4	4	5
" 5	3	4	4	5	5	6
" 6	4	4	5	6	6	7
" 7	4	5	6	7	8	8
" 8	5	6	7	8	9	10
" 9	5	6	8	9	10	11
" 10	6	7	8	10	11	12
" 11	7	8	9	11	12	13
" 12	7	9	10	11	13	14
" 13	8	9	11	12	14	16
" 14	8	10	12	13	15	17
" 15	9	11	13	14	16	18
" 16	10	11	13	15	17	19
" 17	10	12	14	16	18	20
" 18	11	13	15	17	19	22
" 19	11	14	16	18	20	23
" 20	12	14	17	19	22	24
" 21	13	15	18	20	23	25
" 22	13	16	18	21	24	26
" 23	14	16	19	22	25	27
" 24	14	17	20	23	26	29
" 25	15	18	21	24	27	30
" 26	16	19	22	25	28	31
" 27	16	19	23	26	29	32
" 28	17	20	23	27	30	33
" 29	17	21	24	28	31	35
Mos. 1	18	22	25	29	32	36
" 2	36	43	50	57	65	72
" 3	54	65	75	86	97	1.08
" 4	72	86	1.00	1.15	1.29	1.43
" 5	90	1.08	1.25	1.43	1.61	1.79
" 6	1.08	1.29	1.51	1.72	1.94	2.15
" 7	1.25	1.51	1.76	2.01	2.26	2.51
" 8	1.43	1.72	2.01	2.29	2.58	2.87
" 9	1.61	1.94	2.26	2.58	2.90	3.23
" 10	1.79	2.15	2.51	2.87	3.23	3.58
" 11	1.97	2.37	2.76	3.15	3.55	3.94
Yrs. 1	2.15	2.58	3.01	3.44	3.87	4.30
" 2	4.30	5.16	6.02	6.88	7.74	8.60
" 3	6.45	7.74	9.03	10.32	11.61	12.90
" 4	8.60	10.32	12.04	13.76	15.48	17.20
Com. 2	4.41	5.31	6.23	7.16	8.09	9.03
" 3	6.78	8.21	9.68	11.17	12.69	14.23
" 4	9.27	11.29	13.36	15.50	17.70	19.96
" 5	11.88	14.54	17.31	20.18	23.16	26.25
" 6	14.62	18.00	21.53	25.24	29.12	33.18

TIME.	5 %	6 %	7 %	8 %	9 %	10 %
Days 1	1	1	1	1	1	1
" 2	1	1	2	2	2	2
" 3	2	2	3	3	3	4
" 4	2	3	3	4	4	5
" 5	3	4	4	5	6	6
" 6	4	4	5	6	7	7
" 7	4	5	6	7	8	9
" 8	5	6	7	8	9	10
" 9	6	7	8	9	10	11
" 10	6	7	9	10	11	12
" 11	7	8	9	11	12	13
" 12	7	9	10	12	13	15
" 13	8	10	11	13	14	16
" 14	9	10	12	14	15	17
" 15	9	11	13	15	17	18
" 16	10	12	14	16	18	20
" 17	10	12	15	17	19	21
" 18	11	13	15	18	20	22
" 19	12	14	16	19	21	23
" 20	12	15	17	20	22	24
" 21	13	15	18	21	23	26
" 22	13	16	19	22	24	27
" 23	14	17	20	22	25	28
" 24	15	18	21	23	26	29
" 25	15	18	21	24	28	31
" 26	16	19	22	25	29	32
" 27	17	20	23	26	30	33
" 28	17	21	24	27	31	34
" 29	18	21	25	28	32	35
Mos. 1	18	22	26	29	33	37
" 2	37	44	51	59	66	73
" 3	55	66	77	88	99	1.10
" 4	73	88	1.03	1.17	1.32	1.47
" 5	92	1.10	1.28	1.47	1.65	1.83
" 6	1.10	1.32	1.54	1.76	1.98	2.20
" 7	1.28	1.54	1.80	2.05	2.31	2.57
" 8	1.47	1.76	2.05	2.35	2.64	2.93
" 9	1.65	1.98	2.31	2.64	2.97	3.30
" 10	1.83	2.20	2.57	2.93	3.30	3.67
" 11	2.02	2.42	2.82	3.23	3.63	4.03
Yrs. 1	2.20	2.64	3.08	3.52	3.96	4.40
" 2	4.40	5.28	6.16	7.04	7.92	8.80
" 3	6.60	7.92	9.24	10.56	11.88	13.20
" 4	8.80	10.56	12.32	14.08	15.84	17.60
Com. 2	4.51	5.44	6.38	7.32	8.28	9.24
" 3	6.94	8.40	9.90	11.43	12.98	14.56
" 4	9.48	11.55	13.68	15.86	18.11	20.42
" 5	12.16	14.88	17.71	20.65	23.70	26.86
" 6	14.96	18.41	22.03	25.82	29.79	33.95

45 Dollars.

TIME.	5 %	6 %	7 %	8 %	9 %	10 %
Days 1	1	1	1	1	1	1
" 2	1	2	2	2	2	3
" 3	2	2	3	3	3	4
" 4	3	3	4	4	5	5
" 5	3	4	4	5	6	6
" 6	4	5	5	6	7	8
" 7	4	5	6	7	8	9
" 8	5	6	7	8	9	10
". 9	6	7	8	9	10	11
" 10	6	8	9	10	11	13
" 11	7	8	10	11	12	14
" 12	8	9	11	12	14	15
" 13	8	10	11	13	15	16
" 14	9	11	12	14	16	18
" 15	9	11	13	15	17	19
" 16	10	12	14	16	18	20
" 17	11	13	15	17	19	21
" 18	11	14	16	18	20	23
" 19	12	14	17	19	21	24
" 20	13	15	18	20	23	25
" 21	13	16	18	21	24	26
" 22	14	17	19	22	25	28
" 23	14	17	20	23	26	29
" 24	15	18	21	24	27	30
" 25	16	19	22	25	28	31
" 26	16	20	23	26	29	33
" 27	17	20	24	27	30	34
" 28	18	21	25	28	32	35
" 29	18	22	25	29	33	36
Mos. 1	19	23	26	30	34	38
" 2	38	45	53	60	68	75
". 3	56	68	79	90	1.01	1.13
" 4	75	90	1.05	1.20	1.35	1.50
" 5	94	1.13	1.31	1.50	1.69	1.88
" 6	1.13	1.35	1.58	1.80	2.03	2.25
" 7	1.31	1.58	1.84	2.10	2.36	2.62
" 8	1.50	1.80	2.10	2.40	2.70	3.00
" 9	1.69	2.03	2.36	2.70	3.04	3.38
" 10	1.88	2.25	2.63	3.00	3.38	3.75
" 11	2.06	2.48	2.89	3.30	3.71	4.13
Yrs. 1	2.25	2.70	3.15	3.60	4.05	4.50
" 2	4.50	5.40	6.30	7.20	8.10	9.00
" 3	6.75	8.10	9.45	10.80	12.15	13.50
" 4	9.00	10.80	12.60	14.40	16.20	18.00
Com. 2	4.61	5.56	6.52	7.49	8.46	9.45
" 3	7.09	8.60	10.13	11.69	13.28	14.90
" 4	9.70	11.81	13.99	16.22	18.52	20.88
" 5	12.43	15.22	18.11	21.12	24.24	27.47
" 6	15.30	18.83	22.53	26.41	30.47	34.72

TIME.	5 %	6 %	7 %	8 %	9 %	10 %
Days 1	1	1	1	1	1	1
" 2	1	2	2	2	2	3
" 3	2	2	3	3	3	4
" 4	3	3	4	4	5	5
" 5	3	4	4	5	6	6
" 6	4	5	5	6	7	8
" 7	4	5	6	7	8	9
" 8	5	6	7	8	9	10
" 9	6	7	8	9	10	12
" 10	6	8	9	10	12	13
" 11	7	8	10	11	13	14
" 12	8	9	11	12	14	15
" 13	8	10	12	13	15	17
" 14	9	11	13	14	16	18
" 15	10	12	13	15	17	19
" 16	10	12	14	16	18	20
" 17	11	13	15	17	20	22
" 18	12	14	16	18	21	23
" 19	12	15	17	19	22	24
" 20	13	15	18	20	23	26
" 21	13	16	19	21	24	27
" 22	14	17	20	22	25	28
" 23	15	18	21	24	26	29
" 24	15	18	21	25	28	31
" 25	16	19	22	26	29	32
" 26	17	20	23	27	30	33
" 27	17	21	24	28	31	35
" 28	18	21	25	29	32	36
" 29	19	22	26	30	33	37
Mos. 1	19	23	27	31	35	38
" 2	38	46	54	61	69	77
" 3	58	69	81	92	1.04	1.15
" 4	77	92	1.07	1.23	1.38	1.53
" 5	96	1.15	1.34	1.53	1.73	1.92
" 6	1.15	1.38	1.61	1.84	2.07	2.30
" 7	1.34	1.61	1.88	2.15	2.42	2.68
" 8	1.53	1.84	2.15	2.45	2.76	3.07
" 9	1.73	2.07	2.42	2.76	3.11	3.45
" 10	1.92	2.30	2.68	3.07	3.45	3.83
" 11	2.11	2.53	2.95	3.37	3.80	4.22
Yrs. 1	2.30	2.76	3.22	3.68	4.14	4.60
" 2	4.60	5.52	6.44	7.36	8.28	9.20
" 3	6.90	8.28	9.66	11.04	12.42	13.80
" 4	9.20	11.04	12.88	14.72	16.56	18.40
Com. 2	4.72	5.69	6.67	7.65	8.65	9.66
" 3	7.25	8.79	10.35	11.95	13.57	15.23
" 4	9.91	12.07	14.30	16.58	18.93	21.35
" 5	12.71	15.56	18.52	21.59	24.78	28.08
" 6	15.64	19.25	23.03	27.00	31.15	35.49

TIME.	5 %	6 %	7 %	8 %	9 %	10 %
Days 1	1	1	1	1	1	1
" 2	1	2	2	2	2	3
" 3	2	2	3	3	4	4
" 4	3	3	4	4	5	5
" 5	3	4	5	5	6	7
" 6	4	5	5	6	7	8
" 7	5	5	6	7	8	9
" 8	5	6	7	8	9	10
" 9	6	7	8	9	11	12
" 10	7	8	9	10	12	13
" 11	7	9	10	11	13	14
" 12	8	9	11	13	14	16
" 13	8	10	12	14	15	17
" 14	9	11	13	15	16	18
" 15	10	12	14	16	18	20
" 16	10	13	15	17	19	21
" 17	11	13	16	18	20	22
" 18	12	14	16	19	21	24
" 19	12	15	17	20	22	25
" 20	13	16	18	21	24	26
" 21	14	16	19	22	25	27
" 22	14	17	20	23	26	29
" 23	15	18	21	24	27	30
" 24	16	19	22	25	28	31
" 25	16	20	23	26	29	33
" 26	17	20	24	27	31	34
" 27	18	21	25	28	32	35
" 28	18	22	26	29	33	37
" 29	19	23	27	30	34	38
Mos. 1	20	24	27	31	35	39
" 2	39	47	55	63	71	78
" 3	59	71	82	94	1.06	1.18
" 4	78	94	1.10	1.25	1.41	1.57
" 5	98	1.18	1.37	1.57	1.76	1.96
" 6	1.18	1.41	1.65	1.88	2.12	2.35
" 7	1.37	1.65	1.92	2.19	2.47	2.74
" 8	1.57	1.88	2.19	2.51	2.82	3.13
" 9	1.76	2.12	2.47	2.82	3.17	3.53
" 10	1.96	2.35	2.74	3.13	3.53	3.92
" 11	2.15	2.59	3.02	3.45	3.88	4.31
Yrs. 1	2.35	2.82	3.29	3.76	4.23	4.70
" 2	4.70	5.64	6.58	7.52	8.46	9.40
" 3	7.05	8.46	9.87	11.28	12.69	14.10
" '4	9.40	11.28	13.16	15.04	16.92	18.80
Com. 2	4.82	5.81	6.81	7.82	8.84	9.87
" 3	7.41	8.98	10.58	12.21	13.87	15.56
" 4	10.13	12.34	14.61	16.94	19.34	21.81
" 5	12.99	15.90	18.92	22.06	25.31	28.69
" 6	15.98	19.67	23.53	27.58	31.82	36.26

TIME.	5 %	6 %	7 %	8 %	9 %	10 %
Days 1	1	1	1	1	1	1
" 2	1	2	2	2	2	3
" 3	2	2	3	3	4	4
" 4	3	3	4	4	5	5
" 5	3	4	5	5	6	7
" 6	4	5	6	6	7	8
" 7	5	6	7	7	8	9
" 8	5	6	7	9	10	11
" 9	6	7	8	10	11	12
" 10	7	8	9	11	12	13
" 11	7	9	10	12	13	15
" 12	8	10	11	13	14	16
" 13	9	10	12	14	16	17
" 14	9	11	13	15	17	19
" 15	10	12	14	16	18	20
" 16	11	13	15	17	19	21
" 17	11	14	16	18	20	23
" 18	12	14	17	19	22	24
" 19	13	15	18	20	23	25
" 20	13	16	19	21	24	27
" 21	14	17	20	22	25	28
" 22	15	18	21	23	26	29
" 23	15	18	21	25	28	31
" 24	16	19	22	26	29	32
" 25	17	20	23	27	30	33
" 26	17	21	24	28	31	35
" 27	18	22	25	29	32	36
" 28	19	22	26	30	34	37
" 29	19	23	27	31	35	39
Mos. 1	20	24	28	32	36	40
" 2	40	48	56	64	72	80
" 3	60	72	84	96	1.08	1.20
" 4	80	96	1.12	1.28	1.44	1.60
" 5	1.00	1.20	1.40	1.60	1.80	2.00
" 6	1.20	1.44	1.68	1.92	2.16	2.40
" 7	1.40	1.68	1.96	2.24	2.52	2.80
" 8	1.60	1.92	2.24	2.56	2.88	3.20
" 9	1.80	2.16	2.52	2.88	3.24	3.60
" 10	2.00	2.40	2.80	3.20	3.60	4.00
" 11	2.20	2.64	3.08	3.52	3.96	4.40
Yrs. 1	2.40	2.88	3.36	3.84	4.32	4.80
" 2	4.80	5.76	6.72	7.68	8.64	9.60
" 3	7.20	8.64	10.08	11.52	12.96	14.40
" 4	9.60	11.52	13.44	15.36	17.28	19.20
Com. 2	4.92	5.93	6.96	7.99	9.03	10.08
" 3	7.57	9.17	10.80	12.47	14.16	15.89
" 4	10.34	12.60	14.92	17.30	19.76	22.28
" 5	13.26	16.23	19.32	22.53	25.85	29.30
" 6	16.32	20.09	24.04	28.17	32.50	37.03

TIME.	5 %	6 %	7 %	8 %	9 %	10 %
Days 1	1	1	1	1	1	1
" 2	1	2	2	2	2	3
" 3	2	2	3	3	4	4
" 4	3	3	4	4	5	5
" 5	3	4	5	5	6	7
" 6	4	5	6	7	7	8
" 7	5	6	7	8	9	10
" 8	5	7	8	9	10	11
" 9	6	7	9	10	11	12
" 10	7	8	10	11	12	14
" 11	7	9	10	12	13	15
" 12	8	10	11	13	15	16
" 13	9	11	12	14	16	18
" 14	10	11	13	15	17	19
" 15	10	12	14	16	18	20
" 16	11	13	15	17	20	22
" 17	12	14	16	19	21	23
" 18	12	15	17	20	22	25
" 19	13	16	18	21	23	26
" 20	14	16	19	22	25	27
" 21	14	17	20	23	26	29
" 22	15	18	21	24	27	30
" 23	16	19	22	25	28	31
" 24	16	20	23	26	29	33
" 25	17	20	24	27	31	34
" 26	18	21	25	28	32	35
" 27	18	22	26	29	33	37
" 28	19	23	27	30	34	38
" 29	20	24	28	32	36	39
Mos. 1	20	25	29	33	37	41
" 2	41	49	57	65	74	82
" 3	61	74	86	98	1.10	1.23
" 4	82	98	1.14	1.31	1.47	1.63
" 5	1.02	1.23	1.43	1.63	1.84	2.04
" 6	1.23	1.47	1.72	1.96	2.21	2.45
" 7	1.43	1.72	2.00	2.29	2.57	2.86
" 8	1.63	1.96	2.29	2.61	2.94	3.27
" 9	1.84	2.21	2.57	2.94	3.31	3.68
" 10	2.04	2.45	2.86	3.27	3.68	4.08
" 11	2.25	2.70	3.14	3.59	4.04	4.49
Yrs. 1	2.45	2.94	3.43	3.92	4.41	4.90
" 2	4.90	5.88	6.86	7.84	8.82	9.80
" 3	7.35	8.82	10.29	11.76	13.23	14.70
" 4	9.80	11.76	13.72	15.68	17.64	19.60
Com. 2	5.02	6.06	7.10	8.15	9.22	10.29
" 3	7.72	9.36	11.03	12.73	14.46	16.22
" 4	10.56	12.86	15.23	17.66	20.17	22.74
" 5	13.54	16.57	19.73	23.00	26.39	29.91
" 6	16.66	20.51	24.54	28.76	33.18	37.81

TIME.	5 %	6 %	7 %	8 %	9 %	10 %
Days 1	1	1	1	1	1	1
" 2	1	2	2	2	3	3
" 3	2	3	3	3	4	4
" 4	3	3	4	4	5	6
" 5	3	4	5	6	6	7
" 6	4	5	6	7	8	8
" 7	5	6	7	8	9	10
" 8	6	7	8	9	10	11
" 9	6	8	9	10	11	13
" 10	7	8	10	11	13	14
" 11	8	9	11	12	14	15
" 12	8	10	12	13	15	17
" 13	9	11	13	14	16	18
" 14	10	12	14	16	18	19
" 15	10	13	15	17	19	21
" 16	11	13	16	18	20	22
" 17	12	14	17	19	21	24
" 18	13	15	18	20	23	25
" 19	13	16	18	21	24	26
" 20	14	17	19	22	25	28
" 21	15	18	20	23	26	29
" 22	15	18	21	24	28	31
" 23	16	19	22	26	29	32
" 24	17	20	23	27	30	33
" 25	17	21	24	28	31	35
" 26	18	22	25	29	33	36
" 27	19	23	26	30	34	38
" 28	19	23	27	31	35	39
" 29	20	24	28	32	36	40
Mos. 1	21	25	29	33	38	42
" 2	42	50	58	67	75	83
" 3	63	75	88	1.00	1.13	1.25
" 4	83	1.00	1.17	1.33	1.50	1.67
" 5	1.04	1.25	1.46	1.67	1.88	2.08
" 6	1.25	1.50	1.75	2.00	2.25	2.50
" 7	1.46	1.75	2.04	2.33	2.63	2.92
" 8	1.67	2.00	2.33	2.67	3.00	3.33
" 9	1.88	2.25	2.63	3.00	3.38	3.75
" 10	2.08	2.50	2.92	3.33	3.75	4.17
" 11	2.29	2 75	3.21	3.67	4.13	4.58
Yrs. 1	2.50	3.00	3.50	4.00	4.50	5.00
" 2	5.00	6.00	7.00	8.00	9.00	10.00
" 3	7.50	9.00	10.50	12.00	13.50	15.00
" 4	10.00	12.00	14.00	16.00	18.00	20.00
Com. 2	5.13	6.18	7.25	8.32	9.41	10.50
" 3	7.88	9.55	11.25	12.99	14.75	16.55
" 4	10.78	13.12	15.54	18.02	20.58	23.21
" 5	13.81	16.91	20.13	23.47	26.93	30.53
" 6	17.00	20.93	25.04	29.34	33.86	38.58

TIME.	5 %	6 %	7 %	8 %	9 %	10 %
Days 1	1	1	1	1	1	1
" 2	1	2	2	2	3	3
" 3	2	3	3	3	4	4
" 4	3	3	4	5	5	6
" 5	4	4	5	6	6	7
" 6	4	5	6	7	8	9
" 7	5	6	7	8	9	10
" 8	6	7	8	9	10	11
" 9	6	8	9	10	11	13
" 10	7	9	10	11	13	14
" 11	8	9	11	12	14	16
" 12	9	10	12	14	15	17
" 13	9	11	13	15	17	18
" 14	10	12	14	16	18	20
" 15	11	13	15	17	19	21
" 16	11	14	16	18	20	23
" 17	12	14	17	19	22	24
" 18	13	15	18	20	23	26
" 19	13	16	19	22	24	27
" 20	14	17	20	23	26	28
" 21	15	18	21	24	27	30
" 22	16	19	22	25	28	31
" 23	16	20	23	26	29	33
" 24	17	20	24	27	31	34
" 25	18	21	25	28	32	35
" 26	18	22	26	29	33	37
" 27	19	23	27	31	34	38
" 28	20	24	28	32	36	40
" 29	21	25	29	33	37	41
Mos. 1	21	26	30	34	38	43
" 2	43	51	60	68	77	85
" 3	64	77	89	1.02	1.15	1.28
" 4	85	1.02	1.19	1.36	1.53	1.70
" 5	1.06	1.28	1.49	1.70	1.91	2.13
" 6	1.28	1.53	1.79	2.04	2.30	2.55
" 7	1.49	1.79	2.08	2.38	2.68	2.98
" 8	1.70	2.04	2.38	2.72	3.06	3.40
" 9	1.91	2.30	2.68	3.06	3.44	3.83
" 10	2.13	2.55	2.98	3.40	3.83	4.25
" 11	2.34	2.81	3.27	3.74	4.21	4.68
Yrs. 1	2.55	3.06	3.57	4.08	4.59	5.10
" 2	5.10	6.12	7.14	8.16	9.18	10.20
" 3	7.65	9.18	10.71	12.24	13.77	15.30
" 4	10.20	12.24	14.28	16.32	18.36	20.40
Com. 2	5.23	6.30	7.39	8.49	9.59	10.71
" 3	8.04	9.74	11.48	13.25	15.05	16.88
" 4	10.99	13.39	15.85	18.38	20.99	23.67
" 5	14.09	17.25	20.53	23.94	27.47	31.14
" 6	17.34	21.34	25.54	29.93	34.53	39.35

TIME.	5 %	6 %	7 %	8 %	9 %	10 %
Days 1	1	1	1	1	1	1
" 2	1	2	2	2	3	3
" 3	2	3	3	3	4	4
" 4	3	3	4	5	5	6
" 5	4	4	5	6	7	7
" 6	4	5	6	7	8	9
" 7	5	6	7	8	9	10
" 8	6	7	8	9	10	12
" 9	7	8	9	10	12	13
" 10	7	9	10	12	13	14
" 11	8	10	11	13	14	16
" 12	9	10	12	14	16	17
" 13	9	11	13	15	17	19
" 14	10	12	14	16	18	20
" 15	11	13	15	17	20	22
" 16	12	14	16	18	21	23
" 17	12	15	17	20	22	25
" 18	13	16	18	21	23	26
" 19	14	16	19	22	25	27
" 20	14	17	20	23	26	29
" 21	15	18	21	24	27	30
" 22	16	19	22	25	29	32
" 23	17	20	23	27	30	33
" 24	17	21	24	28	31	35
" 25	18	22	25	29	33	36
" 26	19	23	26	30	34	38
" 27	20	23	27	31	35	39
" 28	20	24	28	32	36	40
" 29	21	25	29	34	38	42
Mos. 1	22	26	30	35	39	43
" 2	43	52	61	69	78	87
" 3	65	78	91	1.04	1.17	1.30
" 4	87	1.04	1.21	1.39	1 56	1.73
" 5	1.08	1.30	1.52	1.73	1.95	2.17
" 6	1.30	1.56	1.82	2.08	2.34	2.60
" 7	1.52	1.82	2.12	2.43	2.73	3.03
" 8	1.73	2.08	2.43	2.77	3.12	3.47
" 9	1.95	2.34	2.73	3.12	3.51	3.90
" 10	2.17	2.60	3.03	3.47	3.90	4.33
" 11	2.38	2.86	3.34	3.81	4.29	4.77
Yrs. 1	2.60	3.12	3.64	4.16	4.68	5.20
" 2	5.20	6.24	7.28	8.32	9.36	10.40
" 3	7.80	9.36	10.92	12.48	14.04	15.60
" 4	10.40	12.48	14.56	16.64	18.72	20.80
Com. 2	5.33	6.43	7.53	8.65	9.78	10.92
" 3	8.20	9.93	11.70	13.51	15.34	17.21
" 4	11.21	13.65	16.16	18.75	21.40	24.13
" 5	14.37	17.59	20.93	24.41	28.01	31.75
" 6	17.68	21.76	26.04	30.52	35.21	40.12

TIME.	5 %	6 %	7 %	8 %	9 %	10 %
Days 1	1	1	1	1	1	1
" 2	1	2	2	2	3	3
" 3	2	3	3	4	4	4
" 4	3	4	4	5	5	6
" 5	4	4	5	6	7	7
" 6	4	5	6	7	8	9
" 7	5	6	7	8	9	10
" 8	6	7	8	9	11	12
" 9	7	8	9	11	12	13
" 10	7	9	10	12	13	15
" 11	8	10	11	13	15	16
" 12	9	11	12	14	16	18
" 13	10	11	13	15	17	19
" 14	10	12	14	16	19	21
" 15	11	13	15	18	20	22
" 16	12	14	16	19	21	24
" 17	13	15	18	20	23	25
" 18	13	16	19	21	24	27
" 19	14	17	20	22	25	28
" 20	15	18	21	24	27	29
" 21	15	19	22	25	28	31
" 22	16	19	23	26	29	32
" 23	17	20	24	27	30	34
" 24	18	21	25	28	32	35
" 25	18	22	26	29	33	37
" 26	19	23	27	31	34	38
" 27	20	24	28	32	36	40
" 28	21	25	29	33	37	41
" 29	21	26	30	34	38	43
Mos. 1	22	27	31	35	40	44
" 2	44	53	62	71	80	88
" 3	66	80	93	1.06	1.17	1.33
" 4	88	1.06	1.24	1.41	1.59	1.77
" 5	1.10	1.33	1.55	1.77	1.99	2.21
" 6	1.33	1.59	1.86	2.12	2.39	2.65
" 7	1.55	1.86	2.16	2.47	2.78	3.09
" 8	1.77	2.12	2.47	2.83	3.18	3.53
" 9	1.99	2.39	2.78	3.18	3.58	3.98
" 10	2.21	2.65	3.09	3.53	3.98	4.42
" 11	2.43	2.92	3.40	3.89	4.37	4.86
Yrs. 1	2.65	3.18	3.71	4.24	4.77	5.30
" 2	5.30	6.36	7.42	8.48	9.54	10.60
" 3	7.95	9.54	11.13	12.72	14.31	15.90
" 4	10.60	12.72	14.84	16.96	19.08	21.20
Com. 2	5.43	6.55	7.68	8.82	9.97	11.13
" 3	8.35	10.12	11.93	13.76	15.64	17.54
" 4	11.42	13.91	16.47	19.11	21.81	24.60
" 5	14.64	17.93	21.34	24.87	28.55	32.36
" 6	18.03	22.18	26.54	31.10	35.89	40.89

TIME.	5 %	6 %	7 %	8 %	9 %	10 %
Days 1	1	1	1	1	1	2
" 2	2	2	2	2	3	3
" 3	2	3	3	4	4	5
": 4	3	4	4	5	5	6
" 5	4	5	5	6	7	8
" 6	5	5	6	7	8	9
" 7	5	6	7	8	9	11
" 8	6	7	8	10	11	12
" 9	7	8	9	11	12	14
" 10	8	9	11	12	14	15
" 11	8	10	12	13	15	17
" 12	9	11	13	14	16	18
" 13	10	12	14	16	18	20
" 14	11	13	15	17	19	21
" 15	11	14	16	18	20	23
" 16	12	14	17	19	22	24
" 17	13	15	18	20	23	26
" 18	14	16	19	22	24	27
" 19	14	17	20	23	26	29
" 20	15	18	21	24	27	30
" 21	16	19	22	25	28	32
" 22	17	20	23	26	30	33
" 23	17	21	24	28	31	35
" 24	18	22	25	29	32	36
" 25	19	23	26	30	34	38
" 26	20	23	27	31	35	39
" 27	20	24	28	32	36	41
" 28	21	25	29	34	38	42
" 29	22	26	30	35	39	44
Mos. 1	23	27	32	36	41	45
" 2	45	54	63	72	81	90
" 3	68	81	95	1.08	1.22	1.35
" 4	90	1.08	1.26	1.44	1.62	1.80
" 5	1.13	1.35	1.58	1.80	2.03	2.25
" 6	1.35	1.62	1.89	2.16	2.43	2.70
" 7	1.58	1.89	2.21	2.52	2.84	3.15
" 8	1.80	2.16	2.52	2.88	3.24	3.60
" 9	2.03	2.43	2.84	3.24	3.65	4.05
" 10	2.25	2.70	3.15	3.60	4.05	4.50
" 11	2.48	2.97	3.47	3.96	4.46	4.95
Yrs. 1	2.70	3.24	3.78	4.32	4.86	5.40
" 2	5.40	6.48	7.56	8.64	9.72	10.80
" 3	8.10	9.72	11.34	12.96	14.58	16.20
" 4	10.80	12.96	15.12	17.28	19.44	21.60
Com. 2	5.54	6.67	7.82	8.99	10.16	11.34
" 3	8.51	10.31	12.15	14.02	15.93	17.87
" 4	11.64	14.17	16.78	19.47	22.23	25.06
" 5	14.92	18.26	21.74	25.34	29.09	32.97
" 6	18.37	22.60	27.04	31.69	36.56	41.66

TIME.	5 %	6 %	7 %	8 %	9 %	10 %
Days 1	1	1	1	1	1	2
" 2	2	2	2	2	3	3
" 3	2	3	3	4	4	5
" 4	3	4	4	5	6	6
" 5	4	5	5	6	7	8
" 6	5	6	6	7	8	9
" 7	5	6	7	9	10	11
" 8	6	7	9	10	11	12
" 9	7	8	10	11	12	14
" 10	8	9	11	12	14	15
" 11	8	10	12	13	15	17
" 12	9	11	13	15	17	18
" 13	10	12	14	16	18	20
" 14	11	13	15	17	19	21
" 15	11	14	16	18	21	23
" 16	12	15	17	20	22	24
" 17	13	16	18	21	23	26
" 18	14	17	19	22	25	28
" 19	15	17	20	23	26	29
" 20	15	18	21	24	28	31
" 21	16	19	22	26	29	32
" 22	17	20	24	27	30	34
" 23	18	21	25	28	32	35
" 24	18	22	26	29	33	37
" 25	19	23	27	31	34	38
" 26	20	24	28	32	36	40
" 27	21	25	29	33	37	41
" 28	21	26	30	34	39	43
" 29	22	27	31	35	40	44
Mos. 1	23	28	32	37	41	46
" 2	46	55	64	73	83	92
" 3	69	83	96	1.10	1.24	1.38
" 4	92	1.10	1.28	1.47	1.65	1.83
" 5	1.15	1.38	1.60	1.83	2.06	2.29
" 6	1.38	1.65	1.93	2.20	2.48	2.75
" 7	1.60	1.93	2.25	2.57	2.89	3.21
" 8	1.83	2.20	2.57	2.93	3.30	3.67
" 9	2.06	2.48	2.89	3.30	3.71	4.13
" 10	2.29	2.75	3.21	3.67	4.13	4.58
" 11	2.52	3.03	3.53	4.03	4.54	5.04
Yrs. 1	2.75	3.30	3.85	4.40	4.95	5.50
" 2	5.50	6.60	7.70	8.80	9.90	11.00
" 3	8.25	9.90	11.55	13.20	14.85	16.50
" 4	11.00	13.20	15.40	17.60	19.80	22.00
Com. 2	5.64	6.80	7.97	9.15	10.35	11.55
" 3	8.67	10.51	12.38	14.28	16.23	18.21
" 4	11.85	14.44	17.09	19.83	22.64	25.53
" 5	15.20	18.60	22.14	25.81	29.62	33.58
" 6	18.71	23.02	27.54	32.28	37.24	42.43

TIME.	5 %	6 %	7 %	8 %	9 %	10 %
Days 1	1	1	1	1	1	2
" 2	2	2	2	2	3	3
" 3	2	3	3	4	4	5
" 4	3	4	4	5	6	6
" 5	4	5	5	6	7	8
" 6	5	6	7	7	8	9
" 7	5	7	8	9	10	11
" 8	6	7	9	10	11	12
" 9	7	8	10	11	13	14
" 10	8	9	11	12	14	16
" 11	9	10.	12	14	15	17
" 12	9	11	13	15	17	19
" 13	10	12	14	16	18	20
" 14	11	13	15	17	20	22
" 15	12	14	16	19	21	23
" 16	12	15	17	20	22	25
" 17	13	16	19	21	24	26
" 18	14	17	20	22	25	28
" 19	15	18	21	24	27	30
" 20	16	19	22	25	28	31
" 21	16	20	23	26	29	33
" 22	17	21	24	27	31	34
" 23	18	21	25	29	32	36
" 24	19	22	26	30	34	37
" 25	19	23	27	31	35	39
" 26	20	24	28	32	36	40
" 27	21	25	29	34	38	42
" 28	22	26	30	35	39	44
" 29	23	27	32	36	41	45
Mos. 1	23	28	33	37	42	47
" 2	47	56	65	75	84	93
" 3	70	84	98	1.12	1.26	1.40
" 4	93	1.12	1.31	1.49	1.68	1.87
" 5	1.17	1.40	1.63	1.87	2.10	2.33
" 6	1.40	1.68	1.96	2.24	2.52	2.80
" 7	1.63	1.96	2.29	2.61	2.94	3.27
" 8	1.87	2.24	2.61	2.99	3.36	3.73
" 9	2.10	2.52	2.94	3.36	3.78	4.20
" 10	2.33	2.80	3.27	3.73	4.20	4.67
" 11	2.57	3.08	3.59	4.11	4.62	5.13
Yrs. 1	2.80	3.36	3.92	4.48	5.04	5.60
" 2	5.60	6.72	7.84	8.96	10.08	11.20
" 3	8.40	10.08	11.76	13.44	15.12	16.80
" 4	11.20	13.44	15.68	17.92	20.16	22.40
Com. 2	5.74	6.92	8.11	9.32	10.53	11.76
" 3	8.83	10.70	12.60	14.54	16.52	18.54
" 4	12.07	14.70	17.40	20.19	23.05	25.99
" 5	15.47	18.94	22.54	26.28	30.16	34.19
" 6	19.05	23.44	28.04	32.86	37.92	43.21

TIME.	5 %	6 %	7 %	8 %	9 %	10 %
Days 1	1	1	1	1	1	2
" 2	2	2	2	3	3	3
" 3	2	3	3	4	4	5
" 4	3	4	4	5	6	6
" 5	4	5	5	6	7	8
" 6	5	6	7	8	9	10
" 7	6	7	8	9	10	11
" 8	6	8	9	10	11	13
" 9	7	9	10	11	13	14
" 10	8	10	11	13	14	16
" 11	9	10	12	14	16	17
" 12	10	11	13	15	17	19
" 13	10	12	14	16	18	21
" 14	11	13	16	18	20	22
" 15	12	14	17	19	21	24
" 16	13	15	18	20	23	25
" 17	13	16	19	22	24	27
" 18	14	17	20	23	26	29
" 19	15	18	21	24	27	30
" 20	16	19	22	25	29	32
" 21	17	20	23	27	30	33
" 22	17	21	24	28	31	35
" 23	18	22	25	29	33	36
" 24	19	23	27	30	34	38
" 25	20	24	28	32	36	40
" 26	21	25	29	33	37	41
" 27	21	26	30	34	39	43
" 28	22	27	31	35	40	44
" 29	23	28	32	37	41	46
Mos. 1	24	29	33	38	43	48
" 2	48	57	66	76	86	95
" 3	71	86	1.00	1.14	1.28	1.43
" 4	95	1.14	1.33	1.52	1.71	1.90
" 5	1.19	1.43	1.66	1.90	2.14	2.38
" 6	1.43	1.71	2.00	2.28	2.57	2.85
" 7	1.66	2.00	2.33	2.66	2.99	3.33
" 8	1.90	2.28	2.66	3.04	3.42	3.80
" 9	2.14	2.57	2.99	3.42	3.85	4.28
" 10	2.38	2.85	3.33	3.80	4.28	4.75
" 11	2.61	3.14	3.66	4.18	4.70	5.23
Yrs. 1	2.85	3.42	3.99	4.56	5.13	5.70
" 2	5.70	6.84	7.98	9.12	10.26	11.40
" 3	8.55	10.26	11.97	13.68	15.39	17.10
" 4	11.40	13.68	15.96	18.24	20.52	22.80
Com. 2	5.84	7.05	8.26	9.48	10.72	11.97
" 3	8.98	10.89	12.83	14.80	16.82	18.87
" 4	12.28	14.96	17.72	20.55	23.46	26.45
" 5	15.75	19.28	22.95	26.75	30.70	34.80
" 6	19.39	23.86	28.54	33.45	38.59	43.98

58 DOLLARS.

TIME.	5 %	6 %	7 %	8 %	9 %	10 %
Days 1	1	1	1	1	1	2
" 2	2	2	2	3	3	3
" 3	2	3	3	4	4	5
" 4	3	4	5	5	6	6
" 5	4	5	6	6	7	8
" 6	5	6	7	8	9	, 10
" 7	6	7	8	9	10	11
" 8	6	8	9	10	12	13
" 9	7	9	10	12	13	15
" 10	8	10	11	13	15	16
" 11	9	11	12	14	16	18
" 12	10	12	14	15	17	19
" 13	10	13	15	17	19	21
" 14	11	14	16	18	20	23
" 15	12	15	17	19	22	24
" 16	13	15	18	21	23	26
" 17	14	16	19	22	25	27
" 18	15	17	20	23	26	29
" 19	15	18	21	24	28	31
" 20	16	19	23	26	29	32
" 21	17	20	24	27	30	34
" 22	18	21	25	28	32	35
" 23	19	22	26	30	33	37
" 24	19	23	27	31	35	39
" 25	20	24	28	32	36	40
" 26	21	25	29	34	38	42
" 27	22	26	30	35	39	44
" 28	23	27	32	36	41	45
" 29	23	28	33	37	42	47
Mos. 1	24	29	34	39	44	48
" 2	48	58	68	77	87	97
" 3	73	87	1.02	1.16	1.31	1.45
" 4	97	1.16	1.35	1.55	1.74	1.93
" 5	1.21	1.45	1.69	1.93	2.18	2.42
" 6	1.45	1.74	2.03	2.32	2.61	2.90
" 7	1.69	2.03	2.37	2.71	3.05	3.38
" 8	1.93	2.32	2.71	3.09	3.48	3.87
" 9	2.18	2.61	3.05	3.48	3.92	4.35
" 10	2.42	2.90	3.38	3.87	4.35	4.83
" 11	2.66	3.19	3.72	4.25	4.79	5.32
Yrs. 1	2.90	3.48	4.06	4.64	5.22	5.80
" 2	5.80	6.96	8.12	9.28	10.44	11.60
" 3	8.70	10 44	12.18	13.92	15.66	17.40
" 4	11.60	13.92	16.24	18.56	20.88	23.20
Com. 2	5.95	7.17	8.40	9.65	10.91	12.18
" 3	9.14	11.08	13.05	15.06	17.11	19.20
" 4	12.50	15.22	18.03	20.91	23.87	26.92
" 5	16.02	19.62	23.35	27.22	31.24	35.41
" 6	19.73	24.27	29.04	34.04	39.27	44.75

59 Dollars.

TIME	5 %	6 %	7 %	8 %	9 %	10 %
Days 1	1	1	1	1	1	2
" 2	2	2	2	3	3	3
" 3	2	3	3	4	4	5
" 4	3	4	5	5	6	7
" 5	4	5	6	7	7	8
" 6	5	6	7	8	9	10
" 7	6	7	8	9	10	11
" 8	7	8	9	10	12	13
" 9	7	9	10	12	13	15
" 10	8	10	11	13	15	16
" 11	9	11	13	14	16	18
" 12	10	12	14	16	18	20
" 13	11	13	15	17	19	21
" 14	11	14	16	18	21	23
" 15	12	15	17	20	22	24
" 16	13	16	18	21	24	26
" 17	14	17	20	22	25	28
" 18	15	18	21	24	27	30
" 19	16	19	22	25	28	31
" 20	16	20	23	26	30	33
" 21	17	21	24	28	31	34
" 22	18	22	25	29	32	36
" 23	19	23	26	30	34	38
" 24	20	24	28	31	35	39
" 25	20	25	29	33	37	41
" 26	21	26	30	34	38	43
" 27	22	27	31	35	40	44
" 28	23	28	32	37	41	46
" 29	24	29	33	38	43	48
Mos. 1	25	30	34	39	44	49
" 2	49	59	69	79	89	98
" 3	74	89	1.03	1.18	1.33	1.48
" 4	98	1.18	1.38	1.57	1.77	1.97
" 5	1.23	1.48	1.72	1.97	2.21	2.46
" 6	1.48	1.77	2.07	2.36	2.66	2.95
" 7	1.72	2.07	2.41	2.75	3.10	3.44
" 8	1.97	2.36	2.75	3.15	3.54	3.93
" 9	2.21	2.66	3.10	3.54	3.98	4.43
" 10	2.46	2.95	3.44	3.93	4.43	4.92
" 11	2.70	3.25	3.79	4.33	4.87	5.41
Yrs. 1	2.95	3.54	4.13	4.72	5.31	5.90
" 2	5.90	7.08	8.26	9.44	10.62	11.80
" 3	8.85	10.62	12.39	14.16	15.93	17.70
" 4	11.80	14.16	16.52	18.88	21.24	23.60
Com. 2	6.05	7.29	8.55	9.82	11.10	12.39
" 3	9.30	11.27	13.28	15.32	17.41	19.53
" 4	12.71	15.49	18.34	21.27	24.28	27.38
" 5	16.30	19.96	23.75	27.69	31.78	36.02
" 6	20.07	24.69	29.54	34.63	39.95	45.52

TIME.	5 %	6 %	7 %	8 %	9 %	10 %
Days 1	1	1	1	1	2	2
" 2	2	2	2	3	3	3
" 3	3	3	4	4	5	5
" 4	3	4	5	5	6	7
" 5	4	5	6	7	8	8
" 6	5	6	7	8	9	10
" 7	6	7	8	9	11	12
" 8	7	8	9	11	12	13
" 9	8	9	11	12	14	15
" 10	8	10	12	13	15	17
" 11	9	11	13	15	17	18
" 12	10	12	14	16	18	20
" 13	11	13	15	17	20	22
" 14	12	14	16	19	21	23
" 15	13	15	18	20	23	25
" 16	13	16	19	21	24	27
" 17	14	17	20	23	26	28
" 18	15	18	21	24	27	30
" 19	16	19	22	25	29	32
" 20	17	20	23	27	30	33
" 21	18	21	25	28	32	35
" 22	18	22	26	29	33	37
" 23	19	23	27	31	35	38
" 24	20	24	28	32	36	40
" 25	21	25	29	33	38	42
" 26	22	26	30	35	39	43
" 27	23	27	32	36	41	45
" 28	23	28	33	37	42	47
" 29	24	29	34	39	44	48
Mos. 1	25	30	35	40	45	50
" 2	50	60	70	80	90	1.00
" 3	75	90	1.05	1.20	1.35	1.50
" 4	1.00	1.20	1.40	1.60	1.80	2.00
" 5	1.25	1.50	1.75	2.00	2.25	2.50
" 6	1.50	1.80	2.10	2.40	2.70	3.00
" 7	1.75	2.10	2.45	2.80	3.15	3.50
" 8	2.00	2.40	2.80	3.20	3.60	4.00
" 9	2.25	2.70	3.15	3.60	4.05	4.50
" 10	2.50	3.00	3.50	4.00	4.50	5.00
" 11	2.75	3.30	3.85	4.40	4.95	5.50
Yrs. 1	3.00	3.60	4.20	4.80	5.40	6.00
" 2	6.00	7.20	8.40	9.60	10.80	12.00
" 3	9.00	10.80	12.60	14.40	16.20	18.00
" 4	12.00	14.40	16.80	19.20	21.60	24.00
Com. 2	6.15	7.42	8.69	9.98	11.29	12.60
" 3	9.46	11.46	13.50	15.58	17.70	19.86
" 4	12.93	15.75	18.65	21.63	24.69	27.85
" 5	16.58	20.29	24.15	28.16	32.32	36.63
" 6	20.41	25.11	30.04	35.21	40.63	46.29

TIME.	5 %	6 %	7 %	8 %	9 %	10 %
Days 1	1	1	1	1	2	2
" 2	2	2	2	3	3	3
" 3	3	3	4	4	5	5
" 4	3	4	5	5	6	7
" 5	4	5	6	7	8	8
" 6	5	6	7	8	9	10
" 7	6	7	8	9	11	12
" 8	7	8	9	11	12	14
" 9	8	9	11	12	14	15
" 10	8	10	12	14	15	17
" 11	9	11	13	15	17	19
" 12	10	12	14	16	18	20
" 13	11	13	15	18	20	22
" 14	12	14	17	19	21	24
" 15	13	15	18	20	23	25
" 16	14	16	19	22	24	27
" 17	14	17	20	23	26	29
" 18	15	18	21	24	27	31
" 19	16	19	23	26	29	32
" 20	17	20	24	27	31	34
" 21	18	21	25	28	32	36
" 22	19	22	26	30	34	37
" 23	19	23	27	31	35	39
" 24	20	24	28	33	37	41
' 25	21	25	30	34	38	42
" 26	22	26	31	35	40	44
" 27	23	27	32	37	41	46
" 28	24	28	33	38	43	47
" 29	25	29	34	39	44	49
Mos. 1	25	31	36	41	46	51
" 2	51	61	71	81	92	1.02
" 3	76	92	1.07	1.22	1.37	1.53
" 4	1.02	1.22	1.42	1.63	1.83	2.03
" 5	1.27	1.53	1.78	2.03	2.29	2.54
" 6	1.53	1.83	2.14	2.44	2.75	3.05
" 7	1.78	2.14	2.49	2.85	3.20	3.56
" 8	2.03	2.44	2.85	3.25	3.66	4.07
" 9	2.29	2.75	3.20	3.66	4.12	4.58
" 10	2.54	3.05	3.56	4.07	4.58	5.08
" 11	2.80	3.36	3.91	4.47	5.03	5.59
Yrs. 1	3.05	3.66	4.27	4.88	5.49	6.10
" 2	6.10	7.32	8.54	9.76	10.98	12.20
" 3	9.15	10.98	12.81	14.64	16.47	18.30
" 4	12.20	14.64	17.08	19.52	21.96	24.40
Com. 2	6.25	7.54	8.84	10.15	11.47	12.81
" 3	9.62	11.65	13.73	15.84	18.00	20.19
" 4	13.15	16.01	18.96	21.99	25.11	28.31
" 5	16.85	20.63	24.56	28.63	32.86	37.24
" 6	20.75	25.53	30.54	35.80	41.30	47.07

TIME.	5 %	6 %	7 %	8 %	9 %	10 %
Days 1	1	1	1	1	2	2
" 2	2	2	2	3	3	3
" 3	3	3	4	4	5	5
" 4	3	4	5	6	6	7
" 5	4	5	6	7	8	9
" 6	5	6	7	8	9	10
" 7	6	7	8	10	11	12
" 8	7	8	10	11	12	14
" 9	8	9	11	12	14	16
" 10	9	10	12	14	16	17
" 11	9	11	13	15	17	19
" 12	10	12	14	17	19	21
" 13	11	13	16	18	20	22
" 14	12	14	17	19	22	24
" 15	13	16	18	21	23	26
" 16	14	17	19	22	25	28
" 17	15	18	20	23	26	29
" 18	16	19	22	25	28	31
" 19	16	20	23	26	29	33
" 20	17	21	24	28	31	34
" 21	18	22	25	29	33	36
" 22	19	23	27	30	34	38
" 23	20	24	28	32	36	40
" 24	21	25	29	33	37	41
" 25	22	26	30	34	39	43
" 26	22	27	31	36	40	45
" 27	23	28	33	37	42	47
" 28	24	29	34	39	43	48
" 29	25	30	35	40	45	50
Mos 1	26	31	36	41	47	52
" 2	52	62	72	83	93	1.03
" 3	78	93	1.09	1.24	1.40	1.55
" 4	1.03	1.24	1.45	1.65	1.86	2.07
" 5	1.29	1.55	1.81	2.07	2.33	2.58
" 6	1.55	1.86	2.17	2.48	2.79	3.10
" 7	1.81	2.17	2.53	2.89	3.26	3.62
" 8	2.07	2.48	2.89	3.31	3.72	4.13
" 9	2.33	2.79	3.26	3.72	4.19	4.65
" 10	2.58	3.10	3.62	4.13	4.65	5.17
" 11	2.84	3.41	3.98	4.55	5.12	5.68
Yrs. 1	3.10	3.72	4.34	4.96	5.58	6.20
" 2	6.20	7.44	8.68	9.92	11.16	12.40
" 3	9.30	11.16	13.02	14.88	16.74	18.60
" 4	12.40	14.88	17.36	19.84	22.32	24.80
Com. 2	6.36	7.66	8.98	10.32	11.66	13.02
" 3	9.77	11.84	13.95	16.10	18.29	20.52
" 4	13.36	16.27	19.27	22.35	25.52	28.77
" 5	17.13	20.97	24.96	29.10	33.39	37.85
" 6	21.09	25.95	31.05	36.39	41.98	47.83

TIME.	5 %	6 %	7 %	8 %	9 %	10 %
Days 1	1	1	1	1	2	2
" 2	2	2	2	3	3	4
" 3	3	3	4	4	5	5
" 4	4	4	5	6	6	7
" 5	4	5	6	7	8	9
" 6	5	6	7	8	9	11
" 7	6	7	9	10	11	12
" 8	7	8	10	11	13	14
" 9	8	9	11	13	14	16
" 10	9	11	12	14	16	18
" 11	10	12	13	15	17	19
" 12	11	13	15	17	19	21
" 13	11	14	16	18	20	23
" 14	12	15	17	20	22	25
" 15	13	16	18	21	24	26
" 16	14	17	20	22	25	28
" 17	15	18	21	24	27	30
" 18	16	19	22	25	28	32
" 19	17	20	23	27	30	33
" 20	18	21	25	28	32	35
" 21	18	22	26	29	33	37
" 22	19	23	27	31	35	39
" 23	20	24	28	32	36	40
" 24	21	25	29	34	38	42
" 25	22	26	31	35	39	44
" 26	23	27	32	36	41	46
" 27	24	28	33	38	43	47
" 28	25	29	34	39	44	49
" 29	25	30	36	41	46	51
Mos. 1	26	32	37	42	47	53
" 2	53	63	74	84	95	1.05
" 3	79	95	1.10	1.26	1.42	1.58
" 4	1.05	1.26	1.47	1.68	1.89	2.10
" 5	1.31	1.58	1.84	2.10	2.36	2.63
" 6	1.58	1.89	2.21	2.52	2.84	3.15
" 7	1.84	2.21	2.57	2.94	3.31	3.68
" 8	2.10	2.52	2.94	3.36	3.78	4.20
" 9	2.36	2.84	3.31	3.78	4.25	4.73
" 10	2.63	3.15	3.68	4.20	4.73	5.25
" 11	2.89	3.47	4.04	4.62	5.20	5.78
Yrs. 1	3.15	3.78	4.41	5.04	5.67	6.30
" 2	6.30	7.56	8.82	10.08	11.34	12.60
" 3	9.45	11.34	13.23	15.12	17.01	18.90
" 4	12.60	15.12	17.64	20.16	22.68	25.20
Com. 2	6.46	7.79	9.13	10.48	11.85	13.23
" 3	9.93	12.03	14.18	16.36	18.59	20.85
" 4	13.58	16.54	19.58	22.71	25.93	29.24
" 5	17.41	21.31	25.36	29.57	33.93	38.46
" 6	21.43	26.37	31.55	36.97	42.66	48.61

TIME.	5 %	6 %	7 %	8 %	9 %	10 %
Days 1	1	1	1	1	2	2
" 2	2	2	2	3	3	4
" 3	3	3	4	4	5	5
" 4	4	4	5	6	6	7
" 5	4	5	6	7	8	9
" 6	5	6	7	9	10	11
" 7	6	7	9	0	11	12
" 8	7	9	10	11	13	14
" 9	8	10	11	13	14	16
" 10	9	11	12	14	16	18
" 11	10	12	14	16	18	20
" 12	11	13	15	17	19	21
" 13	12	14	16	18	21	23
" 14	12	15	17	20	22	25
" 15	13	16	19	21	24	27
" 16	14	17	20	23	26	28
" 17	15	18	21	24	27	30
" 18	16	19	22	26	29	32
" 19	17	20	24	27	30	34
" 20	18	21	25	28	32	36
" 21	19	22	26	30	34	37
" 22	20	23	27	31	35	39
" 23	20	25	29	33	37	41
" 24	21	26	30	34	38	43
" 25	22	27	31	36	40	44
" 26	23	28	32	37	42	46
" 27	24	29	34	38	43	48
" 28	25	30	35	40	45	50
" 29	26	31	36	41	46	52
Mos. 1	27	32	37	43	48	53
" 2	53	64	75	85	96	1.07
" 3	80	96	1.12	1.28	1.44	1.60
" 4	1.07	1.28	1.49	1.71	1.92	2.13
" 5	1.33	1.60	1.87	2.13	2.40	2.67
" 6	1.60	1.92	2.24	2.56	2.88	3.20
" 7	1.87	2.24	2.61	2.99	3.36	3.73
" 8	2.13	2.56	2.99	3.41	3.84	4.27
" 9	2.40	2.88	3.36	3.84	4.32	4.80
" 10	2.67	3.20	3.73	4.27	4.80	5.33
" 11	2.93	3.52	4.11	4.69	5.28	5.87
Yrs. 1	3.20	3.84	4.48	5.12	5.76	6.40
" 2	6.40	7.68	8.96	10.24	11.52	12.80
" 3	9.60	11.52	13.44	15.36	17.28	19.20
" 4	12.80	15.36	17.92	20.48	23.04	25.60
Com. 2	6.56	7.91	9.27	10.65	12.04	13.44
" 3	10.09	12.23	14.40	16.62	18.88	21.18
" 4	13.79	16.80	19.89	23.07	26.34	29.70
" 5	17.68	21.65	25.76	30.04	34.47	39.07
" 6	21.77	26.79	32.05	37.56	43.33	49.38

65 Dollars.

TIME.	5 %	6 %	7 %	8 %	9 %	10 %
Days 1	1	1	1	1	2	2
" 2	2	2	3	3	3	4
" 3	3	3	4	4	5	5
" 4	4	4	5	6	7	7
" 5	5	5	6	7	8	9
" 6	5	7	8	9	10	11
" 7	6	8	9	10	11	13
" 8	7	9	10	12	13	14
" 9	8	10	11	13	15	16
" 10	9	11	13	14	16	18
" 11	10	12	14	16	18	20
" 12	11	13	15	17	20	22
" 13	12	14	16	19	21	23
" 14	13	15	18	20	23	25
" 15	14	16	19	22	24	27
" 16	14	17	20	23	26	29
" 17	15	18	21	25	28	31
" 18	16	20	23	26	29	33
" 19	17	21	24	27	31	34
" 20	18	22	25	29	33	36
" 21	19	23	27	30	34	38
" 22	20	24	28	32	36	40
" 23	21	25	29	33	37	42
" 24	22	26	30	35	39	43
" 25	23	27	32	36	41	45
" 26	23	28	33	38	42	47
" 27	24	29	34	39	44	49
" 28	25	30	35	40	46	51
" 29	26	31	37	42	47	52
Mos. 1	27	33	38	43	49	54
" 2	54	65	76	87	98	1.08
" 3	81	98	1.14	1.30	1.46	1.63
" 4	1.08	1.30	1.52	1.73	1.95	2.17
" 5	1.35	1.63	1.90	2.17	2.44	2.71
" 6	1.63	1.95	2.28	2.60	2.93	3.25
" 7	1.90	2.28	2.65	3.03	3.41	3.79
" 8	2.17	2.60	3.03	3.47	3.90	4.33
" 9	2.44	2.93	3.41	3.90	4.39	4.88
" 10	2.71	3.25	3.79	4.33	4.88	5.42
" 11	2.98	3.58	4.17	4.77	5.36	5.96
Yrs. 1	3.25	3.90	4.55	5.20	5.85	6.50
" 2	6.50	7.80	9.10	10.40	11.70	13.00
" 3	9.75	11.70	13.65	15.60	17.55	19.50
" 4	13.00	15.60	18.20	20.80	23.40	26 00
Com. 2	6.66	8.03	9.42	10.82	12.23	13.65
" 3	10.25	12.42	14.63	16.88	19.18	21.52
" 4	14.01	17.06	20.20	23.43	26.75	30.17
" 5	17.96	21.98	26.17	30.51	35.01	39.68
" 6	22.11	27.20	32.55	38.15	44.01	50.15

TIME.	5 %	6 %	7 %	8 %	9 %	10 %
Days 1	1	1	1	1	2	2
" 2	2	2	3	3	3	4
" 3	3	3	4	4	5	6
" 4	4	4	5	6	7	7
" 5	5	6	6	7	8	9
" 6	6	7	8	9	10	11
" 7	6	8	9	10	12	13
" 8	7	9	10	12	13	15
" 9	8	10	12	13	15	17
" 10	9	11	13	15	17	18
" 11	10	12	14	16	18	20
" 12	11	13	15	18	20	22
" 13	12	14	17	19	21	24
" 14	13	15	18	21	23	26
" 15	14	17	19	22	25	28
" 16	15	18	21	23	26	29
" 17	16	19	22	25	28	31
" 18	17	20	23	26	30	33
" 19	17	21	24	28	31	35
" 20	18	22	26	29	33	37
" 21	19	23	27	31	35	39
" 22	20	24	28	32	36	40
" 23	21	25	30	34	38	42
" 24	22	26	31	35	40	44
" 25	23	28	32	37	41	46
" 26	24	29	33	38	43	48
" 27	25	30	35	40	45	50
" 28	26	31	36	41	46	51
" 29	27	32	37	43	48	53
Mos. 1	28	33	39	44	50	55
" 2	55	66	77	88	99	1.10
" 3	83	99	1.16	1.32	1.49	1.65
" 4	1.10	1.32	1.54	1.76	1.98	2.20
" 5	1.38	1.65	1.93	2.20	2.48	2.75
" 6	1.65	1.98	2.31	2.64	2.97	3.30
" 7	1.93	2.31	2.70	3.08	3.47	3.85
" 8	2.20	2.64	3.08	3.52	3.96	4.40
" 9	2.48	2.97	3.47	3.96	4.46	4.95
" 10	2.75	3.30	3.85	4.40	4.95	5.50
" 11	3.03	3.63	4.24	4.84	5.45	6.05
Yrs. 1	3.30	3.96	4.62	5.28	5.94	6.60
" 2	6.60	7.92	9.24	10.56	11.88	13.20
" 3	9.90	11.88	13.86	15.84	17.82	19.80
" 4	13.20	15.84	18.48	21.12	23.76	26.40
Com. 2	6.77	8.16	9.56	10.98	12.41	13.86
" 3	10.40	12.61	14.85	17.14	19.47	21.85
" 4	14.22	17.32	20.51	23.79	27.16	30.63
" 5	18.23	22.32	26.57	30.98	35.55	40.29
" 6	22.45	27.62	33.05	38.73	44.69	50.92

TIME.	5 %	6 %	7 %	8 %	9 %	10 %
Days 1	1	1	1	1	2	2
" 2	2	2	3	3	3	4
" 3	3	3	4	4	5	6
" 4	4	4	5	6	7	7
" 5	5	6	7	7	8	9
" 6	6	7	8	9	10	11
" 7	7	8	9	10	12	13
" 8	7	9	10	12	13	15
" 9	8	10	12	13	15	17
" 10	9	11	13	15	17	19
" 11	10	12	14	16	18	20
" 12	11	13	16	18	20	22
" 13	12	15	17	19	22	24
" 14	13	16	18	21	23	26
" 15	14	17	20	22	25	28
" 16	15	18	21	24	27	30
" 17	16	19	22	25	28	32
" 18	17	20	23	27	30	34
" 19	18	21	25	28	32	35
" 20	19	22	26	30	34	37
" 21	20	23	27	31	35	39
" 22	20	25	29	33	37	41
" 23	21	26	30	34	39	43
" 24	22	27	31	36	40	45
" 25	23	28	33	37	42	47
" 26	24	29	34	39	44	48
" 27	25	30	35	40	45	50
" 28	26	31	36	42	47	52
" 29	27	32	38	43	49	54
Mos. 1	28	34	39	45	50	56
" 2	56	67	78	89	1.01	1.12
" 3	84	1.01	1.17	1.34	1.51	1.68
" 4	1.12	1.34	1.56	1.79	2.01	2.23
" 5	1.40	1.68	1.95	2.23	2.51	2.79
" 6	1.68	2.01	2.35	2.68	3.02	3.35
" 7	1.95	2.35	2.74	3.13	3.52	3.91
" 8	2.23	2.68	3.13	3.57	4.02	4.47
" 9	2.51	3.02	3 52	4.02	4.52	5.03
" 10	2.79	3.35	3.91	4.47	5.03	5.58
" 11	3.07	3.69	4.30	4.91	5.53	6.14
Yrs. 1	3.35	4.02	4.69	5.36	6.03	6.70
" 2	6.70	8.04	9.38	10.72	12.06	13.40
" 3	10.05	12.06	14.07	16.08	18.09	20.10
" 4	13.40	16.08	18.76	21.44	24.12	26.80
Com. 2	6.87	8.28	9.71	11.15	12.60	14.07
" 3	10.56	12.80	15.08	17.40	19.77	22.18
" 4	14.44	17.59	20.82	24.15	27.58	31.09
" 5	18.51	22.66	26.97	31.44	36.09	40.90
" 6	22.79	28.04	33.55	39.32	45.37	51.69

TIME		5 %	6 %	7 %	8 %	9 %	10 %
Days	1	1	1	1	2	2	2
"	2	2	2	3	3	3	4
"	3	3	3	4	5	5	6
"	4	4	5	5	6	7	8
"	5	5	6	7	8	9	9
"	6	6	7	8	9	10	11
"	7	7	8	9	11	12	13
"	8	8	9	11	12	14	15
"	9	9	10	12	14	15	17
"	10	9	11	13	15	17	19
"	11	10	12	15	17	19	21
"	12	11	14	16	18	20	23
"	13	12	15	17	20	22	25
"	14	13	16	19	21	24	26
"	15	14	17	20	23	26	28
"	16	15	18	21	24	27	30
"	17	16	19	22	26	29	32
"	18	17	20	24	27	31	34
"	19	18	22	25	29	32	36
"	20	19	23	26	30	34	38
"	21	20	24	28	32	36	40
"	22	21	25	29	33	37	42
"	23	22	26	30	35	39	43
"	24	23	27	32	36	41	45
"	25	24	28	33	38	43	47
"	26	25	29	34	39	44	49
"	27	26	31	36	41	46	51
"	28	26	32	37	42	48	53
"	29	27	33	38	44	49	55
Mos.	1	28	34	40	45	51	57
"	2	57	68	79	91	1.02	1.13
"	3	85	1.02	1.19	1.36	1.53	1.70
"	4	1.13	1.36	1.59	1.81	2.04	2.27
"	5	1.42	1.70	1.98	2.27	2.55	2.83
"	6	1.70	2.04	2.38	2.72	3.06	3.40
"	7	1.98	2.38	2.78	3.17	3.57	3.97
"	8	2.27	2.72	3.17	3.63	4.08	4.53
"	9	2.55	3.06	3.57	4.08	4.59	5.10
"	10	2.83	3.40	3.97	4.53	5.10	5.67
"	11	3.12	3.74	4.36	4.99	5.61	6.23
Yrs.	1	3.40	4.08	4.76	5.44	6.12	6.80
"	2	6.80	8.16	9.52	10.88	12.24	13.60
"	3	10.20	12.24	14.28	16.32	18.36	20.40
"	4	13.60	16.32	19.04	21.76	24.48	27.20
Com.	2	6.97	8.40	9.85	11.32	12.79	14.28
"	3	10.72	12.99	15.30	17.66	20.06	22.51
"	4	14.65	17.85	21.13	24.51	27.99	31.56
"	5	18.79	23.00	27.37	31.91	36.65	41.51
"	6	23.13	28.46	34.05	39.91	46.04	52.47

TIME.	5 %	6 %	7 %	8 %	9 %	10 %
Days 1	1	1	1	2	2	2
" 2	2	2	3	3	3	4
" 3	3	3	4	5	5	6
" 4	4	5	5	6	7	8
" 5	5	6	7	8	9	10
" 6	6	7	8	9	10	12
" 7	7	8	9	11	12	13
" 8	8	9	11	12	14	15
" 9	9	10	12	14	16	17
" 10	10	12	13	15	17	19
" 11	11	13	15	17	19	21
" 12	12	14	16	18	21	23
" 13	12	15	17	20	22	25
" 14	13	16	19	21	24	27
" 15	14	17	20	23	26	29
" 16	15	18	21	25	28	31
" 17	16	20	23	26	29	33
" 18	17	21	24	28	31	35
" 19	18	22	25	29	33	36
" 20	19	23	27	31	35	38
" 21	20	24	28	32	36	40
" 22	21	25	30	34	38	42
" 23	22	26	31	35	40	44
" 24	23	28	32	37	41	46
" 25	24	29	34	38	43	48
" 26	25	30	35	40	45	50
" 27	26	31	36	41	47	52
" 28	27	32	38	43	48	54
" 29	28	33	39	44	50	56
Mos. 1	29	35	40	46	52	58
" 2	58	69	81	92	1.04	1.15
" 3	86	1.04	1.21	1.38	1.55	1.73
" 4	1.15	1.38	1.61	1.84	2.07	2.30
" 5	1.44	1.73	2.01	2.30	2.59	2.88
" 6	1.73	2.07	2.42	2.76	3.11	3.45
" 7	2.01	2.42	2.82	3.22	3.62	4.03
" 8	2.30	2.76	3.22	3.68	4.14	4.60
" 9	2.59	3.11	3.62	4.14	4.66	5.18
" 10	2.88	3.45	4.03	4.60	5.18	5.75
" 11	3.16	3.80	4.43	5.06	5.69	6.33
Yrs. 1	3.45	4.14	4.83	5.52	6.21	6.90
" 2	6.90	8.28	9.66	11.04	12.42	13.80
" 3	10.35	12.42	14.49	16.56	18.63	20.70
" 4	13.80	16.56	19.32	22.08	24.84	27.60
Com. 2	7.07	8.53	10.00	11.48	12.98	14.49
" 3	10.88	13.18	15.53	17.92	20.36	22.84
" 4	14.87	18.11	21.44	24.87	28.40	32.02
" 5	19.06	23.34	27.78	32.38	37.17	42.13
" 6	23.47	28.88	34.55	40.49	46.72	53.24

TIME.	5 %	6 %	7 %	8 %	9 %	10 %
Days 1	1	1	1	2	2	2
" 2	2	2	3	3	4	4
" 3	3	4	4	5	5	6
" 4	4	5	5	6	7	8
" 5	5	6	7	8	9	10
" 6	6	7	8	9	11	12
" 7	7	8	10	11	12	14
" 8	8	9	11	12	14	16
" 9	9	11	12	14	16	18
" 10	10	12	14	16	18	19
" 11	11	13	15	17	19	21
" 12	12	14	16	19	21	23
" 13	13	15	18	20	23	25
" 14	14	16	19	22	25	27
" 15	15	18	20	23	26	29
" 16	16	19	22	25	28	31
" 17	17	20	23	26	30	33
" 18	18	21	25	28	32	35
" 19	18	22	26	30	33	37
" 20	19	23	27	31	35	39
" 21	20	25	29	33	37	41
" 22	21	26	30	34	39	43
" 23	22	27	31	36	40	45
" 24	23	28	33	37	42	47
" 25	24	29	34	39	44	49
" 26	25	30	35	40	46	51
" 27	26	32	37	42	47	53
" 28	27	33	38	44	49	54
" 29	28	34	39	45	51	56
Mos. 1	29	35	41	47	53	58
" 2	58	70	82	93	1.05	1.17
" 3	88	1.05	1.23	1.40	1.58	1.75
" 4	1.17	1.40	1.63	1.87	2.10	2.33
" 5	1.46	1.75	2.04	2.33	2.63	2.92
" 6	1.75	2.10	2.45	2.80	3.15	3.50
" 7	2.04	2.45	2.86	3.27	3.68	4.08
" 8	2.33	2 80	3.27	3.73	4.20	4.67
" 9	2.63	3.15	3.68	4.20	4.73	5.25
" 10	2.92	3.50	4.08	4.67	5.25	5.83
" 11	3.21	3.85	4.49	5.13	5.78	6.42
Yrs. 1	3.50	4.20	4.90	5.60	6.30	7.00
" 2	7.00	8.40	9.80	11.20	12.60	14.00
" 3	10.50	12.60	14.70	16.80	18.90	21.00
" 4	14.00	16.80	19.60	22.40	25.20	28.00
Com. 2	7.18	8.65	10.14	11.65	13.17	14.70
" 3	11.03	13.37	15.75	18.18	20.65	23.17
" 4	15.09	18.37	21.76	25.23	28.81	32.49
" 5	19.34	23.68	28.18	32.85	37.70	42.74
" 6	23.81	29.30	35.05	41.08	47.40	54.01

TIME.	5 %	6 %	7 %	8 %	9 %	10 %
Days 1	1	1	1	2	2	2
" 2	2	2	3	3	4	4
" 3	3	4	4	5	5	6
" 4	4	5	5	6	7	8
" 5	5	6	7	8	9	10
" 6	6	7	8	9	11	12
" 7	7	8	10	11	12	14
" 8	8	9	11	13	14	16
" 9	9	11	12	14	16	18
" 10	10	12	14	16	18	20
" 11	11	13	15	17	20	22
" 12	12	14	17	19	21	24
" 13	13	15	18	21	23	26
" 14	14	17	19	22	25	28
" 15	15	18	21	24	27	30
" 16	16	19	22	25	28	32
" 17	17	20	23	27	30	34
" 18	18	21	25	28	32	36
" 19	19	22	26	30	34	37
" 20	20	24	28	32	36	39
" 21	21	25	29	33	37	41
" 22	22	26	30	35	39	43
" 23	23	27	32	36	41	45
" 24	24	28	33	38	43	47
" 25	25	30	35	39	44	49
" 26	26	31	36	41	46	51
" 27	27	32	37	43	48	53
" 28	28	33	39	44	50	55
" 29	29	34	40	46	51	57
Mos. 1	30	36	41	47	53	59
" 2	59	71	83	95	1.07	1.18
" 3	89	1.07	1.24	1.42	1.60	1.78
" 4	1.18	1.42	1.66	1.89	2.13	2.37
" 5	1.48	1.78	2.07	2.37	2.66	2.96
" 6	1.78	2.13	2.49	2.84	3.20	3.55
" 7	2.07	2.49	2.90	3.31	3.73	4.14
" 8	2.37	2.84	3.31	3.79	4.26	4.73
" 9	2.66	3.20	3.73	4.26	4.79	5.33
" 10	2.96	3.55	4.14	4.73	5.33	5.92
" 11	3.25	3.91	4.56	5.21	5.86	6.51
Yrs. 1	3.55	4.26	4.97	5.68	6.39	7.10
" 2	7.10	8.52	9.94	11.36	12.78	14.20
" 3	10.65	12.78	14.91	17.04	19.17	21.30
" 4	14.20	17.04	19.88	22.72	25.56	28.40
Com. 2	7.28	8.78	10.29	11.81	13.36	14.91
" 3	11.19	13.56	15.98	18.44	20.95	23.50
" 4	15.30	18.64	22.07	25.59	29.22	32.95
" 5	19.62	24.01	28.58	33.32	38.24	43.35
" 6	24.15	29.71	35.55	41.67	48.07	54.78

72 Dollars.

TIME.	5 %	6 %	7 %	8 %	9 %	10 %
Days 1	1	1	1	2	2	2
" 2	2	2	3	3	4	4
" 3	3	4	4	5	5	6
" 4	4	5	6	6	7	8
" 5	5	6	7	8	9	10
" 6	6	7	8	10	11	12
" 7	7	8	10	11	13	14
" 8	8	10	11	13	14	16
" 9	9	11	13	14	16	18
" 10	10	12	14	16	18	20
" 11	11	13	15	18	20	22
" 12	12	14	17	19	22	24
" 13	13	16	18	21	23	26
" 14	14	17	20	22	25	28
" 15	15	18	21	24	27	30
" 16	16	19	22	26	29	32
" 17	17	20	24	27	31	34
" 18	18	22	25	29	32	36
" 19	19	23	27	30	34	38
" 20	20	24	28	32	36	40
" 21	21	25	29	.34	38	42
" 22	22	26	31	35	40	44
" 23	23	28	32	37	41	46
" 24	24	29	34	38	43	48
" 25	25	30	35	40	45	50
" 26	26	31	36	42	47	52
" 27	27	32	38	43	49	54
" 28	28	34	39	45	50	56
" 29	29	35	41	46	52	58
Mos. 1	30	36	42	48	54	60
" 2	60	72	84	96	1.08	1.20
" 3	90	1.08	1.26	1.44	1.62	1.80
" 4	1.20	1.44	1.68	1.92	2.16	2.40
" 5	1.50	1.80	2.10	2.40	2 70	3.00
" 6	1.80	2.16	2.52	2.88	3.24	3.60
" 7	2.10	2.52	2.94	3.36	3.78	4.20
" 8	2.40	2.88	3.36	3.84	4.32	4.80
" 9	2.70	3.24	3.78	4.32	4.86	5.40
" 10	3.00	3.60	4.20	4.80	5.40	6.00
" 11	3.30	3.96	4.62	5.28	5.94	6.60
Yrs. 1	3.60	4.32	5.04	5.76	6.48	7.20
" 2	7.20	8.64	10.08	11.52	12.96	14.40
" 3	10.80	12.96	15.12	17.28	19.44	21.60
" 4	14.40	17.28	20.16	23.04	25.92	28.80
Com. 2	7.38	8.90	10.43	11.98	13.54	15.12
" 3	11.35	13.75	16.20	18.70	21.24	23.83
" 4	15.52	18.90	22.38	25.96	29.63	33.42
" 5	19.89	24.35	28.98	33.79	38.78	43.96
" 6	24.49	30.13	36.05	42.25	48.75	55.55

TIME.	5 %	6 %	7 %	8 %	9 %	10 %
Days 1	1	1	1	2	2	2
" 2	2	2	3	3	3	4
" 3	3	4	4	5	5	6
" 4	4	5	6	6	7	8
" 5	5	6	7	.8	9	10
" 6	6	7	9	10	11	12
" 7	7	9	10	11	13	14
" 8	8	10	11	13	15	16
" 9	9	11	13	15	16	18
" 10	10	12	14	16	18	20
" 11	11	13	16	18	20	22
" 12	12	15	17	19	22	24
" 13	13	16	18	21	24	26
" 14	14	17	20	23	26	28
" 15	15	18	21	24	27	30
" 16	16	19	23	26	29	32
" 17	17	21	24	28	31	34
" 18	18	22	26	29	33	37
" 19	19	23	27	31	35	39
" 20	20	24	28	32	37	41
" 21	21	26	30	34	38	43
" 22	22	27	31	36	40	45
" 23	23	28	33	37	42	47
" 24	24	29	34	39	44	49
" 25	25	30	35	41	46	51
" 26	26	32	37	42	47	53
" 27	27	33	38	44	49	55
" 28	28	34	40	45	51	57
" 29	29	35	41	47	53	59
Mos. 1	30	37	43	49	5.\	61
" 2	61	73	85	97	1.10	1.22
" 3	91	1.10	1.28	1.46	1.64	1.83
" 4	1.22	1.46	1.70	1.95	2.19	2.43
" 5	1.52	1.83	2.13	2.43	2.74	3.04
" 6	1.83	2.19	2.56	2.92	3.29	3.65
" 7	2.13	2.56	2.98	3.41	3.83	4.26
" 8	2.43	2.92	3.41	3.89	4.38	4.87
" 9	2.74	3.29	3.83	4.38	4.93	5.48
" 10	3.04	3.65	4.26	4.87	5.48	6.08
" 11	3.35	4.02	4.68	5.35	6.02	6.69
Yrs. 1	3.65	4.38	5.11	5.84	6.57	7.30
" 2	7.30	8.76	10.22	11.68	13.14	14.60
" 3	10.95	13.14	15.33	17.52	19.71	21.90
" 4	14.60	17.52	20.44	23.36	26.28	29.20
Com. 2	7.48	9.02	10.58	12.15	13.73	15.33
' 3	11.51	13.94	16.43	18.96	21.54	24.16
" 4	15.73	19.16	22.69	26.32	30.05	33.88
" 5	20.17	24.69	29.39	34.26	39.32	44.57
" 6	24.83	30.55	36.55	42.84	49.43	56.32

TIME.	5 %	6 %	7 %	8 %	9 %	10 %
Days 1	1	1	1	2	2	2
" 2	2	2	3	3	4	4
" 3	3	4	4	5	6	6
" 4	4	5	6	7	7	8
" 5	5	6	7	8	9	10
" 6	6	7	9	10	11	12
" 7	7	9	10	12	13	14
" 8	8	10	12	13	15	16
" 9	9	11	13	15	17	19
" 10	10	12	14	16	19	21
" 11	11	14	16	18	20	23
" 12	12	15	17	20	22	25
" 13	13	16	19	21	24	27
" 14	14	17	20	23	26	29
" 15	15	19	22	25	28	31
" 16	16	20	23	26	30	33
" 17	17	21	24	28	31	35
" 18	19	22	26	30	33	37
" 19	20	23	27	31	35	39
" 20	21	25	29	33	37	41
" 21	22	26	30	35	39	43
" 22	23	27	32	36	41	45
" 23	24	28	33	38	43	47
" 24	25	30	35	39	44	49
" 25	26	31	36	41	46	51
" 26	27	32	37	43	48	53
" 27	28	33	39	44	50	56
" 28	29	35	40	46	52	58
" 29	30	36	42	48	54	60
Mos. 1	31	37	43	49	56	62
" 2	62	74	86	99	1.11	1.23
" 3	93	1.11	1.30	1.48	1.67	1.85
" 4	1.23	1.48	1.73	1.97	2.22	2.47
" 5	1.54	1.85	2.16	2.47	2.78	3.08
" 6	1.85	2.22	2.59	2.96	3.33	3.70
" 7	2.16	2.59	3.02	3.45	3.89	4.32
" 8	2.47	2.96	3.45	3.95	4.44	4.93
" 9	2.78	3.33	3.89	4.44	5.00	5.55
" 10	3.08	3.70	4.32	4.93	5.55	6.17
" 11	3.39	4.07	4.75	5.43	6.11	6.78
Yrs. 1	3.70	4.44	5.18	5.92	6.66	7.40
" 2	7.40	8.88	10.36	11.84	13.32	14.80
" 3	11.10	13.32	15.54	17.76	19 98	22.20
" 4	14.80	17.76	20.72	23.68	26.64	29.60
Com. 2	7.59	9.15	10.72	12.31	13.92	15.54
" 3	11.66	14.14	16.65	19.22	21.83	24.49
" 4	15.95	19.42	23.00	26.68	30.46	34.34
" 5	20.44	25.03	29.79	34.73	39.86	45.18
" 6	25.17	30.97	37.05	43.43	50.11	57.10

75 Dollars.

TIME.	5 %	6 %	7 %	8 %	9 %	10 %
Days 1	1	1	1	2	2	2
" 2	2	3	3	3	4	4
" 3	3	4	4	5	6	6
" 4	4	5	6	7	8	8
" 5	5	6	7	8	9	10
" 6	6	8	9	10	11	13
" 7	7	9	10	12	13	15
" 8	8	10	, 12	13	15	17
" 9	9	11	13	15	17	19
" 10	10	13	15	17	19	21
" 11	11	14	16	18	21	23
" 12	13	15	18	20	23	25
" 13	14	16	19	22	24	27
" 14	15	18	20	23	26	29
" 15	16	19	22	25	28	31
" 16	17	20	23	27	30	33
" 17	18	21	25	28	32	35
" 18	19	23	26	30	34	38
" 19	20	24	28	32	36	40
" 20	21	25	29	33	38	42
" 21	22	26	31	35	39	44
" 22	23	28	32	37	41	46
" 23	24	29	34	38	43	48
" 24	25	30	35	40	45	50
" 25	26	31	36	42	47	52
" 26	27	33	38	43	49	54
" 27	28	34	39	45	51	56
" 28	29	35	41	47	53	58
" 29	30	36	42	48	54	60
Mos. 1	31	38	44	50	56	63
" 2	63	75	88	1.00	1.13	1.25
" 3	94	1.13	1.31	1.50	1.69	1.88
" 4	1.25	1.50	1.75	2.00	2.25	2.50
" 5	1.56	1.88	2.19	2.50	2.81	3.13
" 6	1.88	2.25	2.63	3.00	3.38	3.75
" 7	2.19	2.63	3.06	3.50	3.94	4.38
" 8	2.50	3.00	3.50	4.00	4.50	5.00
" 9	2.81	3.38	3.94	4.50	5.06	5.63
" 10	3.13	3.75	4.38	5.00	5.63	6.25
" 11	3.44	4.13	4.81	5.50	6.19	6.88
Yrs. 1	3.75	4.50	5.25	6.00	6.75	7.50
" 2	7.50	9.00	10.50	12.00	13.50	15.00
" 3	11.25	13.50	15.75	18.00	20.25	22.50
" 4	15.00	18.00	21.00	24.00	27.00	30.00
Com. 2	7.69	9.27	10.87	12.48	14.11	15.75
" 3	11.82	14.33	16.88	19.48	22.13	24.83
" 4	16.16	19.69	23.31	27.04	30.87	34.81
" 5	20.72	25.37	30.19	35.20	40.40	45.79
" 6	25.51	31.39	37.55	44.02	50.78	57.87

TIME.	5 %	6 %	7 %	8 %	9 %	10 %
Days 1	1	1	1	2	2	2
" 2	2.	3	3	3	4	4
" 3	3	4	4	5	6	6
" 4	4	5	6	7	8	8
" 5	5	6	7	8	10	11
" 6	6	8	9	10	11	13
" 7	7	9	10	12	13	15
" 8	8	10	12	14	15	17
" 9	10	11	13	15	17	19
" 10	11	13	15	17	19	21
" 11	12	14	16	19	21	23
" 12	13	15	18	20	23	25
" 13	14	16	19	22	25	27
" 14	15	18	21	24	27	30
" 15	16	19	22	25	29	32
" 16	17	20	24	27	30	34
" 17	18	22	25	29	32	36
" 18	19	23	27	30	34	38
" 19	20	24	28	32	36	40
" 20	21	25	30	34	38	42
" 21	22	27	31	35	40	44
" 22	23	28	33	37	42	46
" 23	24	29	34	39	44	49
" 24	25	30	35	41	46	51
" 25	26	32	37	42	48	53
" 26	27	33	38	44	49	55
" 27	29	34	40	46	51	57
" 28	30	35	41	47	53	59
" 29	31	37	43	49	55	61
Mos. 1	32	38	44	51	57	63
" 2	63	76	89	1.01	1.14	1.27
" 3	95	1.14	1.33	1.52	1.71	1.90
" 4	1.27	1.52	1.77	2.03	2.28	2.53
" 5	1.58	1.90	2.22	2.53	2.85	3.17
" 6	1.90	2.28	2.66	3.04	3.42	3.80
" 7	2.22	2.66	3.10	3.55	3.99	4.43
" 8	2.53	3.04	3.55	4.05	4.56	5.07
" 9	2.85	3.42	3.99	4.56	5.13	5.70
" 10	3.17	3.80	4.43	5.07	5.70	6.33
" 11	3.48	4.18	4.88	5.57	6.27	6.97
Yrs. 1	3.80	4.56	5.32	6.08	6.84	7.60
" 2	7.60	9.12	10.64	12.16	13.68	15.20
" 3	11.40	13.68	15.96	18.24	20.52	22.80
" 4	15.20	18.24	21.28	24.32	27.36	30.40
Com. 2	7.79	9.39	11.01	12.65	14.30	15.96
" 3	11.98	14.52	17.10	19.74	22.42	25.16
" 4	16.38	19.95	23.62	27.40	31.28	35.27
" 5	21.00	25.71	30.59	35.67	40.94	46.40
" 6	25.85	31.81	38.06	44.60	51.46	58.64

TIME.	5 %	6 %	7 %	8 %	9 %	10 %
Days 1	1	1	1	2	2	2
" 2	2	3	3	3	4	4
" 3	3	4	4	5	6	6
" 4	4	5	6	7	8	9
" 5	5	6	7	9	10	11
" 6	6	8	9	10	12	13
" 7	7	9	10	12	13	15
" 8	9	10	12	14	15	17
" 9	10	12	13	15	17	19
" 10	11	13	15	17	19	21
" 11	12	14	16	19	21	24
" 12	13	15	18	21	23	26
" 13	14	17	19	22	25	28
" 14	15	18	21	24	27	30
" 15	16	19	22	26	29	32
" 16	17	21	24	27	31	34
" 17	18	22	25	29	33	36
" 18	19	23	27	31	35	39
" 19	20	24	28	33	37	41
" 20	21	26	30	34	39	43
" 21	22	27	31	36	40	45
" 22	24	28	33	38	42	47
" 23	25	30	34	89	44	49
" 24	26	31	36	41	46	51
" 25	27	32	37	43	48	53
" 26	28	33	39	44	50	56
" 27	29	35	40	46	52	58
" 28	30	36	42	48	54	60
" 29	31	37	43	50	56	62
Mos. 1	32	39	45	51	58	64
" 2	64	77	90	1.03	1.16	1.28
" 3	96	1.16	1.35	1.54	1.73	1.93
" 4	1.28	1.54	1.80	2.05	2.31	2.57
" 5	1.60	1.93	2.25	2.57	2.89	3.21
" 6	1.93	2.31	2.70	3.08	3.47	3.85
" 7	2.25	2.70	3.14	3.59	4.04	4.49
" 8	2.57	3.08	3.59	4.11	4.62	5.13
" 9	2.89	3.47	4.04	4.62	5.20	5.78
" 10	3.21	3.85	4.49	5.13	5.78	6.42
" 11	3.53	4.24	4.94	5.65	6.35	7.06
Yrs. 1	3.85	4.62	5.39	6.16	6.93	7.70
" 2	7.70	9.24	10.78	12.32	13.86	15.40
" 3	11.55	13.86	16.17	18.48	20.79	23.10
" 4	15.40	18.48	21.56	24.64	27.72	30.80
Com. 2	7.89	9.52	11.16	12.81	14.48	16.17
" 3	12.14	14.71	17.33	20.00	22.72	25.49
" 4	16.59	20.21	23.93	27.76	31.69	35.74
" 5	21.27	26.04	31.00	36.14	41.47	47.01
" 6	26.19	32.23	38.56	45.19	52.14	59.41

TIME.	5 %	6 %	7 %	8 %	9 %	10 %
Days 1	1	1	2	2	2	2
" 2	2	3	3	3	4	4
" 3	3	4	5	5	6	7
" 4	4	5	6	7	8	9
" 5	5	7	8	9	10	11
" 6	7	8	9	10	12	13
" 7	8	9	11	12	14	15
" 8	9	10	12	14	16	17
" 9	10	12	14	16	18	20
" 10	11	13	15	17	20	22
" 11	12	14	17	19	21	24
" 12	13	16	18	21	23	26
" 13	14	17	20	23	25	28
" 14	15	18	21	24	27	30
" 15	16	20	23	26	29	33
" 16	17	21	24	28	31	35
" 17	18	22	26	29	33	37
" 18	20	23	27	31	35	39
" 19	21	25	29	33	37	41
" 20	22	26	30	35	39	43
" 21	23	27	32	36	41	46
" 22	24	29	33	38	43	48
" 23	25	30	35	40	45	50
" 24	26	31	36	42	47	52
" 25	27	33	38	43	49	54
" 26	28	34	39	45	51	56
" 27	29	35	41	47	53	59
" 28	30	36	42	49	55	61
" 29	31	38	44	50	57	63
Mos. 1	33	39	46	52	59	65
" 2	65	78	91	1.04	1.17	1.30
" 3	98	1.17	1.37	1.56	1.76	1.95
" 4	1.30	1.56	1.82	2.08	2.34	2.60
" 5	1.63	1.95	2.28	2.60	2.93	3.25
" 6	1.95	2.34	2.73	3.12	3.51	3.90
" 7	2.28	2.73	3.19	3.64	4.10	4.55
" 8	2.60	3.12	3.64	4.16	4.68	5.20
" 9	2.93	3.51	4.10	4.68	5.27	5.85
" 10	3.25	3.90	4.55	5.20	5.85	6.50
" 11	3.58	4.29	5.01	5.72	6.44	7.15
Yrs. 1	3.90	4.68	5.46	6.24	7.02	7.80
" 2	7.80	9.36	10.92	12.48	14.04	15.60
" 3	11.70	14.04	16.38	18.72	21.06	23.40
" 4	15.60	18.72	21.84	24.96	28.08	31.20
Com. 2	8.00	9.64	11.30	12.98	14.67	16.38
" 3	12.29	14.90	17.55	20.26	23.01	25.82
" 4	16.81	20.47	24.24	28.12	32.10	36.20
" 5	21.55	26.38	31.40	36.61	42.01	47.62
" 6	26.53	32.64	39.06	45.78	52.81	60.18

TIME.	5 %	6 %	7 %	8 %	9 %	10 %
Days 1	1	1	2	2	2	2
" 2	2	3	3	4	4	4
" 3	3	4	5	5	6	7
" 4	4	5	6	7	8	9
" 5	5	7	8	9	10	11
" 6	7	8	9	11	12	13
" 7	8	9	11	12	14	15
" 8	9	11	12	14	16	18
" 9	10	12	14	16	18	20
" 10	11	13	15	18	20	22
" 11	12	14	17	19	22	24
" 12	13	16	18	21	24	26
" 13	14	17	20	23	26	29
" 14	15	18	22	25	28	31
" 15	16	20	23	26	30	33
" 16	18	21	25	28	32	35
" 17	19	22	26	30	34	37
" 18	20	24	28	32	36	40
" 19	21	25	29	33	38	42
" 20	22	26	31	35	40	44
" 21	23	28	32	37	41	46
" 22	24	29	34	39	43	48
" 23	25	30	35	40	45	50
" 24	26	32	37	42	47	53
" 25	27	33	38	44	49	55
" 26	29	34	40	46	51	57
" 27	30	36	41	47	53	59
" 28	31	37	43	49	55	61
" 29	32	38	45	51	57	64
Mos. 1	33	40	46	53	59	66
" 2	66	79	92	1.05	1.19	1.32
" 3	99	1.19	1.38	1.58	1.78	1.98
" 4	1.32	1.58	1.84	2.11	2.37	2.63
" 5	1.65	1.98	2.30	2.63	2.96	3.29
" 6	1.98	2.37	2.77	3.16	3.56	3.95
" 7	2.30	2.77	3.23	3.69	4.15	4.61
" 8	2.63	3.16	3.69	4.21	4.74	5.27
" 9	2.96	3.56	4.15	4.74	5.33	5.93
" 10	3.29	3.95	4.61	5.27	5.93	6.58
" 11	3.62	4.35	5.07	5.79	6.52	7.24
Yrs. 1	3.95	4.74	5.53	6.32	7.11	7.90
" 2	7.90	9.48	11.06	12.64	14.22	15.80
" 3	11.85	14.22	16.59	18.96	21.33	23 70
" 4	15.80	18.96	22.12	25.28	28.44	31 60
Com. 2	8.10	9.76	11.45	13.15	14.86	16.59
" 3	12.45	15.09	17.78	20.52	23.31	26.15
" 4	17.03	20.74	24.55	28.48	32.51	36.66
" 5	21.83	26.72	31.80	37.08	42.55	48.23
" 6	26.87	33.06	39.56	46.36	53.49	60.95

TIME.	5 %	6 %	7 %	8 %	9 %	10 %
Days 1	1	1	2	2	2	2
" 2	2	3	3	4	4	4
" 3	3	4	5	5	6	7
" 4	4	5	6	7	8	9
" 5	6	7	8	9	10	11
" 6	7	8	9	11	12	13
" 7	8	9	11	12	14	16
" 8	9	11	12	14	16	18
" 9	10	12	14	16	18	20
" 10	11	13	16	18	20	22
" 11	12	15	17	20	22	24
" 12	13	16	19	21	24	27
" 13	14	17	20	23	26	29
" 14	16	19	22	25	28	31
" 15	17	20	23	27	30	33
" 16	18	21	25	28	32	36
" 17	19	23	26	30	34	38
" 18	20	24	28	32	36	40
" 19	21	25	30	34	38	42
" 20	22	27	31	36	40	44
" 21	23	28	33	37	42	47
" 22	24	29	34	39	44	49
" 23	26	31	36	41	46	51
" 24	27	32	37	·43	48	53
" 25	28	33	39	44	50	56
" 26	29	35	40	46	52	58
" 27	30	36	42	48	54	60
" 28	31	37	44	50	56	62
" 29	32	39	45	52	58	64
Mos. 1	· 33	40	47	53	60	67
" 2	67	80	93	1.07	1.20	1.33
" 3	1.00	1.20	1.40	1.60	1.80	2.00
" 4	1.33	1.60	1.87	2.13	2.40	2.67
" 5	1.67	2.00	2.33	2.67	3.00	3.33
" 6	2.00	2.40	2.80	3.20	3.60	4.00
" 7	2.33	· 2.80	3.27	3.73	4.20	4.67
" 8	2.67	3.20	3.73	4.27	4.80	5.33
" 9	3.00	3.60	4.20	4.80	5.40	6.00
" 10	3.33	4.00	4.67	5.33	6.00	6.67
" 11	3.67	4.40	5.13	5.87	6.60	7.33
Yrs. 1	4.00	4.80	5.60	6.40	7.20	8.00
" 2	8.00	9.60	11.20	12.80	14.40	16.00
" 3	12.10	14.40	16.80	19.20	21.60	24.00
" 4	16.00	19.20	22.40	25.60	28.80	32.00
Com. 2	8.20	9.89	11.59	13.31	15.05	16.80
" 3	12.61	15.28	18.00	20.78	23.60	26.48
" 4	17.24	21.00	24.86	28.84	32.93	37.13
" 5	22.10	27.06	32.20	37.55	43.09	48.84
" 6	27.21	33.48	40.06	46.95	54.17	61.73

TIME.	5 %	6 %	7 %	8 %	,9 %	10 %
Days 1	1	1	2	2	2	2
" 2	2	3	3	4	4	4
" 3	3	4	5	5	6	7
" 4	4	5	6	7	8	9
" 5	6	7	8	9	10	11
" 6	7	8	9	11	12	14
" 7	8	9	11	13	14	16
" 8	9	11	13	14	16	18
" 9	10	12	14	16	18	20
" 10	11	14	16	18	20	23
" 11	12	15	17	20	22	25
" 12	14	16	19	22	24	27
" 13	15	18	20	23	26	29
" 14	16	19	22	25	28	32
" 15	17	20	24	27	30	34
" 16	18	22	25	29	32	36
" 17	19	23	27	31	34	38
" 18	20	24	28	32	36	41
" 19	21	26	30	34	38	43
" 20	23	27	32	36	41	45
" 21	24	28	33	38	43	47
" 22	25	30	35	40	45	50
" 23	26	31	36	41	47	52
" 24	27	32	38	43	49	54
" 25	28	34	39	45	51	56
" 26	29	35	41	47	53	59
" 27	30	36	43	49	55	61
" 28	32	38	44	50	57	63
" 29	33	39	46	52	59	65
Mos. 1	34	41	47	54	. 61	68
" 2	68	81	95	1.08	1.22	1.35
" 3	1.01	1.22	1.42	1.62	1.82	2.03
" 4	1.35	1.62	1.89	2.16	2.43	2.70
" 5	1.69	2.03	2.36	2.70	3.04	3.38
" 6	2.03	2.43	2.84	3.24	3.65	4.05
" 7	2.36	2.84	3.31	3.78	4.25	4.73
" 8	2.70	3.24	3.78	4.32	4.86	5.40
" 9	3.04	3.65	4.25	4.86	5.47	6.08
" 10	3.38	4.05	4.73	5.40	6.08	6.75
" 11	3.71	4.46	5.20	5.94	6.68	7.43
Yrs. 1	4.05	4.86	5.67	6.48	7.29	8.10
" 2	8.10	9.72	11.34	12.96	14.58	16.20
" 3	12.15	14.58	17.01	19.44	21.87	24.30
" 4	16.20	19.44	22.68	25.92	29.16	32.40
Com. 2	8.30	10.01	11.74	13.48	15.24	17.01
" 3	12.77	15.47	18.23	21.04	23 90	26.81
" 4	17.46	21.26	25.17	29.20	33 34	37.59
" 5	22.38	27.40	32.61	38.02	43.63	49.45
" 6	27.55	33.90	40.56	47.54	54.85	62.50

TIME.	5 %	6 %	7 %	8 %	9 % ·	10 %
Days 1	1	1	2	2	2	2
" 2	2	3	3	4	4	5
" 3	3	4	5	5	6	7
" 4	5	5	6	7	8	9
" 5	6	7	8	9	10	11
" 6	7	8	10	11	12	14
" 7	8	10	11	13	14	16
" 8	9	11	13	15	16	18
" 9	10	12	14	16	18	21
" 10	11	14	16	18	21	23
" 11	13	15	18	20	23	25
" 12	14	16	19	22	25	27
" 13	15	18	21	24	27	30
" 14	16	19	22	26	29	32
" 15	17	21	24	27	31	34
" 16	18	22	26	29	33	36
" 17	19	23	27	31	35	39
" 18	21	25	29	33	37	41
" 19	22	26	30	35	39	43
" 20	23	27	32	36	41	46
" 21	24	29	33	38	43	48
" 22	25	30	35	40	45	50
" 23	26	31	37	42	47	52
" 24	27	33	38	44	49	55
" 25	28	34	40	46	51	57
" 26	30	36	41	47	53	59
" 27	31	37	43	49	55	62
" 28	32	38	45	51	57	64
" 29	33	40	46	53	59	66
Mos. 1	34	41	48	55	62	68
" 2	68	82	96	1.09	1.23	1.37
" 3	1.03	1.23	1.44	1.64	1.85	2.05
" 4	1.37	1.64	1.91	2 19	2.46	2.73
" 5	1.71	2.05	2.39	2.73	3.08	3.42
" 6	2.05	2.46	2.87	3.28	3.69	4.10
" 7	2.39	2.87	3.35	3.83	4.31	4.78
" 8	2.73	3.28	3.83	4.37	4.92	5.47
" 9	3.08	3.69	4.31	4.92	5.54	6.15
" 10	3.42	4.10	4.78	5.47	6.15	6.83
" 11	3.76	4.51	5.26	6.01	6.77	7.52
Yrs 1	4.10	4.92	5.74	6.56	7.38	8.20
" 2	8.20	9.84	11.48	13.12	14.76	16.40
" 3	12.30	14.76	17.22	19.68	22.14	24.60
" 4	16.40	19.68	22.96	26.24	29.52	32.80
Com. 2	8.41	10.14	11.88	13.64	15.42	17.22
" 3	12.93	15.66	18.45	21.30	24.19	27.14
" 4	17.67	21.52	25.49	29.56	33.75	38.06
" 5	22.67	27.73	33.01	38.48	44.17	50.06
" 6	27.89	34.32	41.06	48.12	55.52	63.27

TIME.	5 %	6 %	7 %	8 %	9 %	10 %
Days 1	1	1	2	2	2	2
" 2	2	3	3	4	4	5
" 3	3	4	5	6	6	7
" 4	5	6	6	7	8	9
" 5	6	7	8	9	10	12
" 6	7	8	10	11	12	14
" 7	8	10	11	13	15	16
" 8	9	11	13	15	17	18
" 9	10	12	15	17	19	21
" 10	12	14	16	18	21	23
" 11	13	15	18	20	23	25
" 12	14	17	19	22	25	28
" 13	15	18	21	24	27	30
" 14	16	19	23	26	29	32
" 15	17	21	24	28	31	35
" 16	18	22	26	30	33	37
" 17	20	24	27	31	35	39
" 18	21	25	29	33	37	42
" 19	22	26	31	35	39	44
" 20	23	28	32	37	42	46
" 21	24	29	34	39	44	48
" 22	25	30	36	41	46	51
" 23	27	32	37	42	48	53
" 24	28	33	39	44	50	55
" 25	29	35	40	46	52	58
" 26	30	36	42	48	54	60
" 27	31	37	44	50	56	62
" 28	32	39	45	52	58	65
" 29	33	40	47	53	60	67
Mos. 1	35	42	48	55	62	69
" 2	69	83	97	1.11	1.25	1.38
" 3	1.04	1.25	1.45	1.66	1.87	2.08
" 4	1.38	1.66	1.94	2.21	2.49	2.77
" 5	1.73	2.08	2.42	2.77	3.11	3.46
" 6	2.08	2.49	2.91	3.32	3.74	4.15
" 7	2.42	2.91	3.39	3.87	4.36	4.84
" 8	2.77	3.32	3.87	4.43	4.98	5.53
" 9	3.11	3.74	4.36	4.98	5.60	6.23
" 10	3.46	4.15	4.84	5.53	6.23	6.92
" 11	3.80	4.57	5.33	6.09	6.85	7.61
Yrs. 1	4.15	4.98	5.81	6.64	7.47	8.30
" 2	8.30	9.96	11.62	13.28	14.94	16.60
" 3	12.45	14.94	17.43	19.92	22.41	24.90
" 4	16.60	19.92	23.24	26.56	29.88	33.20
Com. 2	8.51	10.26	12.03	13.81	15.61	17.43
" 3	13.08	15.85	18.68	21.56	24.49	27.47
" 4	17.89	21.79	25.80	29.92	34.16	38.52
" 5	22.93	28.07	33.41	38.95	44.71	50.67
" 6	28.23	34.74	41.56	48.71	56.20	64.04

TIME.	5 %	6 %	7 %	8 %	9 %	10 %
Days 1	1	1	2	2	2	2
" 2	2	3	3	4	4	5
" 3	3	4	5	6	6	7
" 4	5	6	7	7	8	9
" 5	6	7	8	9	11	12
" 6	7	8	10	11	13	14
" 7	8	10	11	13	15	16
" 8	9	11	13	15	17	19
" 9	11	13	15	17	19	21
" 10	12	14	16	19	21	23
" 11	13	15	18	21	23	26
" 12	14	17	20	22	25	28
" 13	15	18	21	24	27	30
" 14	16	20	23	26	29	33
" 15	18	21	25	28	32	35
" 16	19	22	26	30	34	37
" 17	20	24	28	32	36	40
" 18	21	25	29	34	38	42
" 19	22	27	31	35	40	44
" 20	23	28	33	37	42	47
" 21	25	29	34	39	44	49
" 22	26	31	36	41	. 46	51
" 23	27	32	38	43	48	54
" 24	28	34	39	45	50	56
" 25	29	35	41	47	53	58
" 26	30	36	42	49	55	61
" 27	32	38	44	50	57	63
" 28	33	39	46	52	59	65
" 29	34	41	47	54	61	68
Mos. 1	35	42	49	56	63	70
" 2	70	84	98	1.12	1.26	1.40
" 3	1.05	1.26	1.47	1.68	1.89	2.10
" 4	1.40	1.68	1.96	2.24	2.52	2.80
" 5	1.75	2.10	2.45	2.80	3.15	3.50
" 6	2.10	2.52	2.94	3.36	3.78	4.20
" 7	2.45	2.94	3.43	3.92	4.41	4.90
" 8	2.80	3.36	3.92	4.48	5.04	5.60
" 9	3.15	3.78	4.41	5.04	5.67	6.30
" 10	3.50	4.20	4.90	5.60	6.30	7.00
" 11	3.85	4.62	5.39	6.16	6.93	7.70
Yrs. 1	4.20	5.04	5.88	6.72	7.56	8.40
" 2	8.40	10.08	11.76	13.44	15.12	16.80
" 3	12.60	15.12	17.64	20.16	22.68	25.20
" 4	16.80	20.16	23.52	26.88	30.24	33.60
Com. 2	8.61	10.38	12.17	13.98	15.80	17.64
" 3	13.24	16.05	18.90	21.82	24.78	27.80
" 4	18.10	22.05	26.11	30.28	34.57	38.98
" 5	23.21	28.41	33.81	39.42	45.24	51.28
" 6	28.57	35.16	42.06	49.30	56.88	64.81

TIME.	5 %	6 %	7 %	8 %	9 %	10 %
Days 1	1	1	2	2	2	2
" 2	2	3	3	4	4	5
" 3	4	4	5	6	6	7
" 4	5	6	7	8	9	9
" 5	6	7	8	9	11	12
" 6	7	9	10	11	13	14
" 7	8	10	12	13	15	17
" 8	9	11	13	15	17	19
" 9	11	13	15	17	19	21
" 10	12	14	17	19	21	24
" 11	13	16	18	21	23	26
" 12	14	17	20	23	26	28
" 13	15	18	21	25	28	31
" 14	17	20	23	26	30	33
" 15	18	21	25	28	32	35
" 16	19	23	26	30	34	38
" 17	20	24	28	32	36	40
" 18	21	26	30	34	38	43
" 19	22	27	31	36	40	45
" 20	24	28	33	38	43	47
" 21	25	30	35	40	45	50
" 22	26	31	36	42	47	52
" 23	27	33	38	43	49	54
" 24	28	34	40	45	51	57
" 25	30	35	41	47	53	59
" 26	31	37	43	49	55	61
" 27	32	38	45	51	57	64
" 28	33	40	46	53	60	66
" 29	34	41	48	55	62	68
Mos. 1	35	43	50	57	64	71
" 2	71	85	99	1.13	1.28	1.42
" 3	1.06	1.28	1.49	1.70	1.91	2.13
" 4	1.42	1.70	1.98	2.27	2.55	2.83
" 5	1.77	2.13	2.48	2.83	3.19	3.54
" 6	2.13	2.55	2.98	3.40	3.83	4.25
" 7	2.48	2.98	3.47	3.97	4.46	4.96
" 8	2.83	3.40	3.97	4.53	5.10	5.67
" 9	3.19	3.83	4.46	5.10	5.74	6.38
" 10	3.54	4.25	4.96	5.67	6.38	7.08
" 11	3.90	4.68	5.45	6.23	7.01	7.79
Yrs. 1	4.25	5.10	5.95	6.80	7.65	8.50
" 2	8.50	10.20	11.90	13.60	15.30	17.00
" 3	12.75	15.30	17.85	20.40	22.95	25.50
" 4	17.00	20.40	23.80	27.20	30.60	34.00
Com. 2	8.71	10.51	12.32	14.14	15.94	17.85
" 3	13.40	16.24	19.13	22.08	25.08	28.14
" 4	18.32	22.31	26.42	30.64	34.98	39.45
" 5	23.48	28.75	34.22	39.89	45.78	51.89
" 6	28.91	35.57	42.56	49.88	57.55	65.58

TIME.	5 %	6 %	7 %	8 %	9 %	10 %
Days 1	1	1	2	2	2	2
" 2	2	3	3	4	4	5
" 3	4	4	5	6	6	7
" 4	5	6	7	8	9	10
" 5	6	7	8	10	11	12
" 6	7	9	10	11	13	14
" 7	8	10	12	13	15	17
" 8	10	11	13	15	17	19
" 9	11	13	15	17	19	22
" 10	12	14	17	19	22	24
" 11	13	16	18	21	24	26
" 12	14	17	20	23	26	29
" 13	16	19	22	25	28	31
" 14	17	20	23	27	30	33
" 15	18	22	25	29	32	36
" 16	19	23	27	31	34	38
" 17	20	24	28	32	37	41
" 18	22	26	30	34	39	43
" 19	23	27	32	36	41	45
" 20	24	29	33	38	43	48
" 21	25	30	35	40	45	50
" 22	26	32	37	42	47	53
" 23	27	33	38	44	49	55
" 24	29	34	40	46	52	57
" 25	30	36	42	48	54	60
" 26	31	37	43	50	56	62
" 27	32	39	45	52	58	65
" 28	33	40	47	54	60	67
" 29	35	42	48	55	62	69
Mos. 1	36	43	50	57	65	72
" 2	72	86	1.00	1.15	1.29	1.43
" 3	1.08	1.29	1.51	1.72	1.94	2.15
" 4	1.43	1.72	2.01	2.29	2.58	2.87
" 5	1.79	2.15	2.51	2.87	3.23	3.58
" 6	2.15	2.58	3.01	3.44	3.87	4.30
" 7	2.51	3.01	3.51	4.01	4.52	5.02
" 8	2.87	3.44	4.01	4.59	5.16	5.73
" 9	3.23	3.87	4.52	5.16	5.81	6.45
" 10	3.58	4.30	5.02	5.73	6.45	7.17
" 11	3.94	4.73	5.52	6.31	7.10	7.88
Yrs. 1	4.30	5.16	6.02	6.88	7.74	8 60
" 2	8.60	10.32	12.04	13.76	15.48	17.20
" 3	12.90	15.48	18.06	20.64	23.22	25.80
" 4	17.20	20.64	24.08	27.52	30.96	34.40
Com. 2	8.82	10.63	12.46	14.31	16.18	18.06
" 3	13.56	16.43	19.35	22.34	25.37	28.47
" 4	18.53	22.57	26.73	31.00	35.40	39.91
" 5	23.76	29.09	34.62	40.36	46.32	52.50
" 6	29.25	35.99	43.06	50.47	58.23	66.35

TIME.	5 %	6 %	7 %	8 %	9 %	10 %
Days 1	1	1	2	2	2	2
" 2	2	3	3	4	4	5
" 3	4	4	5	6	7	7
" 4	5	6	7	8	9	10
" 5	6	7	8	10	11	12
" 6	7	9	10	12	13	15
" 7	8	10	12	14	15	17
" 8	10	12	14	15	17	19
" 9	11	13	15	17	20	22
" 10	12	15	17	19	22	24
" 11	13	16	19	21	24	27
" 12	15	17	20	23	26	29
" 13	16	19	22	25	28	31
" 14	17	20	24	27	30	34
" 15	18	22	25	29	33	36
" 16	19	23	27	31	35	39
" 17	21	25	29	33	37	41
" 18	22	26	30	35	39	44
" 19	23	28	32	37	41	46
" 20	24	29	34	39	44	48
" 21	25	30	36	41	46	51
" 22	27	32	37	43	48	53
" 23	28	33	39	44	50	56
" 24	29	35	41	46	52	58
" 25	30	36	42	48	54	60
" 26	31	38	44	50	57	63
" 27	33	39	46	52	59	65
" 28	34	41	47	54	61	68
" 29	35	42	49	56	63	70
Mos. 1	36	44	51	58	65	73
" 2	73	87	1.02	1.16	1.31	1.45
" 3	1.09	1.31	1.52	1.74	1.96	2.18
" 4	1.45	1.74	2.03	2.32	2.61	2.90
" 5	1.81	2.18	2.54	2.90	3.26	3.63
" 6	2.18	2.61	3.05	3.48	3.92	4.35
" 7	2.54	3.05	3.55	4.06	4.57	5.08
" 8	2.90	3.48	4.06	4.64	5.22	5.80
" 9	3.26	3.92	4.57	5.22	5.87	6.53
" 10	3.63	4.35	5.08	5.80	6.53	7.25
" 11	3.99	4.79	5.58	6.38	7.18	7.98
Yrs. 1	4.35	5.22	6.09	6.96	7.83	8.70
" 2	8.70	10.44	12.18	13.92	15.66	17.40
" 3	13.05	15.66	18.27	20.88	23.49	26.10
" 4	17.40	20.88	24.36	27.84	31.32	34.80
Com. 2	8.92	10.75	12.61	14.48	16.36	18.27
" 3	13.71	16.62	19.58	22.59	25.67	28.80
" 4	18.75	22.84	27.04	31.36	35.81	40.38
" 5	24.04	29.43	35.02	40.83	46.86	53.11
" 6	29.59	36.41	43.56	51.06	58.91	67.13

TIME.	5 %	6 %	7 %	8 %	9 %	10 %
Days 1	1	1	2	2	2	2
" 2	2	3	3	4	4	5
" 3	4	4	5	6	7	7
" 4	5	6	7	8	9	10
" 5	6	7	9	10	11	12
" 6	7	9	10	12	13	15
" 7	9	10	12	14	15	17
" 8	10	12	14	16	18	20
" 9	11	13	15	18	20	22
" 10	12	15	17	20	22	24
" 11	13	16	19	22	24	27
" 12	15	18	21	23	26	29
" 13	16	19	22	25	29	32
" 14	17	21	24	27	31	34
" 15	18	22	26	29	33	37
" 16	20	23	27	31	35	39
" 17	21	25	29	33	37	42
" 18	22	26	31	35	40	44
" 19	23	28	33	37	42	46
" 20	24	29	34	39	44	49
" 21	26	31	36	41	46	51
" 22	27	32	38	43	48	54
" 23	28	34	39	45	51	56
" 24	29	35	41	47	53	59
" 25	31	37	43	49	55	61
" 26	32	38	44	51	57	64
" 27	33	40	46	53	59	66
" 28	34	41	48	55	62	68
" 29	35	43	50	57	64	71
Mos. 1	37	44	51	59	66	73
" 2	73	88	1.03	1.17	1.32	1.47
" 3	1.10	1.32	1.54	1.76	1.98	2.20
" 4	1.47	1.76	2.05	2.35	2.64	2.93
" 5	1.83	2.20	2.57	2.93	3.30	3.67
" 6	2.20	2.64	3.08	3.52	3.96	4.40
" 7	2.57	3.08	3.59	4.11	4.62	5.13
" 8	2.93	3.52	4.11	4.69	5.28	5.87
" 9	3.30	3.96	4.62	5.28	5.94	6.60
" 10	3.67	4.40	5.13	5.87	6.60	7.33
" 11	4.03	4.84	5.65	6.45	7.26	8.07
Yrs. 1	4.40	5.28	6.16	7.04	7.92	8.80
" 2	8.80	10.56	12.32	14.08	15.84	17.60
" 3	13.20	15.84	18.48	21.12	23.76	26.40
" 4	17.60	21.12	24.64	28.16	31.68	35.20
Com. 2	9.02	10.88	12.75	14.64	16.55	18.48
" 3	13.87	16.81	19.80	22.85	25.96	29.13
" 4	18.96	23.10	27.35	31.72	36.22	40.84
" 5	24.31	29.76	35.42	41.30	47.40	53.72
" 6	29.93	36.83	44.06	51.64	59.58	67.90

TIME.	5 %	6 %	7 %	8 %	9 %	10 %
Days 1	1	1	2	2	2	2
" 2	2	3	3	4	4	5
" 3	4	4	5	6	7	7
" 4	5	6	7	8	9	10
" 5	6	7	9	10	11	12
" 6	7	9	10	12	13	15
" 7	9	10	12	14	16	17
" 8	10	12	14	16	18	20
" 9	11	13	16	18	20	22
" 10	12	15	17	20	22	25
" 11	14	16	19	22	24	27
" 12	15	18	21	24	27	30
" 13	16	19	22	26	29	32
" 14	17	21	24	28	31	35
" 15	19	22	26	30	33	37
" 16	20	24	28	32	36	40
" 17	21	25	29	34	38	42
" 18	22	27	31	36	40	45
" 19	23	28	33	38	42	47
" 20	25	30	35	40	45	49
" 21	26	31	36	42	47	52
" 22	27	33	38	44	49	54
" 23	28	34	40	45	51	57
" 24	30	36	42	47	53	59
" 25	31	37	43	49	56	62
" 26	32	39	45	51	58	64
" 27	33	40	47	53	60	67
" 28	35	42	48	55	62	69
" 29	36	43	50	57	65	72
Mos. 1	37	45	52	59	67	74
" 2	74	89	1.04	1.19	1.34	1.48
" 3	1.11	1.34	1.56	1.78	2.00	2.23
" 4	1.48	1.78	2.08	2.37	2.67	2.97
" 5	1.85	2.23	2.60	2.97	3.34	3.71
" 6	2.23	2.67	3.12	3.56	4.01	4.45
" 7	2.60	3.12	3.63	4.15	4.67	5.19
" 8	2.97	3.56	4.15	4.75	5.34	5.93
" 9	3.34	4.01	4.67	5.34	6.01	6.68
" 10	3.71	4.45	5.19	5.93	6.68	7.42
" 11	4.08	4.90	5.71	6.53	7.34	8.16
Yrs. 1	4.45	5.34	6.23	7.12	8.01	8.90
" 2	8.90	10.68	12.46	14.24	16.02	17.80
" 3	13.35	16.02	18.69	21.36	24.03	26.70
" 4	17.80	21.36	24.92	28.48	32.04	35.60
Com. 2	9.12	11.00	12.90	14.81	16.74	18.69
" 3	14.03	17.00	20.03	23.11	26.26	29.46
" 4	19.18	23.36	27.66	32.08	36.63	41.30
" 5	24.59	30.10	35.83	41.77	47.94	54.35
" 6	30.27	37.25	44.57	52.23	60.26	68.67

TIME.	5 %	6 %	7 %	8 %	9 %	10 %
Days 1	1	2	2	2	2	3
" 2	3	3	4	4	5	5
" 3	4	5	5	6	7	8
" 4	5	6	7	8	9	10
" 5	6	8	9	10	11	13
" 6	8	9	11	12	14	15
" 7	9	11	12	14	16	18
" 8	10	12	14	16	18	20
" 9	11	14	16	18	20	23
" 10	13	15	18	20	23	25
" 11	14	17	19	22	25	28
" 12	15	18	21	24	27	30
" 13	16	20	23	26	29	33
" 14	18	21	25	28	32	35
" 15	19	23	26	30	34	38
" 16	20	24	28	32	36	40
" 17	21	26	30	34	38	43
" 18	23	27	32	36	41	45
" 19	24	29	33	38	43	48
" 20	25	30	35	40	45	50
" 21	26	32	37	42	47	53
" 22	28	33	39	44	50	55
" 23	29	35	40	46	52	58
" 24	30	36	42	48	54	60
" 25	31	38	44	50	56	63
" 26	33	39	46	52	59	65
" 27	34	41	47	54	61	68
" 28	35	42	49	56	63	70
" 29	36	44	51	58	65	73
Mos. 1	38	45	53	60	68	75
" 2	75	90	1.05	1.20	1.35	1.50
" 3	1.13	1.35	1.58	1.80	2.03	2.25
" 4	1.50	1.80	2.10	2.40	2.70	3.00
" 5	1.88	2.25	2.63	3.00	3.38	3.75
" 6	2.25	2.70	3.15	3.60	4.05	4.50
" 7	2.63	3.15	3.68	4.20	4.73	5.25
" 8	3.00	3.60	4.20	4.80	5.40	6.00
" 9	3.38	4.05	4.73	5.40	6.08	6.75
" 10	3.75	4.50	5.25	6.00	6.75	7.50
" 11	4.13	4.95	5.78	6.60	7.43	8.25
Yrs. 1	4.50	5.40	6.30	7.20	8.10	9.00
" 2	9.00	10.80	12.60	14.40	16.20	18.00
" 3	13.50	16.20	18.90	21.60	24.30	27.00
" 4	18.00	21.60	25.20	28.80	32.40	36.00
Com. 2	9.23	11.12	13.04	14.98	16.93	18.90
" 3	14.19	17.19	20.25	23.37	26.55	29.79
" 4	19.40	23.62	27.97	32.44	37.04	41.77
" 5	24.87	30.44	36.23	42.24	48.48	54.95
" 6	30.61	37.67	45.07	52.83	60.94	69.44

TIME.	5 %	6 %	7 %	8 %	9 %	10 %
Days 1	1	2	2	2	2	3
" 2	3	3	4	4	5	5
" 3	4	5	5	6	7	8
" 4	5	6	7	8	9	10
" 5	6	8	9	10	11	13
" 6	8	9	11	12	14	15
" 7	9	11	12	14	16	18
" 8	10	12	14	16	18	20
" 9	11	14	16	18	20	23
" 10	13	15	18	20	23	25
" 11	14	17	19	22	25	28
" 12	15	18	21	24	27	30
" 13	16	20	23	26	30	33
" 14	18	21	25	28	32	35
" 15	19	23	27	30	34	38
" 16	20	24	28	32	36	40
" 17	21	26	30	34	39	43
" 18	23	27	32	36	41	46
" 19	24	29	34	38	43	48
" 20	25	30	35	40	46	51
" 21	27	32	37	42	48	53
" 22	28	33	39	44	50	56
" 23	29	35	41	47	52	58
" 24	30	36	42	49	55	61
" 25	32	38	44	51	57	63
" 26	33	39	46	53	59	66
" 27	34	41	48	55	61	68
" 28	35	42	50	57	64	71
" 29	37	44	51	59	66	73
Mos. 1	38	46	53	61	68	76
" 2	76	91	1.06	1.21	1.37	1.52
" 3	1.14	1.37	1.59	1.82	2.05	2.28
" 4	1.52	1.82	2.12	2.43	2.73	3.03
" 5	1.90	2.28	2.65	3.03	3.41	3.79
" 6	2.28	2.73	3.19	3.64	4.10	4.55
" 7	2.65	3.19	3.72	4.25	4.78	5.31
" 8	3.03	3.64	4.25	4.85	5.46	6.07
" 9	3.41	4.10	4.78	5.46	6.14	6.82
" 10	3.79	4.55	5.31	6.07	6.83	7.58
" 11	4.17	5.01	5.84	6.67	7.51	8.34
Yrs. 1	4.55	5.46	6.37	7.28	8.19	9.10
" 2	9.10	10.92	12.74	14.56	16.38	18.20
" 3	13.65	16.38	19.11	21.84	24.57	27.30
" 4	18.20	21.84	25.48	29.12	32.76	36.40
Com. 2	9.33	11.25	13.19	15.14	17.12	19.11
" 3	14.34	17.38	20.48	23.63	26.85	30.12
" 4	19.61	23.89	28.28	32.80	37.45	42.23
" 5	25.14	30.78	36.63	42.71	49.01	55.56
" 6	30.95	38.09	45.57	53.41	61.62	70.21

TIME.	5 %	6 %	7 %	8 %	9 %	10 %
Days 1	1	2	2	2	2	3
" 2	3	3	4	4	5	5
" 3	4	5	5	6	7	8
" 4	5	6	7	8	9	10
" 5	6	8	9	10	12	13
" 6	8	9	11	12	14	15
" 7	9	11	13	14	16	18
" 8	10	12	14	16	18	20
" 9	12	14	16	18	21	23
" 10	13	15	18	20	23	26
" 11	14	17	20	22	25	28
" 12	15	18	21	25	28	31
" 13	17	20	23	27	30	33
" 14	18	21	25	29	32	36
" 15	19	23	27	31	35	38
" 16	20	25	29	33	37	41
" 17	22	26	30	35	39	43
" 18	23	28	32	37	41	46
" 19	24	29	34	39	44	49
" 20	26	31	36	41	46	51
" 21	27	32	38	43	48	54
" 22	28	34	39	45	51	56
" 23	29	35	41	47	53	59
" 24	31	37	43	49	55	61
" 25	32	38	45	51	58	64
" 26	33	40	47	53	60	66
" 27	35	41	48	55	62	69
" 28	36	43	50	57	64	72
" 29	37	44	52	59	67	74
Mos. 1	38	46	54	61	69	77
" 2	77	92	1.07	1.23	1.38	1.53
" 3	1.15	1.38	1.61	1.84	2.07	2.30
" 4	1.53	1.84	2.15	2.45	2.76	3.07
" 5	1.92	2.36	2.68	3.07	3 45	3.83
" 6	2.30	2.76	3.22	3 68	4.14	4.60
" 7	2.68	3.22	3.76	4.29	4.83	5.37
" 8	3.07	3.68	4.29	4.91	5.52	6.13
" 9	3.45	4.14	4.83	5.52	6.21	6.90
" 10	3.83	4.60	5.37	6.13	6.90	7.67
" 11	4.22	5.06	5.90	6.75	7.59	8.43
Yrs. 1	4.60	5.52	6.44	7.36	8.28	9.20
" 2	9.20	11.04	12.88	14.72	16.56	18.40
" 3	13.80	16.56	19.32	22.08	24.84	27.60
" 4	18.40	22.08	25.76	29.44	33.12	36.80
Com. 2	9.43	11.37	13.33	15.31	17.31	19.32
" 3	14.50	17.57	20.70	23.89	27.14	30.45
" 4	19.83	24.15	28.59	33.16	37.87	42.70
" 5	25.42	31.12	37.03	43.18	49.55	56.17
" 6	31.29	38.50	46.07	53.99	62.29	70.98

TIME.	5 %	6 %	7 %	8 %	9 %	10 %
Days 1	1	2	2	2	2	3
" 2	3	3	4	4	5	5
" 3	4	5	5	6	7	8
" 4	5	6	7	8	9	10
" 5	6	8	9	10	12	13
" 6	8	9	11	12	14	16
" 7	9	11	13	14	16	18
" 8	10	12	14	17	19	21
" 9	12	14	16	19	21	23
" 10	13	16	18	21	23	26
" 11	14	17	20	23	26	28
" 12	16	19	22	25	28	31
" 13	17	20	24	27	30	34
" 14	18	22	25	29	33	36
" 15	19	23	27	31	35	39
" 16	21	25	29	33	37	41
" 17	22	26	31	35	40	44
" 18	23	28	33	37	42	47
" 19	25	29	34	39	44	49
" 20	26	31	36	41	47	52
" 21	27	33	38	43	49	54
" 22	28	34	40	45	51	57
" 23	30	36	42	48	53	59
" 24	31	37	43	50	56	62
" 25	32	39	45	52	58	65
" 26	34	40	47	54	60	67
" 27	35	42	49	56	63	70
" 28	36	43	51	58	65	72
" 29	37	45	52	60	67	75
Mos. 1	39	47	54	62	70	78
" 2	78	93	1.09	1.24	1.40	1.55
" 3	1.16	1.40	1.63	1.86	2.09	2.33
" 4	1.55	1.86	2.17	2.48	2.79	3.10
" 5	1.94	2.33	2.71	3.10	3.49	3.88
" 6	2.33	2.79	3.26	3.72	4.19	4.65
" 7	2.71	3.26	3.80	4.34	4.88	5.43
" 8	3.10	3.72	4.34	4.96	5.58	6.20
" 9	3.49	4.19	4.88	5.58	6.28	6.98
" 10	3.88	4.65	5.43	6.20	6.98	7.75
" 11	4.26	5.12	5.97	6.82	7.67	8.53
Yrs. 1	4.65	5.58	6.51	7.44	8.37	9.30
" 2	9.30	11.16	13.02	14.88	16.74	18.60
" 3	13.95	16.74	19.53	22.32	25.11	27.90
" 4	18.60	22.32	26.04	29.76	33.48	37.20
Com. 2	9.53	11.49	13.48	15.48	17.49	19.53
" 3	14.66	17.76	20.93	24.15	27.44	30.78
" 4	20.04	24.41	28.90	33.53	38.28	43.16
" 5	25.69	31.45	37.44	43.65	50.09	56.78
" 6	31.63	38.92	46.57	54.58	62.97	71.76

TIME.	5 %	6 %	7 %	8 %	9 %	10 %
Days 1	1	2	2	2	2	3
" 2	3	3	4	4	5	5
" 3	4	5	5	6	7	8
" 4	5	6	7	8	9	10
" 5	7	8	9	10	12	13
" 6	8	9	11	13	14	16
" 7	9	11	13	15	16	18
" 8	10	13	15	17	19	21
" 9	12	14	16	19	21	24
" 10	13	16	18	21	24	26
" 11	14	17	20	23	26	29
" 12	16	19	22	25	28	31
" 13	17	20	24	27	31	34
" 14	18	22	26	29	33	37
" 15	20	24	27	31	35	39
" 16	21	25	29	33	38	42
" 17	22	27	31	36	40	44
" 18	24	28	33	38	42	47
" 19	25	30	35	40	45	50
" 20	26	31	37	42	47	52
" 21	27	33	38	44	49	55
" 22	29	34	40	46	52	57
" 23	30	36	42	48	54	60
" 24	31	38	44	50	56	63
" 25	33	39	46	52	59	65
" 26	34	41	48	54	61	68
" 27	35	42	49	56	63	71
" 28	37	44	51	58	66	73
" 29	38	45	53	61	68	76
Mos. 1	39	47	55	63	71	78
" 2	78	94	1.10	1.25	1.41	1.57
" 3	1.18	1.41	1.65	1.88	2.12	2.35
" 4	1.57	1.88	2.19	2.51	2.82	3.13
" 5	1.96	2.35	2.74	3.13	3.53	3.92
" 6	2.35	2.82	3.29	3.76	4.23	4.70
" 7	2.74	3.29	3.84	4.39	4.94	5.48
" 8	3.13	3.76	4.39	5.01	5.64	6.27
" 9	3.53	4.23	4.94	5.64	6 35	7.05
" 10	3.92	4.70	5.48	6.27	7.05	7.83
" 11	4.31	5.17	6.03	6.89	7.76	8.62
Yrs. 1	4.70	5.64	6.58	7.52	8.46	9.40
" 2	9.40	11.28	13.16	15.04	16.92	18.80
" 3	14.10	16.92	19.74	22.56	25.38	28.20
" 4	18.80	22.56	26.32	30.08	33.84	37.60
Com. 2	9.64	11.62	13.62	15.64	17.68	19.74
" 3	14.82	17.96	21.15	24 41	27.73	31.11
" 4	20.26	24.67	29.21	33.89	38.69	43.63
" 5	25.97	31.79	37.84	44.12	50.63	57.39
" 6	31.97	39.34	47.07	55.17	63.65	72.53

TIME.	5 %	6 %	7 %	8 %	9 %	10 %
Days 1	1	2	2	2	2	3
" 2	3	3	4	4	5	5
" 3	4	5	6	6	7	8
" 4	5	6	7	8	10	11
" 5	7	8	9	11	12	13
" 6	8	10	11	13	14	16
" 7	9	11	13	15	17	18
" 8	11	13	15	17	19	21
" 9	12	14	17	19	21	24
" 10	13	16	18	21	24	26
" 11	15	17	20	23	26	29
" 12	16	19	22	25	29	32
" 13	17	21	24	27	31	34
" 14	18	22	26	30	33	37
" 15	20	24	28	32	36	40
" 16	21	25	30	34	38	42
" 17	22	27	31	36	40	45
" 18	24	29	33	38	43	48
" 19	25	30	35	40	45	50
" 20	26	32	37	42	48	53
" 21	28	33	39	44	50	55
" 22	29	35	41	46	52	58
" 23	30	36	42	49	55	61
" 24	32	38	44	51	57	63
" 25	33	40	46	53	59	66
" 26	34	41	48	55	62	69
" 27	36	43	50	57	64	71
" 28	37	44	52	59	67	74
" 29	38	46	54	61	69	77
Mos. 1	40	48	55	63	71	79
" 2	79	95	1.11	1.27	1.43	1.58
" 3	1.19	1.43	1.66	1.90	2.14	2.38
" 4	1.58	1.90	2.22	2.53	2.85	3.17
" 5	1.98	2.38	2.77	3.17	3.56	3.96
" 6	2.38	2.85	3.33	3.80	4.28	4.75
" 7	2.77	3.33	3.88	4.43	4.99	5.54
" 8	3.17	3.80	4.43	5.07	5.70	6.33
" 9	3.56	4.28	4.99	5.70	6.41	7.13
" 10	3.96	4.75	5.54	6.33	7.13	7.92
" 11	4.35	5.23	6.10	6.97	7.84	8.71
Yrs. 1	4.75	5.70	6.65	7.60	8.55	9.50
" 2	9.50	11.40	13.30	15.20	17.10	19.00
" 3	14.25	17.10	19.95	22.80	25.65	28.50
" 4	19 00	22.80	26.60	30.40	34.20	38.00
Com. 2	9.74	11.74	13.77	15.81	17.87	19.95
" 3	14.97	18.15	21.38	24.67	28.03	31.45
" 4	20.47	24.94	29.53	34.25	39.10	44.09
" 5	26.25	32.13	38.24	44.59	51.17	58.00
" 6	32.31	39.76	47.57	55.75	64.32	73.30

TIME.	5 %	6 %	7 %	8 %	9 %	10 %
Days 1	1	2	2	2	2	3
" 2	3	3	4	4	5	5
" 3	4	5	6	6	7	8
" 4	5	6	7	9	10	11
" 5	7	8	9	11	12	13
" 6	8	10	11	13	14	16
" 7	9	11	13	15	17	19
" 8	11	13	15	17	19	21
" 9	12	14	17	19	22	24
" 10	13	16	19	21	24	27
" 11	15	18	21	23	26	29
" 12	16	19	22	26	29	32
" 13	17	21	24	28	31	35
" 14	19	22	26	30	34	37
" 15	20	24	28	32	36	40
" 16	21	26	30	34	38	43
" 17	23	27	32	36	41	4b
" 18	24	29	34	38	43	48
" 19	25	30	35	41	46	51
" 20	27	32	37	43	48	53
" 21	28	34	39	45	50	56
" 22	29	35	41	47	53	59
" 23	31	37	43	49	55	61
" 24	32	38	45	51	58	64
" 25	33	40	47	53	60	67
" 26	35	42	49	55	62	69
" 27	36	43	50	58	65	72
" 28	37	45	52	60	67	75
" 29	39	46	54	62	70	77
Mos. 1	40	48	56	64	72	80
" 2	80	96	1.12	1.28	1.44	1.60
" 3	1.20	1.44	1.68	1.92	2.16	2.40
" 4	1.60	1.92	2.24	2.56	2.88	3.20
" 5	2.00	2.40	2.80	3.20	3.60	4.00
" 6	2.40	2.88	3.36	3.84	4.32	4.80
" 7	2.80	3.36	3.92	4.48	5.04	5.60
" 8	3.20	3.84	4.48	5.12	5.76	6.40
" 9	3.60	4.32	5.04	5.76	6.48	7.20
" 10	4.00	4.80	5.60	6.40	7.20	8.00
" 11	4.40	5.28	6.16	7.04	7.92	8.80
Yrs. 1	4.80	5.76	6.72	7.68	8.64	9.60
" 2	9.60	11.52	13.44	15.36	17.28	19.20
" 3	14.40	17.28	20.16	23.04	25.92	28.80
" 4	19.20	23.04	26.88	30.72	34.56	38.40
Com. 2	9.84	11.87	13.91	15.97	18 06	20.16
" 3	15.13	18.34	21.60	24.93	28.32	31.78
" 4	20.69	25.20	29.84	34.61	39.51	44.55
" 5	26.52	32.47	38.64	45.06	51.71	58.61
" 6	32.65	40.18	48.07	56.34	65.00	74.07

TIME		5 %	6 %	7 %	8 %	9 %	10 %
Days	1	1	2	2	2	2	3
"	2	3	3	4	4	5	5
"	3	4	5	6	6	7	8
"	4	5	6	8	9	10	11
"	5	7	8	9	11	12	13
"	6	8	10	11	13	15	16
"	7	9	11	13	15	17	19
"	8	11	13	15	17	19	22
"	9	12	15	17	19	22	24
"	10	13	16	19	22	24	27
"	11	15	18	21	24	27	30
"	12	16	19	23	26	29	32
"	13	18	21	25	28	32	35
"	14	19	23	26	30	34	38
"	15	20	24	28	32	36	40
"	16	22	26	30	34	39	43
"	17	23	27	32	37	41	46
"	18	24	29	34	39	44	49
"	19	26	31	36	41	46	51
"	20	27	32	38	43	49	54
"	21	28	34	40	45	51	57
"	22	30	36	41	47	53	59
"	23	31	37	43	50	56	62
"	24	32	39	45	52	58	65
"	25	34	40	47	54	61	67
"	26	35	42	49	56	63	70
"	27	36	44	51	58	65	73
"	28	38	45	53	60	68	75
"	29	39	47	55	63	70	78
Mos.	1	40	49	57	65	73	81
"	2	81	97	1.13	1.29	1.46	1.62
"	3	1.21	1.46	1.70	1.94	2.18	2.43
"	4	1.62	1.94	2.26	2.59	2.91	3.23
"	5	2.02	2.43	2.83	3.23	3.64	4.04
"	6	2.43	2.91	3.40	3.88	4.37	4.85
"	7	2.83	3.40	3.96	4.53	5.09	5.66
"	8	3.23	3.88	4.53	5.17	5.82	6.47
"	9	3.64	4.37	5.09	5.82	6.55	7.28
"	10	4.04	4.85	5.66	6.47	7.28	8.08
"	11	4.45	5.34	6.22	7.11	8.00	8.89
Yrs.	1	4.85	5.82	6.79	7.76	8.73	9.70
"	2	9.70	11.64	13.58	15.52	17.46	19.40
"	3	14.55	17.46	20.37	23.28	26.19	29.10
"	4	19.40	23.28	27.16	31.04	34.92	38.80
Com.	2	9.94	11.99	14.06	16.14	18.25	20.37
"	3	15.29	18.53	21.83	25.19	28.62	32.11
"	4	20.90	25.46	30.15	34.97	39.92	45.02
"	5	26.80	32.81	39.05	45.52	52.25	59.22
"	6	32.99	40.60	48.57	56.93	65.68	74.84

TIME.	5 %	6 %	7 %	8 %	9 %	10 %
Days 1	1	2	2	2	2	3
" 2	3	3	4	4	5	5
" 3	4	5	6	7	7	8
" 4	5	7	8	9	10	11
" 5	7	8	10	11	12	14
" 6	8	10	11	13	15	16
" 7	10	11	13	15	17	19
" 8	11	13	15	17	20	22
" 9	12	15	17	20	22	25
" 10	14	16	19	22	25	27
" 11	15	18	21	24	27	30
" 12	16	20	23	26	29	33
" 13	18	21	25	28	32	35
" 14	19	23	27	30	34	38
" 15	20	25	29	33	37	41
" 16	22	26	30	35	39	44
" 17	23	28	32	37	42	46
" 18	25	29	34	39	44	49
" 19	26	31	36	41	47	52
" 20	27	33	38	44	49	54
" 21	29	34	40	46	51	57
" 22	30	36	42	48	54	60
" 23	31	38	44	50	56	63
" 24	33	39	46	52	59	65
" 25	34	41	48	54	61	68
" 26	35	42	50	57	64	71
" 27	37	44	51	59	66	74
" 28	38	46	53	61	69	76
" 29	39	47	55	63	71	79
Mos. 1	41	49	57	65	74	82
" 2	82	98	1.14	1.31	1.47	1.63
" 3	1.23	1.47	1.72	1.96	2.21	2.45
" 4	1.63	1.96	2.29	2.61	2.94	3.27
" 5	2.04	2.45	2.86	3.27	3.68	4.08
" 6	2.45	2.94	3.43	3.92	4.41	4.90
" 7	2.86	3.43	4.00	4.57	5.15	5.72
" 8	3.27	3.92	4.57	5.23	5.88	6.53
" 9	3.68	4.41	5.15	5.88	6.62	7.35
" 10	4.08	4.90	5.72	6.53	7.35	8.17
" 11	4.49	5.39	6.29	7.19	8.09	8.98
Yrs. 1	4.90	5.88	6.86	7.84	8.82	9.80
" 2	9.80	11.76	13.72	15.68	17.64	19.60
" 3	14.70	17.64	20.58	23.52	26.46	29.40
" 4	19.60	23.52	27.44	31.36	35.28	39.20
Com. 2	10.05	12.11	14.20	16.31	18.43	20.58
" 3	15.45	18.72	22.05	25.45	28.91	32.44
" 4	21.12	25.72	30.46	35.33	40.33	45.48
" 5	27.08	33.15	39.45	45.99	52.79	59.83
" 6	33.33	41.01	49.07	57.52	66.36	75.61

TIME.		5 %	6 %	7 %	8 %	9 %	10 %
Days	1	1	2	2	2	2	3
"	2	3	3	4	4	5	6
'	3	4	5	6	7	7	8
"	4	6	7	8	9	10	11
"	5	7	8	10	11	12	14
"	6	8	10	12	13	15	17
"	7	10	12	13	15	17	19
"	8	11	13	15	18	20	22
"	9	12	15	17	20	22	25
"	10	14	17	19	22	25	28
"	11	15	18	21	24	27	30
"	12	17	20	23	26	30	33
"	13	18	21	25	29	32	36
"	14	19	23	27	31	35	39
"	15	21	25	29	33	37	41
"	16	22	26	31	35	40	44
"	17	23	28	33	37	42	47
"	18	25	30	35	40	45	50
"	19	26	31	37	42	47	52
"	20	28	33	39	44	50	55
"	21	29	35	40	46	52	58
"	22	30	36	42	48	54	61
"	23	32	38	44	51	57	63
"	24	33	40	46	53	59	66
"	25	34	41	48	55	62	69
"	26	36	43	50	57	64	72
"	27	37	45	52	59	67	74
"	28	39	46	54	62	69	77
"	29	40	48	56	64	72	80
Mos.	1	41	50	58	66	74	83
"	2	83	99	1.16	1.32	1.49	1.65
"	3	1.24	1.49	1.73	1.98	2.23	2.48
"	4	1.65	1.98	2.31	2.64	2.97	3.30
"	5	2.06	2.48	2.89	3.30	3.71	4.13
"	6	2.48	2.97	3.47	3.96	4.46	4.95
"	7	2.89	3.47	4.04	4.62	5.20	5.78
"	8	3.30	3.96	4.62	5.28	5.94	6.60
"	9	3.71	4.46	5.20	5.94	6.68	7.43
"	10	4.13	4.95	5.78	6.60	7.43	8.25
"	11	4.54	5.45	6.35	7.26	8.17	9.08
Yrs.	1	4.95	5.94	6.93	7.92	8.91	9.90
"	2	9.90	11.88	13.86	15.84	17.82	19.80
"	3	14.85	17.82	20.79	23.76	26.73	29.70
"	4	19.80	23.76	27.72	31.68	35.64	39.60
Ccm.	2	10.15	12.24	14.35	16.47	18.62	20.79
"	3	15.60	18.91	22.28	25.71	29.21	32.77
"	4	21.34	25.99	30.77	35.69	40.75	45.95
"	5	27.35	33.48	39.85	46.46	53.32	60.44
"	6	33.67	41.43	49.57	58.10	67.03	76.38

100 Dollars.

TIME.	5 %	6 %	7 %	8 %	9 %	10 %
Days 1	1	2	2	2	3	3
" 2	3	3	4	4	5	6
" 3	4	5	6	7	8	8
" 4	6	7	8	9	10	11
" 5	7	8	10	11	13	14
" 6	8	10	12	13	15	17
" 7	10	12	14	16	18	19
" 8	11	13	16	18	20	22
" 9	13	15	18	20	23	25
" 10	14	17	19	22	25	28
" 11	15	18	21	24	28	31
" 12	17	20	23	27	30	33
" 13	18	22	25	29	33	36
" 14	19	23	27	31	35	39
" 15	21	25	29	33	38	42
" 16	22	27	31	36	40	44
" 17	24	28	33	38	43	47
" 18	25	30	35	40	45	50
" 19	26	32	37	42	48	53
" 20	28	33	39	44	50	56
" 21	29	35	41	47	53	58
" 22	31	37	43	49	55	61
" 23	32	38	45	51	58	64
" 24	33	40	47	53	60	67
" 25	35	42	49	56	63	69
" 26	36	43	51	58	65	72
" 27	38	45	53	60	68	75
" 28	39	47	54	62	70	78
" 29	40	48	56	64	73	81
Mos. 1	42	50	58	67	75	83
" 2	83	1.00	1.17	1.33	1.50	1.67
" 3	1.25	1.50	1.75	2.00	2.25	2.50
" 4	1.67	2.00	2.33	2.67	3.00	3.33
" 5	2.08	2.50	2.92	3.33	3.75	4.17
" 6	2.50	3.00	3.50	4.00	4.50	5.00
" 7	2.92	3.50	4.08	4.67	5.25	5.83
" 8	3.33	4.00	4.67	5.33	6.00	6.67
" 9	3.75	4.50	5.25	6.00	6.75	7.50
" 10	4.17	5.00	5.83	6.67	7.50	8.33
" 11	4.58	5.50	6.42	7.33	8.25	9.17
Yrs. 1	5.00	6.00	7.00	8.00	9.00	10.00
" 2	10.00	12.00	14.00	16.00	18.00	20.00
" 3	15.00	18.00	21.00	24.00	27.00	30.00
" 4	20.00	24.00	28.00	32.00	36.00	40.00
Com. 2	10.25	12.36	14.49	16.64	18.81	21.00
" 3	15.76	19.10	22.50	25.97	29.50	33.10
" 4	21.55	26.25	31.08	36.05	41.16	46.41
" 5	27.63	33.82	40.26	46.93	53.86	61.05
" 6	34.01	41.85	50.07	58.69	67.71	77.16

TIME.	5 %	6 %	7 %	8 %	9 %	10 %
Days 1	3	3	4	4	5	6
" 2	6	7	8	9	10	11
" 3	8	10	12	13	15	17
" 4	11	13	16	18	20	22
" 5	14	17	19	22	25	28
" 6	17	20	23	27	30	33
" 7	19	23	27	31	35	39
" 8	22	27	31	36	40	44
" 9	25	30	35	40	45	50
" 10	28	33	39	44	50	56
" 11	31	37	43	49	55	61
" 12	33	40	47	53	60	67
" 13	36	43	51	58	65	72
" 14	39	47	54	62	70	78
" 15	42	50	58	67	75	83
" 16	44	53	62	71	80	89
" 17	47	57	66	76	85	94
" 18	50	60	70	80	90	1.00
" 19	53	63	74	84	95	1.06
" 20	56	67	78	89	1.00	1.11
" 21	58	70	82	93	1.05	1.17
" 22	61	73	86	98	1.10	1.22
" 23	64	77	89	1.02	1.15	1.28
" 24	67	80	93	1.07	1.20	1.33
" 25	69	83	97	1.11	1.25	1.39
" 26	72	87	1.01	1.16	1.30	1.44
" 27	75	90	1.05	1.20	1.35	1.50
" 28	78	93	1.09	1.24	1.40	1.56
" 29	81	97	1.13	1.29	1.45	1.61
Mos. 1	83	1.00	1.17	1.33	1.50	1.67
" 2	1.67	2.00	2.33	2.67	3.00	3.33
" 3	2.50	3 00	3.50	4.00	4.50	5.00
" 4	3.33	4.00	4.67	5.33	6.00	6.67
" 5	4.17	5.00	5.83	6.67	7.50	8.33
" 6	5.00	6.00	7.00	8.00	9.00	10.00
" 7	5.83	7.00	8.17	9.33	10.50	11.67
" 8	6.67	8.00	9.33	10.67	12.00	13.33
" 9	7.50	9.00	10.50	12.00	13.50	15.00
" 10	8.33	10.00	11.67	13.33	15.00	16.67
" 11	9.17	11.00	12.83	14.67	16.50	18.33
Yrs. 1	10.00	12.00	14.00	16.00	18.00	20.00
" 2	20.00	24.00	28.00	32.00	36.00	40.00
" 3	30.00	36.00	42.00	48.00	54.00	60 00
" 4	40.00	48.00	56.00	64.00	72.00	80.00
Com. 2	20.50	24.72	28.98	33.28	37.62	42.00
" 3	31.53	38.20	45.01	51.94	59.01	66.20
" 4	43.10	52.50	62.16	72.10	82.32	92.82
" 5	55.26	67.65	80.51	93.87	107.72	122.10
" 6	68.02	83.70	100.15	117.37	135.42	154.31

300 Dollars.

TIME.	5 %	6 %	7 %	8 %	9 %	10 %
Days 1	4	5	6	7	8	8
" 2	8	10	12	13	15	17
" 3	13	15	18	20	23	25
" 4	17	20	23	27	30	33
" 5	21	25	29	33	38	42
" 6	25	30	35	40	45	50
" 7	29	35	41	47	53	58
" 8	33	40	47	53	60	67
" 9	38	45	53	60	68	75
" 10	42	50	58	67	75	83
" 11	46	55	64	73	83	92
" 12	50	60	70	80	90	1.00
" 13	54	65	76	87	98	1.08
" 14	58	70	82	93	1.05	1.17
" 15	63	75	88	1.00	1.13	1.25
" 16	67	80	93	1.07	1.20	1.33
" 17	71	85	99	1.13	1.28	1.42
" 18	75	90	1.05	1.20	1.35	1.50
" 19	79	95	1.11	1.27	1.43	1.58
" 20	83	1.00	1.17	1.33	1.50	1.67
" 21	88	1.05	1.23	1.40	1.58	1.75
" 22	92	1.10	1.28	1.47	1.65	1.83
" 23	96	1.15	1.34	1.53	1.73	1.92
" 24	1.00	1.20	1.40	1.60	1.80	2.00
" 25	1.04	1.25	1.46	1.67	1.88	2.08
" 26	1.08	1.30	1.52	1.73	1.95	2.17
" 27	1.13	1.35	1.58	1.80	2.03	2.25
" 28	1.17	1.40	1.63	1.87	2.10	2.33
" 29	1.21	1.45	1.69	1.93	2.18	2.42
Mos. 1	1.25	1.50	1.75	2.00	2.25	2.50
" 2	2.50	3.00	3.50	4.00	4.50	5.00
" 3	3.75	4.50	5.25	6.00	6.75	7.50
" 4	5.00	6.00	7.00	8.00	9.00	10.00
" 5	6.25	7.50	8.75	10.00	11.25	12.50
" 6	7.50	9.00	10.50	12.00	13.50	15.00
" 7	8.75	10.50	12.25	14.00	15.75	17.50
" 8	10.00	12.00	14.00	16.00	18.00	20.00
" 9	11.25	13.50	15.75	18.00	20.25	22.50
" 10	12.50	15.00	17.50	20.00	22.50	25.00
" 11	13.75	16.50	19.25	22.00	24.75	27.50
Yrs. 1	15.00	18.00	21.00	24.00	27.00	30.00
" 2	30.00	36.00	42.00	48.00	54.00	60.00
" 3	45.00	54.00	63.00	72.00	81.00	90.00
" 4	60.00	72.00	84.00	96.00	108.00	120.00
Com. 2	30.75	37.08	43.47	49.92	56.43	63.00
" 3	47.29	57.30	67.51	77.91	88.51	99.20
" 4	64.65	78.74	93.24	108.15	123.47	139.23
" 5	82.88	101.47	120.77	140.80	161.59	183.15
" 6	102.03	125.56	150.22	176.06	203.13	231.47

400 Dollars.

TIME.	5 %	6 %	7 %	8 %	9 %	10 %
Days 1	6	7	8	9	10	11
" 2	11	13	16	18	20	22
" 3	17	20	23	27	30	33
" 4	22	27	31	36	40	44
" 5	28	33	39	44	50	56
" 6	33	40	47	53	60	67
" 7	39	47	54	62	70	78
" 8	44	53	62	71	80	89
" 9	50	60	70	80	90	1.00
" 10	56	67	78	89	1.00	1.11
" 11	61	73	86	98	1.10	1.22
" 12	67	80	93	1.07	1.20	1.33
" 13	72	87	1.01	1.16	1.30	1.44
" 14	78	93	1.09	1.24	1.40	1.56
" 15	83	1.00	1.17	1.33	1.50	1.67
" 16	89	1.07	1.24	1.42	1.60	1.78
" 17	94	1.13	1.32	1.51	1.70	1.89
" 18	1.00	1.20	1.40	1.60	1.80	2.00
" 19	1.06	1.27	1.48	1.69	1.90	2.11
" 20	1.11	1.33	1.56	1.78	2.00	2.22
" 21	1.17	1.40	1.63	1.87	2.10	2.33
" 22	1.22	1.47	1.71	1.96	2.20	2.44
" 23	1.28	1 53	1.79	2.04	2.30	2.56
" 24	1.33	1.60	1.87	2.13	2.40	2.67
" 25	1.39	1.67	1.94	2.22	2.50	2.78
" 26	1.44	1.73	2.02	2.31	2.60	2.89
" 27	1.50	1.80	2.10	2.40	2.70	3.00
" 28	1.56	1.87	2.18	2.49	2.80	3.11
" 29	1.61	1.93	2.26	2.58	2.90	3.22
Mos. 1	1.67	2.00	2.33	2.67	3.00	3.33
" 2	3.33	4.00	4.67	5.33	6.00	6.67
" 3	5.00	6.00	7.00	8.00	9.00	10.00
" 4	6.67	8.00	9.33	10.67	12.00	13.33
" 5	8.33	10.00	11.67	13.33	15.00	16.67
" 6	10.00	12.00	14.00	16.00	18.00	20.00
" 7	11.67	14.00	16.33	18.67	21.00	23.33
" 8	13.33	16.00	18.67	21.33	24.00	26.67
" 9	15.00	18.00	21.00	24.00	27.00	30.00
" 10	16.67	20.00	23.33	26.67	30.00	33.33
" 11	18.33	22.00	25.67	29.33	33.00	36.67
Yrs. 1	20.00	24.00	28.00	32.00	36.00	40.00
" 2	40.00	48.00	56.00	64.00	72.00	80.00
" 3	60.00	72.00	84.00	96.00	108.00	120.00
" 4	80.00	96.00	112.00	128.00	144.00	160.00
Com. 2	41.00	49.44	57.96	66.56	75.24	84.00
" 3	63.05	76.41	90.02	103.88	118.01	132.40
" 4	86.20	104.99	124.32	144.20	164.63	185.64
" 5	110.51	135.29	161.02	187.73	215.45	244.20
" 6	136.04	167.41	200.29	234.75	270.84	308.62

500 Dollars.

TIME.	5 %	6 %	7 %	8 %	9 %	10 %
Days 1	7	8	10	11	13	14
" 2	14	17	19	22	25	28
" 3	21	25	29	33	38	42
" 4	28	33	39	44	50	56
" 5	35	42	49	56	63	69
" 6	42	50	58	67	75	83
" 7	49	58	68	78	88	97
" 8	56	67	78	89	1.00	1.11
" 9	63	75	88	1.00	1.13	1.25
" 10	69	83	97	1.11	1.25	1.39
" 11	76	92	1.07	1.22	1.38	1.53
" 12	83	1.00	1.17	1.33	1.50	1.67
" 13	90	1.08	1.26	1.44	1.63	1.81
" 14	97	1.17	1.36	1.56	1.75	1.94
" 15	1.04	1.25	1.46	1.67	1.88	2.08
" 16	1.11	1.33	1.56	1.78	2.00	2.22
" 17	1.18	1.42	1.65	1.89	2.13	2.36
" 18	1.25	1.50	1.75	2.00	2.25	2.50
" 19	1.32	1.58	1.85	2.11	2.38	2.64
" 20	1.39	1.67	1.94	2.22	2.50	2.78
" 21	1.46	1.75	2.04	2.33	2.63	2.92
" 22	1.53	1.83	2.14	2.44	2.75	3.06
" 23	1.60	1.92	2.24	2.56	2.88	3.19
" 24	1.67	2.00	2.33	2.67	3.00	3.33
" 25	1.74	2.08	2.43	2.78	3.13	3.47
" 26	1.81	2.17	2.53	2.89	3.25	3.61
" 27	1.88	2.25	2.63	3.00	3.38	3.75
" 28	1.94	2.33	2.72	3.11	3.50	3.89
" 29	2.01	2.42	2.82	3.22	3.63	4.03
Mos. 1	2.08	2.50	2.92	3.33	3.75	4.17
" 2	4.17	5.00	5.83	6.67	7.50	8.33
" 3	6.25	7.50	8.75	10.00	11.25	12.50
" 4	8.33	10.00	11.67	13.33	15.00	16.67
" 5	10.42	12.50	14.58	16.67	18.75	20.83
" 6	12.50	15.00	17.50	20.00	22.50	25.00
" 7	14.58	17.50	20.42	23.33	26.25	29.17
" 8	16.67	20.00	23.33	26.67	30.00	33.33
" 9	18.75	22.50	26.25	30.00	33.75	37.50
" 10	20.83	25.00	29.17	33.33	37.50	41.67
" 11	22.92	27.50	32.08	36.67	41.25	45.83
Yrs. 1	25.00	30.00	35.00	40.00	45.00	50.00
" 2	50.00	60.00	70.00	80.00	90.00	100.00
" 3	75.00	90.00	105.00	120.00	135.00	150.00
" 4	100.00	120.00	140.00	160.00	180.00	200.00
Com. 2	51.25	61.80	72.45	83.20	94.05	105.00
" 3	78.81	95.51	112.52	129.86	147.51	165.50
" 4	107.75	131.24	155.40	180.24	205.79	232.05
" 5	138.14	169.11	201.28	234.66	269.31	305.26
" 6	170.05	209.26	250.37	293.44	338.55	385.78

600 DOLLARS.

TIME.	5 %	6 %	7 %	8 %	9 %	10 %
Days 1	8	10	12	13	15	17
" 2	17	20	23	27	30	33
" 3	25	30	35	40	45	50
" 4	33	40	47	53	60	67
" 5	42	50	58	67	75	83
" 6	50	60	70	80	90	1.00
" 7	58	70	82	93	1.05	1.17
" 8	67	80	93	1.07	1.20	1.33
" 9	75	90	1.05	1.20	1.35	1.50
" 10	83	1.00	1.17	1.33	1.50	1.67
" 11	92	1.10	1.28	1.47	1.65	1.83
" 12	1.00	1.20	1.40	1.60	1.80	2.00
" 13	1.08	1.30	1.52	1.73	1.95	2.17
" 14	1.17	1.40	1.63	1.87	2.10	2.33
" 15	1.25	1.50	1.75	2.00	2.25	2.50
" 16	1.33	1.60	1.87	2.13	2.40	2.67
" 17	1.42	1.70	1.98	2.27	2.55	2.83
" 18	1.50	1.80	2.10	2.40	2.70	3.00
" 19	1.58	1.90	2.22	2.53	2.85	3.17
" 20	1.67	2.00	2.33	2.67	3.00	3.33
" 21	1.75	2.10	2.45	2.80	3.15	3.50
" 22	1.83	2.20	2.57	2.93	3.30	3.67
" 23	1.92	2.30	2.68	3.07	3.45	3.83
" 24	2.00	2.40	2.80	3.20	3.60	4.00
" 25	2.08	2.50	2.92	3.33	3.75	4.17
" 26	2.17	2.60	3.03	3.47	3.90	4.33
" 27	2.25	2.70	3.15	3.60	4.05	4.50
" 28	2.33	2.80	3.27	3.73	4.20	4.67
" 29	2.42	2.90	3.38	3.87	4.35	4.83
Mos. 1	2.50	3.00	3.50	4.00	4.50	5.00
" 2	5.00	6.00	7.00	8.00	9.00	10.00
" 3	7.50	9.00	10.50	12.00	13.50	15.00
" 4	10.00	12.00	14.00	16.00	18.00	20.00
" 5	12.50	15.00	17.50	20.00	22.50	25.00
" 6	15.00	18.00	21.00	24.00	27.00	30.00
" 7	17.50	21.00	24.50	28.00	31.50	35.00
" 8	20.00	24.00	28.00	32.00	36.00	40.00
" 9	22.50	27.00	31.50	36.00	40.50	45.00
" 10	25.00	30.00	35.00	40.00	45.00	50.00
" 11	27.50	33.00	38.50	44.00	49.50	55.00
Yrs. 1	30.00	36.00	42.00	48.00	54.00	60.00
" 2	60.00	72.00	84.00	96.00	108.00	120.00
" 3	90.00	108.00	126.00	144.00	162.00	180.00
" 4	120.00	144.00	168.00	192.00	216.00	240.00
Com. 2	61.50	74.16	86.94	99.84	112.86	126.00
" 3	94.58	114.61	135.03	155.83	177.02	198.60
" 4	129.30	157.49	186.48	216.29	246.95	278.46
" 5	165.77	202.94	241.53	281.60	323.17	366.31
" 6	204.06	251.11	300.43	352.12	406.26	462.94

TIME.	5 %	6 %	7 %	8 %	9 %	10 %
Days 1	10	12	14	16	18	19
" 2	19	23	27	31	35	39
" 3	29	35	41	47	53	58
" 4	39	47	54	62	70	78
" 5	49	58	68	78	88	97
" 6	58	70	82	93	1.05	1.17
" 7	68	82	95	1.09	1.23	1.36
" 8	78	93	1.09	1.24	1.40	1.56
" 9	88	1.05	1.23	1.40	1.58	1.75
" 10	97	1.17	1.36	1.56	1.75	1.94
" 11	1.07	1.28	1.50	1.71	1.93	2.14
" 12	1.17	1.40	1.63	1.87	2.10	2.33
" 13	1.26	1.52	1.77	2.02	2.28	2.53
" 14	1.36	1.63	1.91	2.18	2.45	2.72
" 15	1.46	1.75	2.04	2.33	2.63	2.92
" 16	1.56	1.87	2.18	2.49	2.80	3.11
" 17	1.65	1.98	2.31	2.64	2.98	3.31
" 18	1.75	2.10	2.45	2.80	3.15	3.50
" 19	1.85	2.22	2.59	2.96	3.33	3.69
" 20	1.94	2.33	2.72	3.11	3.50	3.89
" 21	2.04	2.45	2.86	3.27	3.68	4.08
" 22	2.14	2.57	2.99	3.42	3.85	4.28
" 23	2.24	2.68	3.13	3.58	4.03	4.47
" 24	2.33	2.80	3.27	3.73	4.20	4.67
" 25	2.43	2.92	3.40	3.89	4.38	4.86
" 26	2.53	3.03	3.54	4.04	4.55	5.06
" 27	2.63	3.15	3.68	4.20	4.73	5.25
" 28	2.72	3.27	3.81	4.36	4.90	5.44
" 29	2.82	3.38	3.95	4.51	5.08	5.64
Mos. 1	2.92	3.50	4.08	4.67	5.25	5.83
" 2	5.83	7.00	8.17	9.33	10.50	11.67
" 3	8.75	10.50	12.25	14.00	15.75	17.50
" 4	11.67	14.00	16.33	18.67	21.00	23.33
" 5	14.58	17.50	20.42	23.33	26.25	29.17
" 6	17.50	21.00	24.50	28.00	31.50	35.00
" 7	20.42	24.50	28.58	32.67	36.75	40.83
" 8	23.33	28.00	32.67	37.33	42.00	46.67
" 9	26.25	31.50	36.75	42.00	47.25	52.50
" 10	29.17	35.00	40.83	46.67	52.50	58.33
" 11	32.08	38.50	44.92	51.33	57.75	64.17
Yrs. 1	35.00	42.00	49.00	56.00	63.00	70.00
" 2	70.00	84.00	98.00	112.00	126.00	140.00
" 3	105.00	126.00	147.00	168.00	189.00	210.00
" 4	140.00	168.00	196.00	224.00	252.00	280.00
Com. 2	71.75	86.52	101.43	116.48	131.67	147.00
" 3	110.34	133.71	157.53	181.80	206.52	231.70
" 4	150.85	183.73	217.56	252.34	288.11	324.87
" 5	193.40	236.76	281.79	328.53	377.04	427.38
" 6	238.07	292.96	350.51	410.81	473.97	540.09

TIME.	5 %	6 %	7 %	8 %	9 %	10 %
Days 1	11	13	16	18	20	22
" 2	22	27	31	36	40	44
" 3	33	40	47	53	60	67
" 4	44	53	62	71	80	89
" 5	56	67	78	89	1.00	1.11
" 6	67	80	93	1.07	1.20	1.33
" 7	78	93	1.09	1.24	1.40	1.56
" 8	89	1.07	1.24	1.42	1.60	1.78
" 9	1.00	1.20	1.40	1.60	1.80	2.00
" 10	1.11	1.33	1.56	1.78	2.00	2.22
" 11	1.22	1.47	1.71	1.96	2.20	2.44
" 12	1.33	1.60	1.87	2.13	2.40	2.67
" 13	1.44	1.73	2.02	2.31	2.60	2.89
" 14	1.56	1.87	2.18	2.49	2.80	3.11
" 15	1.67	2.00	2.33	2.67	3.00	3.33
" 16	1.78	2.13	2.49	2.84	3.20	3.56
" 17	1.89	2.27	2.64	3.02	3.40	3.78
" 18	2.00	2.40	2.80	3.20	3.60	4.00
" 19	2.11	2.53	2.96	3.38	3.80	4.22
" 20	2.22	2.67	3.11	3.56	4.00	4.44
" 21	2.33	2.80	3.27	3.73	4.20	4.67
" 22	2.44	2.93	3.42	3.91	4.40	4.89
" 23	2.56	3.07	3.58	4.09	4.60	5.11
" 24	2.67	3.20	3.73	4.27	4.80	5.33
" 25	2.78	3.33	3.89	4.44	5.00	5.56
" 26	2.89	3.47	4.04	4.62	5.20	5.78
" 27	3.00	3.60	4.20	4.80	5.40	6.00
" 28	3.11	3.73	4.36	4.98	5.60	6.22
" 29	3.22	3.87	4.51	5.16	5.80	6.44
Mos. 1	3.33	4.00	4.67	5.33	6.00	6.67
" 2	6.67	8.00	9.33	10.67	12.00	13.33
" 3	10.00	12.00	14.00	16.00	18.00	20.00
" 4	13.33	16.00	18.67	21.33	24.00	26.67
" 5	16.67	20.00	23.33	26.67	30.00	33.33
" 6	20.00	24.00	28.00	32.00	36.00	40.00
" 7	23.33	28.00	32.67	37.33	42.00	46.67
" 8	26.67	32.00	37.33	42.67	48.00	53.33
" 9	30.00	36.00	42.00	48.00	54.00	60.00
" 10	33.33	40.00	46.67	53.33	60.00	66.67
" 11	36.67	44.00	51.33	58.67	66.00	73.33
Yrs. 1	40.00	48.00	56.00	64.00	72.00	80.00
" 2	80.00	96.00	112.00	128.00	144.00	160.00
" 3	120.00	144.00	168.00	192.00	216.00	240.00
" 4	160.00	192.00	224.00	256.00	288.00	320.00
Com. 2	82.00	98.88	115.92	133.12	150.48	168 00
" 3	126.10	152.81	180.03	207.77	236.02	264.80
" 4	172.41	209.98	248.64	288.39	329.27	371.28
" 5	221.03	270.58	322.04	375.46	430.90	488.41
" 6	272.08	334.82	400.58	469.50	541.68	617.25

TIME.	5 %	6 %	7 %	8 %	9 %	10 %
Days 1	13	15	18	20	23	25
" 2	25	30	35	40	45	50
" 3	38	45	53	60	68	75
" 4	50	60	70	80	90	1.00
" 5	63	75	88	1.00	1.13	1.25
" 6	75	90	1.05	1.20	1.35	1.50
" 7	88	1.05	1.23	1.40	1.58	1.75
" 8	1.00	1.20	1.40	1.60	1.80	2.00
" 9	1.13	1.35	1.58	1.80	2.03	2.25
" 10	1.25	1.50	1.75	2.00	2.25	2.50
" 11	1.38	1.65	1.93	2.20	2.48	2.75
" 12	1.50	1.80	2.10	2.40	2.70	3.00
" 13	1.63	1.95	2.28	2.60	2.93	3.25
" 14	1.75	2.10	2.45	2.80	3.15	3.50
" 15	1.88	2.25	2.63	3.00	3.38	3.75
" 16	2.00	2.40	2.80	3.20	3.60	4.00
" 17	2.13	2.55	2.98	3.40	3.83	4.25
" 18	2.25	2.70	3.15	3.60	4.05	4.50
" 19	2.38	2.85	3.33	3.80	4.28	4.75
" 20	2.50	3.00	3.50	4.00	4.50	5.00
" 21	2.63	3.15	3.68	4.20	4.73	5.25
" 22	2.75	3.30	3.85	4.40	4.95	5.50
" 23	2.88	3.45	4.03	4.60	5.18	5.75
" 24	3.00	3.60	4.20	4.80	5.40	6.00
" 25	3.13	3.75	4.38	5.00	5.63	6.25
" 26	3.25	3.90	4.55	5.20	5.85	6.50
" 27	3.38	4.05	4.73	5.40	6.08	6.75
" 28	3.50	4.20	4.90	5.60	6.30	7.00
" 29	3.63	4.35	5.08	5.80	6.53	7.25
Mos. 1	3.75	4.50	5.25	6.00	6.75	7.50
" 2	7.50	9.00	10.50	12.00	13.50	15.00
" 3	11.25	13.50	15.75	18.00	20.25	22.50
" 4	15.00	18.00	21.00	24.00	27.00	30.00
" 5	18.75	22.50	26.25	30.00	33.75	37.50
" 6	22.50	27.00	31.50	36.00	40.50	45.00
" 7	26.25	31.50	36.75	42.00	47.25	52.50
" 8	30.00	36.00	42.00	48.00	54.00	60.00
" 9	33.75	40.50	47.25	54.00	60.75	67.50
" 10	37.50	45.00	52.50	60.00	67.50	75.00
" 11	41.25	49.50	57.75	66.00	74.25	82.50
Yrs. 1	45.00	54.00	63.00	72.00	81.00	90.00
" 2	90.00	108.00	126.00	144.00	162.00	180.00
" 3	135.00	162.00	189.00	216.00	243.00	270.00
" 4	180.00	216.00	252.00	288.00	324.00	360.00
Com. 2	92.25	111.24	130.41	149.76	169.29	189.00
" 3	141.86	171.91	202.54	233.74	265.53	297.90
" 4	193.96	236.23	279.72	324.44	370.42	417.69
" 5	248.65	304.40	362.30	422.40	484.76	549.46
" 6	306.09	376.67	450.66	528.19	609.39	694.41

1000 Dollars.

TIME.	5 %	6 %	7 %	8 %	9 %	10 %
Days 1	14	17	19	22	25	28
" 2	28	33	39	44	50	56
" 3	42	50	58	67	75	83
" 4	56	67	78	89	1.00	1.11
" 5	69	83	97	1.11	1.25	1.39
" 6	83	1.00	1.17	1.33	1.50	1.67
" 7	97	1.17	1.36	1.56	1.75	1.94
" 8	1.11	1.33	1.56	1.78	2.00	2.22
" 9	1.25	1.50	1.75	2.00	2.25	2.50
" 10	1.39	1.67	1.94	2.22	2.50	2.78
" 11	1.53	1.83	2.14	2.44	2.75	3.06
" 12	1.67	2.00	2.33	2.67	3.00	3.33
" 13	1.81	2.17	2.53	2.89	3.25	3.61
" 14	1.94	2.33	2.72	3.11	3.50	3.89
" 15	2.08	2.50	2.92	3.33	3.75	4.17
" 16	2.22	2.67	3.11	3.56	4.00	4.44
" 17	2.36	2.83	3.31	3.78	4.25	4.72
" 18	2.50	3.00	3.50	4.00	4.50	5.00
" 19	2.64	3.17	3.69	4.22	4.75	5.28
" 20	2.78	3.33	3.89	4.44	5.00	5.56
" 21	2.92	3.50	4.08	4.67	5.25	5.83
" 22	3.06	3.67	4.28	4.89	5.50	6.11
" 23	3.19	3.83	4.47	5.11	5.75	6.39
" 24	3.33	4.00	4.67	5.33	6.00	6.67
" 25	3.47	4.17	4.86	5.56	6.25	6.94
" 26	3.61	4.33	5.06	5.78	6.50	7.22
" 27	3.75	4.50	5.25	6.00	6.75	7.50
" 28	3.89	4.67	5.44	6.22	7.00	7.78
" 29	4.03	4.83	5.64	6.44	7.25	8.06
Mos. 1	4.17	5.00	5.83	6.67	7.50	8.33
" 2	8.33	10.00	11.67	13.33	15.00	16.67
" 3	12.50	15.00	17.50	20.00	22.50	25.00
" 4	16.67	20.00	23.33	26.67	30.00	33.33
" 5	20.83	25.00	29.17	33.33	37.50	41.67
" 6	25.00	30.00	35.00	40.00	45.00	50.00
" 7	29.17	35.00	40.83	46.67	52.50	58.33
" 8	33.33	40.00	46.67	53.33	60.00	66.67
" 9	37.50	45.00	52.50	60.00	67.50	75.00
" 10	41.67	50.00	58.33	66.67	75.00	83.33
" 11	45.83	55.00	64.17	73.33	82.50	91.67
Yrs. 1	50.00	60.00	70.00	80.00	90.00	100.00
" 2	100.00	120.00	140.00	160.00	180.00	200.00
" 3	150.00	180.00	210.00	240.00	270.00	300.00
" 4	200.00	240.00	280.00	320.00	360.00	400.00
Com. 2	102.50	123.60	144.90	166.40	188.10	210.00
" 3	157.63	191.02	225.04	259.71	295.03	331.00
" 4	215.51	262.48	310.80	360.49	411.58	464.10
" 5	276.28	338.23	402.55	469.33	538.62	610.51
" 6	340.10	418.52	500.73	586.87	677.10	771.66

TIME.	5 %	6 %	7 %	8 %	9 %	10 %
Day» 1	28	33	39	44	50	56
" 2	56	67	78	89	1.00	1.11
" 3	83	1.00	1.17	1.33	1.50	1.67
" 4	1.11	1.33	1.56	1.78	2.00	2.22
" 5	1.39	1.67	1.94	2.22	2.50	2.78
" 6	1.67	2.00	2.33	2.67	3.00	3.33
" 7	1.94	2.33	2.72	3.11	3.50	3.89
" 8	2.22	2.67	3.11	3.56	4.00	4.44
" 9	2.50	3.00	3.50	4.00	4.50	5.00
" 10	2.78	3.33	3.89	4.44	5.00	5.56
" 11	3.06	3.67	4.28	4.89	5.50	6.11
" 12	3.33	4.00	4.67	5.33	6.00	6.67
" 13	3.61	4.33	5.06	5.78	6.50	7.22
" 14	3.89	4.67	5.44	6.22	7.00	7.78
" 15	4.17	5.00	5.83	6.67	7.50	8.33
" 16	4.44	5.33	6.22	7.11	8.00	8.89
" 17	4.72	5.67	6.61	7.56	8.50	9.44
" 18	5.00	6.00	7.00	8.00	9.00	10.00
" 19	5.28	6.33	7.39	8.44	9.50	10.56
" 20	5.56	6.67	7.78	8.89	10.00	11.11
" 21	5.83	7.00	8.17	9.33	10.50	11.67
" 22	6.11	7.33	8.56	9.78	11.00	12.22
" 23	6.39	7.67	8.94	10.22	11.50	12.78
" 24	6.67	8.00	9.33	10.67	12.00	13.33
" 25	6.94	8.33	9.72	11.11	12.50	13.89
" 26	7.22	8.67	10.11	11.56	13.00	14.44
" 27	7.50	9.00	10.50	12.00	13.50	15.00
" 28	7.78	9.33	10.89	12.44	14.00	15.56
" 29	8.06	9.67	11.28	12.89	14.50	16.11
Mos. 1	8.33	10.00	11.67	13.33	15.00	16.67
" 2	16.67	20.00	23.33	26.67	30.00	33.33
" 3	25.00	30.00	35.00	40.00	45.00	50.00
" 4	33.33	40.00	46.67	53.33	60.00	66.67
" 5	41.67	50.00	58.33	66.67	75.00	83.33
" 6	50.00	60.00	70.00	80.00	90.00	100.00
" 7	58.33	70.00	81.67	93.33	105.00	116.67
" 8	66.67	80.00	93.33	106.67	120.00	133.33
" 9	75.00	90.00	105.00	120.00	135.00	150.00
" 10	83.33	100.00	116.67	133.33	150.00	166.67
" 11	91.67	110.00	128.33	146.67	165.00	183.33
Yrs. 1	100.00	120.00	140.00	160.00	180.00	200.00
" 2	200.00	240.00	280.00	320.00	360.00	400.00
" 3	300.00	360.00	420.00	480.00	540.00	600.00
" 4	400.00	480.00	560.00	640.00	720.00	800.00
Com. 2	205.00	247.20	289.80	332.80	376.20	420.00
" 3	315.25	382.03	450.09	519.42	590.06	662.00
" 4	431.01	524.95	621.59	720.98	823.16	928.20
" 5	552.56	676.45	805.10	938.66	1077.25	1221.02
" 6	680.19	837.04	1001.46	1173.75	1354.20	1543.12

3000 Dollars.

TIME.	5 %	6 %	7 %	8 %	9 %	10 %
Days 1	42	50	58	67	75	83
" 2	83	1.00	1.17	1.33	1.50	1.67
" 3	1.25	1.50	1.75	2.00	2.25	2.50
" 4	1.67	2.00	2.33	2.67	3.00	3.33
" 5	2.08	2.50	2.92	3.33	3.75	4.17
" 6	2.50	3.00	3.50	4.00	4.50	5.00
" 7	2.92	3.50	4.08	4.67	5.25	5.83
" 8	3.33	4.00	4.67	5.33	6.00	6.67
" 9	3.75	4.50	5.25	6.00	6.75	7.50
" 10	4.17	5.00	5.83	6.67	7.50	8.33
" 11	4.58	5.50	6.42	7.33	8.25	9.17
" 12	5.00	6.00	7.00	8.00	9.00	10.00
" 13	5.42	6.50	7.58	8.67	9.75	10.83
" 14	5.83	7.00	8.17	9.33	10.50	11.67
" 15	6.25	7.50	8.75	10.00	11.25	12.50
" 16	6.67	8.00	9.33	10.67	12.00	13.33
" 17	7.08	8.50	9.92	11.33	12.75	14.17
" 18	7.50	9.00	10.50	12.00	13.50	15.00
" 19	7.92	9.50	11.08	12.67	14.25	15.83
" 20	8.33	10.00	11.67	13.33	15.00	16.67
" 21	8.75	10.50	12.25	14.00	15.75	17.50
" 22	9.17	11.00	12.83	14.67	16 50	18.33
" 23	9.58	11.50	13.42	15.33	17.25	19.17
" 24	10.00	12.00	14.00	16.00	18.00	20.00
" 25	10.42	12.50	14.58	16.67	18.75	20.83
" 26	10.83	13.00	15.17	17.33	19.50	21.67
" 27	11.25	13.50	15.75	18.00	20 25	22.50
" 28	11.67	14.00	16.33	18.67	21.00	23.33
" 29	12.08	14.50	16.92	19.33	21.75	24.17
Mos. 1	12.50	15.00	17.50	20.00	22.50	25.00
" 2	25.00	30.00	35.00	40.00	45.00	50.00
" 3	37.50	45.00	52.50	60.00	67.50	75.00
" 4	50.00	60.00	70.00	80.00	90.00	100.00
" 5	62.50	75.00	87.50	100.00	112.50	125.00
" 6	75.00	90.00	105.00	120.00	135.00	150.00
" 7	87.50	105.00	122.50	140.00	157.50	175.00
" 8	100.00	120.00	140.00	160.00	180.00	200.00
" 9	112.50	135.00	157.50	180.00	202.50	225.00
" 10	125.00	150.00	175 00	200.00	225.00	250.00
" 11	137.50	165.00	192.50	220.00	247.50	275.00
Yrs. 1	150.00	180.00	210.00	240.00	270.00	300.00
" 2	300.00	360.00	420.00	480.00	540.00	600.00
" 3	450.00	540.00	630.00	720.00	810.00	900.00
" 4	600.00	720.00	840.00	960.00	1080.00	1200.00
Com. 2	307.50	370.80	434.70	499.20	564.30	630.00
" 3	472.88	573.05	675.13	779.14	885.09	993.00
" 4	646.52	787.43	932.39	1081.47	1234.75	1392.30
" 5	828.85	1014.68	1207.66	1407.98	1615.87	1831.53
" 6	1020.29	1255.56	1502.19	1760.62	2031.30	2314.68

4000 DOLLARS.

TIME.	5 %	6 %	7 %	8 %	9 %	10 %
Days 1	56	67	78	89	1.00	1.11
" 2	1.11	1.33	1.56	1.78	2.00	2.22
" 3	1.67	2.00	2.33	2.67	3.00	3.33
" 4	2.22	2.67	3.11	3.56	4.00	4.44
" 5	2.78	3.33	3.89	4.44	5.00	5.56
" 6	3.33	4.00	4.67	5.33	6.00	6.67
" 7	3.89	4.67	5.44	6.22	7.00	7.78
" 8	4.44	5.33	6.22	7.11	8.00	8.89
" 9	5.00	6.00	7.00	8.00	9.00	10.00
" 10	5.56	6.67	7.78	8.89	10.00	11.11
" 11	6.11	7.33	8.56	9.78	11.00	12.22
" 12	6.67	8.00	9.33	10.67	12.00	13.33
" 13	7.22	8.67	10.11	11.56	13.00	14.44
" 14	7.78	9.33	10.89	12.44	14.00	15.56
" 15	8.33	10.00	11.67	13.33	15.00	16.67
" 16	8.89	10.67	12.44	14.22	16.00	17.78
" 17	9.44	11.33	13.22	15.11	17.00	18.89
" 18	10.00	12.00	14.00	16.00	18.00	20.00
" 19	10.56	12.67	14.78	16.89	19.00	21.11
" 20	11.11	13.33	15.56	17.78	20.00	22.22
" 21	11.67	14.00	16.33	18.67	21.00	23.33
" 22	12.22	14.67	17.11	19.56	22.00	24.44
" 23	12.78	15.33	17.89	20.44	23.00	25.56
" 24	13.33	16.00	18.67	21.33	24.00	26.67
" 25	13.89	16.67	19.44	22.22	25.00	27.78
" 26	14.44	17.33	20.22	23.11	26.00	28.89
" 27	15.00	18.00	21.00	24.00	27.00	30.00
" 28	15.56	18.67	21.78	24.89	28.00	31.11
" 29	16.11	19.33	22.56	25.78	29.00	32.22
Mos. 1	16.67	20.00	23.33	26.67	30.00	33.33
' 2	33.33	40.00	46.67	53.33	60.00	66.67
' 3	50.00	60.00	70.00	80.00	90.00	100.00
" 4	66.67	80.00	93.33	106.67	120.00	133.33
" 5	83.33	100.00	116.67	133.33	150.00	166.67
" 6	100.00	120.00	140.00	160.00	180.00	200.00
" 7	116.67	140.00	163.33	186.67	210.00	233.33
" 8	133.33	160.00	186.67	213.33	240.00	266.67
" 9	150.00	180.00	210.00	240.00	270.00	300.00
" 10	166.67	200.00	233.33	266.67	300.00	333.33
" 11	183.33	220.00	256.67	293.33	330.00	366.67
Yrs. 1	200.00	240.00	280.00	320.00	360.00	400.00
" 2	400.00	480.00	560.00	640.00	720.00	800.00
" 3	600.00	720.00	840.00	960.00	1080.00	1200.00
" 4	800.00	960.00	1120.00	1280.00	1440.00	1600.00
Com. 2	410.00	494.40	579.60	665.60	752.40	840.00
" 3	630.50	764.06	900.17	1038.85	1180.12	1324.00
" 4	862.03	1049.91	1243.18	1441.96	1646.33	1856.40
" 5	1105.13	1352.90	1610.21	1877.31	2154.50	2442.04
" 6	1360.38	1674.08	2002.92	2347.50	2708.40	3086.24

TIME.	5 %	6 %	7 %	8 %	9 %	10 %
Days 1	69	83	97	1.11	1.25	1.39
" 2	1.39	1.67	1.94	2.22	2.50	2.78
" 3	2.08	2.50	2.92	3.33	3.75	4.17
" 4	2.78	3.33	3.89	4.44	5.00	5.56
" 5	3.47	4.17	4.86	5.56	6.25	6.94
" 6	4.17	5.00	5.83	6.67	7.50	8.33
" 7	4.86	5.83	6.81	7.78	8.75	9.72
" 8	5.56	6.67	7.78	8.89	10.00	11.11
" 9	6.25	7.50	8.75	10.00	11.25	12.50
" 10	6.94	8.33	9.72	11.11	12.50	13.89
" 11	7.64	9.17	10.69	12.22	13.75	15.28
" 12	8.33	10.00	11.67	13.33	15.00	16.67
" 13	9.03	10.83	12.64	14.44	16.25	18.06
" 14	9.72	11.67	13.61	15.56	17.50	19.44
" 15	10.42	12.50	14.58	16.67	18.75	20.83
" 16	11.11	13.33	15.56	17.78	20.00	22.22
" 17	11.81	14.17	16.53	18.89	21.25	23.61
" 18	12.50	15.00	17.50	20.00	22.50	25.00
" 19	13.19	15.83	18.47	21.11	23.75	26.39
" 20	13.89	16.67	19.44	22.22	25.00	27.78
" 21	14.58	17.50	20.42	23.33	26.25	29.17
" 22	15.28	18.33	21.39	24.44	27.50	30.56
" 23	15.97	19.17	22.36	25.56	28.75	31.94
" 24	16.67	20.00	23.33	26.67	30.00	33.33
" 25	17.36	20.83	24.31	27.78	31.25	34.72
" 26	18.06	21.67	25.28	28.89	32.50	36.11
" 27	18.75	22.50	26.25	30.00	33.75	37.50
" 28	19.44	23.33	27.22	31.11	35.00	38.89
" 29	20.14	24.17	28.19	32.22	36.25	40.28
Mos. 1	20.83	25.00	29.17	33.33	37.50	41.67
" 2	41.67	50.00	58.33	66.67	75.00	83.33
" 3	62.50	75.00	87.50	100.00	112.50	125.00
" 4	83.33	100.00	116.67	133.33	150.00	166.67
" 5	104.17	125.00	145.83	166.67	187.50	208.33
" 6	125.00	150.00	175.00	200.00	225.00	250.00
" 7	145.83	175.00	204.17	233.33	262.50	291.67
" 8	166.67	200.00	233.33	266.67	300.00	333.33
" 9	187.50	225.00	262.50	300.00	337.50	375.00
" 10	208.33	250.00	291.67	333.33	375.00	416.67
" 11	229.17	275.00	320.83	366.67	412.50	458.33
Yrs. 1	250.00	300.00	350.00	400.00	450.00	500.00
" 2	500.00	600.00	700.00	800.00	900.00	1000.00
" 3	750.00	900.00	1050.00	1200.00	1350.00	1500.00
" 4	1000.00	1200.00	1400.00	1600.00	1800.00	2000.00
Com. 2	512.50	618.00	724.50	832.00	940.50	1050.00
" 3	788.13	955.08	1125.22	1298.56	1475.15	1655.00
" 4	1077.53	1312.39	1553.98	1802.45	2057.91	2320.50
" 5	1381.41	1691.13	2012.76	2346.64	2693.12	3052.55
" 6	1700.48	2092.60	2503.65	2934.37	3385.50	3857.81

6000 Dollars.

TIME.	5 %	6 %	7 %	8 %	9 %	10 %
Days 1	83	1.00	1.17	1.33	1.50	1.67
" 2	1.67	2.00	2.33	2.67	3.00	3.33
" 3	2.50	3.00	3.50	4.00	4.50	5.00
" 4	3.33	4.00	4.67	5.33	6.00	6.67
" 5	4.17	5.00	5.83	6.67	7.50	8.33
" 6	5.00	6.00	7.00	8.00	9.00	10.00
" 7	5.83	7.00	8.17	9.33	10.50	11.67
" 8	6.67	8.00	9.33	10.67	12.00	13.33
" 9	7.50	9.00	10.50	12.00	13.50	15.00
" 10	8.33	10.00	11.67	13.33	15.00	16.67
" 11	9.17	11.00	12.83	14.67	16.50	18.33
" 12	10.00	12.00	14.00	16.00	18.00	20.00
" 13	10.83	13.00	15.17	17.33	19.50	21.67
" 14	11.67	14.00	16.33	18.67	21.00	23.33
" 15	12.50	15.00	17.50	20.00	22.50	25.00
" 16	13.33	16.00	18.67	21.33	24.00	26.67
" 17	14.17	17.00	19.83	22.67	25.50	28.33
" 18	15.00	18.00	21.00	24.00	27.00	30.00
" 19	15.83	19.00	22.17	25.33	28.50	31.67
" 20	16.67	20.00	23.33	26.67	30.00	33.33
" 21	17.50	21.00	24.50	28.00	31.50	35.00
" 22	18.33	22.00	25.67	29.33	33.00	36.67
" 23	19.17	23.00	26.83	30.67	34.50	38.33
" 24	20.00	24.00	28.00	32.00	36.00	40.00
" 25	20.83	25.00	29.17	33.33	37.50	41.67
" 26	21.67	26.00	30.33	34.67	39.00	43.33
" 27	22.50	27.00	31.50	36.00	40.50	45.00
" 28	23.33	28.00	32.67	37.33	42.00	46.67
" 29	24.17	29.00	33.83	38.67	43.50	48.33
Mos. 1	25.00	30.00	35.00	40.00	45.00	50.00
" 2	50.00	60.00	70.00	80.00	90.00	100.00
" 3	75.00	90.00	105.00	120.00	135.00	150.00
" 4	100.00	120.00	140.00	160.00	180.00	200.00
" 5	125.00	150.00	175.00	200.00	225.00	250.00
" 6	150.00	180.00	210.00	240.00	270.00	300.00
" 7	175.00	210.00	245.00	280.00	315.00	350.00
" 8	200.00	240.00	280.00	320.00	360.00	400.00
" 9	225.00	270.00	315.00	360.00	405.00	450.00
" 10	250.00	300.00	350.00	400.00	450.00	500.00
" 11	275.00	330.00	385.00	440.00	495.00	550.00
Yrs. 1	300.00	360.00	420.00	480.00	540.00	600.00
" 2	600.00	720.00	840.00	960.00	1080.00	1200.00
" 3	900.00	1080.00	1260.00	1440.00	1620.00	1800.00
" 4	1200.00	1440.00	1680.00	1920.00	2160.00	2400.00
Com. 2	615.00	741.60	869.40	998.40	1128.60	1260.00
" 3	945.75	1146.10	1350.26	1558.27	1770.17	1986.00
" 4	1293.04	1574.86	1864.78	2162.93	2469.49	2784.60
" 5	1657.69	2029.35	2415.31	2815.97	3231.74	3663.06
" 6	2040.57	2511.12	3004.38	3521.25	4062.60	4629.37

TIME.	5 %	6 %	7 %	8 %	9 %	10 %
Days 1	97	1.17	1.36	1.56	1.75	1.94
" 2	1.94	2.33	2.72	3.11	3.50	3.89
" 3	2.92	3.50	4.08	4.67	5.25	5.83
" 4	3.89	4.67	5.44	6.22	7.00	7.78
" 5	4.86	5.83	6.81	7.78	8.75	9.72
" 6	5.83	7.00	8.17	9.33	10.50	11.67
" 7	6.81	8.17	9.53	10.89	12.25	13.61
" 8	7.78	9.33	10.89	12.44	14.00	15.56
" 9	8.75	10.50	12.25	14.00	15.75	17.50
" 10	9.72	11.67	13.61	15.56	17.50	19.44
" 11	10.69	12.83	14.97	17.11	19.25	21.39
" 12	11.67	14.00	16.33	18.67	21.00	23.33
" 13	12.64	15.17	17.69	20.22	22.75	25.28
" 14	13.61	16.33	19.06	21.78	24.50	27.22
" 15	14.58	17.50	20.42	23.33	26.25	29.17
" 16	15.56	18.67	21.78	24.89	28.00	31.11
" 17	16.53	19.83	23.14	26.44	29.75	33.06
" 18	17.50	21.00	24.50	28.00	31.50	35.00
" 19	18.47	22.17	25.86	29.56	33.25	36.94
" 20	19.44	23.33	27.22	31.11	35.00	38.89
" 21	20.42	24.50	28.58	32.67	36.75	40.83
" 22	21.39	25.67	29.94	34.22	38.50	42.78
" 23	22.36	26.83	31.31	35.78	40.25	44.72
" 24	23.33	28.00	32.67	37.33	42.00	46.67
" 25	24.31	29.17	34.03	38.89	43.75	48.61
" 26	25.28	30.33	35.39	40.44	45.50	50.56
" 27	26.25	31.50	36.75	42.00	47.25	52.50
" 28	27.22	32.67	38.11	43.56	49.00	54.44
" 29	28.19	33.83	39.47	45.11	50.75	56.39
Mos. 1	29.17	35.00	40.83	46.67	52.50	58.33
" 2	58.33	70.00	81.67	93.33	105.00	116.67
" 3	87.50	105.00	122.50	140.00	157.50	175.00
" 4	116.67	140.00	163.33	186.67	210.00	233.33
" 5	145.83	175.00	204.17	233.33	262.50	291.67
" 6	175.00	210.00	245.00	280.00	315.00	350.00
" 7	204.17	245.00	285.83	326.67	367.50	408.33
" 8	233.33	280.00	326.67	373.33	420.00	466.67
" 9	262.50	315.00	367.50	420.00	472.50	525.00
" 10	291.67	350.00	408.33	466.67	525.00	583.33
" 11	320.83	385.00	449.17	513.33	577.50	641.67
Yrs. 1	350.00	420.00	490.00	560.00	630.00	700.00
" 2	700.00	840.00	980.00	1120.00	1260.00	1400.00
" 3	1050.00	1260.00	1470.00	1680.00	1890.00	2100.00
" 4	1400.00	1680.00	1960.00	2240.00	2520.00	2800.00
Com. 2	717.50	865.20	1014.30	1164.80	1316.70	1470.00
" 3	1103.38	1337.11	1575.30	1817.98	2065.20	2317.00
" 4	1508.54	1837.34	2175.57	2523.42	2881.07	3248.70
" 5	1933.97	2367.58	2817.86	3285.30	3770.37	4273.57
" 6	2380.67	2929.63	3505.11	4108.12	4739.70	5400.93

8000 Dollars.

TIME.	5 %	6 %	7 %	8 %	9 %	10 %
Days 1	1.11	1.33	1.56	1.78	2.00	2.22
" 2	2.22	2.67	3.11	3.56	4.00	4.44
" 3	3.33	4.00	4.67	5.33	6.00	6.67
" 4	4.44	5.33	6.22	7.11	8.00	8.89
" 5	5.56	6.67	7.78	8.89	10.00	11.11
" 6	6.67	8.00	9.33	10.67	12.00	13.33
" 7	7.78	9.33	10.89	12.44	14.00	15.56
" 8	8.89	10.67	12.44	14.22	16.00	17.78
" 9	10.00	12.00	14.00	16.00	18.00	20.00
" 10	11.11	13.33	15.56	17.78	20.00	22.22
" 11	12.22	14.67	17.11	19.56	22.00	24.44
" 12	13.33	16.00	18.67	21.33	24.00	26.67
" 13	14.44	17.33	20.22	23.11	26.00	28.89
" 14	15.56	18.67	21.78	24.89	28.00	31.11
" 15	16.67	20.00	23.33	26.67	30.00	33.33
" 16	17.78	21.33	24.89	28.44	32.00	35.56
" 17	18.89	22.67	26.44	30.22	34.00	37.78
" 18	20.00	24.00	28.00	32.00	36.00	40.00
" 19	21.11	25.33	29.56	33.78	38.00	42.22
" 20	22.22	26.67	31.11	35.56	40.00	44.44
" 21	23.33	28.00	32.67	37.33	42.00	46.67
" 22	24.44	29.33	34.22	39.11	44.00	48.89
" 23	25.56	30.67	35.78	40.89	46.00	51.11
" 24	26.67	32.00	37.32	42.67	48.00	53.33
" 25	27.78	33.33	38.89	44.44	50.00	55.56
" 26	28.89	34.67	40.44	46.22	52.00	57.78
" 27	30.00	36.00	42.00	48.00	54.00	60.00
" 28	31.11	37.33	43.56	49.78	56.00	62.22
" 29	32.22	38.67	45.11	51.56	58.00	64.44
Mos. 1	33.33	40.00	46.67	53.33	60.00	66.67
' 2	66.67	80.00	93.33	106.67	120.00	133.33
" 3	100.00	120.00	140.00	160.00	180.00	200.00
" 4	133.33	160.00	186.67	213.33	240.00	266.67
" 5	166.67	200.00	233.33	266.67	300.00	333.33
" 6	200.00	240.00	280.00	320.00	360.00	400.00
" 7	233.33	280.00	326.67	373.33	420.00	466.67
" 8	266.67	320.00	373.33	426.67	480.00	533.33
" 9	300.00	360.00	420.00	480.00	540.00	600.00
" 10	333.33	400.00	466.67	533.33	600.00	666.67
" 11	366.67	440.00	513.33	586.67	660.00	733.33
Yrs. 1	400.00	480.00	560.00	640.00	720.00	800.00
" 2	800.00	960.00	1120.00	1280.00	1440.00	1600.00
" 3	1200.00	1440.00	1680.00	1920.00	2160.00	2400.00
" 4	1600.00	1920.00	2240.00	2560.00	2880.00	3200.00
Com. 2	820.00	988.80	1159.20	1331.20	1504.80	1680.00
" 3	1261.00	1528.13	1800.34	2077.70	2360.23	2648.00
" 4	1724.05	2099.82	2486.37	2883.91	3292.65	3712.80
" 5	2210.25	2705.81	3220.41	3754.63	4308.99	4884.08
" 6	2720.77	3348.15	4005.84	4694.99	5416.80	6172.49

TIME.	5 %	6 %	7 %	8 %	9 %	10 %
Days 1	1.25	1.50	1.75	2.00	2.25	2.50
" 2	2.50	3.00	3.50	4.00	4.50	5.00
" 3	3.75	4.50	5.25	6.00	6.75	7.50
" 4	5.00	6.00	7.00	8.00	9.00	10.00
" 5	6.25	7.50	8.75	10.00	11.25	12.50
" 6	7.50	9.00	10.50	12.00	13.50	15.00
" 7	8.75	10.50	12.25	14.00	15.75	17.50
" 8	10.00	12.00	14.00	16.00	18.00	20.00
" 9	11.25	13.50	15.75	18.00	20.25	22.50
" 10	12.50	15.00	17.50	20.00	22.50	25.00
" 11	13.75	16.50	19.25	22.00	24.75	27.50
" 12	15.00	18.00	21.00	24.00	27.00	30.00
" 13	16.25	19.50	22.75	26.00	29.25	32.50
" 14	17.50	21.00	24.50	28.00	31.50	35.00
" 15	18.75	22.50	26.25	30.00	33.75	37.50
" 16	20.00	24.00	28.00	32.00	36.00	40.00
" 17	21.25	25.50	29.75	34.00	38.25	42.50
" 18	22.50	27.00	31.50	36.00	40.50	45.00
" 19	23.75	28.50	33.25	38.00	42.75	47.50
" 20	25.00	30.00	35.00	40.00	45.00	50.00
" 21	26.25	31.50	36.75	42.00	47.25	52.50
" 22	27.50	33.00	38.50	44.00	49.50	55.00
" 23	28.75	34.50	40.25	46.00	51.75	57.50
" 24	30.00	36.00	42.00	48.00	54.00	60.00
" 25	31.25	37.50	43.75	50.00	56.25	62.50
" 26	32.50	39.00	45.50	52.00	58.50	65.00
" 27	33.75	40.50	47.25	54.00	60.75	67.50
" 28	35.00	42.00	49.00	56.00	63.00	70.00
" 29	36.25	43.50	50.75	58.00	65.25	72.50
Mos. 1	37.50	45.00	52.50	60.00	67.50	75.00
" 2	75.00	90.00	105.00	120.00	135.00	150.00
" 3	112.50	135.00	157.50	180.00	202.50	225 00
" 4	150.00	180.00	210.00	240.00	270.00	300 00
" 5	187.50	225.00	262.50	300.00	337.50	375.00
" 6	225.00	270.00	315.00	360.00	405.00	450.00
" 7	262.50	315.00	367.50	420.00	472.50	525.00
" 8	300.00	360.00	420.00	480.00	540.00	600.00
" 9	337.50	405.00	472.50	540.00	607.50	675.00
" 10	375.00	450.00	525.00	600.00	675.00	750.00
" 11	412.50	495.00	577.50	660.00	742.50	825.00
Yrs. 1	450.00	540.00	630.00	720.00	810.00	900.00
" 2	900.00	1080.00	1260.00	1440.00	1620.00	1800.00
" 3	1350.00	1620.00	1890.00	2160 00	2430.00	2700.00
" 4	1800.00	2160.00	2520.00	2880.00	3240.00	3600.00
Com. 2	922.50	1112.40	1304.10	1497.60	1692.90	1890.00
" 3	1418.63	1719.14	2025.39	2337.41	2655.26	2979.00
" 4	1939.56	2362.29	2797.16	3244.40	3704.23	4176.90
" 5	2486.53	3044.03	3622.97	4223.95	4847.62	5494.59
" 6	3060.86	3766.67	4506.57	5281.87	6093.90	6944.05

TIME.	5 %	6 %	7 %	8 %	9 %	10 %
Days 1	1.39	1.67	1.94	2.22	2.50	2.78
" 2	2.78	3.33	3.89	4.44	5.00	5.56
" 3	4.17	5.00	5.83	6.67	7.50	8.33
" 4	5.56	6.67	7.78	8 89	10.00	11.11
" 5	6.94	8.33	9.72	11.11	12.50	13.89
" 6	8.33	10.00	11.67	13.33	15.00	16.67
" 7	9.72	11.67	13.61	15.56	17.50	19.44
" 8	11.11	13.33	15.56	17.78	20.00	22.22
" 9	12.50	15.00	17.50	20 00	22.50	25.00
" 10	13.89	16.67	19.44	22.22	25.00	27.78
" 11	15.28	18.33	21.39	24.44	27.50	30.56
" 12	16.67	20.00	23.33	26.67	30.00	33.33
" 13	18.06	21.67	25.28	28 89	32.50	36.11
" 14	19.44	23.33	27.22	31.11	35.00	38.89
" 15	20.83	25.00	29.17	33.33	37.50	41.67
" 16	22.22	26.67	31.11	35.56	40.00	44.44
" 17	23.61	28.33	33.06	37.78	42.50	47.22
" 18	25.00	30.00	35.00	40.00	45.00	50.00
" 19	26.39	31.67	36.94	42.22	47.50	52.78
" 20	27.78	33.33	38.89	44.44	50.00	55.56
" 21	29.17	35.00	40.83	46.67	52.50	58.33
" 22	30.56	36.67	42.78	48.89	55.00	61.11
" 23	31.94	38.33	44.72	51.11	57.50	63.89
" 24	33.33	40.00	46.67	53 33	60.00	66.67
" 25	34.72	41.67	48.61	55.56	62.50	69.44
" 26	36.11	43.33	50.56	57.78	65.00	72.22
" 27	37.50	45.00	52.50	60.00	67.50	75.00
" 28	38.89	46.67	54.44	62.22	70.00	77.78
" 29	40.28	48.33	56.39	64.44	72.50	80.56
Mos. 1	41.67	50.00	58.33	66.67	75.00	83.33
" 2	83.33	100.00	116.67	133.33	150.00	166 67
" 3	125.00	150.00	175.00	200.00	225.00	250.00
" 4	166.67	200.00	233.33	266.67	300.00	333.33
" 5	208.33	250.00	291.67	333.33	375.00	416.67
" 6	250.00	300.00	350.00	400.00	450.00	500.00
" 7	291.67	350.00	408.33	466.67	525.00	583.33
" 8	333.33	400.00	466.67	533.33	600.00	666.67
" 9	375.00	450.00	525.00	600.00	675.00	750.00
" 10	416.67	500.00	583.33	666.67	750 00	833.33
" 11	458.33	550.00	641.67	733.33	825.00	916.67
Yrs. 1	500.00	600.00	700.00	800.00	900.00	1000.00
" 2	1000.00	1200.00	1400.00	1600.00	1800.00	2000.00
" 3	1500.00	1800.00	2100.00	2400.00	2700.00	3000.00
" 4	2000.00	2400.00	2800.00	3200.00	3600.00	4000.00
Com. 2	1025.00	1236.00	1449.00	1664.00	1881.00	2100.00
" 3	1576.25	1910.16	2250.43	2597.12	2950.29	3310.00
" 4	2155.06	2624.77	3107.96	3604.89	4115.82	4641.00
" 5	2762.82	3382.26	4025.52	4693.28	5386.24	6105.10
" 6	3400.96	4185.19	5007.30	5868.74	6771.00	7715.61

www.ingramcontent.com/pod-product-compliance
Lightning Source LLC
Chambersburg PA
CBHW030936110726
47900CB00004B/1022